The Three

Meghan O'Brien

Quest Books

Nederland, Texas

ISBN 978-1-932300-51-2
1-932300-51-1

First Printing 2006

9 8 7 6 5 4 3 2 1

Cover design by Donna Pawlowski

Published by:

Quest Books
4700 Highway 365, Suite A, PMB 210
Port Arthur, Texas 77642

Find us on the World Wide Web at
http://www.regalcrest.biz

Printed in the United States of America

Acknowledgments

I want to thank everyone who helped me with this novel along the way. First, to the members of my Yahoo group online, who are always eager to offer encouragement and suggestions. They have no idea how much I appreciate that.

I'd also like to thank Ty, who participated in all kinds of discussions with me about what this world might look like. I had almost as much fun talking and brainstorming with her as I did actually writing it down. Every writer should have a Ty around.

Thank you to Angie, who is always willing to read my stuff, offer suggestions, and provide endless support. I love you and appreciate everything.

A quick nod to my sister Kathleen, the English teacher, who wishes I'd write something she could teach in her high school classroom. I'm sorry this isn't it, but I'm glad you're proud of me anyway.

And, as always: Jennifer Knight, for her continued help and support, in matters both writing and life. Lori Lake, for all her advice and assistance, and for being a great role model.

Finally, I want to again thank those who read. You're my favorite people.

For Angie, my source of endless support and love.

And for Ty, who will always be in my heart.

Chapter One

THE ONLY REASON Anna knew she was still alive was because her feet hurt so damn much. She limped along through the forest, eyes vacantly on the trees ahead, almost past the point of caring that she could be caught unaware by an attack from either flank. Her feet hurt and she was breathing. She was alive.

And Garrett is dead. This time, it didn't even slow her pace. She felt empty inside; there was no more hurt left. *Garrett is dead and I'm alive.* She kicked at the slippery green and yellow leaves beneath her feet. *What the fuck is the point of it all?*

She stumbled and winced at the dull pain in her ankle. Almost a week old, the injury still ached. She felt sure it wasn't broken, but feared it was more serious than she'd first thought. Gritting her teeth, she trudged on. Not that she had anywhere in particular to go. She was walking for the sake of walking, for no other reason than habit.

Less than a quarter mile later, she stopped and sniffed the air. *Water.* A grin tugged at her lips for the first time in days. She hadn't stopped to bathe since the fight. Sobering, she ran a hand through her tangled hair and studied the reddish-brown stains that still marred her brown skin. *Those guys left me feeling filthy, inside and out.*

She shook her head to chase away the memories. All she wanted was a long, lazy soak in a cool lake. Instinctively cautious, she moved through the woods on quiet feet, attempting stealth despite her injury, blocking out the pain that radiated from her left ankle. She knew that venturing close to a water source would increase the odds of running into people, and the very last thing she wanted to do was see another person.

Not when she wasn't in any shape to defend herself.

She crept through the thick vegetation until she reached a clearing. Hesitating, she peered past a low branch at a small lake that lay beyond. Spruce trees surrounded the water on all sides, except for a break in the forest across the lake where a wide path was forged. The sun illuminated the surface of the water, and the sparkling blue of it captivated Anna where she stood.

Just as she was about to leave the safety of the trees, she zeroed in on exactly what she hadn't wanted to see. She was not alone.

An auburn-haired woman lay stretched out on a blanket next to the lake. Anna's mouth dropped open as she stared at creamy pale skin exposed by a light tank top above snug blue jeans. She was beautiful. Anna glanced anxiously around. *What's a beautiful woman like her doing out here all alone? Doesn't she know how dangerous that is?* Anna took a step backwards. The woman was lucky it was just she who had found her. *And she's lucky the only thing I'm taking from her is a mental snapshot to remind me that, for better or worse, I am still alive.*

With that, she turned away, already feeling lighter for having gazed upon the ethereal redhead for a couple of minutes. Sometimes all it took was a little beauty to give her the will to get through another day.

She began to retreat, intent on setting up camp so she could return to bathe later, but she sensed something in the forest with her and stopped in her tracks, listening.

They weren't alone.

She searched the trees for some hint of the presence she could feel. The redheaded woman by the lake still lay prone, seemingly oblivious to the approaching threat.

Anna bit her lip, torn. She didn't want the woman to be attacked while she hesitated, but she didn't know what kind of danger they were facing. Giving away her position might not be a wise move, and more than likely, the redhead knew how to fight. *At least I hope so, being foolish enough to get caught sunbathing alone. These guys will be on her so fast...*

Anna stopped her train of thought, shuddering. They were men; she was certain of that. She would guess three or four. Stealthy enough to evade all but the barest tickling of her senses, approaching from multiple directions. Darting her eyes from the redhead to the surrounding trees, she shifted her weight cautiously from her good ankle to the bad. The pain made her cringe, and she swallowed hard. *What if they have weapons? I don't even have my baseball bat anymore. What if I can't defend her? What if I run out there and get captured?* Hot tears stung her eyes. *I can't go through that again.*

When the moment came, she was still frozen with indecision. She heard the rustling of leaves to the north of her position and spotted the three men creeping along the shore toward the unsuspecting woman. Anna stared at the curve of her lower back, at the swell of her hip. She willed her to lift her head and see the danger, but the woman didn't stir.

Goddamn it. Anna lifted her eyes to the leering men who slunk ever closer. *This may be the biggest damn mistake I ever make, but I can't just leave her to them.*

She had taken only two steps when the woman looked up and instantly pushed herself into a crouching position, staring the men down. She glanced backwards, as though considering the possibility of escape, then tipped her head back to let loose a shrill, high-pitched whistle.

The men stopped short no more than twenty feet from her, obviously startled. After a moment, the man in front chuckled.

"Was that supposed to be a warning or a cry for help?" He folded his arms and gave the redhead a condescending look. "Either way, it looks to me like you're all alone out here."

Still in a crouch, the woman cocked her head to the side. "I suggest you boys keep moving along." Her calm, gentle voice raised gooseflesh on Anna's arms. "You don't want to cause trouble here, I promise."

From behind the leader, a stocky, bearded man stepped closer and raised an eyebrow. "Yeah? What's gonna stop us? You?"

The woman leapt to her feet in a lightning-quick move that made even Anna step back in surprise. She held a slim black object in one hand. "If I have to."

The leader took an aggressive step forward. "All you have to do, honey, is cooperate with us. Nobody gets hurt that way. I promise."

The redhead appeared to relax, but Anna watched her slightly widen her stance. She recognized the stillness before the strike and held her breath in anticipation.

"No, thanks." The woman extended a long, steel baton with the flick of her wrist and delivered a hard strike to the legs of the man leading the pack.

He roared in pain and fell to the ground, clutching his shin.

"Fucking bitch!" the bearded man behind him growled.

He lunged with a large hunting knife in his hand, and his buddy followed. The woman was good, but she struggled against the two larger men. She struck out with her baton, forcing one to jump back to avoid the blow. The other punched her shoulder, and she immediately countered with a fierce strike to his arm. He let go a scream of genuine pain and bent at the waist to cradle the injured limb against his stomach. The bearded man rushed her once more, and she landed a quick, hard punch to the face. He barely hesitated before moving forward again, just as his friend recovered and straightened where he stood.

Anna was weighing her options — go and help finish them off, or let the redhead take care of them on her own — when she saw something that chilled her blood. A fourth man was sneaking up behind the woman with what looked to be a crowbar clutched in his hands. Preoccupied with the other attackers, she seemed unaware of his approach.

Anna burst out of the bushes where she hid. "Hey!" she yelled. "Behind you!"

The redhead turned just in time to duck a violent swing of the crowbar. For a split second, she stared at Anna, wide-eyed, then returned to defending herself. Anna didn't waste any time. She ran as fast as her injured ankle would allow, stumbling down a small hill overgrown with plants.

"Lucky day, boys." The fourth man leered at Anna's approach. "Looks like you won't have to wait to get your turns."

Anna's blood turned to ice at the casual comment. Eyes narrowing, she stalked up to the curly-haired man with a cold smile. She forced away her fear until numbness took over. "You going first?"

The man gave her a soulless grin. "Count on it."

Anna nodded, buying herself a moment's grace. She could almost feel fear and adrenaline masking her pain. As she detected a slight lowering of the man's guard, she feinted left, then delivered a solid kick to his midsection with her right foot. He didn't see it coming. He bent at the waist and curled his arms around his stomach, gagging at the blow. Anna followed up with a hard strike to his right shoulder that forced him to drop his weapon to the ground.

Busy with thug number four, she glimpsed the first man struggling to his feet, but could not react before he delivered a vicious backhand across the redhead's face, throwing her off balance. Distracted by the woman's grunt of pain as she hit the ground, Anna paid dearly for her momentary lapse when a foot kicked out and made contact with her injured left ankle. She screamed in agony and went down beside the redhead, who was already rolling back into a crouching position.

"Stay down!" The bearded man slapped the woman across the face as she rose to her feet.

She stumbled but remained standing, pinning him with cold eyes so in contrast to the innocent beauty of her face. "Stop this now," she warned. "Walk away or I promise you'll regret it."

The man cocked his head. Blood ran down his face from a gash above his eye, and his lip was split, streaming another trail of blood over his chin. He grinned, showing teeth covered in red, and gestured at Anna. "Go ahead and start with this one. I'll get the other under control."

Anna's throat went dry, and she quickly scrabbled backwards, getting to her feet despite the throbbing pain in her ankle. The curly-haired man took a step closer and unbuckled his belt, winding it around his fist.

I'd rather die. Anna set her feet apart in a defensive stance and gave her attacker the most chilling glare she could muster. *I'd rather die than get hurt like that again.*

The redhead flew back into action, delivering furious punches and kicks against the man's assault. Anna clenched her fists, ready to fight no matter the pain from her ankle. She was so full of terrified rage that she almost didn't hear the quiet growl from the trees until after it raised the hairs on the back of her neck.

"What the fuck do you think you're doing with *my* women?"

The low, dangerous voice floated to them on the late afternoon breeze, easily cutting through the noise of the fight and stopping everyone dead in their tracks. A young man emerged from among the trees without a sound, so close that Anna felt shaken at not having noticed his approach. Dark eyes shone with cold malevolence as he scanned the four men who surrounded them. Anna shivered when the young man's emotionless gaze swept over her, assessing. She checked the redhead's reaction to the stranger.

Her smile was so sunny that Anna blinked in surprise and looked at the glowering young man again. He was dressed in a baggy black T-shirt and dark blue jeans. She couldn't tell what color his hair was, as it was shaved close to his head. His eyebrows were dark and drawn together in quiet anger.

The leader of the men chuckled, and his buddies joined in after a brief hesitation. "I'm sorry, boy. *Your* women?"

The young man took a step forward and fixed Anna with possessive eyes. "*My* women."

"Looks to me like you've got more women than a boy like you can handle," the man next to Anna said. He grabbed at her and squeezed her flesh with cruel fingers. "How about you let us take one off your hands?"

Anna drew back and threw an elbow at his face, catching him hard in the jaw. He recoiled with a grunt of pain, then lunged with his belt held aloft in an upraised fist.

His blow never connected, and for a stunned moment, Anna stood frozen as she waited for her brain to catch up with the action. The man who had tried to hit her was lying on the ground. An instant later, the leader of the thugs was engaged in a whirlwind attack that ended when he dropped to his knees and the young man snapped his neck with merciless hands.

"Didn't my women warn you that you shouldn't cause trouble here?" he growled, and reached behind his shoulder to unsheathe a long sword that was strapped to his back.

The fight was over within seconds.

Fight? More like a massacre. The redhead's friend was the best fighter Anna had ever seen. He moved so fast that she could barely keep up, and his technique was like nothing she had ever witnessed before. When the last of the thugs hit the ground, the young man stopped, breathing hard, and dropped his bloody sword. He examined his hands briefly and wiped them on his pants before taking a tentative step toward the redhead.

"Are you okay, Elin?" His voice was low, urgent.

The redhead, Elin, turned with a tender smile and held out her arms. "I'm fine, baby. Are you okay?"

Eyes flashing with pure relief, their savior stepped into Elin's embrace, pulling her tight against his body. "If you're fine, I'm fine." They held one another quietly while Anna stood by in awed silence.

When the couple broke apart, Elin gave Anna a bright grin. "I'm sorry. How about you? Are you okay?"

With an embarrassed nod, Anna mumbled, "I'm okay."

The man scanned Anna with stormy eyes. "I don't know what the hell you were thinking, running into the middle of a fight like that."

That set her on the defensive. "I can fight."

"Yeah, you can fight so well that you were about to get raped right here on the ground in front of me."

Anna's chin trembled at his harsh comment, and she swiped an angry hand across her face to hide her weakness. "Fuck you." She felt raw, exposed by the cruel words, and her chest stung. "You don't know anything about me."

"I know that you're damn lucky Elin held them off until I got back." He stared at her with a blank gaze that made her feel even more the hysterical woman.

"Kael," Elin said, "she probably saved my life. I didn't see the fourth guy sneaking up behind me. If she hadn't warned me, I most likely would've gotten a crowbar to the back of the head."

Momentary panic flashed in the young man's eyes, then his expression softened, and he engulfed Elin in another hug.

Elin squirmed and giggled within his embrace. "I said I'm fine."

He dropped a tender kiss on her hair. "Bloody," he observed, and dabbed at a cut above her eyebrow.

"A little. So much for my sunny, relaxing afternoon."

Anna folded her arms across her chest, still hurt and upset by Kael's comment. "Speaking of bad decisions, I don't know what the hell *you* were doing, leaving her alone out here like that. You can't be so thickheaded as to think *that's* safe."

He glanced at her. "I don't answer to you."

"Kael can't be with me every second," Elin responded with a gentle shake of her head. "Nor do I *want* Kael with me every second. I think you saw that I'm rather capable in my own right."

"You're right," Anna said. "I'm sorry."

She met warm hazel eyes when Elin stepped close and lifted Anna's face with a hand under her chin. "Hey, don't be sorry. I'm just glad you were here when I needed you. Kael got back fast, but it could've been a lot worse if you hadn't decided to help me."

Kael gave a quiet snort. "I'm just wondering what she's doing out here alone in the first place."

"Just walking," Anna mumbled.

"Well, I left dinner in the woods. I should go back and get it." Kael nodded at Elin, eyes shining with affection. "I caught you a rabbit."

Elin clapped and a wide smile lit up her whole face. "My perfect afternoon is back on track." She placed a gentle hand on Anna's arm. "And now we have a dinner guest and everything. You will stay for dinner, won't you?"

Anna blinked in surprise. She glanced at Kael, but his face betrayed no emotion. Thanking Elin for the offer, she said, "My name's Anna, by the way."

"Nice to meet you, Anna." Elin pressed a hand against the blood that still oozed from the cut above her eyebrow. "I don't know about you, but I could use a bath."

Anna blushed and ran a hand self-consciously through her hair. "That's what I was planning when I happened upon this whole sordid mess."

Elin nudged her playfully. "What do you say you and I wash off while Kael gets dinner ready?"

Kael nodded. "No offense, but it looks like you're both in desperate need of a good soak."

As he picked up his sword, Anna lowered her eyes to the prone bodies sprawled on the ground around them. "Are they all dead?"

"Yeah." There was a hint of sadness in Kael's dark eyes.

Anna gazed down at the curly-haired man at her feet, remembering the feeling of his hand groping her body. "Good." She was surprised to catch Kael staring at her with quiet sorrow, and asked, wondering if she'd missed a comment, "I'm sorry, did you say something?"

"I'm just glad you're both okay." Kael tipped his head, serious, and walked away. As he passed Elin, he said, "I set up camp in that clearing we passed through earlier. The one with the" — he dropped his voice — "pretty flowers."

Elin grinned, waving him away. "We'll be there in no time." Walking toward the lake, she called, "Hey, Anna! Come on, the water's fantastic."

ANNA WATCHED ELIN dive into the water, and her throat went unexpectedly dry at the glimpse of pale, naked skin. Still trembling with adrenaline from the fight, stomach in knots over her confrontation with Kael, she summoned her strength and limped to the shore.

Elin's head broke the surface of the water. "This feels wonderful." She slicked back her hair with both hands. "You hurt your ankle?"

"About a week ago, during a fight. I keep thinking it should feel better —"

Elin stood and Anna watched breathlessly as water sluiced over her bare skin. "I'll look at it after dinner. Maybe I can help. Now take off your clothes and get in here. You don't know what you're missing."

Anna licked her lips and stared at the dark pink nipples only yards from where she stood on shore. This was the closest she'd ever been to a real live naked woman. *You're right, I probably don't.* As much as she wanted to dive into the water and get closer to Elin, shyness held her back. She dropped her eyes to her own chest. Her green T-shirt was torn and dirty, her light brown skin smudged with blood and filth. She rubbed her hands over the seat of her pants, remembering all too well the scars that littered her body.

"Not used to being naked in front of someone else?" Elin's voice was full of quiet sympathy. "You have nothing to be embarrassed about." At Anna's quick backwards glance to where Kael had disappeared into the woods, she added, "And you have no reason to be afraid."

"He doesn't like me, does he?" Anna pulled her T-shirt over her head after a brief hesitation. She folded her arms over her stomach, skin burning beneath Elin's gaze.

"Kael just doesn't know you. It isn't easy for him to trust. Give him some time."

Anna unsnapped her pants, stepped out of them quickly,

and shot another look at the trees around them. "He's one hell of a fighter."

"One hell of a person." Elin held one hand playfully in front of her eyes. "I'm not peeking. Get the rest of those clothes off, and get your ass in here, girl!"

With a nervous giggle, Anna shed her bra and panties, then, putting as much weight on her left ankle as she could bear, she moved into the water. She was submerged safely to her upper chest when Elin uncovered her eyes.

"Feel good?"

"Wonderful."

"Want to feel even better?"

Anna tried hard not to stare at Elin's creamy collarbones. She worked her jaw for a moment, unable to produce a sound. *If she had any idea what I was thinking, she'd hate me.* Playing it safe, she croaked, "That depends."

Elin brought a hand out of the water and displayed a small, capped bottle with a triumphant grin. It was half full of thick amber liquid. "Shall I wash your hair?"

Anna couldn't remember the last time she'd experienced the luxury of shampoo. She skimmed one hand over the surface of the water. "I don't want you to waste—"

Elin clicked her tongue in disapproval and put a soothing hand on Anna's shoulder. "Don't be silly. It'd make me really happy to give you this simple pleasure. Given that you saved my life and all."

"But—"

Encouraging Anna to face away from her, Elin said, "Dunk."

Anna did, bending her knees until her head was underwater. She held the position for only a moment, until a powerful feeling of vulnerability propelled her to the surface. Sputtering, she pushed away the wet locks of dark hair that hung in her face.

"I'm not sure I saved your life," she said, keeping her back to Elin. She jerked in surprise when Elin touched her head, then released an involuntary moan when strong fingers rubbed fragrant shampoo into her hair. "My fighting skills aren't exactly up to par these days."

"You saved my life." Elin scratched at Anna's scalp, and Anna had to fight hard not to whimper in pleasure. "So it's just your ankle that's hurt?"

"Among other things." *My head. My heart. My will.*

"Well, you look exhausted." Resting a hand on Anna's shoulder, Elin encouraged her to bend her knees and crouch. She scooped up fresh water to pour over Anna's soapy hair and asked, "Where are you headed?"

"I'm not sure." Anna closed her eyes to enjoy the slow rinsing of her hair.

Elin was quiet for a minute, then asked, "Where are you from?"

Anna flashed on a nightmare image of her last day at home, unable to suppress a shudder. "Near the Pennsylvania-Maryland border. I grew up in a tribe that settled in that area."

"Nomadic?"

Anna managed a weak shrug. "Not nomadic enough, I guess."

For a moment Elin's movement faltered, and then she began rubbing one hand over Anna's upper back. Anna blinked and brought her hands to the surface of the water, scrubbing at the dried blood that still clung to them.

"Your tribe was attacked?"

"Last year." To Anna's surprise, it all came tumbling out. "Nearly everyone was killed. The rest were captured by raiders. My best friend Garrett and I managed to escape." She hesitated, then murmured, "He was killed last month."

"I'm sorry." Elin curled her fingers around Anna's shoulder, giving her a tender squeeze. "So you're alone now?"

"Yeah," Anna whispered. It was the first time she had spoken it aloud. "I'm alone."

Anna wasn't even aware that she was crying until Elin tightened her grip on her shoulder and pulled her around into a warm embrace. Then she felt the wetness of her cheek pressed against Elin's, and her shoulders shook within the circle of Elin's slim arms. She barely registered the thrill of naked breasts pressed against her own, she was so overcome with her private agony.

"It's okay, sweetheart," Elin cooed, and rocked her where they stood. "It's okay. You're not alone anymore."

The whispered words, and Elin's fingers stroking the small of her back, shocked Anna out of their embrace. Wiping at her tears with both hands, she glanced around at the trees once more. Her whole body trembled at the thought of Kael coming back and finding them like that.

Elin interlaced delicate fingers with Anna's battle-roughened ones. "I never lived in a tribe," she said, pulling Anna's attention back to her face. This close, she could see the furious smattering of freckles across pale skin. "I grew up all alone with my father. He took us to the country just as the sickness reached its peak, then spent years teaching me how to hide from other people. It must have been amazing for you, growing up around so many others."

"Your biological father?" Anna had never met an adult raised by a biological parent before. Her own parents died early on, shortly after the President had declared a state of emergency for the entire country. Anna couldn't remember a lot of the details, but Uncle Roberto had sometimes talked about it on those nights when he got drunk enough to summon up that time without breaking down.

It had taken only months for the country to dissolve into chaos. There were so many dead and dying, the hospitals had to close their doors. Anarchy erupted and the military struggled to maintain order amid rising violence from a citizenry driven to blind panic. The president was assassinated, and the federal government imposed martial law. But it was too late to stem the spread of rebellion. Throughout the nation, state and local government collapsed and small competing militias emerged, vying for power in shattered communities.

Eventually, the army turned on the White House and deposed the administration, and a series of generals attempted to run the country and combat the militias. But the army and the National Guard were decimated by illness and had no hope of winning the guerilla wars that followed. Uncle Roberto often said he wasn't sure who the lucky ones were: those who lived through the sickness and the factional warfare, or those who never had to adapt to this barren new world.

"I was lucky," Elin said. "My father survived the sickness and the troubles. I was only two years old at the time, so I barely remember my mother."

"I remember my family. Not as much as I'd like. One of my uncles survived. I always thought I was really lucky for that. He's the one who took me with him to the tribe."

"We were both lucky." Elin took Anna's hand and walked them to shore. For a moment, her eyes looked haunted. "There are much worse ways to grow up."

Anna nodded. She trailed behind Elin, trying not to stare at her shapely bottom as they reached shallow water. "So how long have you been traveling with Kael?"

Elin gave her a serene smile. "Well, I guess it would be just over two years now. My father died just before that—natural causes, I think—and I set out on my own. I wanted to explore the world, see new things. I found Kael, or we found each other, a couple of months later."

Anna grew bashful as they emerged from the water and stepped onto the shore. She covered her breasts with one arm, desperate to hide the ugly white scars on the left one, and dropped an awkward hand to conceal the curly triangle of hair between her thighs. "You must feel really safe with him."

Elin knelt to collect their clothing from the ground. "Kael makes me feel safe, yes. In every way."

Anna blushed at the obvious adoration in Elin's voice and cast her eyes to the grassy shore. Feeling shy, and not knowing how to talk about love, she stayed quiet, looking up only when Elin thrust her soiled clothing at her.

"I'm sorry you've got to put these things on again. Unless you have something clean with your stuff?"

"No." Anna accepted her dirty clothes, with red-tinged cheeks. She had nothing now.

"I guess it's time for some new clothes, huh?" Elin pulled on her tank top. "I've got a shirt you can borrow for now, back at camp."

Anna tried not to stare at erect nipples outlined against the cotton of Elin's top. "Thanks."

When they were both dressed, Elin asked, "Where'd you leave your stuff?"

Anna's face grew hot with shame. "I don't have anything."

"Nothing?"

"Not since I was attacked last week. The men who jumped me...I left my bags behind when I escaped them. My weapon. Everything I had—" She stopped, not wanting to dwell on the thought of all that she had lost. After Garrett was killed, nothing had mattered anymore. Not even what little she had left in life.

"Oh, sweetheart," Elin breathed, and rubbed her thumb along the back of Anna's hand. "I'm so glad you found us."

Anna allowed herself to be pulled into another spontaneous hug. This time she pressed her nose into Elin's neck and inhaled, soaking up the comfort. Despite her reservations about Kael, she found herself agreeing with the soft words. "Me, too."

"Are you hungry?" Elin slid her hands casually down Anna's sides, sending a rush of shivered pleasure through her body. "You feel like you could use a good meal."

"I'm starving." A simple statement, and Elin would never know how true it was.

"Come on, then," Elin said. "I saw some fresh cuts on your back when we were bathing. I want to look at those when we get to camp, okay?"

Anna followed the chattering redhead with a dazed smile on her face. For the first time since Garrett had drawn his last breath—perhaps for the first time since the attack last year—she felt a tingling of something deep in her belly. It was a feeling she thought she'd never know again. It was hope.

Chapter
Two

KAEL WAS LOUNGING in front of a crackling fire when they got back to camp. He leaned against a log, long legs stretched out in front of him and lean, muscled arms folded across his chest. Tearing his intense gaze away from the flames, he gave them a friendly nod. "Dinner's almost ready."

Now that she was out of danger and had seen the depth of Elin's love for Kael in her bright hazel eyes, Anna studied him as if for the first time. As much as she didn't want to admit it, he was an attractive guy. His face was smooth and defined, almost beautiful, even despite the darkness he exuded.

"Two rabbits!" Elin's exclamation pulled Anna's attention to the fire, where two skinned rabbits cooked on spits. "You've been busy."

"It's not every day we have a dinner guest."

Elin strode over to a pile of supplies and searched through a duffel bag. "Anna, here's that shirt I promised."

Anna accepted the T-shirt with a shy nod. It looked like it would fit. She glanced over her shoulder into the woods.

"Kael, turn your head."

Anna's cheeks flushed in embarrassed horror at Elin's command. "No, I...I can just —"

"No, you can stay right there. Kael will look away."

"Sure," he said, and faced away from Anna.

Elin also averted her eyes, though Anna wasn't nearly as self-conscious with her as she had been before their naked swim. She moved quickly, eager to release her hosts from their forced inattention.

"We'll have to figure something out," Elin said once Anna had pulled on the T-shirt and given the okay. She gave Kael a meaningful look. "She doesn't have any supplies. She lost everything after she was attacked about a week ago."

"Attacked?" His eyes were full of concern. "Are you hurt?"

Anna was touched by the change in his demeanor and

understood the underlying question. "Just some cuts and bruises, and I think my ankle's sprained. I was lucky to get away."

Kael held her gaze for a few moments. "Elin's a wonderful healer. She'll see to your injuries."

"Yes, she told me she'll be taking a look at them after dinner." Anna glanced over at Elin and blushed when she saw her smoothing out two sleeping bags that had been zipped together to make a double bed.

"We can unzip these and give you one," the lovely redhead said. "Kael has an extra blanket we can use, and next time we have the chance, we'll find something you can use to sleep. We'll also get you new clothes."

Anna blinked rapidly at Elin's words and the promise in them. She peeked over at Kael, who had a similarly stunned look on his face.

Elin gave him a beatific smile. "Right, Kael?"

Anna watched an entire conversation unfold in their shared gaze. She shifted where she stood, almost uncomfortable at the intimacy of the exchange. After a long moment, Kael and Elin both wore smiles that spoke of a mutual understanding.

"Right," Kael rumbled. Without a word to Anna, he looked back at the fire. "Rabbits are done."

ANNA COULDN'T SLEEP. Lying on her side in Elin's thick sleeping bag, she stared out at the shadowy forest that surrounded their campsite. Despite her utter exhaustion, she couldn't turn her brain off.

Maybe I should sneak away while they're sleeping. She wiped at the dampness under one eye with the fingers that lay curled near her face. *I may have nowhere else to go, but I'm not sure I should stay here.*

Kael didn't want her. She saw it in his eyes, though he treated her with quiet respect. He didn't trust her, and she couldn't blame him a bit. She didn't trust him, either. But Elin wanted her to stay. And suddenly that was what Anna wanted, deep down, so badly it hurt. Thinking about leaving Elin so soon after finding her made her chest ache. To have that light in her life when she'd been so certain that there was nothing but darkness in a future without Garrett...she sighed and eased onto her back. It would be amazing.

If she stayed, she would just have to deal with Kael. And how bad could he be? If a woman like Elin loved him, was there any reason for Anna not to trust him? Her body tensed at the thought, and it took some deep breathing to relax again. *Not all men are bad men.*

She couldn't leave. She had nothing and no one. Twenty-four hours ago, she had been wondering why she was still alive. Since then, she'd been held by the most beautiful woman she'd ever met, and made to feel cared for. It was as good a reason to live as any. And she didn't really want to die.

So I'll learn to live with Kael, for now. And who knows? Maybe he can teach me how to fight like him.

Decision made, she relaxed. Just as she began to drift to sleep, she was pulled back to awareness by a whispered conversation across the campfire. Cracking one eyelid open, she spotted Elin propped up on her side, leaning over Kael and murmuring under her breath. A moment later, the low sound of Kael's quiet voice floated through the air.

She wondered if they were talking about her. *I'm not causing tension between them, am I?*

Unable to rein in her curiosity, she peeked over with half-closed eyes. She couldn't hear their words, but she could see Elin smiling down on Kael as she spoke. At first his demeanor was distant, reserved, but soon he began to run his fingers through her red hair as they spoke. Then they were chuckling quietly, Elin wearing a wide grin and Kael nodding his head with a peaceful smile.

He doesn't seem too upset. Anna didn't dare move and kept her breathing deep and even. Seeing Kael unguarded like this, interacting with Elin, she felt her anxiety about him ease even further. *She must be one hell of a communicator. He almost looks happy.* Anna studied their tender looks and touches. *I hope she's convincing him that I'm not so bad, after all.*

She was shocked when, moments later, Elin bent down and captured Kael's mouth in a passionate kiss. She nearly slammed her eyes shut on instinct, but her curiosity won out and she remained still, watching. Kael released a muffled groan, and Elin pulled back with a soft giggle. She held a finger on her lips, urging him to be silent.

Then Elin sat up on their sleeping bag, and the extra blanket that was draped over their bodies fell down around her lap. She was still wearing her light tank top, but her upper thighs were bare. She reached down and pulled off her panties, tossing them on top of her bag with a mischievous smile. Anna watched Kael's answering smile grow wide as Elin moved over to straddle his hips and settle on top of him. Elin leaned down and kissed him again as Anna lay frozen in awe.

Anna had never made love with anybody. She had never even seen two people making love. She knew sex, and she knew violence, but she was a stranger to the intimate dance that was happening across the fire. As much as she knew that she should close her eyes, she was riveted to the scene.

Kael reached down between their bodies, grinning up at Elin. The firelight played off the muscles of his arm as he worked his hand between her legs. Elin squeezed her eyes closed, and her breathing hitched loud enough for Anna to hear.

Anna flexed her thigh muscles, and her own breathing became erratic for just a moment before she brought it under control. She lay, unmoving, feeling a familiar ache between her legs, made almost unfamiliar by its strength. The look on Elin's face was intense and sensual. Kael's eyes were glued to her, flashing with heat that Anna could see as clear as day.

Then he withdrew his hand, drawing a quiet groan of protest from Elin. He gripped Elin's bare hips with both hands and whispered something up at her, and she nodded in response. Elin reached down between them and planted her knees farther apart, shifting on top of Kael. Her eyes grew wide, and her mouth opened in a soundless cry.

My God, Anna thought. She watched Kael slide a hand up the middle of Elin's back to encourage her to lean down and meet him in a hungry kiss. Elin's hips continued to move as they got lost in the joining of lips and tongues, and she rode Kael in a steady rhythm. One of Kael's hands twined in Elin's hair, while the other slid down her back to grip her pale bottom. *I've never seen anything so beautiful in my entire life.*

Anna told herself again that she should close her eyes, but she was rapt. She couldn't tear her attention away from the lovemaking any more than she could stop breathing. Her heart pounded so hard that she was afraid that Kael and Elin would hear it and discover her watching.

Elin broke their kiss and sat up, riding Kael's hips with increasing urgency. She leaned back a little and smiled down at Kael from beneath hooded eyes. Anna's mouth fell open at the pure heat of that look, and she listened to Kael's soft moan float out into the cool night air. Elin broke into a wide grin that quickly turned into a grimace of pleasure.

As though he knew just what she needed, Kael reached between their bodies again, and Anna watched in amazement as Elin tipped back her head, opened her mouth, and arched her back in silent release. Kael kept his other hand pressed against her lower back and supported her trembling body. Elin continued a slow, erotic grinding against Kael until he seemed to stiffen beneath her, and the two lovers sent a mutual silent cry out into the night.

Anna's body was alive with feeling. She worried that her hosts would know she was awake because she was so out of control; she was shaking, and she couldn't get her heartbeat to slow back to normal. Across the campfire, Elin whispered a quiet *I love you* down to Kael, who mouthed a reverent response in reply and pulled Elin down into a full-body hug, turning his face toward Anna and squinting hard in an expression of pure bliss.

She knew she shouldn't have watched, but it had been the most incredible thing she'd ever seen. They were so beautiful together. Even Kael, who had frightened and enraged her earlier that day, had been transformed into something entirely different by their lovemaking. Suddenly, powerfully, Anna trusted these two strangers with her life. To find love out here in such a cold, hard world was a clear sign that these were people who could become a home. Homeless for over a year, and alone for a month, Anna couldn't think of anything she wanted more. A family. A place where she belonged.

I hope Kael can grow to like me. She directed the thought out to the universe, an uncharacteristic prayer. She listened to another few moments of murmured endearments from across the fire before forcibly turning her mind off and waiting for the refuge of sleep.

WHEN ANNA AWOKE the next morning, it was to the sound of faint laughter coming from just beyond the campsite. She regarded the cold fire pit and empty sleeping bag with a smile, remembering what had taken place there the night before. Yawning, she dragged her tongue across her teeth. *I wish I still had a toothbrush.*

She visited the bushes, then returned to her sleeping bag and picked up the half-full canteen of water Elin had given her. She took a long pull of cool liquid, swirled it around in her mouth, then spat it on the ground. She swallowed the second sip. Feeling a little awkward, she decided to seek out the laughter and voices she could hear just inside the trees. She crept, hesitant to surprise her new companions. *After all, they could be having a repeat performance of last night.*

When she found them, she thought for a moment that she'd been right. They were rolling around on the ground in a small clearing not far from their campsite, wrapped in a fierce embrace. Anna stopped in her tracks, surprised, but she soon realized that what she was seeing was a playful wrestling match.

"No way, pal." Elin panted with exertion from her position beneath Kael. She squirmed until she was able to free herself from his hold, then scrambled to her feet and said, "I don't think so."

Kael sprang to his feet with a feral smile, charging at his lover in another attack. He brought her down hard and immediately pinned her wrists above her head. "Get out of this one, baby."

Okay, maybe not so playful. Anna took a step back at the unexpected fierceness of the attack and at the position Elin was now in. Her mouth fell open a little, and her heart pounded in her chest. Painful tears stung her eyes, an instinctive reaction to the scene of dominance.

At first Elin appeared to go limp. Kael shifted his body a bit, and she began to squirm and twist beneath him, then brought her knee up to catch him in the crotch. He released a high-pitched grunt at the blow and struggled to keep Elin pinned as she fought against him like a woman possessed.

"Damn, honey," Kael gasped, his voice high and breathy. "You've gotten *good* at this."

A few moments more and Elin was free. Kael lay on his side on the ground, heaving, both arms curled over his stomach. "Good job," he praised. He opened his mouth and rolled onto his back, spreading his arms wide as he regained his breath.

Elin laughed, then caught sight of Anna still standing among the trees. With a calm smile, she rose to her feet. "Anna, good morning."

Kael lifted his head from the ground, managing a sheepish grin. "Good morning."

Anna willed her hands to stop trembling. "Good morning."

"Are you okay?" Elin approached and took one of Anna's hands, giving it a squeeze. "I hope we didn't scare you."

"I'm fine. It's just when I saw you at first—"

Kael sat up at the words, then clambered to his feet. He remained standing behind Elin, staring at Anna with genuine concern.

"Kael's taught me almost everything I know about self-defense," Elin said. "My dad, well, he taught me to hide and to run."

"And he did a good job of it," Kael praised.

Elin shot him a pleased look. "Kael teaches me how to protect myself when he can't."

Eyes intense, Kael stepped closer to them, compelling Anna to lean into Elin for support. "I can teach you some moves, if you want."

Anna remembered the sting of Kael's comments about her fighting skills and fought not to get defensive about his offer. But despite her wounded pride, she knew an opportunity when she saw one. "Thanks." She hesitated, then said, "I was one of the best fighters in my tribe. I do know a little, even if it didn't look like it yesterday."

Kael gave her the barest hint of an apologetic smile. "I can show you some great strategies for fighting with an injured ankle. With all kinds of injuries, really. I know it's hard to rely on your regular moves when you're hurt."

Anna released Elin's fingers and held out her hand, grateful when Kael shook it gently. Elin looked like she was ready to bounce up and down beside them, and she flashed white teeth back and forth between Kael and Anna.

"Awesome," Elin said. "Listen, I'm going to go to the bathroom before breakfast." To Anna, she said, "I have a toothbrush you can borrow, if you'd like."

Anna exhaled in relief, grinning harder than she had in a long time. "Yes, please."

"Give me a minute or so head start so I can find it in that disaster I call a bag, okay?" Elin left them with a wave and a sweet kiss blown in their direction.

Aware that she was wearing a goofy grin, Anna forced it down with effort. When she looked at Kael, she could see that he was struggling to wipe a similar smile from his handsome face. When she was all of a sudden alone with him, Anna's discomfort kicked in. Wondering if she would ever feel at ease with him, she waited long enough that she wouldn't appear totally rude, then turned to follow Elin back to the campsite. She had taken only two steps when Kael spoke in a low voice.

"Anna?"

She looked back warily

"I'm sorry about yesterday." His expression was softer. "What I said...I was harsh."

Anna shrugged. "You probably had a point."

Kael shook his head and held up a hand to forestall her words. "I was an asshole about it, so let me apologize. It just shook me up, not only finding Elin in trouble with four men, but also seeing someone else who could get hurt." When Anna opened her mouth to speak, he continued, "Elin told me you saved her life. She wouldn't exaggerate something like that. For that I thank you, from the bottom of my heart. I'm glad you were there." He paused, his eyes guilty. "I should have been."

The emotion in his voice made Anna feel as if she were a voyeur once again. "Apology accepted," she whispered. "And remember, like the lady said, you can't always be there. She's capable in her own right."

Kael snickered and jammed both hands deep into the pockets of his jeans. "You don't know how often I get to hear that. Just wait. You'll see."

With that, he sauntered off in the opposite direction of their campsite, and Anna turned the other way, following the path Elin had taken. She wore a slight smile, feeling worlds better after the short conversation with the man she'd been certain disliked her.

ELIN AND KAEL had an obvious routine forged from two years of traveling together. After eating a small breakfast prepared by Elin, they packed their things and walked until the sun hung directly overhead. Anna didn't know where they were going, and she didn't care to ask. It didn't matter. She had more direction today than she'd had yesterday, and for that she was so grateful she would follow them anywhere.

Around noon, Kael slowed his brisk walk as they entered a clearing and found a green field overgrown with pansies. The purple flowers provided yet another point of color in an already brilliant autumn day.

Elin's hazel eyes grew wide, and her face lit up at the discovery. A light breeze whipped red hair around her pale face, and she pulled a strand away from where it had blown into her mouth. "You guys, isn't this *beautiful*?"

Aware of Kael gazing with adoration at Elin, Anna found herself equally unable to tear her eyes from the sight of her. "Yeah, it is. Gorgeous."

Elin stepped into the field and shot a sunny grin over her shoulder. "I'm just going to go on ahead for a minute, okay?" Before either of them could answer, she gave an elated whoop and took off running through the flowers.

Anna watched her simple, uninhibited joy with amazement. She couldn't remember ever possessing that kind of innocent wonder, even as a child.

"You've never met anyone like her, right?"

At the soft question, Anna glanced cautiously at Kael, wondering if her warmth for his lover was too close to the surface. "No, I can't say that I have. She's so genuine."

Kael hefted the large pack that was strapped to his shoulders and gave her the first real grin she had ever elicited from him, his whole face lighting up with it. "Elin came into my life at a very dark time. She was — she is — a breath of fresh air."

Anna stared ahead at the edge of the field. Elin was crouching near the wide trunk of a tree, bending low to inhale the scent of the violet blooms. Daylight played upon her hair and her pale skin, and she looked so lovely it made Anna's heart hurt.

"How does she do it?" She glanced at Kael. "How does she stay so happy when the world is the way it is?"

"She hasn't had to experience a lot of what makes the world so bad. Her father did a wonderful job protecting her."

"Good for him."

"I thank him every day."

When they reached Elin, she was stretched out on the grass with her hands planted next to her hips. She watched their approach with an amused smirk. "Slowpokes."

Anna jammed her hands in the pockets of her torn jeans. "I just enjoy nature at a decelerated pace, I guess."

Elin grinned and lifted a delicate hand. "Help me up?"

"Lazy thing," Kael admonished with good humor, as Anna pulled her to her feet. More soberly, he said, "We're coming up on Sullivan, if I'm reading my map right. I'm going to scout ahead. We can stop for supplies there."

"All right." Elin tugged Anna closer by their enjoined hands. "Anna and I will take the opportunity to have some girl talk."

"Knock yourselves out."

Elin giggled, sending Kael off with a gentle slap on his bottom. His only reaction was to raise an eyebrow at her as he passed them by. He rolled his neck from side to side as he walked away, cracking the vertebrae with a quiet groan. Elin shuddered at the sound.

When he'd disappeared into the trees, she took one last look at the field of flowers, sighed, then said, "He hates going into cities. Expect him to get a little edgy."

A little edgy? As far as Anna could tell, Kael was always edgy. Peering ahead, she confirmed that he was no longer within earshot. "Elin?"

"Yeah?" Elin squeezed her hand.

"Is Kael uncomfortable having me around? You can tell me the truth."

"No, of course not. Did he do anything to make you feel that way?"

"No, I...no. I mean, I know we got off to a rocky start, but he's been really great today."

"He knows I like you," Elin said as they strolled slowly in his wake. "He's trying. I know it may take some time, but I hope you'll give him a chance. He's one of the strongest, most amazing people you'll ever meet. But he can be tough to get to know. He keeps his distance unless he really trusts you."

"Does he trust anyone but you?"

"Not yet."

Anna caught a flicker of hope in Elin's eyes. "But you're

optimistic?"

"I am." Elin smiled. "One thing I've always wanted is a big family. Growing up, I only ever had my dad. That was hard. I would've given anything for a little brother or sister, or even just a friend. I loved Dad so, so much, and when he died, I felt like I had nothing left. Now I have Kael, and I love him more than I ever knew I could love anything in the world. And it feels so good to love someone, and to be loved back. I want as much of that in my life as I can get. Kael knows that."

Anna accepted the pronouncement at face value, although she thought Elin could be overestimating her lover's understanding nature. They walked a little farther in silence, their hands still lightly clasped, then Elin stopped abruptly.

"Anna, I want to say something. I don't know what your plans are, but I want you to know you're welcome to stay with me and Kael for as long as you want." She squeezed Anna's hand as she started to voice doubts, and said, "I guess what I'm saying is you could be part of our family."

Anna's vision blurred as emotion flooded her. Blinking, she stopped walking, and Elin halted alongside. It was exactly what she wanted, crazy as it seemed. She was almost afraid to believe that it was possible. "You want me to be your family? How can you say that so soon? You just met me."

"You risked your life to help me yesterday. You were brave and good. I know I've only just met you, but I feel a connection with you. I feel like you belong with us, and I can tell you're a good person."

They started walking again, Anna deep in thought. For the first time since Garrett's death, she allowed herself to experience the hole his absence left in her heart. She would give anything for it to be filled up again. The emptiness she had been feeling before she met Elin had scared the hell out of her. She kept her fingers entangled with Elin's, enjoying the simple human contact.

"I'm not sure that what I did yesterday makes me a good person," she said after some hesitation. "After Garrett was killed, I felt like I had no more reason to live. When I lost all my stuff in the attack last week, I figured it was a sign that there was nothing left for me anymore. Yesterday...I don't know if I was being brave or just suicidal."

"Death wouldn't necessarily have been the worst thing to happen to you yesterday," Elin said. "But you helped me anyway."

Anna basked in the warm glow of Elin's sincere words. "I wouldn't want to cause any problem between you and Kael. I don't want to be a source of tension."

"Don't worry, nothing could ever come between Kael and me. Our love is too real for anything to weaken it."

Anna felt her face flush as she once again remembered their lovemaking, and she cast a shy grin down at the ground. "I think it's wonderful that you've found something like that. How did you meet him?"

"After my father died, I decided to set out on my own. I knew it was dangerous. Dad told me every day how dangerous traveling could be, but I couldn't stand hiding out alone."

"I understand. Being alone...is horrible."

Elin wrapped an arm around Anna's waist. "I don't know what I hoped to find. God knows I never imagined finding someone like Kael. I just walked and started seeing a little of the world. Mostly I tried to stay away from people, and then one day I was walking through the forest and found a campsite. There was a small fire going, and Kael was just sitting there, cooking dinner."

"Weren't you scared, coming on a strange man in the woods like that?"

Elin shook her head. "Not really. I was curious. He was staring into the fire, so deep in thought. All I wanted was to know what was going on inside his head."

"Did you actually approach him?"

Elin giggled. "No. I was hiding behind a tree debating the wisdom of trusting my gut on Kael when I noticed that he was gone. Then suddenly there's this low voice coming from behind me, whispering in my ear. 'It's dangerous for a beautiful girl to be out here all alone.'" Elin affected a dramatic swoon. "Oh my God, my knees almost gave out on me."

"That would be terrifying." Anna shivered at the thought of being caught off guard like that.

"A little terrifying, but mostly exciting. I thought Kael was the sexiest person I had ever seen."

Anna bit her lip, trying to suppress a bashful grin at that. She wanted to ask Elin more, but she was hesitant to move their conversation toward a subject she knew very little about. It didn't take long before curiosity won out over shyness. "When...um, when did you become lovers?"

"It took us two weeks to get there. Kael invited me to dinner that first night, and we talked for hours. The next morning, he insisted that I travel with him. He didn't want to let me go off alone, and I didn't want to leave him, so that worked out. Everything happened so fast. I knew almost immediately that I was meant to be with him."

"Were you nervous?" She couldn't help but ask. Elin had experienced things that Anna had only fantasized about, and she hadn't experienced the things that gave Anna nightmares. "I mean, was he your first?"

"Kael was my first, and yes, I was a little nervous." Elin's eyes twinkled. "Not that Kael would hurt me or anything, but I think it must always be a little nerve-wracking, making love with someone for the first time."

Anna's stomach flip-flopped at how quickly Elin was creeping into her heart. She'd never felt comfortable talking about sex with anyone, ever, but this almost felt easy. *I never thought I'd have a friend again after Garrett. How is it possible to have found something so amazing, so soon?*

"Your friend Garrett," Elin asked, "was he your lover?"

Anna shook her head. "No. I've never had a lover before."

"Never?" Elin sounded surprised. "I can't believe that. You're so gorgeous."

Anna felt her cheeks go hot at the compliment. "No. I've never...found anyone who interested me."

"He wasn't your type?"

Anna chuckled at the thought and at the bittersweet flash of memory of her blond, curly-haired friend. "No. Garrett was like my brother. And I was like his sister." *And one of the only things we didn't have in common was loving men. He did, I didn't.* A familiar wave of melancholy swept through her.

"So what is your type?" Elin stroked her hand. "What interests you?"

By this point, Anna's face was on fire. She struggled not to look over and meet Elin's hazel eyes, terrified that her own attraction would be obvious. "I don't know." *Why did I open this can of worms?*

"How about Kael?" Elin asked in a hushed whisper and nudged Anna with her hip.

Anna's breathing picked up at the question. "Kael, uh...Kael—"

"Don't worry," Elin hastened to say. "I'm just curious about what you find attractive. Do you think Kael is sexy? I won't be jealous or anything if you do."

"Kael is very good-looking. He...I guess he's—"

Elin stopped Anna's rambling speech with another squeeze of her hand. "How about me?" she asked after a quiet moment. "Am I more your type?"

Anna felt her stomach drop at Elin's query. *She could be trying to trick me into saying something,* was her first irrational thought. *She's crazy if she thinks I'll admit to that when it will get me hated or killed by most people.* An instant of heart-thumping paranoia, and then Anna remembered how at ease Elin had made her feel at every other moment since they'd met. *Elin wouldn't do that to me. I'm not sure Elin could hate anyone. But what does she want to hear?*

"You're a very attractive woman," Anna said. Her palm felt sweaty in Elin's hand, and her voice shook. "I'm sure Kael is just as happy that he found you as you are that you found him."

"Am I making you uncomfortable?"

Anna avoided her eyes. "I'm just not used to talking about this stuff."

"We don't have to if you don't want to, but I want you to know that you can talk to me about everything. I promise to never judge you or make you feel bad about anything you want to tell me, okay?"

Anna gave her an embarrassed nod. "I do want to talk about it. I just don't know how."

Elin laughed and brought Anna's hand to her lips to plant a soft kiss on her knuckles. "Stick with me, babe. If there's one thing I do, it's talk. Sex and love are two of my favorite subjects."

"Great." Anna's fingers tingled where silky lips had pressed against them, bringing a grin to her face. "Two I don't know much about."

Elin stopped and faced Anna, looking into her eyes. "There's a lot I can teach you," she said, and pressed a gentle kiss to Anna's lips. "Like I said, stick with me."

They started walking again, Elin still holding onto Anna's hand.

I can die happy now, Anna thought in wonderment. She resisted the urge to touch her lips with her free hand, amazed at the sensation from the simple gesture. *I guess that was lesson number one.*

KAEL REJOINED THEM as they strode up a gravel path that led to the main road into Sullivan. Still reeling from girl talk, Anna blushed a little as he stalked toward them. Elin greeted him with a wide grin.

"Looks quiet," he said. "I haven't seen a soul."

"Where are we?" Anna asked. *God, I have no fucking idea even what state I'm in anymore.*

Kael gave her an odd look. "Indiana."

"And where are we going?"

"We're going south for the winter." Elin took Kael's hand. "Got to keep moving, or Kael gets antsy. Kentucky or Tennessee,

I think. How does that sound to you?"

"Fine." Anna tried not to stare at their clasped hands. Already she missed Elin's attention and wished she could grab her other hand

"Anna." Kael's dark, expressionless eyes moved over her. "When we go into a city, you stick close to me. We don't separate. There are too many places for people to hide, too much chance I won't hear someone coming."

Anna frowned, feeling a twinge of annoyance at Kael's commanding tone. Before yesterday, she'd been master of her own destiny. Nobody told her what to do. Even Garrett had never tried; she would've slugged him, and he'd known it. Though Kael was the best fighter she'd ever seen, and he'd already saved her life once, she was long past being told what she was allowed to do as if she were a child.

Kael must have seen her internal struggle. "Please don't argue with me," he insisted. "There's a reason Elin and I do things the way we do, and it's kept us safe for two years now. Okay?"

Anna bit her lip. "Fine. But do you think we could start sparring together in the next couple days, so you can see that I'm not quite as helpless as I may have appeared by the lake?"

"Deal," he said with a brief nod. "But this isn't about thinking you're helpless. This is about safety in numbers. In cities, that's what matters. And that's final."

Elin shot Anna a soothing smile. "Besides, shopping isn't nearly as much fun alone."

"Thank God." Kael released a quiet snort. "At last we've found you a good shopping partner."

Elin turned to Anna with a long-suffering sigh. "Kael thinks shopping is boring. Well, some shopping." She raised herself up on her tiptoes and kissed his cheek. "I didn't hear you complaining when we found that Victoria's Secret store in Dayton, Ohio."

Kael's blush rivaled Anna's. "Yeah, well—" He cleared his throat, gave Elin a scolding look, then dropped her hand and walked to the trees that lined the main road. "Who in their right mind would complain about that?"

Not me. Anna had heard of Victoria's Secret. Uncle Roberto had kept a stack of catalogues from the lingerie store under his sleeping pallet. As a teenager, Anna found and fell in love with his collection.

Having scouted ahead, Kael knew right where to lead them. There was a sporting goods store near the edge of the city, requiring them to walk only three blocks on deserted sidewalks.

The glass front door had been smashed in some time ago, and the interior was dark. Kael led them to the entrance, then lifted his arm to stop their progress.

"You two wait out here. I want to take a walk through before we go inside." He gave them a stern look. "Stay out of sight."

"No problem," Elin said. "We'll just wait for your signal."

Jaw tense, Anna said nothing. She walked over to the brick wall at the side of the store and folded her arms over her stomach. Elin came to lean against the wall beside her.

"Is this what you mean by 'a little edgy'?" Staring toward the abandoned parking lot, Anna resisted the urge to glower.

"He doesn't mean anything by it." Elin's kind voice drew Anna's attention to her face and her tender hazel eyes. "He's...been through a lot. He's cautious. Please believe that Kael just doesn't want to see any of us hurt."

"I'm sorry." Anna exhaled steadily. "I don't mean to be difficult. I just have a hard time with being ordered around like that."

"I understand — believe me, I do. I used to get frustrated sometimes, too, but now...I know Kael. I know where he's coming from. He just wants to protect us from the bad things in this world."

"Well, it's a bit late for me. I know all about the bad things the world has to offer."

Elin's eyes flashed with pain. "I'm sorry. I'm sorry that nobody was there to help protect you when you needed it, but please...let us help protect you now." She placed her hand on Anna's arm. "And you can help protect us."

Elin's warm gaze melted away the last of her anger, and Anna said, "You're right. I'm sorry. I'm oversensitive." *I just hate having a man telling me what to do all the time. It feels a little too much like home.*

Kael poked his head out the front door and gestured to them. "Ladies, are you ready to shop?"

"You said the magic words." Elin jumped away from the wall and went to him, rising up on her tiptoes to kiss his cheek as she walked through the smashed door.

Anna followed, hissing sharply when she took her first step. Her limp was still pronounced, though Elin had carefully wrapped her ankle the night before. The kick she'd received at the lake left her gritting her teeth in pain after only half a day of walking.

"How's the ankle?" Kael asked.

"Fine. No sweat."

Kael held her stare for a moment before turning to walk back into the store. "We'll set up camp once we get far enough outside of town."

"I said it's fine. Look, I don't want to be the dead weight who slows you two down. I can keep up. I promise."

"Anna." Kael paused and rubbed his palm over his shaven head. "I know that you and I are still...adjusting to this situation. I don't want you to feel like I have a problem with you or like I'm questioning your abilities. I just have a certain way that I like to do things, and being careful is very important to me. For all of us. If you don't let your ankle heal properly, you'll be at a disadvantage if something unexpected happens."

Anna released a frustrated breath. "I know, but—"

"But nothing. I only walked us as far as I did today so that we could get some supplies. If we hadn't needed them, I'd have insisted you rest for at least a day." Before Anna could respond, he continued, "Listen, you're with us now. That means you're going to have to put up with me and my moods. It means I care about you and how you're doing. I know that Elin is better at this stuff than I am. Please don't take anything I say or do personally. I'm not the bad guy, I swear."

Anna couldn't suppress a smile at that. Once again, Kael had reached out and smoothed over her hurt and anger, and despite his brusque manner, she heard the truth of his words. *He's not the bad guy. Elin wouldn't be with a bad guy.*

"I'm sorry. You're right," she said. "I guess you're going to have to put up with my moods, and me, too. I just have an aversion to feeling like someone is telling me what to do." She wrinkled her nose in distaste. "Bad memories."

Kael gave her a humorless smile. "I understand."

"Hey, Anna!" Elin's excited voice came from somewhere inside the store. "This place still has a few sleeping bags. Come check it out."

Anna ducked her head in a quick nod to Kael, then followed the sound of Elin's voice. Gazing around, she noted that the shelves were still relatively full of random sporting goods items, everything covered with a thick layer of dust. This was one of the more untouched stores she'd seen. It wasn't unusual for a place like this to be well picked through.

"What do you think?" Elin held up two rolled sleeping bags. "Red or green?"

"Green." Anna shot her a half-grin. "I don't want to be too easy to spot when I'm unconscious."

"Good call. You know, I saw some clothing up near the counter. I don't know what they have, but maybe you could find something. I'll look for a backpack for your stuff."

"Thanks." Anna limped to the racks of clothing at the other side of the store. As she walked past a center aisle, she caught sight of something that immediately captured her interest: a row of baseball bats, both wooden and aluminum. She disappeared between the tall shelves for a closer look and emerged a moment later with a sturdy wooden baseball bat gripped in her hand. *I have a weapon again.* Relieved, she set out in search of something to wear.

On her way past a cash register, she glanced down at a folded newspaper that sat on the counter. The headline was similar to the headlines of every paper she had seen from right before they had stopped printing them twenty years earlier: *The Attack That Never Ends: Billions Dead As A Result of Biological Agent.* She read the subtitle. *Are These The Last Days?*

"Not for all of us," she muttered under her breath. "God knows why." A tired sigh, and she limped off to go shopping for new clothes.

Chapter
Three

AFTER ONLY A day and a half of rest at their campsite just out of Sullivan, Anna felt stronger and healthier than she had in months and decided it was time to start fighting lessons. She left Elin cooking breakfast by the fire, deeply engrossed in a tattered paperback book, and set off in search of Kael.

She found him standing in a small clearing, and as she looked on, he nocked an arrow and drew the compound bow he'd picked up in the sporting goods store in Sullivan. Anna stopped about fifteen feet from where he stood. As he aimed at something in the distance, she took the opportunity to study him in a way she didn't feel comfortable doing when he could watch her in return. His body was lean and strong, muscled shoulders in stark relief beneath his black T-shirt. Dark energy radiated from his tense frame; his concentration on his target was silent and intense.

Do you think Kael is sexy?

Anna took in the unrelenting strength of her traveling companion, and her cheeks flushed at the sudden heat in her belly. She dropped her eyes to her feet, confused, then raised them again so she could keep watching.

Kael released the arrow, keeping his upper body straight and in line with his hips. His posture was impeccable, his entire presence cool and confident. The arrow whizzed through the air and landed with a thwack in the narrow trunk of a tree amongst dozens of others, just below the juncture of the branches. He held his position momentarily after the arrow hit its mark, then lowered his impressive bow with a quiet sigh.

"So, was that a hit or a miss?" Anna leaned against a tree, arms folded over her chest.

"Hit," Kael said, not even reacting to her sudden presence. "I think I'm getting the hang of this thing."

"Looks like it." They stood in silence for a beat until Anna gave an awkward cough and cleared her throat. "Anyway, I was wondering if maybe you were up to helping me practice fighting this morning. Elin told me I'd find you out here."

"Sounds good." He walked over and set his new bow down near the tree, standing as close to her as he had ever been.

For the first time, Anna noticed the startling indigo color of his eyes. She blinked, entranced, then dropped her gaze. "Cool."

"But I'm going to take it a little easy on you today." Kael raised his arms above his head and stretched. "I think we should concentrate on good strategies for fighting with an injured ankle. No weapons."

Anna stripped off her light jacket, laid her toiletries down upon it, and straightened to begin her own stretching. "Don't go too easy on me. The point isn't just for me to learn some new moves, but also for you to see that I already know a few things."

Kael gave her a friendly smile. "Of course." After some mutual stretching, he gestured to the clearing. "You ready?"

"Sure thing." Anna bounced up and down on the balls of her feet, shaking out her arms. "Let's go."

Facing Kael, she took in his relaxed posture, his confident half-smile, and met his gaze in silent challenge. *I need to show him that I can do this. I need to show him that I can hold my own in this group.*

"Why don't you show me what you've got?" Kael said. "Standard sparring rules apply. No elbow or knee strikes, attacks to the neck, spine, or eyes. Obviously I'm going to avoid that ankle."

Anna nodded. "Okay."

"Now, I want you to work around your pain, not fight through it. You got that? In a perfect world, you'd be able to rest up before needing to use that ankle again. I know this isn't a perfect world, and I understand why you need to get back on your feet. But take it easy. Concentrate on using your arms, your hands. Try to keep that ankle out of the strike zone. Try to get an early advantage by going for vulnerable areas—crotch, eyes, throat."

"Wait. I thought there were no attacks to the neck or eyes?"

Kael gave her a small smile. "I don't expect you to go full-out, but you can try to hit me. If you want to avoid those areas, go for my feet or my head."

Anna's upper lip twitched at his utter calm. "Deal."

Kael beckoned her with his hand. "Come on. Knock me down."

Anna hesitated only briefly, then threw a punch at Kael's face. She pulled it before it could connect and used her good foot to stomp on his instep. He grunted at the move, and she stepped forward to bring her knee into his crotch. He moved sideways, avoiding her, and she spun around to give him a wicked smile.

"Nice. Try again."

Anna exhaled, then swung at Kael's head. He ducked her fist and countered with a light punch to her shoulder. Anna scowled. "You can hit me for real, you know."

"That's not what this is about. Listen, let's concentrate on self-defense. What's normally your first reaction to a threat?"

"I listen," Anna said. "I don't normally get surprised. I'm very good at listening."

"Good. That's important. But what if you're in a situation already? The threat is approaching. You know a confrontation is imminent."

Anna considered. "I try to catch them off guard. Attack before they have a chance to realize I'm not just going to let myself be taken."

Kael frowned. "Your first move should always be to try for an escape. First, be alert to your surroundings. Second, run away from danger if you can."

Anna let out a disgusted snort. Taking advantage of Kael's distraction, she jabbed at his midsection. He absorbed the blow and grabbed her arm as she retreated. She jerked back to escape his grasp, but he spun them around so that he was behind her. Wrapping muscular arms around her chest, he pulled her to his body and immobilized her with startling strength.

"If you get into a fight, you can lose. If you escape from needing to have to fight, you win no matter what." Kael's lips brushed her ear; his warm breath tickled her neck.

Anna shivered at the sensation, remembering her confusing flash of attraction for him earlier. Stiffening in discomfort, she squirmed in an attempt to get out of his hold. "What if I can't run away? What if I'm trying to protect my tribe from slavers who are attacking us?" Her voice rose, and her heart pounded at the unwelcome assault of nightmarish memories that overtook her at the words. "What if women and children are depending on me?"

"Then you fight." Kael's voice was calm, his grip sure.

Anna seethed at being restrained. She continued to struggle for a moment, her heart rate rising as panic set in. "Goddamn you, Kael," she growled, kicking back at him with her uninjured foot.

"So fight." Kael lifted her off her feet, and she flailed her legs uselessly. "Get out of this."

Anna closed her eyes, trying hard not to focus on the way his crotch pressed into her bottom. Her breathing increased as she remembered the smell of blood and male sweat, the sound of her tribe mates screaming in the distance. Summoning all of her righteous fear and anger, she went limp in Kael's arms.

Obviously surprised, Kael shifted and Anna immediately drew her foot forward then kicked back hard, striking him in the shin to cause him to loosen his hold. She pressed her advantage, slipping down through his grip as her feet hit the ground. Turning her left hip forward, she drove her elbow into his solar plexus, escaped from his stranglehold, and stumbled backwards away from him.

He bent over at the waist, holding his stomach with one hand. "Christ," he gasped. "You pack one hell of a punch when you're pissed off."

Anna shook out her arms and rolled her head from side to side. Facing him, she tried to push back her lingering fear. She didn't want him to see how much he'd terrified her with his physical dominance. Somehow she managed a cocky grin. "So don't piss me off."

"Nah, it's good to get mad. If someone is attacking you, and especially if you find yourself overpowered, you need to feel that anger. Get pissed off. Use that rage. Sometimes it's the only thing that'll save you." Kael straightened, his hand lingering over his belly. "Use your fear, too."

"Who say's I'm afraid?"

"There's nothing wrong with being afraid." He took a careful step closer. "All animals, including humans, need to feel fear. Those without fear don't live very long."

Anna blinked rapidly as her eyes flooded. *I've spent a year trying to block out my fear. Don't tell me I should just live with it.*

"And right now, we're not going to worry about protecting others. This is about protecting yourself." Kael feinted left, as though he were going to attack, then danced backwards. "Fight me off."

"I'm not afraid of you." Anna threw her shoulders back and raised her chin in defiance.

"Prove it." Kael lunged forward and grabbed her arm, pulling her to him.

Startled, she allowed her body to be moved forward, using the momentum to drive her shoulder into his chest. He jumped backwards, clearly shaken by the blow, then grabbed her around the waist to pull her to the ground. Anna stumbled, going down with a muted cry of despair.

Kael followed her as she fell, quickly scrambled on top of her body, and pinned her wrists above her head. "Tell me you wouldn't be afraid if someone got you into this position," he said into her ear.

"Fuck you, Kael," she spat, squirming beneath his heavier bulk.

"It's okay, Anna." He kept her arms pinned on the ground, his hips pressed hard against hers. "But I want you to use what you're feeling right now. It's not about the right moves or the perfect strategy. It's about channeling everything inside of you into getting out of this situation."

Anna closed her eyes, no longer able to focus on Kael's voice through her panic. She felt the hard ground beneath her back, rocks and plants digging into her skin through her T-shirt. She felt his heart pounding against her breasts, his thigh insinuating itself between her legs as she struggled.

"Fight me off," he said. "Go crazy. Do whatever you need to do, just get me off of you. I can do anything to you right now. You need to get out of this, Anna."

"Don't," Anna whispered. Every move she made left her feeling more vulnerable than before.

"Look to press any advantage you can," Kael continued, seemingly oblivious to her rising panic. He transferred both of her wrists to one hand and used the other to reach between their bodies. "Changes in my position, distractions, fumbling with clothing—"

Pure, animal terror rampaged through her. Her entire body stiffened at the familiarity of Kael's movements. She no longer had control over her reactions to his words and actions. Razor-sharp memories of the last time she'd been overpowered and held down on the ground flashed through her mind.

The first one had lank, greasy hair that hung down and tickled her face as he moved on top of her. The pain had been traumatic, a shocking entry into a whole new world of agony. The second had a chin full of overgrown stubble that had scratched her tender cheek as his face rubbed against hers. He whispered to her, filthy words, the entire time. The third one, she swore, would kill her.

All of a sudden the weight above her was gone, and Anna instinctively drew her knees up to her chest and rolled onto her side, blind fear leaving her uncertain and confused. She felt tears streaming down her cheeks, heard the harshness of her gasping as she struggled to breathe. A worried voice penetrated the frantic hammer of her pulse in her ears. Elin was there.

"My God, Kael. What happened?"

"I don't know," Anna heard Kael answer. "We were wrestling, and I was trying to get her to use her fear and...maybe I went a little too far."

Anna squinted her eyes closed, face hot with shame. Her

entire body shook with the power of the flashbacks that had consumed her. Caught up in memories, she was unable to relax and assure her companions that she was all right. She choked back a sob and curled into a tighter ball.

A soft hand landed on her back, and she cringed instinctively away before she realized that it was Elin and allowed herself to be pulled up into a tender embrace.

"Anna, baby. It's okay, sweetheart. You're okay. You're safe." Elin rubbed her hands up and down Anna's back.

"I'm sorry," Anna mumbled into Elin's T-shirt. "I don't know what...I'm sorry."

"Anna, you know Kael would never hurt you for real. Right?" Elin asked in a gentle voice.

Anna gave a miserable nod. "I know." She tried to back out of Elin's embrace, utterly mortified that she had broken down in front of Kael. *And this after I tell him that I'm not afraid.* She stole a cautious look at Kael and was shocked by the pain in his indigo eyes.

He sat on the ground, arms resting on his legs, looking wholly devastated by her distress. As she watched, he swiped at the dampness on his face with the back of his hand. When he saw her looking, he dropped his gaze to the leaves and murmured, "I'm sorry." His voice was quiet, tremulous, and he sounded more vulnerable than Anna had ever heard him before. "I didn't mean to...I didn't know."

"It's okay, Kael," Elin said. "Anna knows you didn't mean to scare her like that."

"But I did mean to scare her," Kael mumbled, looking so miserable that Anna couldn't suppress a tentative smile. "I just didn't know —"

"Kael," Anna interrupted in a whisper, "I know you were only trying to help me fight back. You had no reason to think I would react like that. I'm sorry, I —" Her words died away as she struggled for a way to explain what had happened. She had never talked about it with anyone, and Kael wasn't going to be the first.

"Okay," Elin soothed. "Both of you stop apologizing. Nobody meant for that to happen. There are no hard feelings, right?"

"Right." Anna remained within Elin's embrace, too exhausted to even think about moving away anymore.

After a moment, Kael added his agreement. "Right."

Elin gave each of them a tender smile. "Breakfast is ready. Can you go back to the fire and take care of it, Kael? We'll be there in a few minutes, okay?"

"Right. No problem." Kael got to his feet and brushed his hands over the seat of his jeans. He hesitated a moment, then said, "I really am sorry, Anna. I never want to make you feel unsafe like that."

Anna tipped her head in acknowledgement. Her entire body burned with her humiliation. "It's not your fault," she said, voice breaking. "Please, let's just forget it, okay?"

"Okay." Kael gathered his things and exited the clearing without another word.

"Do you want to talk about it?" Elin asked after they were left alone.

"No." *That's not something I talk about.*

"Have you ever talked about it?"

A bead of sweat rolled down Anna's spine, tickling her back. She shifted within the circle of Elin's arms. "No."

"Maybe it would help." Elin rubbed one hand over Anna's side, while the other combed through her hair. "Do you think?"

"I can't." Anna closed her eyes, shuddering at the idea of putting words to the images that still assaulted her so many months later. "I can't right now, Elin." Her panic began to rise again, forcing her breathing to come out in harsh gasps.

"Shh." Elin pressed her lips to Anna's forehead. "It's okay, baby. Really. I was just asking. You don't have to talk about anything you don't want to talk about. But if you ever do—"

"It'll be you." Anna eased out of Elin's lap, and they both stood.

"Do you want to visit the stream and clean up before you come to breakfast?" Elin asked.

"Yeah, that sounds good."

"Okay. We'll see you back at the campsite."

Anna stopped Elin from leaving with a hand on her arm. "Elin, could you...tell Kael again that I'm sorry?"

Elin caressed the side of Anna's face with her hand. "You have nothing to be sorry about, baby. I will make sure that he's all right, though. Don't worry."

"Thanks."

Minutes later, Anna felt refreshed enough to consider rejoining her friends and crept through the forest, lost in thought. *I've never had a flashback that bad before. Nightmares, sure, but never something like that. I felt like it was happening all over again.*

Approaching the campsite, she heard Elin's voice first. She couldn't make out the words, but the tone was low, soothing, and insistent. With her emotion still close to the surface, fear sent her slipping into stealth mode and she slowed her steps and tiptoed closer, peering through the branches to see what was going on before she made her presence known.

She saw Elin first, facing Kael, and for a moment Anna could only see his boots, planted on the ground on either side of Elin's legs. Then Elin moved, revealing Kael sitting on a rolled double sleeping bag with his head in his hands. From where Anna was standing, she could see the almost uncontrollable trembling of Kael's fingers where they were pressed against his shaven scalp. Tears slid down his cheeks unchecked, drawing a silent gasp from Anna.

Elin knelt down and encircled Kael's broad shoulders with one arm, leaning her head against his, speaking to him in a low voice that Anna couldn't hear. *Is this because of me?* she wondered, thunderstruck. She knew her breakdown must have been startling for Kael, but she'd never dreamed the depth of the effect it would have on him. *I never could have imagined Kael losing control like this. Over anything.*

Kael shook his head at something Elin said. "I'll be okay," he said, loud enough for Anna to hear. "I just...it triggered so much—"

Elin placed her whole hand on top of Kael's head, caressing his shaven scalp with her palm. She kept whispering and trailed a string of kisses along his jaw.

His posture was tense, ramrod straight. "I wanted to comfort her so bad, but I couldn't—"

Anna couldn't hear the rest and blushed when Kael captured Elin's mouth in a long, slow kiss. She crept backwards into the woods, then rustled leaves and stomped around as she approached their campsite. By the time she walked into the clearing, Elin was tending to breakfast and Kael was sitting on the rolled sleeping bag with stoic eyes pinned on the fire.

"Ready to eat, Anna?" Elin greeted her with an affectionate smile.

Anna nodded and gave Kael a nervous glance. "Yeah. Your man over there worked up my appetite, kicking my ass."

The corner of Kael's mouth twitched in amusement. "I don't know. You got a couple of good hits in there. I think my belly is going to ache all day."

"As long as you don't blame breakfast," Elin said playfully.

Anna chuckled, dropping down to sit beside the fire. "It looks great," she said, as Elin spooned breakfast into the plastic bowls they carried with them. Rabbit again, and fresh vegetables they'd snagged from a field. "You know, maybe if Kael gets good enough with that bow, we could have deer for dinner sometime."

Kael lifted his head. "That would be awesome." He shot her

a smile full of grateful wonder. "You're right. I bet I could totally do that."

Elin frowned. "But deer are so cute."

"And tasty," Anna said, sharing a knowledgeable nod with Kael.

Elin scowled. "Well, I'm not cleaning it."

"That's fine. I've got to be good for something around here. Kael can shoot it, I can clean it, and you can enjoy the fruits of our labors."

"Because we love you," Kael said.

Anna gave Elin a serious nod. "It's true."

Elin handed Kael his bowl, and Anna hers, then picked up her fork with a resigned sigh. "All right. Go kill your deer. You boys," she said, and turned to Anna, "and warriors...I'll never understand you."

By instinct, Anna turned to share a conspiratorial grin with Kael. As their eyes met, she saw recognition in his, the knowledge of what she was thinking, and he opened his gaze to her, truly, for the first time since she had known him. She read such depth of emotion, such sorrow and quiet empathy, that her heart momentarily stopped in her chest. They both broke their gaze then, turning to listen to Elin as she launched into a story about the book she was reading.

SHE WAS LIVING it again. That day.

She saw the blue sky, smelled the acrid smoke as their belongings burned. She heard the screams of the women who were being attacked and captured by the large group of men who had raided their community. She felt the thrum of combat in the ground beneath her feet. The fighters of her tribe were locked in a fierce struggle with men carrying weapons. There were more than twenty of the raiders.

She was one of only nine trying to protect her people. She carried a wooden baseball bat. It was the only weapon she had ever used in training. She gripped it with her right hand, so hard that her knuckles turned white with tension. Next to her, Pete Jamison grunted as a bearded man thrust a long blade into his gut. Scared blue eyes found hers as the light went out of them.

She was overtaken, not killed. One blow to the back of her head that drove her to her knees, then a backhanded punch across the face that sent her to the ground. She didn't even recall being moved away from the fighting.

The sky was so blue. It was the first thing she saw when she regained consciousness. Blue sky, tree branches and leaves above her. Then a sneering face looking down at her with an ugly grin, and then

*another one. She closed her eyes, cold fear clutching at her belly. She
knew what was going to happen.*

She thought she could endure it, stoic and silent. She was wrong.

ANNA JERKED AWAKE with a panicked gasp, cold sweat
beaded on her hairline. She half-sat in her sleeping bag, caught
somewhere between waking and dreaming. Nightmare images
merged with reality for a long moment, pulling her eyes to the
surrounding trees in a desperate scan for enemies. The breath
she'd been holding escaped from her mouth in a pathetic
whimper, a foreign noise that shocked her into awareness.

Elin knelt beside her. "You're awake?" she whispered.

It took Anna a beat to nod. "I hope so."

"Do you want some water?"

"Please," she croaked, embarrassed.

Elin crawled away, then returned with a canteen of water.
She gave it to Anna and scooted over to sit with her on her
sleeping bag.

"Is this okay?" She eased a careful arm around Anna's waist.

"Wonderful." Anna put the canteen down after a couple of
deep gulps, not wanting to take a trip to the bushes in the still-
dark night. She sat in silence and worked on steadying her
breathing, still keyed up from the nightmare and the emotional
turmoil of the past day and a half.

"Do you think you can get back to sleep?" Elin stroked
Anna's side and back through her T-shirt, tracing random
designs with her fingers.

Anna relaxed into the contact. "No. I don't think so."

"Would it help if I stayed?"

Warmth rushed through Anna's body at the affection in
Elin's gaze. "You need your sleep. We don't want to both be dead
on our feet tomorrow because I had a nightmare."

"I could sleep next to you."

Anna bit her lip, overcome by Elin's offer. She glanced over
at the lump Kael made in their double sleeping bag. "That's okay,
Elin. I think Kael would miss you."

Elin gave her a sweet smile. "Kael would want me to be here
with you tonight. Trust me."

Anna looked over to Kael again, this time glimpsing shining
eyes in the darkness before he rolled over onto his back. To Elin,
she murmured, "I'd like that. Very much."

"Come on, then." Elin took the canteen from Anna's lap and
placed it on the ground. "Let's see if we can both squeeze into
this sleeping bag."

Anna flushed at Elin's words. She didn't even have the presence of mind to hide her expression of dazed arousal, drawing a soft giggle from Elin.

"Lie down, baby," Elin said. "I'm looking forward to holding you, too."

Anna moved to the very edge of her blankets to make room, and Elin crawled under the thick material and turned on her side. She wrapped her arm around Anna's middle, pulling her close. Soft breasts pressed against her back and warm hips cradled her bottom. Anna released a deep sigh, desire mingling with comfort to create a pleasant heat in her belly. She twitched in surprise when Elin brushed the hair away from her neck to drop a gentle kiss on her shoulder.

"Nobody's going to hurt you anymore," Elin whispered.

The way she said it, Anna almost believed her. Not knowing how to respond, she pushed her bottom backwards in an effort to get even closer. Elin pressed her palm flat against Anna's belly, drawing her near, and a moment later, Anna felt a careful leg ease its way between her calves. She lifted one leg slightly, and Elin slipped her thigh between Anna's, entangling them in a thorough embrace.

"This feels so good," Anna murmured some time later. "I never thought I would feel anything like this."

Elin nuzzled her earlobe. "Just wait until you get to the really good parts."

Anna broke into a grin and felt her face glow with embarrassment. She really didn't know what to say to that, so she said nothing.

"Has anyone ever held you before?" Elin asked.

Anna shook her head. "Garrett and I hugged a few times. It always felt a little awkward. My uncle really wasn't affectionate."

"I'm sorry," Elin said as she kissed Anna's earlobe again. "I'll be sure to remedy that in the future. Deal?"

Anna beamed out at the trees. "Deal."

In the silence that followed, Anna had time to think. She didn't dare close her eyes, afraid of what she might see if she did. The memories were just below the surface of every thought she had, every breath she took. She sighed in frustration.

"Do you want to talk?" Elin asked in a whisper, and tightened her arm around Anna. "About anything."

"I don't know how to talk about it," Anna admitted in a broken whisper. She had never wanted to talk about it before, but something in the safety of Elin's arms almost had her willing to go there.

"Take your time. Say whatever you want to say."

"I should be over it by now." Anna stared out at the dark forest with a sad smile. "You know what happened, right?"

"I have a good idea."

"Yeah, well, it's not like I'm the first woman to go through that."

"That doesn't make it any less horrible."

"It was always this specter hanging over my head, you know?" She kept her voice low, not wanting Kael to overhear them. "It was the reason I never strayed far from my tribe alone. But when it actually happened, I just lay there at first. It was like I just couldn't believe it."

Elin stroked Anna's belly. "I can't imagine."

"I don't want you to even try. I never want you to know." Anna shook her head, frustrated with her inability to express her jumbled emotions. "I had no idea what it would be like. I thought it would be just another injury, a battle scar. I thought I would be able to handle it better."

"Even the strongest people...that's a lot more than a simple injury. It doesn't matter how strong you are, Anna, it's going to hurt. It can hurt for a long time. Please believe me that everyone, even the strongest person you could imagine, would hurt after that."

Anna closed her eyes, letting her mind travel back in time. Her nightmare. That day. "They were so mad at me. I fought with a baseball bat then, too, and I killed one of their companions. Hit him right in the head. I heard his skull crack."

Elin flinched, and for a moment Anna was frightened that her innocent friend would pull away from her in revulsion. Instead, she tugged Anna closer. "Had you ever killed someone before?"

"He was my first." Anna flashed back on his face for a moment, his dark hair. "It didn't even feel real to me. I was knocked out only a minute or two later."

"So they took it out on you."

Anna rolled onto her back. Elin drew away to let her adjust, then repositioned herself with one arm across Anna's chest and one leg insinuated between her thighs. "See?" she murmured as she settled her head down on Anna's shoulder. "You're getting good at this cuddling thing."

Anna held her breath as her body reacted to the new position, humming in pleasure when she finally exhaled. After only a slight hesitation, she eased her arm around Elin's narrow shoulders, grateful that Elin couldn't see the rising color of her cheeks in the dark. "You make everything easy. Even talking."

Elin lifted her head so she could look into Anna's eyes. "I'm glad."

Soaking up the warmth of the soft body pressed against hers, Anna stared up at the stars that were visible through the treetops over their heads. "I thought they were going to kill me," she said eventually. "The third one, especially. He had a knife. That's how I got the scars."

Elin pressed the palm of her hand flat against Anna's upper chest, just above the breast that bore two jagged white reminders of that day. "I wondered." Her voice took on a profound sadness, and she nuzzled her face into the side of Anna's other breast. "You're beautiful, you know."

Anna bit her lip as traitorous tears slipped from her eyes and rolled down her cheeks. "I don't feel that way sometimes."

"You are. So, so beautiful. Inside and out. Every line, every curve, every scar."

"You're the beautiful one." Anna blushed at the boldness of her words, but Elin made her confident, and she let herself be carried along by that feeling. "I've never met such a beautiful person."

Elin gave her a loving smile and leaned up to plant a slow kiss on her lips. Anna closed her eyes at the first touch of Elin's mouth, trembling when the warm lips didn't pull away until after long moments of breathless connection. Her heart thumped hard beneath Elin's hand.

"How did you escape?" Elin asked when she'd settled back down with her head on Anna's shoulder.

The question snapped her back into the moment, hitting her directly in the gut. "Garrett."

"He found you?"

"He stopped them. One of them had left, and the other two were arguing about what to do with me. The man with the knife wanted to kill me. The first one wanted to take me with the other women from my tribe." She had lain on the ground, bleeding and in pain, listening to the two men argue her fate. She remembered praying they would just kill her. "Then, all of sudden I heard a sound. One of the men was on the ground. Garrett killed the other one in front of me. He shoved his knife right into his stomach."

"Thank God he was there."

"Yeah. Thank God." Recalling that terrible day, she felt a familiar pang of guilt. "It was too late to save the others. Garrett had been knocked out during the fighting, and they left him for dead. That's how he came to survive and save me."

"And then you lost him." Elin's voice broke with sorrow on

her next words. "God, Anna, I'm so sorry, baby."

"It was my fault." Anna closed her eyes, even as she felt the unburdening of a giant weight from her soul at the confession. "There were only three of them, not many. They ambushed us while we were eating. I don't know what happened. One minute we were fighting, then the next...Garrett got hit. Right in the head, like the man I killed. I watched him fall. I knew right away that he was dead."

"That's not your fault," Elin whispered. "You were outnumbered. Please don't ever think it was your fault."

"He saved my life. I couldn't save his."

"Sometimes there's nothing you can do to stop something horrible from happening." Elin stayed curled around Anna's body, her steady heartbeat thumping against Anna's side. "You can't play God, no matter how much you may wish you could. And that means you can't accept that responsibility, either."

"But I did play God." Anna swallowed in a desperate attempt to moisten her throat and ease the way for a final confession. "I went crazy. I killed every one of them. I still don't know how I did it. It was like I was possessed. Judge, jury, executioner...they killed Garrett, and so I made sure they died."

"Do you feel guilty about that?"

Anna met Elin's gaze in the dark. Her eyes shone with empathetic emotion. "Only that I don't feel more guilty, I think."

"Do you feel better now that you've said it out loud?"

Anna didn't even have to think about that one. "Yeah." She stared deep into Elin's eyes. "Do you...are you—" *Do I disgust you?*

"I love you, Anna." Elin brushed away Anna's fears with three little words. "You're a survivor. You've got a good heart. You've had a lot of bad things happen to you, but you're a good person. I know I haven't known you long, but...I love you very much."

Anna started to cry, but these were different from any tears she'd ever shed before. It was joy. It welled up inside of her, filling her heart until she had no choice but to release the pressure through quiet sobbing. "I love you, too," she managed to say, and grabbed Elin with both arms, holding on tight.

Elin cooed nonsense words of comfort into her ear and stroked her hair, slow and measured, until Anna nearly felt hypnotized by the peace her touch instilled. "Close your eyes, baby," she whispered after some time, and Anna was helpless to do anything but obey. "Let's see if we can't get a couple more hours of sleep, okay? I promise nothing is going to hurt you tonight."

Believing every word that came out of Elin's mouth, Anna slipped into an exhausted, but surprising, slumber. There were no more dreams that night.

Chapter
Four

TWO DAYS OUTSIDE of Sullivan, an hours-long hike through thick forest ended with the most spectacular view of a sparkling blue lake. Kael broke through the trees first and stopped, staring out at the water while he wiped sweat from his brow. Elin and Anna followed, and their friendly chatter died as they took in the blue horizon.

"Wow." Elin put her hand on Kael's lower back and grinned behind his shoulders at Anna, who stood on his other side gazing open-mouthed at the stretch of water.

"I don't know about you girls," Kael drawled, "but I could really use a bath."

Elin grabbed his hand and lifted it into the air, ducking her head to take a whiff of his underarm. She wrinkled her nose. "That's the truth."

He spun around, grabbed her around the waist, and tickled her sides. "You're feeling a little sweaty there yourself, sweet girl."

Anna grinned at their easy affection and swiped the back of her hand across her forehead. Droplets of perspiration rolled down her hairline, a testament to the arduous walking they'd done that day.

"Well, you're making it worse!" Elin twisted out of Kael's grip and took Anna's hand. "A bath sounds fantastic to me. How about you?"

Without waiting for an answer, she led Anna down the gentle hill to shore, calling back to Kael over her shoulder, "It's okay to swim here?"

"I don't think there's anyone around. We should be fine. How about we walk out to that vantage point before we get in? Then we can easily see if anyone's approaching."

Elin nodded and tugged Anna along to the spot Kael indicated. Anna kept her eyes forward, already feeling awkward about the idea of bathing in front of Kael. She had never gotten naked in front of a man before. The idea of seeing him naked was also vaguely unsettling.

Elin stopped when they reached a stretch of land that jutted out into the water and formed a wide area of treeless shore. Stepping in front of Anna, she took both her hands and gave them a gentle squeeze. "You're nervous, aren't you?"

Anna managed a weak smile. "Nervous, yeah."

"About Kael? Or are you still nervous about being naked with me, too?"

"I'm not nervous with you." That much was true. Her comfort with Elin was absolute. And it wasn't that she didn't trust Kael, but memories of her worst flashback still lingered in her head.

She started to explain, but Elin looked over her shoulder to Kael and exchanged a nod with him. "Anna, there's something we want to tell you."

"Okay."

"Sweetheart, I want you to look at Kael."

"Elin?" *Why should I look at him? Has he started undressing?*

"Please just trust me."

Anna turned to see Kael standing less than ten feet behind them. He rubbed at the back of his neck with his hand, uncharacteristically shy, then he dropped his hands to grip the bottom of his T-shirt and pulled it off over his head. He wore a sports bra beneath.

Anna blinked as the sports bra was torn off and discarded. She didn't see it fall; she was too focused on the small, delicate-looking breasts Kael had revealed. Female breasts.

Kael stared at her with a naked vulnerability that shook Anna to the core. All at once the cocky, self-assured man who had defeated four thugs with unthinking ease was reduced to trembling hands, tense broad shoulders, and a reddened face.

Uncertain of what else to do, Anna continued to watch. The blue jeans went next, eased down over narrow hips and kicked away by a long leg. Coarse dark hair covered pale shins and thighs, disappearing beneath the navy blue boxer shorts that Kael wore. Anna met Kael's uneasy gaze and gave him an uncertain smile.

Kael hooked both thumbs in the waistband of the boxer shorts and pushed them down to fall around his ankles. His eyes dropped as well, and he stared so hard at the ground that Anna swore he would split the earth open with his gaze. It only took a moment for her to shift her attention to the triangle of curly dark hair between Kael's legs, where she didn't see what she had expected to see.

She looked at Elin in numb shock. "I don't understand." She glanced back to Kael, who was trying and failing to look nonchalant about his nudity. *Her nudity.* With some confusion, she remembered the way that Elin had ridden astride Kael that first night. She shook her head, unable to put the pieces together in any way that made sense.

"Kael feels more comfortable living as a man," Elin explained in a gentle voice. "It's really a lot easier when people assume she's male, and people always do."

Kael folded her arms over her breasts. "I'm going to get in the water," she mumbled. "You two can follow me when you're ready."

Anna was silent as Kael stalked to the shore and strode into the water until she was waist deep, then dove beneath the surface to swim away from them.

"I know this must come as a surprise," Elin said, "and I'm sorry we lied to you. But since she escaped, Kael has always presented herself as a man. You're only the second person to know, after me."

Anna shook her head. "But I saw...you were—"

Elin raised an interested eyebrow. "What?"

Anna wore a fierce blush when she realized what she was trying to explain to Elin. "Um, no. It's nothing. Never mind."

One side of Elin's mouth twitched. " 'Fess up. You saw what?"

Anna glanced out at the water, making sure that Kael was far enough away, and leaned close to murmur into Elin's ear, "The first night, I couldn't sleep and, well, I don't understand how..."

"You saw us making love?" Elin's eyes danced with amusement.

"I'm sorry. I didn't mean to watch, but—"

"You're confused because you saw me riding him."

Anna's face burned. "Well, yeah."

Elin tipped her head back and released a musical peal of laughter. "I'm sorry, you're just so—" When Anna looked down, humiliated, Elin grabbed her hand. "You're wonderful, really." She leaned over to give Anna a soft kiss on the lips. "To answer your question, Kael and I spent some time in Michigan last year. We picked something up in a shop in Ann Arbor. A toy and a harness for strapping it on." Tilting her head, she stroked her thumb over the side of Anna's hand. "Do you know what I mean?"

Anna wasn't entirely sure she understood how such a thing would work, but she imagined that these objects helped Kael simulate the anatomy of a biological male. She wondered what kind of store would have carried something like that. "Um, yeah. I get it."

"You don't have a problem with this, do you? That we're both women?"

"You know I don't." A sudden, strong feeling of safety overwhelmed her. "I never thought I would meet another woman who...felt the same way I did."

"A woman who loves other women?"

"Yes," Anna whispered. Speaking her own secret for the first time since one teenaged afternoon with Garrett, she felt her whole body relax and she broke into an unthinking grin at the joy of it. "Or who hopes to."

Elin gave her a sly smile, then stepped back and stripped off her T-shirt. "We should probably think about getting in the water. I'm sure Kael would appreciate not being the only one who's naked and swimming."

Anna managed a nod as Elin reached behind her back and unhooked her bra. She didn't even try to tear her eyes from Elin's bare breasts when her pink nipples darkened and contracted under her heated stare. Finally dragging her gaze to Elin's face, she said, "It was hard for Kael to take off his...her clothes in front of me, wasn't it?"

Elin nodded, cheeks rosy after Anna's intense appraisal. "Yeah, it was. He's shy about his body."

The words bolstered Anna's courage, so she pulled off her own T-shirt and cast it to the ground. "Um, does Kael prefer to be called 'he'?" She kept her hands moving, trying not to concentrate on the fact that she was baring her body.

"Kael...can go either way. If it's just the three of us, it's okay to acknowledge that Kael is a woman. He doesn't mind. But in general, I use male pronouns. He likes it, and it's less confusing that way. It's also safer if we're in a situation where there's any chance we could be overheard."

Fascinated, Anna shed her jeans. "You said that Kael has presented himself as a man since he escaped. Where did he escape from?"

Elin stepped out of her panties and stood nude before her. "That's not really my story to tell." Her eyes flicked out across the water to where Kael floated on her back, some distance from shore. "All I can say is that he spent most of his life in a very bad place. He wasn't as lucky as you and I were after the sickness. There are some very evil things out there. Before I met Kael, I had no idea."

Anna shook her head, a million questions flooding her mind.

"So that's why he pretends to be a man? He escaped from someone and doesn't want to be found?"

"That's part of it. Mostly, though, it's just who Kael is. He's not really a woman, and he's not really man. He's just...Kael."

Naked now, Anna gestured to the water. "Let's get in, all right?"

"I know it's confusing," Elin said as they walked into the lake. "And I know I'm not telling you very much, but I think some of this needs to come from Kael himself."

Anna gasped as the cool water hit her inner thighs. "I'm not sure that Kael would want to talk to me about stuff like that."

"Why do you say that?"

Anna's eyes strayed to Kael, who was slowly paddling toward them. "Kael and I aren't as comfortable with one another as I am with you. Or like Kael is with you. I just don't know that he—"

"Anna," Elin whispered, keeping her voice low at Kael's approach, "now that there are no more secrets between you, maybe you can get closer. Kael knows that you've felt uncomfortable with him, and that...well, that's affected him, too."

Anna thought back to seeing Kael trembling and in tears with Elin after her flashback of the other day. It was yet another piece of the puzzle of Kael that she still struggled to put together. "I know."

"You should try to talk to him. He's an amazing person, really. And you two have more in common than maybe either of you realize."

Anna couldn't help a soft giggle at that. "One pretty major thing, for sure." She looked down at her own breasts bobbing in the water. *Kael is a woman. I never saw that one coming,*

"Pretty is right," Elin drawled.

Anna glanced up to find hazel eyes assessing her breasts. "Stop," she whispered, blushing hard at the blatant flirtation.

With a wide grin, Elin asked, "Do you really want me to stop?"

Anna considered for a moment. "No."

"I can't ignore a beautiful woman," Elin said as the shaven-haired Kael swam up beside her, "can I, sweetheart?"

"Not in my experience, no." Kael leaned in to give her a slow kiss.

Anna felt her center throb. Something about knowing Kael's true sex made the sight of them kissing charged and erotic in a way that left her breathless. Kael's delicate masculinity had always intrigued her, but now it fascinated her beyond words.

Kael's gender took on an ambiguity that left her dizzy with arousal.

"Lucky me." Elin drew back and flicked a glance at Anna. "I'm surrounded by beauty."

Anna blushed. *Lucky us.* Remembering what Elin had said about Kael's shyness, she said, "Thank you for trusting me, Kael."

Despite her best effort to resist, her eyes dropped down to take in Kael's small breasts once again. That's when she saw something she had been too flustered to notice before. Scars. Kael's chest and shoulders were littered with faded scars.

Anna had a feeling there was a lot more to understand.

THREE DAYS AFTER the revelation, Kael sought Anna out for a private talk, the first time they'd spent alone since their morning of sparring.

"Listen, I wanted to tell you again how sorry I am about that morning," Kael said. "I never meant to scare you so bad."

"I told you to forget about it. I was just being stupid."

"You weren't being stupid, at all. I was the stupid one. I pushed you way too far."

"You want to know that I can defend myself. I understand that, Kael, I really do."

Kael rubbed her palm over her shaven scalp. "I was being an asshole. You'd just hit me in the chest, and I thought you could feel my breasts and so I pushed. I was trying to break down a little of your defiance. In the ugliest way possible."

"You couldn't know how I would react."

"I've been hurt like that before," Kael murmured. "There are things, if someone did them to me, I would react the same way. Triggers. I should have realized that you might react like that."

Anna looked over to Kael in surprise. *Someone hurt her like that?* She tried to reconcile Kael's deadly strength with that kind of ugly violation. Though she couldn't imagine it, she felt an instinctive agreement with Kael's words. "Yeah. A trigger. That's exactly it."

Kael nodded. "When I looked down and saw that fear in your eyes, I couldn't believe I'd caused it. It really shook me. Knowing I had done that to you." Her eyes shone with emotion. "I never, ever wanted to make you feel like that. It nearly killed me to know I did."

"Is that why you decided to tell me you're a woman?"

"I was always going to tell you, sooner or later. You're here with us to stay, after all. After what happened, I decided I couldn't wait any longer. I wanted you to know that I understand."

They fell silent and enjoyed the quiet evening for a few moments, smiling at one another when the sweet humming of an unfamiliar melody floated over to them. Elin was cooking dinner at their campsite, within shouting distance. When she got really involved with her food preparation, music was usually a part of it.

"Do you have nightmares?" Anna asked after a while.

"I used to have them all the time. Before I met Elin. Now, just sometimes."

"Elin said you've been living as a man since you escaped...from somewhere bad. Is that...where it happened?"

Kael sucked in a deep breath and gazed up at the starry night. "Not the first time. But many times, yes."

Anna wanted to keep asking questions, but she was afraid to push. It wasn't like she enjoyed talking about her own life, and she didn't expect that Kael did either. Still, Kael had brought it up, and Anna had never spoken before to anyone who could really understand.

"You don't have to talk about it," she said. "I don't mean to pry."

Kael shook her head. "No, it's okay. How long ago did it happen to you?"

"A little over a year. They were with the men who attacked my tribe. I killed one of their buddies, when I was defending my people."

Kael gave her a respectful nod. After a long hesitation, she said, "I was ten years old the first time. Everyone was dead. My mother lasted longer than my father. He died almost right away. Mom hung on for a while, but she passed away and then I was alone. Nobody else in my family survived."

"I can't imagine what might have happened to me if I'd been left alone that young." *Uncle Roberto may not have been the nicest guy in the world, but he was someone who cared whether I lived or died.*

"I don't remember a lot about when mom died," Kael said. "I think I lived in our house for a while, ate whatever food we still had. To be honest, I think I've repressed a lot of that time. A neighbor found me. Mr. Jacobs. He took me with him. He decided to leave the city, to find other people. I was just a kid, so I—I let him take me."

"And he hurt you?" Anna guessed in a whisper.

"He told me that as long as he was taking care of me, I had to...do stuff for him. He was a sick fucking bastard."

"Ten years old," Anna whispered. At ten, her biggest concern had been keeping up with Garrett when they ran foot races around camp. "Did you even understand what was happening?"

Kael's lip twitched, and she picked at a slight rip in the knee of her jeans. "No, of course not. All I knew was that I didn't like my new *daddy* very much."

Anna shuddered at the venomous inflection of the murmured word. She could feel hatred pouring out of Kael for a brief, startling instant, then the stoic mask slipped back into place. "Kael, I'm sorry." Her own experience seemed almost insignificant now, and she felt a familiar self-recrimination at letting it shake her so badly. "I don't know what to say."

"I'm not sure there's anything to say about it. It's just...how I grew up."

"So you escaped from him? Mr. Jacobs?"

"No." Kael snorted. "Mr. Jacobs," she repeated, almost under her breath. "Funny how I've never used his first name." She shook her head. "No, I didn't escape from him. He had me until I was twelve, and then, when we were passing through Philadelphia, he found the Procreation Movement."

"The Procreation Movement?"

"You haven't heard of it?"

"No. I mean, the people in my tribe used to talk about procreation all the time. It was why my uncle and everyone else threw a fit when I told them I wanted to train as a fighter. I was supposed to find a mate and have babies."

Kael let out a strangled half-sob, somewhere between laughing and crying. "Imagine the people of your tribe, except there's a whole community of them, and their single-minded purpose is procreation at all costs — repopulating the planet. And they're so focused on that one goal that they will go to any length to promote it. That's the Procreation Movement. It started near Philadelphia, and every year it gained members and got stronger."

"How many people?" Anna was astounded by this piece of news; she had never heard of any kind of organized community like that.

"When I escaped? Honestly, there's no way for me to know. One hundred? Two? There were always more trickling in. Mr. Jacobs sold me — well, he allowed the good religious folks of the Procreation Movement to convince him that abusing a child was morally wrong. Especially one he had adopted. They gave him a place in the community, food, supplies...in exchange for me."

Anna breathed a sigh of relief. "At the very least, it's good that they don't believe in raping children."

Kael turned to her with a hard smile. "No, sex was for procreation. They waited until I started menstruating when I was thirteen. Then I was a woman."

Anna gasped in shock. "How could they claim to be religious and do something like that? How could they claim to be *human*?"

"I was serving the greater good," Kael said in an emotionless voice. "That's what they used to tell me. God wanted us to repopulate the earth, and so I had to stay at the Eve Institute and let them try to impregnate me. I was a girl without anyone in the world. What other reason did I have to exist?"

"That makes me sick," Anna spat. "How can they even think—"

"Desperate times call for desperate measures," Kael said with a painful smile. "It was my duty. And they thought it was their duty to see that I fulfilled mine. I used to wonder why I was here. From a very young age, I knew I was different from other girls. I didn't like men, and I don't think it's just because I didn't have a very good experience with them. I can remember having crushes on the girls when I went to school. So yeah, there were times when I wondered...maybe I really was useless. If I wasn't at the Eve Institute, what could I contribute to the world? Maybe that really was the only thing I was good for."

Anna looked up the sky and a few tears escaped despite her best effort to suppress them. "I can't understand how people who claimed to care about God and the greater good could treat you like that."

"Oh, they were really very civilized about it." Kael's voice was harsh, sarcastic. "At least they thought they were. It wasn't about sex. It wasn't intended to be violent. They wouldn't come to our rooms unless we were fertile. When we were, they would send someone nightly. If a girl got pregnant, she was moved to a special ward and left alone."

"How did you escape?"

"By the end, I was 'out of control.' That's what they labeled it. I was resisting. While alone in my cell, I had been practicing fighting, and I realized that I was getting strong enough to maybe really hurt someone. One night I gave the guy they sent to me a black eye. By this point the guards had concluded I was trouble anyway, and one of them decided to sneak into my room the next day and teach me a lesson." Her eyes glinted in the darkness. "I killed him. I disarmed him and stabbed him in the neck as he laid on top of me. I was twenty-two years old."

"Wow. I bet that felt...amazing."

"It did. I still have nightmares about it. I killed five people to escape. It took me two weeks to make my way out of the city. I was so scared to travel during the day. And all those buildings, I was incredibly paranoid."

Anna managed a slow nod, feeling numb after all she had been told. Her head started to pound when she thought of all that Kael had suffered. "This is an evil world."

Kael stretched her long legs out and leaned back with her palms against the ground. "Sometimes. I used to think that was all there was to it, but now I know better."

"What do you know?" *Please explain to me what's so great about a world where things like this can happen.*

"I know beauty," Kael said, and smiled. "I know pleasure. Before Elin, I never did. Now that I do, I know the world isn't evil."

"Just some people in it?"

"Yeah." Kael gave her a friendly nudge with her shoulder. "I used to want to kill just about everyone I met. I was so full of anger. And fear. I still feel the fear sometimes, but I'm healing. You will, too."

"What happened to me is nothing compared to what happened to you. You're so strong."

The night breeze picked up, whipping a long piece of brunette hair in front of Anna's eyes. Kael reached over and tucked it behind her ear. "It's not a matter of degrees. Hurt is hurt. I'm no stronger than you are. I've just had more time to heal, that's all. Don't give up, okay? I know it's hard, but it can get better. It just takes work."

"And love?"

"Love helps," Kael said.

"You're very lucky to have found Elin," Anna said. *I can't say that I'm not at least a little jealous. I'd give anything to feel that kind of pleasure just one time.*

"She's helped me a lot. I never knew that my body could be a source of joy before I met her. And I never knew that I could feel the things she makes me feel."

"Hey, Kael?"

"Yeah?"

"It can really...feel good?" Anna blushed even as the question left her mouth.

Kael chuckled and eased a careful arm around Anna's waist. The affectionate touch took her by surprise, but she leaned into Kael's strength on instinct. "It can feel *very* good. If it's someone you trust—someone you love—it can be just about the best thing in the world."

Anna gazed at Kael through different eyes. The stoicism, the attitude, the distance, every aspect of the dark woman's personality took on an entirely new spin. Anna was left with a deep sense of admiration, as well as a burgeoning attraction that she didn't yet understand.

"How are you two doing?" Elin's soft voice pulled their attention over their shoulders, to where she stood leaning against a tree with her arms folded over her chest.

"Damn, baby," Kael drawled, "you're too good at being sneaky. I'm sure glad you're on my side."

"You're going to have to teach me your tricks," Anna said. She hadn't heard Elin's approach, which should have unnerved her. Instead, it sent a deep rush of warmth through her body. *She's amazing.* "I've never seen someone so light on her feet before."

Kael released Anna and stood. "Well, I've always told her that her head is in the clouds."

"Smart-ass," Elin said. "Are you two ready for dinner?"

"Starving." Anna allowed Kael to pull her to her feet.

"Perfect." Elin stepped between them, taking Kael's left hand and Anna's right. "Then let's sit down and have a nice family dinner."

"Lead the way," Anna said. *I could get used to this.*

Chapter
Five

ANNA WOKE UP disoriented, burrowed deep within her
sleeping bag, and stared at a wood ceiling high overhead. *Right.
We're in farmland now.* The best part about farmland was the
barns. Despite the hay smell, that was one of the most
comfortable nights of sleep she'd had in a long time.

Turning her head, she confirmed that Kael and Elin's double
sleeping bag was empty. She looked past the dark canvas
material and an abandoned sweatshirt to the door of the run-
down barn. It was ajar, letting bright sunshine through to paint
the floor with light. Anna crept out of the barn and squinted into
the sunlight before gazing around at the overgrown fields that
stretched as far as she could see. There was no sign of her
companions, so she walked to the farmhouse. The water pump
was where she remembered it, and she spent a peaceful ten
minutes going to the bathroom, brushing her teeth, and washing
up before she felt human enough to start the day.

As she returned to the barn, a muffled noise from the rear of
the building drew a hesitant smirk from her. *Behind the barn.
Great.* She stopped at the corner and listened to soft, indistinct
voices. *They're probably making love. God knows, having me around
hasn't allowed for much privacy.* Her heart swelled with emotion as
she went indoors. *Just once. I hope I can feel the way they do just one
time before I die.* She plodded to her sleeping bag. *Yeah, no
problem. There'll be plenty of opportunities for me to meet women.*

Not knowing what else to do, she lay back down on the
blankets and stared at the ceiling, counting the wooden planks
from left to right. She had only counted twenty-three when the
barn door opened, casting a rectangle of warm light over the
abandoned double sleeping bag. Anna sat up and gave Elin a shy
smile.

"Damn," Elin said. "So I'm not going to get the pleasure of
waking you up, I guess."

"Sorry to disappoint you. I've been awake for a little while.

Visited the water pump and everything."

"I didn't even hear you." Elin shut the barn door. "Kael's off practicing with his bow. I decided I wanted to be lazy with you, if you're in the mood."

"I'm always in the mood to be with you."

Elin beamed as she crossed the floor to offer Anna a hand. Pulling Anna to her feet, she said, "I've got an idea. Grab your sleeping bag, okay?"

"Okay." Anna did as she was told. Elin gestured over to an old ladder that leaned against a loft at the far end of the barn. "Does that thing look sturdy to you?"

"The ladder or the hayloft?"

"Either. Both."

"I'm game if you are."

"Then come on." Elin scampered to the loft, taking the first three steps of the ladder before Anna had a chance to blink. "Race you to the top."

"I think you had an unfair advantage," Anna said as she walked to the bottom of the ladder. "Knowing the idea in advance and all." She lifted her eyes and admired the view as Elin climbed up ahead of her. *Then again, I'm not complaining.*

Elin disappeared into the loft, then peeked her head over the edge. "You're just a sore loser. Now hand me the sleeping bag. I'm setting us up a proper lazy spot."

Anna hefted the sleeping bag up to Elin. "It's a good thing I'm not afraid of heights."

"I was eyeing this place when I woke up this morning. I've always liked exploring." Elin spread the sleeping bag out and lay on her side, gesturing to Anna. "Now come here. Let's cuddle."

Anna blushed, but obeyed the command without hesitation. She sank down to her knees, then stretched out on her back beside Elin. The ceiling was less than ten feet above them. She stared up at it, unsure of what to do next.

"Is it all right if I hold you?" Elin touched Anna's arm with her fingers, stroking up and down in a lazy pattern. "I'd really like to hold you. I've been wanting to since I woke up this morning."

"Really?"

"Really." Elin tugged her into an embrace, wrapping both arms around her.

Anna reciprocated by resting her arm across Elin's stomach. Then she curled her fingers and caressed the skin that was exposed where Elin's T-shirt had ridden up above her belly button. Elin released a soft moan that raised the hair on the back of Anna's neck. She pressed her face into Elin's T-shirt, inhaling the sweet scent of her. "Well, I'd really like to be held," she murmured.

Elin pressed her lips to Anna's forehead and drew her closer. "I had a wonderful dream last night. It's put me in the most incredible mood today."

Anna snorted. "I dreamt that I was climbing this enormous tree to get to these big, red apples that were growing at the very top. But no matter how much I climbed, I never got any higher off the ground. I'm not sure what that's done for my mood."

"That's not a very fun dream."

"It was better than some I've had."

"I guess it probably was. But I'm telling you, mine was a lot better."

Anna took the bait. "What did you dream?"

Elin shifted onto her back. "It was about you. I was kissing you."

Anna's heartbeat stuttered at the soft words, then continued on in a crazy staccato that beat in accompaniment with her ragged breathing. *She couldn't have meant that like it sounded.*

"Kissing me?" Anna squeaked.

"Yeah. And I mean *really* kissing you. Making out, really. I woke up so aroused, I had to touch myself. Then I practically attacked Kael before he went out with his bow and arrows. Kissed him until he couldn't see straight. Still, I've spent all morning wondering how it would feel, kissing you." Elin twisted a strand of Anna's hair around her fingers.

Thoughts of Kael shocked Anna back to reality. "What do you think Kael would say about your dream?"

Elin gave her a wicked grin. "He thought it sounded pretty sexy, actually. I think he got just as worked up as I did, when I told him."

"You told him?" Anna's face flooded with heat. "He doesn't care?"

Elin became serious and took Anna's hand between both of her own. "Anna, listen. Kael knows exactly how I feel about you. There is complete honesty between us. He isn't threatened by the fact that I care about you. That I love you. He cares about you, too." She squeezed Anna's hand. "Kael knows I'll never leave him. I love him. I belong with him."

Anna bit her lip as tears filled her eyes. "What about me? Where do I belong?"

"I hope—I mean, I think, and I hope you think, too—well, that you belong with me." Elin actually blushed. "At least it feels like you do. I'm...very attracted to you."

"Why?"

Elin frowned. "What kind of question is that?"

"You're not just saying this because you feel sorry for me, are you?" Anna was too ashamed to even look at Elin. "Because I'm all alone."

A firm pinch on her hip startled her. "How can you even think that?" Elin said.

"I worry." It was as simple as that.

"Well, I love your stubborn streak, for one thing. You aren't about to let anyone tell you what to do. You're independent. I find that very attractive."

Anna said nothing. One corner of her mouth twitched into a reluctant smile.

"I love your fierce loyalty. I hear it in your voice when you talk about Garrett. I see it every time you look at me. And I see it when you look at Kael, too. You've been a part of this family since that first day when you risked your life for me."

"Elin—"

"And I love your shyness. I love your innocence." When Anna cast an ashamed look to the barn wall, Elin reclaimed her attention with a gentle hand on her chin. "You are innocent. I see so much love and passion in you, just waiting to come out. You excite me."

"You excite me, too."

"I love your brown skin." Elin rested a careful hand on Anna's stomach. "I love your dark, curly hair. Your big, brown eyes. Your body...God, you're gorgeous."

"Elin?"

"Yes, Anna?" Elin stroked Anna's belly, then traced over the hem of her T-shirt. "Do you need to hear more reasons why I'm so attracted to you?"

"No. I believe you."

"Are you attracted to me?"

"You know I am. I love you."

"I love you, too." Elin bent so their mouths nearly touched. "May I kiss you?"

Anna blinked, then choked out, "Yes."

Elin moved even closer, and her breath blew warm across Anna's lips. "Have you ever kissed anyone?"

Anna shook her head, hardly able to breathe with Elin so near. "No. Well, Garrett once. Kinda. A peck on the lips."

Elin closed her eyes. "I want to give you more than a peck on the lips, sweetheart. I want to taste you. I want you to taste me."

Gasping, Anna arched her back and brought her face up the scant distance that separated them. She brushed her mouth over Elin's, barely applying pressure to warm, full lips. Elin surged

forward and pressed Anna down against the blankets, dropping
a string of gentle kisses over her mouth.

"Is this okay?" she murmured.

Is she kidding me? "Yes."

Elin's tongue traced over Anna's top lip, then the bottom,
teasing until Anna felt dizzy with need. She threaded her fingers
in Elin's auburn hair and pulled her close, opening her mouth to
let Elin inside, sucking hard on her tongue. A jolt of arousal shot
through her body, hitting her right between the legs. When Elin
retreated, Anna pushed forward. She slipped her tongue into
Elin's mouth, stroking her, moaning in pleasure at the taste and
feel of her. Elin whimpered, and Anna realized that her pale
arms were trembling as she struggled to hold herself above
Anna's body.

She broke the kiss with a shaky sigh against Elin's lips.
"Wow."

Elin collapsed onto the blankets and threw the back of her
hand against her forehead. "Wow," she echoed. "You're a great
kisser already. I can't imagine how you'll be with a little
practice."

"Does that mean you're volunteering to practice with me?"

"Whenever you want. For as long as you want. That
was...amazing. Just as good as I hoped it would be."

"It was even better than I hoped it would be," Anna
whispered.

Elin's hazel eyes twinkled with happiness. "So you've
thought about it?"

"Only all the time. I've...never felt anything like this before."

"I'd like to do a lot more with you than kiss. But I don't want
to push you into anything. I don't want to move you too fast."

Anna shook her head eagerly. "You're not pushing."
Blushing, she calmed her excited tone. "I mean, you're not
moving me too fast. As long as — you know, Kael —"

"Kael knows that I'm hoping to do more than just kiss you.
He's attracted to you, too, Anna. He doesn't have any
expectations, and he'd probably be upset with me for even
telling you that, but I want you to know. But he'll understand if
you only want to share this kind of thing with me. Nobody is
going to try to pressure you to do anything you don't want to
do." She stared deep into Anna's eyes. "No matter what, we're
family."

Anna felt strangely reassured. "Thank you."

Elin traced her fingertips down Anna's face, sliding them
across her skin and over her throat. She smiled when Anna's
breathing hitched at the caress. "I think you're going to be very

responsive. Do you ever touch yourself?"

Anna went bright red at the frank question. "Uh—"

Elin giggled and tickled Anna's upper chest with blunt fingernails. "I already told you that I do. Don't be embarrassed."

Anna shook her head. "No. Not really. I tried a few times, but...I don't think it worked."

Elin gave her a kind smile. "Have you ever had an orgasm?"

"I don't think so."

"If you have to think about it, you haven't."

"Then I guess I haven't."

"I'd like to give you your first," Elin murmured. "I want to make you feel good, sweetheart."

Her trust in Elin was unthinking, immediate, and it eased any nervousness about her inexperience. "Tell me what to do," Anna said. "I want to learn how to make you feel good, too."

Elin sat up on the sleeping bag with a beaming smile, then grasped the hem of her shirt. "How about we start by taking off our shirts?"

I'm almost used to this by now. Anna sat up as Elin pulled off her T-shirt, then tugged her own over her head. Elin reached behind her back and unhooked her bra, giving a playful smile when Anna stared hungrily at her bare breasts.

"Let me get yours." Elin gave Anna a slow, wet kiss as she unhooked the silky green bra they'd found in a clothing store back in Sullivan.

"You practice that move?" Anna murmured as Elin drew back with the bra in her hands.

"That, lover, was pure improvisation." Elin dropped her gaze, taking in Anna's bare skin with intense eyes. "God, you have beautiful breasts. And your nipples—" She pushed Anna back onto the sleeping bag, moving with her and taking her mouth once more in a sensual kiss.

Anna groaned in astonishment when Elin's breasts pressed against her own. It was the softest, sexiest, most intoxicating thing she'd ever experienced in her life. She could feel startling wetness between her thighs, and when Elin parted them with one leg, Anna bucked her hips against the pressure.

Elin pulled back with a lick to Anna's earlobe. "Is it all right that I'm on top of you, baby?"

Anna wrapped her arms around Elin's shoulders and hugged her tight. "Yeah. It feels amazing. You're so soft."

Elin giggled and kissed down the side of Anna's throat. "So are you. But listen, if you get nervous at any point, or if I do anything you don't like, I want you to tell me. Okay? Stop me. You won't hurt my feelings. I want this to be so good for you."

Anna gasped as Elin's mouth slid down the slope of her left breast. She stiffened slightly when Elin used her tongue to trace over the ugly white scars that marred her brown skin.

Elin glanced up at her reaction and whispered, "You're beautiful. Every inch of you."

Anna gasped again when Elin lowered her mouth to lick around her left nipple. She held Elin's head to her breast, releasing a harsh cry of pleasure as her nipple was suckled and scraped with gentle teeth. "Oh, Elin, I'm...I'm..."

Elin released her nipple with a coy grin. "Wet, I hope. Are you getting wet, baby?"

"I think so." Breathing hard, she dropped her gaze to Elin's breasts, smashed against her body. "I want to—"

"What do you want to do? You can do anything you want."

"I want to...to use my mouth on your breasts."

Elin rolled onto her back and beckoned Anna over with a lazy hand. "Come here."

Her breasts were pale, slightly smaller than Anna's, and topped with light pink nipples. They looked delicious, and Anna needed to know how they tasted. She bent to kiss the slope of Elin's left breast, then took creamy skin into her mouth and sucked hard. Elin cried out and arched her back, and Anna pulled away, concerned.

"Did I hurt you?"

"Oh, no. God. Be rough, I don't care. I love having my breasts worshiped. Hard, soft, whatever you do will feel good, I promise."

Shyly, Anna wrapped her lips around a now dark pink nipple, batting at the hard nub with the tip of her tongue. She brought her hand up to Elin's other breast, squeezing and tugging at her nipple with gentle fingers.

"Oh, yeah," Elin whimpered. "That's so perfect. You're so good at this."

Anna's chest swelled with pride. She scraped her teeth over the turgid flesh in her mouth, then made wet circles around it with her tongue. She groaned in pleasure at the feeling of Elin's hand coming to rest on the back of her head. She spent long moments moving her mouth from one breast to the other, thoroughly loving each until her breathing grew heavy and she felt a powerful craving rise within. Startled by the force of it, she broke off and gasped, "I want more." She barely knew what she was asking for. She just wanted more.

"How about we take the rest of our clothes off?" Elin suggested.

Anna murmured her agreement and reached down to unzip

Elin's blue jeans. "Lift your hips," she said, tugging at the waistband.

The first thing that she noticed after tossing the jeans aside was the large wet spot soaking the cotton material between Elin's legs. Then she smelled the sweet scent of her arousal.

"Oh, God," she breathed, stripping off her own jeans and throwing them aside. She didn't spare a thought to her own nudity, instead exploring Elin's delicious skin. She slid her palm down Elin's gently rounded belly, over the damp cotton of the light blue panties, then flexed her fingers over the heat of Elin's center.

Remembering herself, she glanced up in mild alarm. "Is that okay?"

"Wonderful," Elin choked out. "Don't you dare stop."

"I don't know what to do," Anna whispered. She'd touched herself for pleasure occasionally, but never someone else.

"I'm sure you've thought about this before. Just follow your instincts. Do what feels natural."

Anna bit her lip, afraid to voice her deepest desire. Rubbing the palm of her hand over Elin, she cupped her and gave her a gentle squeeze.

As if sensing her fear, Elin said, "What's wrong, baby? Tell me what you want."

"Will you—" Anna paused, then gathered her courage. "Will you show me how you touch yourself? So I know...so I can see how to do it?"

Elin's cheeks flushed light pink. "I could touch you first, Anna. Then you would see—"

She shook her head. "No, I...I'd love to watch you touch yourself. I want to see how you make yourself feel good."

"All right," Elin murmured. When Anna removed her hand, she groaned her disappointment. "You're good at getting me nice and worked up, by the way."

Anna managed a nervous giggle. "Awesome."

Without hesitation or preamble, Elin slid her right hand down beneath the waistband of her panties. She closed her eyes as her fingers began moving beneath the material, stroking her center in practiced rhythm.

Anna quickly decided that the situation, as it was, would never do. She hooked one finger in the leg of Elin's panties and pulled the sodden cotton material aside, exposing swollen pink flesh and busy fingers. She watched Elin's unashamed pleasuring for only a minute or two before she was overwhelmed with the need for more.

"Elin...I need to touch you." She pushed Elin's hand away

and dragged the panties down, leaving her bare and exposed.

Dark brown curls between pale thighs, sparkling with evidence of Elin's arousal.

Slick pink flesh, so wet that Anna could only gape in mute shock.

Pale skin flushed with desire; ragged breathing that signaled painful need.

With a trembling hand, Anna slid her fingertips over the slippery folds. She closed her eyes and hissed in pleasure when she made contact with Elin's wetness. Almost immediately, she opened her eyes again, unwilling to miss one instant of what was happening.

"Yes." Elin covered Anna's hand with wet fingers and pressed her firmly into the slippery, swollen bundle of nerves that lay just beneath her touch. "Feel what you do to me?"

Anna stared hard at her hand between Elin's legs. "You're so wet. I want..."

"What do you want, baby?" Elin's breasts rose and fell with her rapid breathing, her cheeks flushed with color.

"I want to look at you." Anna pulled her fingers away from the silky heat between Elin's thighs, causing hooded hazel eyes to flash with unspoken need.

"Go ahead, sweetheart."

Anna shifted down the sleeping bag until her face was level with the damp curls between Elin's legs. The pale thighs parted in willing surrender, and Anna sucked in a reverent breath at the sight, then traced curious fingers over wet, swollen flesh.

Elin gasped and her whole body jerked at the touch. Anna continued her caresses. She didn't really know what she was doing, but if the rolling of Elin's hips were any indication, she was doing it right. She slid her fingers up to the swollen nub where Elin had guided her before, tracing slow circles around it until she drew a breathy moan from Elin.

"Like this?" she whispered.

"Just like that. It feels so nice when you rub my clit like that." Elin spread her legs farther apart and pushed her hips toward Anna's hand. "God, Anna...you're gonna make me come."

Anna whimpered and rested her face against Elin's thigh. *She's so incredibly soft.* Full of love, she redoubled her efforts and stroked Elin in a steady rhythm set by the undulation of the supple hips. She stared as she worked, disbelieving that she was causing the pleasure and wetness she could see and feel.

"Anna, do you want to put your fingers inside of me?"

Anna gasped and squeezed her thighs together when she felt a literal surge of wetness at the question. She slowed her hand to a gradual stop. "Yes." Her head spun at the very thought. "But I—"

"You won't hurt me." Elin moved Anna's hand down until her trembling fingers were poised at her entrance. "Start with one, okay? I promise you won't hurt me. I want it so bad."

Gathering her courage, Anna explored the tight opening with her index finger, then buried her face in Elin's hip when the sensation grew overwhelming. She pressed forward, just barely going inside, and murmured in contentment as Elin threaded her fingers in her hair and pulled lightly.

"Please..." Elin shifted and arched her back to draw Anna's finger deeper inside. "Please, baby."

With a low groan of excitement, Anna pushed her whole finger inside. She squinted her eyes closed as she was enveloped by tight, wet heat. A shockwave of pleasure coursed through her body when Elin cried out and tugged on her hair.

"Oh, fuck," Elin groaned.

Anna grew wide-eyed at the rough language, something she had never heard from Elin before. A pulse of pleasure-pain between her own legs wrenched a surprised whimper from her mouth.

Elin grasped her wrist with a frantic hand, encouraging her to withdraw and then press inside once again. "Fuck, baby...God, you feel so good. Just...like that."

Anna picked up Elin's motion, thrusting slowly. Elin began to writhe around on the blankets, eyes closed, a constant stream of mewling pleasure falling from her lips. "Your thumb." She bucked her hips, meeting Anna's thrusts with growing urgency. "On my clit."

Anna nodded, but first pulled her finger out of Elin, which drew a soft cry of alarm. "Don't worry, I'm not leaving you." She returned to Elin's opening with two fingers, pushing deep inside. "You are so beautiful," she said in a voice made low with desire. "I want to feel your release."

Elin planted her feet on the sleeping bag and arched her back even farther into the air. Anna stayed with her, thrusting and rubbing as her lover twisted and turned in ecstasy. When Elin cried out as she orgasmed, Anna felt it right between her legs, and joined her with a throaty moan of pleasure. She collapsed onto Elin's chest and panted hard against impossibly soft breasts. Eyes closed, she smiled at the throbbing and pulsing that continued around her fingers and the trembling of Elin's hands on her bare back. They lay in the sweet silence of that moment, Anna still buried deep between Elin's legs. She couldn't speak. *I'm happy. If I died right now, I'd be happy.*

Eventually, Elin gripped Anna's wrist and helped her withdraw, bringing her hand to her mouth. Anna's face grew hot with a mixture of shock and arousal as she watched Elin's silky tongue lick her own juices from the wet fingers, and she was certain that she was right on the verge of her first orgasm.

"What are you doing?" she gasped.

"Tasting myself." Elin released Anna's fingers with a mischievous smile and shifted to lie closer. She leaned forward and captured Anna's lips in a slow kiss. Her mouth tasted sweet, and the new flavor made Anna's heart pound with hunger.

After some time, Elin pulled away and they both gasped for air. "Lie back, sweetheart." Elin pushed on Anna's shoulder until she lay on the sleeping bag.

Now the center of attention, Anna stared up at Elin and took deep, calming breaths. Her nipples hardened, pebbling under Elin's heated stare.

"Are you nervous, baby?"

It didn't even occur to Anna to deny it. "Yes."

"Don't be." Elin crawled on top of Anna's body, settling her weight between Anna's spread legs. Anna still wore her pale yellow panties, and they were soaked. "I'm going to make you feel so good."

Elin bent her head to take Anna's nipple into her mouth, before running her tongue from one breast to the other, peppering brown skin with wet kisses. "How do you feel?"

"Like...I'm going to explode." With a whimper, Anna thrust her hips into Elin's naked abdomen. The feeling of her swollen clit rubbing against the cotton of her panties left her gritting her teeth in desperation.

"My poor girl." Elin kissed the corner of Anna's mouth, then began a new trail of kisses over her throat, between her breasts, down the center of her belly. She took the waistband of Anna's panties between her teeth and gave it a gentle tug. Mouth full, she mumbled, "May I take these off?"

Anna giggled. "Please."

Elin tugged the panties down with an excited growl. When Anna was bare, Elin laid the palms of her hands on her warm inner thighs and looked up at her with a loving smile. "May I see you?"

Anna cleared her throat, nervous. "Okay."

"I won't hurt you. I'm not even going to go inside of you, okay?"

Anna relaxed. *Of course she won't hurt me.* She allowed Elin to press her thighs apart with gentle hands. The hazel gaze dropped and took in her center, and Anna felt herself growing wetter.

"You look delicious." Elin shifted so that she was on her belly between Anna's legs, her face close to where Anna throbbed with need. "Do you want me to taste you, baby?"

Anna managed a dazed nod, barely hearing the question. At that moment, Elin could do anything to her. She felt beside herself with wanting, confused and aroused and straining for something she didn't quite understand. Elin bent forward to drop a gentle kiss on her damp curls, and Anna gasped at the feeling of her lips in such an intimate place. She moaned out loud when Elin dragged her tongue up the length of her sex. Her thighs trembled, and her face flushed hot in reaction.

When Elin covered her swollen folds with her whole mouth, Anna's legs shook beyond her control. She felt a building pressure deep in her belly and she knew — she just knew — that this was the unmistakable pleasure Elin had told her about. She rolled her hips desperately and cried out, all shyness gone; only nonsense words and noises remained, pouring forth as if to ease the growing ache low in her belly. She threaded her fingers in Elin's hair and held her face close, grinding against her lover's mouth, drawing out her pleasure until she yelled out as her entire body shuddered in overwhelming release.

When the rush of sensation finally ebbed, Anna collapsed back with a weak moan and loosened her grip on Elin's hair. Bright eyes gazed down at her, and Elin's lips were swollen red, shining with juices. At the look of pure love in Elin's eyes, Anna began to cry. Ashamed, she immediately tried to roll onto her side, but Elin crawled up and pulled her into a strong embrace.

"I'm sorry." Anna swiped her hand across her cheek. "I don't know...it was just so amazing. I don't know why I'm — "

"It's okay. It's just your body's reaction to the intensity of what you experienced. It's perfectly natural." Elin gave her a slow kiss. "I love you, Anna," she whispered, kissing her sweat-dampened hair. "Thank you for sharing that with me."

"I love you, too." Anna grinned, then rumbled out quiet laughter.

Elin gave her an indulgent smile. "See? The other end of the emotional spectrum."

Anna laughed harder, still crying. "You're right." She burrowed deeper into Elin's warm embrace. "This was a perfect lazy morning."

Chapter
Six

KAEL WAS SITTING on the ground, butt planted in the dirt at the base of a tree. Her knees were bent, big feet set apart on the ground. Her dark blue jeans were worn slightly in the knees, and her leather boots were scuffed. She wore a dark green T-shirt that was tighter on her torso than most of her other clothing, barely hinting at the small breasts concealed beneath. She was thrumming with edgy, tense energy. Several dead rabbits lay to one side of her. Anna smiled, almost hearing Elin's mutters. Occasionally Kael produced a couple of pheasants after a hunt, but rabbit stew was their staple food.

Kael's deep voice broke the stillness of the evening. "You gonna come over here and talk to me or just hide back there in the trees all night?"

"I was coming," Anna said, then blushed hard at the double entendre. *Well, not since Elin woke me up this morning while you were out running.* "I mean, I wasn't hiding."

"Then move closer so I don't have to shout, okay?"

Anna flushed at Kael's gentle tone. While their relationship was still nowhere near as close as what she had with Elin, she and Kael were slowly building a mutual trust. Loving Elin gave them a common purpose, and so far, their growing friendship was based on a mutual adoration of their lover. But even that was starting to change. Anna could see genuine interest in Kael's eyes, and she herself felt a timid attraction that grew stronger every day.

"Sit down." Kael patted the ground at her side. "I was just catching dinner."

"You don't mind the company?"

"Of course not. We don't spend much time together, do we?"

"Alone? No, not much." Tugging nervously on her earlobe, Anna risked the question that gnawed at her every time Kael made an excuse to go off somewhere rather than stay with her. "Why is that?"

Kael gave a sheepish grin. "I guess it just feels like you're Elin's...friend, and I'm not the easiest person to be around. I know I can be a pain in the ass."

Anna chewed on her lip as she contemplated how to respond. *Well, Kael is kind of a pain in the ass sometimes. Then again, I'd say he has good reason to be worried about all the bad things that can happen to us. After all, he lived through so many of them.*

"Being a pain in the ass...is part of your charm," she chanced to say after a few moments.

"Gee, thanks," Kael said in a droll voice. "That makes me feel better. I guess."

Anna wrapped an arm awkwardly around her shoulders. "I mean that in the nicest way possible."

"Is this how you won Elin over?"

Anna's face grew hot at the teasing question. She was still anxious about talking about her love for Elin with Elin's other lover. "Nah, I think that was a fluke. There's nothing I could have done to win Elin over unless she already had it in her mind to take me as I am."

"I know exactly what you mean." A subtle twitch of Kael's lips signaled her gentle humor. "So...was I right?"

Anna bit her lower lip, uncertain how to interpret the question. "About what?"

Kael smiled. It was unforced, genuine, and one of the most thrilling things Anna had ever seen. "That it can feel good?"

"Oh." Anna's face flooded with heat. "Yeah, you were right."

"Are you okay?"

"I'm very okay." Anna hesitated a moment, then asked, "Are...are you okay?"

"Yeah." She drew her dark eyebrows together in concern. "Didn't Elin tell you? You didn't have to worry about me?"

"She did, but I just wanted to make sure."

"Anna...I'm happy for you. I'm happy for Elin. In a world this hard, how could I ever be upset about love?"

"You're a remarkable person," Anna commented. "Someone like Elin...not everyone would be willing to share that with someone else."

Kael touched her arm, drawing her gaze upwards. "Well, first of all...you're not just *anyone* else. Elin loves you. Besides, it's not for me to *share* Elin. I don't own her."

"But you love her."

"Yes, and so I want her to be happy. You make her happy." Cheeks flushed, Kael toyed with the knife she was cleaning. "And Anna, I think you deserve love, very much. I want you to be happy, too."

Anna's throat felt tight at the sentiment, and she cleared it before hastily changing the subject. "How did you learn to hunt like this?"

"I had a lot of time to practice when I was on my own."

"After you escaped from the Eve Institute?" Anna hoped it was okay to bring that up.

Kael nodded. "Yeah. I was alone for a long time. And I spent all my time learning how to fight, how to hunt. I'd choose something I wanted to master, and I would practice and practice until I had it."

"How long were you alone before you met Elin?"

"Six years."

"That's a lot of practice."

"It was a very dark time. A very long time."

Anna did some quick mental math. "So you're thirty years old?"

Kael lowered her voice. "Hasn't anyone ever told you not to ask a lady her age?"

"Lady?" Anna giggled.

Kael gave her a cocky grin and ran her hand over her buzzed hair, flexing muscular arms. "You're right. On both counts. How old are you?"

"Twenty-five."

"So you were five when it happened. Do you remember anything?"

Anna closed her eyes. *Mama's dark hair. Dad's mustache tickling my face. Marina, the most amazing big sister a five-year-old tagalong ever had.* She smiled sadly. "A little bit."

"Elin was lucky. Only two years old—it's one reason she's so untouched by things. She doesn't have to remember everyone dying."

Anna shuddered at some vague flashes of memory. Mama sick. Soldiers breaking into their home. People dying in the streets. *Elin really is so lucky.* When Kael didn't say anything more, Anna steeled her nerve. There was so much she wanted to know about her companion, but she wasn't yet certain what she could ask. "Do you—"

Kael lifted a thick eyebrow when Anna's words trailed off. "Just lay it on me, Anna. And sit back. Get comfortable."

With a shy nod, Anna scooted backwards until her bottom touched the tree, so close to Kael that their bodies touched from shoulder to hip. "Is this okay?"

Kael exhaled and folded her arms across her stomach. "Yeah." Her voice was uncharacteristically soft. "It's very okay. Now ask me."

"Do you...enjoy living as a man?"

Chuckling, Kael said, "I wondered when this might come up."

"Yeah, well, you're so good at it. I mean, I really never even imagined up until you showed me. I had no idea."

"Thanks." Kael beamed. "Don't get me wrong. I don't want to actually *be* a man. I just enjoy being masculine."

"Is it because...because of what happened to you?"

Cool indigo eyes searched Anna's face, and for a few moments she was afraid she'd said something wrong. But Kael just shook her head. "I don't think so. I suppose it may have something to do with it, but I never quite felt like a normal little girl. Normal like the other little girls in my class were normal, I mean."

"Because you liked other girls?"

Kael nodded. "Yeah, but also...I felt more like a boy. At least how I thought they must feel. I always wanted short hair. I wanted to play soccer in the streets with the neighborhood boys. When Mr. Jacobs took me...well, that may have intensified those feelings, but those feelings were always there inside of me."

Recalling Elin's words, Anna asked, "So you don't feel like a woman?" Now that she had started down this path with Kael, she wanted to keep going.

"Not quite like a woman, no. Not quite like a man, either. I don't know what I am. I just know that I'm masculine, and I prefer being seen as a man in this society. And I love women, even if they sometimes seem like foreign creatures to me."

"I can truly say that you're one of the most interesting people I've ever known," Anna said. "I'm so lucky to have met you and Elin. I don't know what I would've done without you two." Anna twisted her hands in her lap, unable to admit how close she had been to giving up.

Kael captured Anna's hand in both of hers and gave it a gentle squeeze. "I understand that, too. If it hadn't been for Elin—" Kael shuddered, and Anna instinctively leaned into her solid body. "I don't want to imagine what I would have become."

Anna struggled to regulate her breathing as she stared at her hand between Kael's. The whole of her concentration seemed suddenly riveted on the scent of her companion and the light pressure of Kael's hip pressing against hers. "What do you mean?"

"The practicing, when I was alone—" Kael exhaled harshly. "One of the most important things I tried to master was becoming the best killer I could be. And I practiced a *lot*."

That wasn't hard to imagine. Kael radiated dark rage at

times, and Anna had been witness to the efficiency with which she dispatched her enemies. She watched the naked pain in Kael's eyes. *It looks like it's disturbing to remember, though.*

"Does Elin know?"

"I've spared her the details." Kael shifted to sheath her knife, her warm breath tickling Anna's cheek and neck, raising gooseflesh on her arms. "She knows she saved me. I tell her all the time."

Anna said, "I've killed people, too." She fought to keep her mind away from the powerful sensuality of full lips brushing accidentally against her ear. "Not a lot, really. Four. And only in self-defense." She remembered Garrett's killers and cast weary eyes to the ground. "Mostly."

Kael's mouth twitched into a wistful smile. "I don't always feel bad about doing it. I don't talk to Elin much about that, but...sometimes I think people deserve to die."

Anna's eyes slipped momentarily shut in reaction to the scent and faint heat coming from Kael's lean body, and she had to force herself to concentrate on her words. "I know what you mean," she replied, feeling short of breath. "I do love how Elin sees the world so innocently. But I just don't see it the same way. I'm trying, for her sake."

"I'm glad she has you, Anna. I really am."

"I'm glad she has you, too." It was the truth.

Kael seemed embarrassed and bent to retrieve the rabbits. "I like hanging out with you. Maybe we can start sparring lessons again."

Since the morning when wrestling had triggered Anna's flashback, she'd only practiced light sparring with Elin. Her gut tugged at her to try fighting with Kael again. *He could teach me so much more than Elin ever could. And I trust Kael. I really do.*

"Okay," she said. "Tomorrow morning?"

"Sounds good." Kael stood, then helped Anna up.

Anna hesitated only a moment before wrapping her arms around Kael's solid body. Kael brought rabbit-filled hands behind Anna's back in an effort to return the hug. She nuzzled into Anna's neck, simply breathing.

"Thanks for coming after me today," Kael murmured. "It feels good to have another friend."

Beaming, Anna gave her a squeeze. "Yes, it does." She brought her mouth close to Kael's ear. Closing her eyes, she whispered, "You make masculinity beautiful, you know."

Kael caught her breath and stepped backwards, stumbling slightly. "Thanks. I, uh...I should go clean these rabbits." Red-faced and holding the rabbits aloft, she added, "And you know...you're beautiful, too. Really beautiful. And, uh...you should go tell Elin we're getting ready for dinner." Another backwards step, and then she turned to stalk away from Anna. "Thanks for the company," she called back over her shoulder.

"It was my pleasure."

DEEPLY INVOLVED IN her book, Elin didn't lift her eyes from her reading until Anna reached the high branches of the oak tree where she sat. When Anna clambered onto the branch beside her, she relaxed into a welcoming grin, folded the corner of a page to mark her place, and closed her book. "Hey, sweetheart. How are you doing?"

"I'm good. I've been with Kael."

Sparkling hazel eyes studied Anna's face with such scrutiny that she squirmed.

Elin smiled big as she watched Anna's discomfort grow. "Did you kiss him?"

Anna gasped. "No."

Elin leaned forward with a conspiratorial grin. "Did you want him to kiss you?"

Anna lowered her head, certain that her face was about to burst into flames. "Stop teasing me."

Elin kissed one heat-infused cheek. "I'm not teasing you." She caught Anna's earlobe between gentle teeth and tugged lightly. "I'm curious. I see the way you look at him sometimes."

Anna shrugged one shoulder. "Maybe."

"Yeah?" Elin rubbed a hand tenderly over Anna's side, then slid it up to caress her breast. "He wants to kiss you," she whispered.

Distracted by the feeling of Elin's fingers stroking her nipple through the cotton of her shirt, Anna murmured, "Is he a good kisser?"

Elin moaned and rolled her eyes heavenward. "Oh God, yes. He's an excellent kisser." Giving Anna's breast a playful squeeze, she said, "So are you. I think if you and Kael kissed...nothing would be hotter than that."

"Yeah? You think so?"

"The two sexiest, most beautiful people I know, kissing? Yeah, that'd be amazingly hot. Are you kidding me?"

Anna broke into an embarrassed giggle. "Well, whatever. I don't know if we'll ever get to that point."

"Would you let me watch if you do?"

With a burst of shocked laughter, Anna poked her in the side. "Depends on how nicely you ask." *Would I let her watch?* She blushed at the idea. *I'd let her do more than watch.*

"Sounds like I'd better be nice, then. If you two finally get over your shyness and make out, I want a front-row seat."

Anna closed the distance between them and traced the tip of her tongue over Elin's bottom lip. "Or maybe you could join us onstage," she mumbled.

Elin's breathing picked up. "I've fantasized about it, you know."

"You fantasize about *everything*." *And, lucky me, you're not embarrassed to tell me about it.*

"Especially you. And just so you know," Elin said with an innocent smile, "Kael really likes a lot of tongue when he's being kissed."

Chapter
Seven

A COLD BREEZE blew over Anna's lower leg and pulled her from deep sleep. She shivered in displeasure, and aware of the faint heat of the body to her right, she shifted closer, half-smiling at the drowsy thought of Elin and her soft curves. An arm reached out and met her halfway, tugging her close and lazily covering her with a blanket. Content, she floated off into light sleep within moments.

The next time she awoke, it was because a gentle hand was stroking her belly. She could feel Elin spooning her from behind, one arm curled over her hip, fingers splayed over her stomach. Anna opened one eye and registered the twilight through the tops of the trees and the darkness that still permeated their campsite. *It's not time to wake up yet,* she managed to think, and pressed her bottom backwards into Elin's hips.

Elin's fingers moved down to the hem of her T-shirt, pushed inside, and traced aimless patterns over her bare skin. As if sensing her rising arousal, the fingers tickled the skin around her belly button before moving up to stroke her breast. The fuzziness around the edges of Anna's mind receded a bit, and her heartbeat picked up.

Rather than lingering on her breast, the hand slid down over her belly to the waistband of her panties. A single fingertip traced a path along the elastic across her abdomen, then moved to her hip and made its way over her panties to her bare thigh. Anna shifted her right leg, opening herself to further exploration. Invitation extended, the fingers responded by tickling a light path to the sensitive skin of her inner thigh, before dipping inside her panties to tease before withdrawing.

Anna lifted her hips in a silent plea, answered almost immediately when a big, strong hand reached between her legs and cupped her firmly. Snapped to instant awareness, she blinked in confusion, rolling back so that she could look over her shoulder.

"Kael?"

"I'm sorry, Anna." Kael's red face and panicked eyes were just barely visible in the darkness of the early morning. "I was half-asleep. I thought you were Elin."

"Me, too." Anna knew she should pull away, but the dimness of the morning and the sensual warmth of Kael's body made her linger. "Where is she?"

"She's sitting over there grinning at us like the cat that ate the canary," Kael rumbled into her ear.

"Do you think she did this on purpose?" Anna stared at Kael's dark hair. It had been growing out and was the longest she'd seen it.

"That little shit?" Kael whispered. "Probably." She sat up and asked, "Elin, what are you doing out of bed?"

"I wasn't feeling well." Elin's beaming grin cut through the dimness of the morning. She was sitting on a fallen log over on the other side of camp, dressed in her jeans and a thick sweatshirt. "I decided to get up and sit for a while, see if I felt better."

Anna lifted her head. "And do you feel better?"

Elin's grin widened. "Much. How do you feel?"

Kael cleared her throat, and Anna smirked at the chuckle she heard suppressed. "Baby," Kael said in a stern voice, "I know you haven't gotten enough sleep. How long have you been out of bed?"

"I don't know. I could probably sleep some more." Elin got to her feet and crossed to their sleeping bags.

Anna crawled back over to her side of their makeshift bed, embarrassed to see how far she had traveled to seek out Kael in Elin's absence. She shot Elin a playful scowl. "Then get back in here, goofball."

"And take off those jeans." Kael shifted over to make room. "We're keeping you here for at least another two hours of sleep. Get comfortable."

"Hey, I'm not complaining." Elin removed her sweatshirt and jeans and tossed them onto her backpack. She slid into the gap between them with a contented sigh. "I missed you both."

"We missed you, too." Anna watched Kael's arm reach over Elin's waist and pull her into a close embrace.

"I want to feel you, Anna." Elin encouraged her closer.

Anna scooted in, groaning in bliss when Elin's hand slipped under the elastic of her panties to cup one buttock. She leaned in to share a sleepy kiss that ended when she nuzzled her face into Elin's throat. Smiling, Anna fell back asleep within the safety created by her new family.

MUCH LATER IN the day, they traveled through a more developed area than they had seen in weeks. Log houses were scattered throughout lush forest that hummed with wildlife, providing brief distraction and plenty of curiosity each time they saw one.

"It's ugly up there, you guys." Elin stopped walking and looked up at the dark clouds that painted the late afternoon sky. "It's gonna pour."

Anna and Kael joined in her study. A cool breeze had picked up, swirling fallen leaves around their ankles. The air smelled damp, and Anna could tell Elin's prediction was dead-on. "I think a storm is on its way," she said.

"Let's hope this isn't a bad sign as far as Kentucky weather goes," Kael muttered.

Elin looked delighted. "We're in Kentucky now? You didn't tell me."

Kael gave her a playful wink. "You were lagging behind with Anna, or else I would've."

"Cool." Elin craned her neck and pointed. "Look, another cabin."

It was probably the fifteenth they had seen that day. Anna and Elin had lingered to gaze longingly at each they passed, but until now Kael had paid them no mind.

"Pretty," Anna commented. It was large, at least two stories, and constructed with sturdy-looking logs. A red vehicle was parked next to it. "Looks like there's a road just on the other side of it. I wonder if we're close to a town."

"Getting closer, I think," Kael said.

"We should stay inside tonight," Elin implored Kael. "Baby, you know it's going to be miserable outside. What do you say we bask in the luxury of a roof over our heads while it storms?"

"That does sound nice," Anna said.

Kael sighed. "We could try to find a nice cave to wait out the rain."

Frowning, Elin shook her head. "Come on, Kael. What're the odds there's anyone in there? We'll let you walk through and check it out. If it doesn't feel safe to you, we'll leave. No questions asked. I'd just *really* love to be warm and dry tonight." She cast a sheepish gaze to the ground and kicked at a plant. "And it's been so long since we've gotten to explore someplace like this. I'd like to see what's in there."

Anna felt a rush of affection. Elin had a fascination with pre-sickness artifacts. Anything, really: books, toys, even non-working appliances. She had entertained Anna more than once by regaling her with tales of the things she and Kael had discovered in their travels.

Kael's broad shoulders slumped in defeat. "Okay. You two stay outside while I walk through the cabin. Don't come in until I signal."

She set off up an incline covered with fallen leaves and overgrown vegetation, and Anna and Elin followed. The steep walk strained Anna's thigh muscles, making her glad that they were stopping for the night. Kael led them around one side of the cabin, signaling them to keep cover in some nearby trees, then she moved stealthily to the front door, sword drawn. After a brief struggle with the handle, she vanished inside.

Anna and Elin waited for a few moments, attuned to any hint of trouble, then they edged closer, moving alongside the red sports utility vehicle that was parked in the driveway.

"I don't think this has been driven for a while," Elin whispered as she traced a hand over the weathered paint.

"Doesn't look like it." Anna swung her baseball bat in a gentle arc at her side. A brief flash of memory came to her: her mother, driving her and Marina...someplace. *It was practice of some kind, wasn't it? Soccer? Gymnastics?*

" 'Support Our Troops,' " Elin read, staring at the faded stickers that were still stuck to the bumper. "I wonder what war that was from?"

Anna snorted in disgust. "There were so many in the end. Who knows?"

"Do you think they realized what would happen?"

"I don't know." Anna took her hand and gave it a tender squeeze. "It's hard to believe that nobody could have imagined where it would lead. When you mix war and technology like that—"

"Elin, Anna." Kael poked her head out of the front door. "It's clear. Come on."

Elin raised Anna's hand to her lips and kissed her knuckles, then skipped away over to the front porch steps. Taking them two at a time, she leaned in and gave Kael a grateful kiss when she reached the top.

Kael returned her sword to its sheath. "I don't want anyone going in the third room on the left upstairs. Other than that...go explore, baby."

Elin clapped in excitement and walked inside. Kael remained on the porch as Anna climbed the steps, then opened the front door for her.

"Body upstairs?" Anna murmured.

Kael gave her a somber nod. "Only bones at this point. I moved the remains into the closet, but still...I don't want Elin seeing that."

Anna walked inside the dark cabin. "Think there are any candles around here?"

"Actually, yeah." Kael closed the door behind them. "Plenty. This isn't a bad place to stop, to tell you the truth. I saw candles, I saw MREs, and I definitely saw a wood-burning stove. I also saw a big tub for bathing."

"Are you telling me I can take a warm bath tonight?" Anna's thigh muscles practically sang in relief.

"I'm telling you that both you and Elin could fit into that tub at the same time, if you wanted."

Anna hummed in pleasure at the thought. "Oh, I'm *so* glad we stopped here."

"Good. I like seeing you two happy."

"I know you do." Anna touched Kael's hand briefly. "We...love that about you."

Kael gave her a look full of awed surprise, but before she could make a sound, Elin's joyful shout echoed from another room.

"Anna, there's a *bathtub* in here! And it's huge!"

Kael broke into a toothy grin. "I think Elin needs someone to explore with her right now." Her hand found the back of Anna's neck. "Come on."

She walked them back into the cabin, releasing Anna when they found a small room lit by candlelight and gently illuminated by the gray light that shone in from a large window.

Elin stood in the center of the room with a burning candle. She was wide-eyed. "You wouldn't believe all the great stuff they have here."

Kael struck a match and lit a few more candles that sat around the room. "The stove is in the next room. I'm going to go see if there's enough wood to heat bath water or if I need to go out and get some more."

Elin looked like she was ready to burst with excitement. "Awesome. Anna, I've found books and photo albums and an old French horn—"

"French horn?" Anna joined Elin over in front of a closet built into the far wall. "What's that?"

Elin pulled an intricately shaped brass object from the closet. "It's a musical instrument. My dad had a book full of pictures and information about all kinds of different instruments...woodwinds, brass, string."

"I don't know a lot about music," Anna admitted. "Just what people in my tribe told me about. Nobody ever mentioned French horns."

"Have you heard a lot of music?"

"I can remember music from when I was very little. After we moved to the forest, just singing. My people didn't believe in electricity, modern things. So for as long as I can remember, just singing. Garrett's adoptive mother used to sing to both of us sometimes. She called it Motown. I think they were pretty old songs."

Elin smiled fondly as she continued examining the contents of the closet. "My dad used car batteries to power an old CD player he had in the house. I love classic rock. It was his favorite, too."

Anna wasn't entirely certain what classic rock was, but nodded. She spotted a door leading to another room. "I'm going to go check out what's in here."

Elin gave her a distracted nod. "Let me know if you find anything really cool."

Anna made a quick detour next to Elin and delivered a light smack to her bottom. Elin giggled and gave Anna's nipple a gentle tweak. Anna was still smirking when she entered the next room. This one also had a window, and she could make out bulky furniture arranged in a semicircle in the center of the floor. She made her way cautiously around the perimeter of the room and smiled when she discovered a shelf full of decorative candles.

"I don't think anyone would mind if I borrowed these," she murmured, using the candle she held to light one after another, until she had the entire shelf ablaze and generating warm light.

Anna turned to face the interior of the room, then collected lit candles and started a slow dispersal of light throughout the room. When done, she could easily see two leather couches that faced one another, and an overstuffed leather chair at the head of the room. A large bookcase sat opposite the armchair. The shelves were crammed with various knickknacks and old volumes. Everything was covered by a thin layer of dust.

Near the windows, a low shelf ran along the wall a foot or two beneath the windowsills. The objects on it appeared to be mostly small home appliances, and unlike the dead technology she normally saw, none of them seemed to be electrically operated. It took only a few minutes of study before Anna realized she'd found something extraordinary. "Elin!"

Elin poked her auburn head inside the room. "Yeah?"

"I've got something for you." Anna examined the object in her lap, trying to decide how it worked. "I think you're going to love this if I can figure it out."

Bounding over, Elin knelt on the floor and rubbed Anna's

lower back through her sweatshirt. "What is it?"

"I think it's a movie projector. I found some reels of film, too. It doesn't look like this thing needs electricity, either. I think it's hand-operated."

"That's so cool. Nice find."

Anna pulled a reel of film from the box. "If I can just figure out how to get the reel on there—"

"Ready for a bath, girls?"

Anna glanced up at Kael's low voice. "I found a movie projector."

"Hand-operated," Elin said excitedly. "We might be able to watch some movies tonight."

Kael gave them an indulgent grin. "That sounds great. There's a lot of room in here. What do you two say we set up our sleeping bags in this room for the night?"

I guess that answers where he found the body. Of course it'd be in the nice, soft bed. Still, carpet sounded like a dream.

"Okay," Elin said. "We can take our baths and then watch movies. How about that?"

"As you wish, sweet girl," Kael said.

Elin rose to her feet and offered Anna her hand. "What do you say we go get wet, Anna?"

Blushing, Anna took in Kael's hooded gaze. "Okay."

Kael stepped back to allow them through the door. "The water may still be a bit hot. Let me check before you get in, okay?"

She led Elin and Anna to a room Anna hadn't yet seen, lit not only by a candle, but also by a wood-burning stove. At one side of the room sat a large wooden tub, three-quarters full of steaming water. The giant pot Kael must have used to heat the water sat on the floor next to the tub, empty.

"There's a water pump out back," Kael said. "It was cold as hell coming out of the ground, but I boiled it before pouring it into the tub. Be careful when you get in."

Elin nodded, then shivered. "It'll cool off pretty quickly, I imagine." She stepped closer to the stove and held out her hands to warm them.

Anna dipped one hand inside the tub just as Kael did the same. "Feels good to me." She couldn't remember the last time she'd had a hot bath.

Kael nodded. "I think it's fine. I put some towels in front of the stove for when you get out."

Elin looked up at Kael with a frown. "You're not taking a bath?"

Kael shot Anna a cautious look, then turned back to Elin

with a shake of her head. "I figured I'd worry about dinner while you two bathed."

"I thought you said there were MREs in here somewhere," Anna said. "You don't need to hunt for us tonight."

Kael hesitated. "Well, I could get our beds set up. And I could go out and gather some more wood for this stove—"

Elin began stripping off her clothes. "Kael, why don't you just stay here? You should get a bath, too."

Kael shot Anna a nervous look. "There's only room enough for two in there at a time. I'd just be...watching, anyway."

Anna bit her lower lip. *You know you don't want him to leave.* "You could keep us company," she murmured. "There's no reason for you to have to go off on your own all the time. We both want you around."

"You do?" Kael stared at them with a solemn look on her face.

"I know I do," Elin said, blue jeans bunched around her ankles. She kicked them away with a flourish. Reaching behind her back, she unclasped her bra and bared her breasts.

Anna met Kael's gaze once again. "I want you around, Kael." *More than you know.* Now that they'd started sparring again, it wasn't flashbacks that Anna worried about. It was her arousal, and how the look and feel of Kael's lean body inspired it. Not to mention the intense indigo eyes, the low, sensual voice, and the genuine caring that she felt every time Kael was near. "There's no reason for you to leave."

"Then it's settled." Elin stood gloriously nude with a beaming smile on her face. She patted the seat of Anna's jeans. "Take your clothes off."

Anna raised an eyebrow at Kael. "Has she always been this bossy?"

"Always."

"We call it 'decisive,' where I come from," Elin said. With a smirk, she climbed onto a bench that sat next to the tub and eased one shapely leg into the steaming water before lowering her body into the bath. "Oh my God, this is heavenly."

Anna's eagerness to bathe overrode most of her modesty, and she began shedding her clothing with relative ease. She could feel Kael's eyes on her body as she undressed, and she felt her face flush with the realization that she enjoyed the attention. A lot. She caught a momentary glimpse of the two hated scars on her breast when her bra fell to the ground, and she lifted her eyes to watch Kael's reaction. Kael wet her lips with her tongue, and she didn't look away. Anna's nipples hardened, but whether from Kael's heated stare or the frigid air, she wasn't sure.

"Anna has the prettiest skin, doesn't she?" Elin murmured. "So smooth."

"And the color." Kael stood with her hands clasped in front of her narrow hips, knuckles white. "It's beautiful."

Anna dropped her eyes to look at her brown skin. She and her uncle had been the only ones in her tribe so dark, and she had only ever seen one man darker than her. She had been at first fascinated by him, and then horrified that she had to kill him.

"Uncle Roberto told me we were Latino." She eased her body into the water with a grateful sigh. "All I knew was that I never looked like anyone else except my uncle. The other kids in the tribe would tease me sometimes, for being so dark."

Elin floated over to wrap her arms around Anna. "They were crazy." Reaching out, she covered one bare breast with pale fingers. "I'm especially fond of your brown nipples."

Anna whimpered in pleasure when Elin captured one erect nipple between gentle fingertips, squeezing and rolling it in a slow tease. "Responsive brown nipples," Elin murmured. She gave Kael a mischievous grin, and then affected innocence at Kael's stern look. "What?"

"Who are you trying to tease?" Kael shifted where she stood and folded her arms over her chest.

"Everyone?" Elin answered.

"It's working," Kael and Anna said in unison.

"Good." Elin beckoned to Kael. "Baby, will you come make sure that I'm clean?"

"Elin," Kael said in soft warning. "Be good."

Anna studied Elin with an amused half-smile. "She's never good. You know that, Kael. You might as well make sure that she's clean, though. At the very least, if she can't be good, she should be clean."

"Definitely." Kael approached the tub and pushed the sleeve of her Henley shirt above the elbow. Staring at Elin's breasts, she held a sponge aloft for a moment before lowering her hand into the water to soak it. "Surprise," she murmured, and brought the sponge up to brush across Elin's breasts. "I found it still wrapped in plastic earlier, if you want to use it."

Elin closed her eyes, groaning in pleasure. "That feels so fucking good."

Anna blinked. *Elin hardly ever swears unless we're —* Her eyes went wide and she felt a rush of sensation between her legs as she took in the scene across from her. *Well, I know Elin is aroused.*

"Dirty mouth." Kael dropped the sponge and cupped Elin's breast with her large hand. "And here I thought I was supposed to be getting you clean."

Anna's breathing faltered, and her heart began to pound.

Elin arched her back to push her breast harder against Kael's hand. "You're doing an excellent job, too."

"What do you think?" Kael glanced at Anna. Her nostrils flared as she twisted a dark pink nipple between her fingertips.

Flustered, Anna met Kael's evil smirk with a shy smile. "I think she could probably be cleaner."

Kael held Anna's gaze as she released Elin's breast and slid her hand down over the center of Elin's belly, deep underwater. Arm muscles flexing, she leaned in and kissed Elin's cheek at the same time working her hand between Elin's legs.

Though the room was dim, the pale skin of her companions was visible underwater, and the sight made Anna crave a lover's touch. She let her thighs fall open and slipped one of her hands between them.

"I think you're clean enough. For now," Kael said after a short while. Her face was serious, almost stern, and Elin dissolved into obedience.

Anna was intrigued by their interplay. *Elin's always so in control when she's with me. I wonder how it is between her and Kael?*

Kael turned desire-filled eyes onto Anna. "Elin, why don't you make sure Anna is clean?"

How can I refuse that? Anna felt water lap her breasts as Elin moved to sit next to her. "You are so bad," she murmured.

Elin wrapped her arms around Anna's shoulders and pulled their wet bodies together in a tight hug. "You and Kael seem to be enjoying it." In a louder voice, she said, "I love you, Anna."

Anna dissolved into a helpless grin. "I love you, too, Elin."

Elin gave her a slow, wet kiss. Anna moaned into the joining and wrapped her arms around Elin, sliding one hand down to palm Elin's bottom while the other stayed planted on Elin's lower back to keep her close. When Elin finally broke the kiss, the room was filled with the sound of heavy breathing. Anna darted a look over to Kael, finally remembering that she had been watching.

"I knew it," Kael drew a breath. "You two are beautiful together. Though I'm not sure that had anything to do with making Anna clean."

Elin tilted her head to kiss Anna again, this time sliding her hand between Anna's thighs to palm her center. Anna gasped into the kiss and sought out Kael with her eyes. Kael looked like she was ready to implode. Elin's fingers parted Anna, and one fingertip grazed along her swollen labia. Anna uttered a breathy moan just as Elin's stomach sent a long, loud growl into the air.

Anna jerked a little in surprise when her own stomach gurgled in sympathy.

Kael's laughter was the next sound to fill the room. Arms folded over her stomach, she bent at the waist, braying helpless guffaws. "That was priceless." She swiped at her wet cheeks with the back of her hand. "Probably the sexiest thing I'd ever seen in my life, and then..." Her shoulders quaked as a fresh round of laughter overtook her.

Anna kissed a pouting Elin on the cheek. "It's okay, baby. It *was* pretty cute."

"But I totally killed the mood."

"You didn't kill it, you just postponed it." Kael wiped the tears from her face. "I think that until I make sure that two girls have full bellies, there'll be no more thinking about sex."

"I doubt that." Elin shot Kael a mischievous smile. "I'm sure I'll keep thinking about it."

Anna's face flushed at the promise in Kael's words. *Postponed.* Her legs felt weak at the thought of where Elin's seductions could lead them. "I am pretty hungry." *And I don't mind slowing down for right now.* "Kael, where did you say you saw those MREs? I'll start worrying about dinner while you take your bath."

"If you go out the door to this room and down the hallway to your left, it's the second door. It's a storage closet, and the MREs are on the middle shelf or so."

Anna snagged the sponge from the surface of the water and gave her body a brisk scrubbing, then rose from the water into the chilly night air. Teeth chattering, she turned to find Kael with a large towel held in two hands. She didn't even hesitate to step out of the tub and into the towel, leaning into Kael's warmth as large hands rubbed her up and down and squeezed her buttocks through the towel.

When finished, Kael undressed and lifted a smaller pot of warm water from its place on the stove and poured it into the tub.

"After dinner, we can figure out that movie projector, okay, Anna?" Elin said.

"Sure," Anna replied.

She would make the fastest dinner in the history of mankind, she decided as she left the room. *After all, once we eat dinner and watch movies...anything could happen.*

Chapter
Eight

ANNA BROUGHT THE movie projector to life with the push of a button after turning its crank until her arm was sore. The reel of film she'd selected at random projected onto a blank wall, a smallish square of light that was at once filled with familiar sights in a surreal reality. A young man in extremely old-fashioned clothing stood grinning and waving in front of an antique vehicle, shoulders thrown back in obvious pride.

"That's a 1965 Ford Mustang," Elin said. At Anna's surprised look, she explained, "My dad taught me everything he knew about cars. He had a lot of books." She folded her hands under her chin to continue watching.

"It's a cool car," Kael murmured from her spot on the sleeping bag beside Elin. She also lay on her stomach, head propped on an upturned palm.

"Yeah, it is." Anna sat cross-legged next to the projector, ready to crank it up again when the power ran down.

Outside, hard rain pounded against the windows, providing a muted soundtrack for the silent film. The movie changed from a scene of the young man and his car to the same man and a running, jumping dog. He held a disc high above the dog's head, and every once in a while he would toss it so that it glided through the air. Most of the time, the dog would catch it in his mouth and return it to the man.

Anna grinned. "A guy called Jack in my tribe had a dog that survived the sickness somehow...and he was really sweet. We called him Lucky."

"Could he do that?" Kael asked. Her eyes were glued to the screen, where the dog leapt into the air and snagged the disc between its teeth.

Anna smiled at the wonder in Kael's gaze, so much more like Elin than Anna had ever seen her. "He would fetch a stick if you threw it, but he was too slow to catch it in the air."

"I think it'd be really cool to train an animal to hunt with me."

"You'd be good at that," Elin said.

"Hell, yeah, you would," Anna agreed. *Kael's good at just about everything he does.* The thought made her flush as she considered it on an increasingly familiar level. *From the way Elin acted when he had his hand between her legs earlier, sex is one of them.*

Kael grunted, but her eyes stayed glued to the movie. The young man had been joined by a number of other young men in some kind of game. They ran around one another, tossing a ball and running it down the length of the grassy field where they played. Anna watched aggressive tackles from players on the opposing side stop the ball carrier time and again, sending them all crashing down to the ground in writhing piles.

"Okay, Garrett would have *loved* that game."

Elin guffawed, familiar with Anna's anecdotes about the boy-crazy young man. "I don't know what else there is to like about football."

"It looks pretty fun to me," Kael said.

Elin bumped Kael's shoulder with hers. "Boys."

They watched the young man participate in a ceremony that Anna recognized as a high school graduation, and then they watched the party afterwards in which the camera followed him around and an older woman beamed at him proudly. Anna felt a tug deep in her stomach at the sight of something she barely remembered in her own life. Her uncle had never looked at her like that. In his eyes, she was a constant source of shame.

"His mother," Kael whispered, sharing a quick look of sympathetic loss with Anna.

From the graduation party, the video moved into a much darker scene, that of the young man dressed in a military uniform and smiling as he had in front of his Mustang. Pride radiated from his lean body, and he held himself like a swaggering hero. Anna dropped her eyes, sick from the sight of the uniform. If there was one thing she had learned to fear, it was war, and the soldiers who waged it.

The film reel ran to its end, flapping in the air upon each revolution until Anna stopped the projector. Kael cleared her throat, awkward.

Elin sighed deeply and deposited a kiss on Kael's temple. "Well, I thought it was pretty good up until the bummer ending. I think he should've found a girl and settled down. That going-to-war story is *so* played out."

"I agree," Anna said. "Maybe there's a better one in this box." She smiled at her companions, allowing her eyes to linger on their contrasting forms. Kael was dressed in a T-shirt and boxer shorts, stretched out tall and lanky on her belly. Her body was lean muscle, solid, with narrow hips. Elin lay in just a tank top and her panties, all soft curves and warmth. Anna desired both so intensely that she felt weak.

She selected a reel of film at random and loaded it into the projector, cranking the handle to charge the machine. As she worked, she watched Kael's hand tickle the back of Elin's upper thigh. Starting the movie with the press of a button, she dragged her eyes from Kael and Elin to the images being projected on the wall. At once, there was complete silence in the room as they all watched what Anna had discovered.

Children. Three of them, tearing shiny paper from boxes stacked beneath a Christmas tree. The imagery was familiar to Anna. Christmas was something nearly everyone in her tribe had celebrated in some way.

"Christmas." Elin's eyes shone with emotion as she watched the screen, seemingly lost in her own memories of the past.

A little boy sat beneath the Christmas tree with a miniature guitar that looked like it had been designed specifically for a child. His upper body swayed back and forth as he strummed the strings, and his mouth opened and closed in silent song. The other two children, both long-haired girls, danced in a circle for the camera. Each had a brand-new doll clutched in eager hands to serve as a dancing partner.

Anna stared at the images in rapt fascination. It had been over a year since she'd seen a child, and the movie brought home some memories she had tried to push aside. There had been eight children born into her tribe over the past twenty years. Growing up, she and Garrett had been two of only four pre-sickness children raised by the tribe. The new births in the years since the sickness had been a sign of hope, if not a source of constant worry for those charged with protecting the tribe and its future.

She wondered what had happened to the children that day. It wasn't the first time she'd had the thought. Janice and Owen always said they would hide the kids if trouble came, but Anna hadn't seen whether they got away. Swallowing, she watched the carefree innocence of the children in the movie, not sure whether she preferred to think that the children she remembered were captured or just killed.

Elin released a wistful sigh. "I'd like to raise children someday."

Anna swung her eyes over to Elin and tried to imagine her lover as a mother and found that it wasn't very difficult. *She'd be wonderful with a child.*

"No." Kael stared at the movie in silence, her eyes hard and expressionless, her face tight with pain. "There is no way I will ever help bring a child into this world. No child deserves that."

"No?" Elin responded sharply. "Since when do you get to just tell me what's going to happen? I thought we talked about things."

Kael turned dark eyes to Elin. "Some things aren't worth talking about."

Anna stayed quiet, uncertain of her own feelings on the subject. On the one hand, Elin's desire to raise a child was so utterly Elin-like that she found it hard to imagine her lover never getting that chance, and especially when she would do such a good job. On the other hand, Anna wasn't sure what kind of legacy past generations had left for the three of them, let alone what they could leave for children. *Maybe it is best that we just...stop. There's so much pain in the world that I don't want a child to have to feel.*

"Not worth talking about?" Elin murmured. "Something that I want—that I've dreamed about—isn't worth talking about?"

Kael's eyes flashed with anger. "If you think I'm letting some man fuck you so that you can have a baby, then—"

"Then what?" Elin's shoulders rose and fell with her rapid breathing, a sign that she was more upset than Anna had ever seen her. "And who said I needed to actually have a baby? I'm not talking about having a baby, necessarily, just raising a child—"

"Same difference." Kael sat up and scooted backwards until she leaned against the couch, arms folded defensively. "And the answer is still no."

"So your issue isn't with the idea of a man *fucking* me, as if there weren't other ways to solve that particular problem—"

"My 'issue,' " Kael interrupted in a cold voice, "is that it's a completely selfish desire that I want no part in."

Elin recoiled as if Kael had slapped her across the face. Anna watched the hurt flash in her lover's eyes, and it elicited her protective instincts. *If there's one thing you could never call Elin, it's selfish.*

"Kael," Anna murmured. When Kael gave her a cold stare, she said, "You know that's not fair."

"I'm selfish?" Elin's eyes filled with tears, even as her face grew hard with anger.

"Wanting a child is selfish," Kael said. "What do we have to offer a child?"

"Love," Elin replied.

On the wall, the movie faded away when the projector ran out of charge. Anna made no move to crank it up again.

"Love?" Kael scoffed. "Well, what does the world have to

offer a child?"

"The same thing it offers us. I thought you agreed that the world isn't a wholly awful place." Elin shifted back to sit against the couch, a couple of feet from Kael. Their separation seemed far vaster to a silent Anna. "Loving you, loving Anna. Watching the sun rise in the morning or swimming in a cool lake on a hot summer day. There are a million things to love about life, and you know it."

"Just because it isn't wholly awful, that doesn't mean we should start ushering kids into it," Kael said. "Your child will never have a Christmas like that, Elin. That's gone now. Over. What do you think your child is going to have to celebrate?"

"*My* child?" Elin stared at Kael as if looking at a stranger.

"Not mine." Kael's jaw tightened. "I refuse to watch a child grow up in this world. Do you really want to have to worry about what's going to happen to your little girl when she grows up? Or about what your little boy could become?"

"But if there was a child who was already here, who *needed* someone—"

Kael wasn't about to listen. "What about you?" she asked Anna. "You want to watch a child grow up so she can be gang-raped on the ground like you were?"

Shamed, Anna looked at the floor. Hot tears stung her eyes, and she blinked, desperately trying to clear her vision. She didn't want Kael to see how much the comment had cut her.

"What the *fuck* is wrong with you, Kael?" Elin's voice rose. "How could you say something like that? What did Anna ever do to you?"

Anna couldn't meet Kael's gaze, but watched her tense jaw work in silence, and her fists clench and unclench in her lap. After a moment of awkward silence, Kael stood and strode over to her discarded blue jeans. She tugged them on angrily.

"Where are you going?" Elin asked, tears rolling down her pale cheeks.

"Out," Kael said in a rough voice.

"Don't go far, please," Elin whispered.

"I won't." Without turning around, Kael left the room, and a few moments later a door opened and closed in another part of the house.

"Did he just go outside in this rain?" Elin's shoulders shook, and she lifted a hand to cover her eyes.

"I think so." Anna had never seen Elin anywhere close to this upset. She gathered her into a gentle embrace.

Elin buried her face in Anna's neck. "I know it's silly to cry, but we've never fought like that before. I feel sick to my stomach."

"He was really upset," Anna said. It was an understatement. Kael had looked transported to another place with her pain and anger. "I can't blame him, given what he's experienced. Having to worry about his own child maybe going through some of the things he did...I'm sure it's a scary thought."

"That doesn't excuse what he said to you. There was no reason for that."

Anna focused on one of a myriad of freckles on Elin's chin. "I'm okay."

"He hurt you."

"Yes, he did."

"He hurt me, too," Elin said in a quiet, sorrowful voice. "Do you think I'm selfish?"

"You're the least selfish person I've ever known."

"Do you think wanting a child is selfish?"

Anna hesitated, then shrugged cautiously. "I don't know. I think if you wanted to adopt a child who needed someone, then no, not at all. As far as bringing new life into this world...sometimes I wonder what people think those children have to look forward to. Sometimes I wonder if I would have chosen to be born, knowing what I do now."

Elin's eyes turned sad. "Oh, Anna, I hope you don't mean that. Every moment I've spent with you has made me happy to be alive."

Anna hastened to explain, heart stuttering at the thought of never having lived her time with Elin. "Me too, every moment. Well, except maybe the first ten minutes or so." She managed to crack a brief smile. "Definitely once I bathed with you that first time."

Elin chuckled. "You take the good with the bad, I guess. But doesn't the good make it all worthwhile?"

Anna considered Elin's question. The bad times in her life had once left her wishing to die; the good times she'd found with Elin and Kael made her grateful that nobody had listened to her wishes. Fear tugged at her gut at the thought of losing either Elin or Kael like she had lost Garrett, but fear wasn't enough to keep her from basking in the joy of them for as long as she could.

"I guess so," she said. *I hope so.*

"I would be just as happy adopting a child in need," Elin said. "Maybe happier. I don't need to get pregnant and have a baby. I'm not saying that I wouldn't want that, maybe, but it's not about that for me. I tried to make Kael understand that."

"I know you did. He just wasn't listening." Lightning flashed, and both women turned their heads to gaze out the window at the pouring rain. "For the record, I'm not sure I'd be okay with a man being with you, either," Anna said.

Elin gave her a gentle shove. "The sickness may have taken us back to the dark ages in some ways, but there are options when it comes to inseminating a woman. We could work around that, if need be."

"You really want a baby someday?"

Elin nodded shyly. "Someday. I'm not ready now, because traveling is no way to raise a child and right now I want to see the world. But someday, whether it's because a situation arises or we just decide to settle down and have a family...yes, someday I would like to raise a child. I think about it sometimes, and it just feels right to me. With you and Kael."

"With me?" Responsibility crashed down upon Anna, before being replaced by elation at being given a gift she had never thought she would receive. "Really?"

"Of course. I think you'd be wonderful with a child."

The words brought unexpected tears to Anna's eyes as she contended with another memory, this one pushed so deep inside that she had steadfastly refused to think about it since the day it happened. She pulled Elin into a quick hug so she wouldn't see her rising emotion.

Elin tightened her arms around Anna's body. "So would Kael."

Anna tried to imagine Kael with a child. Kael had taught her so much about fighting and hunting; their sparring matches had grown competitive and laughter-filled. Anna learned something new nearly every day they spent together. *I love being around him. Once he lets down his guard a little—and I let down mine—he really is one of the most amazing people I've ever met.*

"He would be great," she said. "There's not a question in my mind about that. He's just scared, I think."

Elin drew back and twisted her hands together. "I still love Kael, and Kael still loves me, it's just...I totally ruined tonight. It was such a good night, too."

Anna lifted Elin's face with a hand under her chin and gave her a reassuring kiss. "You didn't ruin anything. Like you said, you still love him and he still loves you."

"But he's standing out there in the rain pissed off at me. We *yelled* at each other."

"Honey, sometimes people who love one another fight. If you didn't love him, he wouldn't be able to make you so angry. The same goes for him. If he didn't love you more than anything in the world, there's no way you could elicit such emotion. And you know that."

"I know. But it doesn't seem right somehow."

"Trust me," Anna said. "John and Moira back in my tribe loved each other so much it was crazy. The only thing louder than their lovemaking was their arguing."

"Do you think *we'll* ever fight?"

"Probably. But I'll love you until the day I die, no matter what."

Elin's face flushed with pleasure. "I'll love you until the day I die, too."

"I think I should go after Kael," Anna said.

"Will you tell him that I love him? No matter what?"

"He knows that."

"Tell him anyway. Sometimes he forgets."

"I'll tell him." Anna stroked her lover's fiery hair. "And then I'll bring him back inside so you can tell him again."

WHEN ANNA STEPPED onto the back porch of the cabin, now in blue jeans and a thick sweatshirt, she thought at first that Kael had broken her word and wandered off. Having already checked the front porch and around the sides of the cabin, she started to weigh the pros and cons of venturing through the rain into the surrounding forest when a quiet sniffling noise drew her attention to the ground just below the porch. She stepped to the railing and looked down at a freshly shaven head. Kael stood shivering in the pouring rain.

Goddamn it, Kael.

She got to the bottom of the back porch steps just as Kael turned to walk away. "Hold it," she called out. "You're not leaving. You're coming out of the rain with me. You're going to get sick, for Christ's sake."

Kael stopped walking, and her shoulders dropped in defeat. She let Anna grab her arm and lead her onto the porch. Then she turned, revealing reddened eyes and an expressionless face. "I honestly don't know why you care." Her voice was almost swept away by the sound of the storm. "Hit me," she whispered.

Anna blinked. "What?"

"Hit me, Anna. Please. I deserve it for what I said to you."

Anna stared at Kael's heaving chest and the way her wet T-shirt clung to her lean body. "That's not going to make me feel better."

"It'd make me feel better." Tears spilled from Kael's eyes, and she swiped at them with an angry hand. "I'm such a fucking asshole sometimes. Even as I was saying the words, I knew what they would do to you."

"So why did you say them?" Anna whispered, still raw from having such ugliness thrown at her by someone she trusted.

Kael balled one hand into a fist and rubbed it over her scalp. "Because I was scared. I thought you might tell Elin that you would raise a child with her. And that Elin might decide to leave me if I couldn't give her what she wanted. I wanted you to hate the idea, too."

"Elin's not going to leave you, Kael. You know that. And for the record, I'm not competing with you for her. I don't want to leave you, either."

"You don't?"

"No, I don't." She blew out a nervous breath. "Before I came out here to find you, Elin made me promise to tell you something. She told me that she loves you no matter what. She said sometimes you forget that."

Kael released a quiet half-sob. "Sometimes I do."

Anna took a deep breath, steeling herself for the talk she knew they needed to have. "Elin really wasn't saying that she has to have a baby. She's just saying that she hopes to have the opportunity to raise a child someday."

Kael raised haunted eyes to Anna. "And I'm saying that I don't think I can do it."

"I don't deny that it would be hard. And it would be scary as hell. But it's something she genuinely wants, and if we could find a child who needed parents, would it really be such a horrible thing?"

"Yes," Kael exploded, anguished. "One more person to worry about? Another person to protect? But this one is completely helpless and dependent upon me? I don't know if I can take it, Anna. Do you know how hard it is?"

"To love?" She allowed herself to imagine Elin being hurt for just an instant, and her bones ached with pain at the idea. "Yeah, it's hard, but what's the alternative? Not to love?"

"I don't know." Kael turned dark eyes to the wet forest that surrounded them. "I never—"

"What?"

"I never thought I would feel...these things I do. And it terrifies me. After I met Elin, I swore I would never let another person inside of me like I did her. Loving her was the best thing I'd ever felt, but it scared me in a way I had never experienced when I only had to think of myself. When we found you...I didn't want to care about you, but goddamn it, I do. And that's fine, because what can I do about that, anyway? But now Elin's asking me to think about adding a child to this family? Why? So I can worry constantly about what could happen to my babies?"

"Kael..." Anna placed a calming hand on her arm.

Kael's whole body trembled beneath her touch, and a low, keening noise escaped from her lips. For a moment the raw emotion paralyzed Anna, then, uncertain of how else to respond, she pulled a soaking-wet Kael into her arms, murmuring, "It's okay. You still love Elin, and she still loves you. I promise."

Anna sighed at the feeling of holding her strong friend. In one earth-tilting moment, Kael had gone from stoic protector to fiercely protected, and Anna felt the fundamental change deep in her soul. *That's exactly how I feel about him, isn't it? Protective. Just like with Elin.*

Leaning into Anna, Kael cleared her throat before making a hushed confession. "There's something I've never really talked about with Elin. It's one reason I got so upset back there."

Anna's instinctive suspicion that Kael was withholding something was confirmed by those tortured words. "Tell me."

Kael's body grew tense in Anna's embrace. "Guess how many children I have?" Her voice was so low that Anna could hardly make out the question over the noise of the thunderstorm.

Anna squinted her eyes closed in reaction to the sinking feeling in the pit of her stomach. She had a hard time reconciling the idea of masculine Kael being a mother. "How many?"

"Three." Kael's voice broke. "I don't even know whether the first two were girls or boys. The third was a little girl. I managed to catch a glimpse of her before they took her away from me."

"I'm sorry," Anna murmured into Kael's ear. *I guess it makes sense. Kael was at the Eve Institute for ten years and forced to procreate for nine of them.* "Elin doesn't know?"

"I don't talk about it." The words were flat and clipped.

"You can talk about it with me," Anna said. "I don't know why you haven't told Elin, and I understand that you must have your reasons, but...talking about it might make you feel better."

"You learned that from Elin, huh?"

"That and other things." Anna traced her fingers over the side of Kael's face, the hard line of her jaw. "And, by the way, you have to know I could never hit you. I have a feeling you've been hit far too many times."

Kael gave her a fond half-smile. "I don't know. You do get pretty brutal when we spar. You're better every day."

Anna chuckled. "Thanks. That's not the same, though."

After a brief hesitation, Kael leaned her forehead against Anna's. Voice tremulous, she said, "I worry about my babies all the time. Where they are, what might be happening to them. I know it's strange. I never wanted to have them, and I hated being forced to carry them, but...nine months is a long time to spend with somebody and not care at all."

"It makes sense," Anna murmured, though she wasn't sure whether she would have felt the same way or not. *I'm glad I never had to find out.*

"I worry about them all, but that last little girl the most. Because I saw her, she's the most real to me. She'd be almost nine years old now."

"How about the oldest?"

"Fifteen."

"I'm sorry," Anna said.

With a helpless shrug, Kael pulled her closer and pressed her rain-dampened face into Anna's hair. "It didn't give me an excuse to get so upset with Elin back there. Or to take my fears out on you. I said what I did to get a reaction, nothing more. Using something like that against you wasn't fair. It was unforgivable."

"But I already told you, Kael. I forgive you."

"I'm not sure I deserve a friend like you." Kael hugged her tighter, then released her so she could look into Anna's eyes. "Hey, Anna?"

"Yeah?"

"Can...can you at least understand where I'm coming from, though? How do you think you would feel about raising children, if—"

"I was pregnant once." The confession left her mouth before she even realized she was going to make it. It was the first time she had ever said it out loud. "I...lost it maybe three or four months after...that day."

"Oh." Kael broke their eye contact at her soft words. "Did you realize you were? Before you lost it?"

"I knew I hadn't menstruated, and I worried, but I thought maybe they had just damaged me inside. I almost hoped they had. And then one morning I woke up, and I just wouldn't stop bleeding. Garrett was scared to death."

"I bet he was," Kael said. "That must have been really frightening."

"I was glad I didn't have to have that baby."

"What am I going to say to Elin?"

Anna gave Kael a patient smile. "You're going to tell her you love her no matter what, too. You're going to tell her you're not mad at her. Tell her you were scared. Tell her whatever you feel comfortable telling her, but make sure she knows this isn't something that could tear you two apart." She paused, framing what she wanted to say most. "Kael, I could help protect a baby.

You don't have to bear that responsibility alone. And in fact, I think the three of us together...well, I think we could do anything. We complement each other."

Kael's lower lip quivered. "Anna—"

"No, listen to me," Anna continued, not allowing Kael even one moment to protest. "I'll spar with you every day until I can hold my own, if it means you could feel better about letting us give Elin a child to raise. Because, I mean...what's one thing we love so much about Elin? It's that part of her that *is* so untouched, right? And that's exactly what makes her want to share her life with a child, I think. So if we want to honor that piece of Elin, then maybe the way to do that is to figure out how we can—"

Kael stopped the rambling speech by covering Anna's mouth with her own. The kiss was slow and gentle, and when it ended long moments later, it left Anna breathless. Kael pulled away and pressed her forehead to Anna's, both of them gasping. Her hands slid down Anna's sides and came to rest on her waist.

"I'm sorry." Kael made no move to pull away. "I just...had to do that."

"Don't be sorry." Anna's voice was low with sudden, startling arousal. "I'm glad you did."

Nodding, Kael raised her eyes to meet Anna's, only inches from her own. Her timid smile almost broke Anna's heart. "I just wanted you to know...thank you. I would appreciate the help. Elin and I are so lucky to have you."

Anna could feel the solemnity of Kael's words, and her heart beat faster as her commitment to her family was solidified by her promises of the night. "You're welcome." At Kael's loving gaze, she relaxed into a playful smile. "Elin was right, by the way. You are one hell of a kisser."

Kael grinned, then took Anna's lips in another lingering kiss. She pushed her tongue inside of Anna's mouth with a groan of pleasure. Anna brought one hand up to rub over the back of Kael's shaven head, keeping her close. Their kiss ended with more mutual gasping, bringing both Kael and Anna to panting laughter.

"You have no idea how long I've wanted you to do that," Anna murmured.

"Not as long as I've wanted to do it, I bet."

"I don't know about that." Anna drew back. "As much as I'd like to kiss you again, I think you need to get inside, tough guy."

"Yes. I need to make things right with Elin."

Anna stepped out of Kael's embrace. "We need to get out of these wet clothes, anyway." Her nipples tightened as Kael's eyes grew heavy-lidded and dark with desire. "We're going to catch our deaths out here like this."

Kael cleared her throat and rubbed her hand over her head. All of the emotion of the evening still hung around them, but the air felt charged in an entirely different way. "Anna?"

"Yeah?"

"Let's go make love to Elin."

For a moment the only sound was the thunderstorm that raged on around them.

"Both of us?" Anna asked when she could speak again.

Nodding, Kael held her gaze with intense indigo eyes. "Together."

Without hesitation, Anna took her hand. "Let's go."

Chapter
Nine

ELIN WAS ON her feet the instant they returned to their sleeping room. Still dressed in her tank top and panties, her auburn hair was mussed and her hazel eyes red-rimmed and watery. She was utter misery tinged with fearful hope, searching out Kael's face as soon as they walked through the door.

"I'm sorry," she said immediately, and took a cautious step forward. "Kael, baby, I'm so —"

"No, I'm sorry." Kael released Anna's hand and strode across the room to meet Elin halfway and wrap her in a crushing embrace. "I was a complete jerk. You have nothing to be sorry about."

Anna walked across the room in silence, leaving Kael and Elin to their apologies. She pulled off her wet T-shirt, shivering, then stripped off her damp blue jeans. Clad in only a bra and panties, she climbed into a sleeping bag and sat cross-legged beneath the warm material. She never considered leaving the room. She finally felt enough a part of the family to bear witness to these emotional apologies.

Kael rubbed her hands up and down Elin's back. "I was scared. I should have just told you how I was feeling."

"Scared of what?" Elin asked. "Caring for a child?"

"And losing you if I can't do it."

Elin leaned back to see Kael's face. "I don't *need* to raise a child, Kael. I do need you. You're not going to lose me, I promise. I'm here to stay."

Kael looked solemn. "I'm just not ready to raise a child right now, but I promise to keep an open mind about it, okay?"

Elin gave Kael a careful smile. "Okay. I'm not ready, either."

"You still love me?"

Elin leaned forward and took Kael's mouth in a long, passionate kiss that left Anna breathless where she sat. She knew a million words were spoken in that kiss: apologies, endearments, and promises of forever. Her heart thumped, and she felt her soul lighten.

Elin broke away from their kiss and giggled, squirming within the circle of Kael's arms. "God, Kael...you're soaking wet!"

Kael gave her a broad, mischievous grin. "You know your kisses always do that to me, sweet girl."

Elin slapped the wet T-shirt that left no part of Kael's chest to the imagination. "Stop."

Anna chuckled. "Fair's fair. He got me all wet out on the porch after he was done apologizing."

Elin laughed, then insisted, "Come here to us. You look cold."

Anna hesitated, then stood and crossed to them, taking the hand Kael extended. When their eyes met, she was transfixed by the vulnerability she saw in those indigo depths. Kael was truly letting her inside as never before. The thought flooded Anna with fierce emotion, and she leaned up to press a gentle kiss to Kael's lips. She heard Elin's soft intake of air beside them and felt Kael's large hand settle on her hip. In a moment of amused panic, she remembered that she was only wearing her bra and panties. Even that thought was lost when Kael's tongue caressed her lips apart and moved inside of her mouth. Anna sucked on it deliberately, provoking a soft moan.

"Okay, well now *I'm* soaking wet," Elin said.

Instantly, they stepped apart, silly grins plastered on their faces.

Kael tipped her head back and laughed. "Me, too."

Anna smiled shyly. "I'm glad I'm not the only one."

"Was that your first kiss?" Elin asked. "I was right. It was the hottest thing ever."

Anna flushed. "The third."

Kael's low chuckle caused her to blush harder. "Is she always this sweet?" Kael asked Elin with a loving half-smile.

"Always." Elin ran hungry eyes down Anna's barely clad body. "Sweeter, even."

Kael cleared her throat. "Well, now that I've gotten both of you girls nice and wet, maybe you should get out of those clothes."

"You think so?" Elin asked, giving Kael a playful smile.

Anna cast her gaze to the floor. She was painfully turned on, but now that the moment was here, she felt all the shyness of her first time with Elin return. *I thought I was over this timid virgin bullshit.* She could feel Kael's eyes on her, and she folded bare arms over her goose-pimpled flesh, uncertain whether it was the cold or Kael's candid stare that was making her shiver.

She raised her eyes to the erect nipples that were visible through Elin's damp tank top and desire hollowed her stomach. As if reading an unspoken invitation, Elin closed the distance between them, and wrapped her arms around Anna's body.

Staring past her to Kael, she said, "Kael's just a horny boy who wants to see us naked and making out."

"Maybe I'm just a horny girl who thinks that sounds like a pretty good idea, too," Anna whispered against Elin's lips.

She moaned when Elin pressed her tongue into her mouth. Warm fingers covered her skin, pressing into her and sending shock waves rolling through her body at the friction against her rock-hard nipple. Gasping, Anna broke away from the kiss. Her heart accelerated even more when she saw that Kael had removed her T-shirt, exposing small breasts, the nipples erect and dusky pink.

"Take off Anna's bra, Elin," Kael instructed.

Elin reached around to Anna's back and found the clasp of her damp bra. "This okay?"

"Yes, very okay." Anna glanced back to Kael, who removed soggy blue jeans and hung them over the back of the armchair. Kael's eyes sought out her bare breasts as Elin removed the bra.

"Now take off Elin's tank top," Kael murmured. She stood a few feet away from them, wearing only dark boxer shorts. "Please, Anna."

Anna grinned and reached down to grasp the hem of Elin's tank top. Tugging it over Elin's head, she immediately stepped in and pulled her lover into an embrace, crushing their naked breasts together. Her mouth found Elin's in a hard, hungry kiss. Knowing that Kael was watching enflamed her, and soon she was struggling to remain standing on trembling legs.

"I need to lie down," she gasped out. "I'm going to fall over if I don't."

Elin beamed. "I'll take that as a compliment." She slowly stepped back as Kael crossed to them.

Kael gave Elin a quick kiss, then dropped to her knees and slid Elin's panties down over pale thighs and shapely legs. She placed a reverent kiss on the curly hair between Elin's legs before rising to her feet. "Get on the sleeping bags, baby," she whispered to Elin.

Elin obeyed the command, and Kael joined Anna in gazing down at her bare, creamy skin. "You want to get her ready?"

"More than anything."

Kael smirked, then leaned close to whisper in Anna's ear, "Get her nice and wet for us, okay?"

Anna almost forgot to keep breathing, aware of the slick

wetness that already painted her inner thighs. "No problem." She gave Elin a sheepish smile as she got to her knees. "Hi."

"Hi." Elin's smile spread slowly, creeping across her face as if she wanted to enjoy every second of its unfolding. "Are you sure you're okay with this, honey? You feel comfortable? One word from you is all it'll take to stop things if you don't feel good about what's happening. Understand?"

Anna trailed a hand over the gentle roundness of Elin's belly. "I understand. I do want this. It just feels...right."

"It is." Elin stroked the side of Anna's face. "I love you both so much."

"I love you, too," Anna said.

She moved on top of Elin, settling her hips between Elin's thighs when she spread them to accommodate her. She cradled Elin's face in both hands, lowering her own face to lick at her full bottom lip. Elin raised her head to deepen the kiss, and soon Anna was thrusting desperate hips into Elin's wetness, driven by a mindless intensity, her only desire to taste and touch and feel her lover. Every time she touched Elin, she savored it like it might be her only chance. Impatiently, she rid herself of her panties, groaning at the feel of Elin's soft skin against hers, at the way the thatch of wiry hair between Elin's legs tangled with her own wet curls. Reluctantly, she lifted her mouth from Elin's and moved down to settle on her stomach again with her head between Elin's thighs.

"May I?" She pulled her lover's legs over her shoulders to gain better access.

Elin giggled and tangled a hand in Anna's hair. "You'd better. You know you don't have to ask, sweetheart. If you want to put your mouth on me, anytime, anywhere, just say the word. I'll drop what I'm doing and come running. Or just come."

Anna bent and planted a wet kiss on the tender skin of Elin's inner thigh. "I don't know if that's such a good idea." She moved over to nibble at Elin's other thigh, then sank gentle teeth into the skin until Elin gasped. Swiping her tongue across the captured flesh, she pulled back with a low groan. "You'd never get anything done. We'd never go anywhere. We'd both starve to death."

"But what a way to go." The hand in Anna's hair tightened and tried to pull her into wet, swollen flesh. "God, Anna. Who taught you to tease this well?"

Anna held strong. She parted her lips and blew warm air on the pink flesh Elin presented without shame. Elin's hips bucked, and Anna pulled back, drawing out her torture.

"I have a great teacher," Anna said. "She's taught me

everything I know."

"Show me," Elin pleaded, and pushed her hips into Anna's face. This time Anna didn't move away, and Elin managed to brush the damp curls against Anna's chin.

Anna's ability to draw this out fractured at the painful need in hooded hazel eyes. She met Elin's stare and lowered her face, dragging the flat of her tongue up the length of Elin's sex. She moaned into Elin's flesh at the familiar taste. Elin tightened her hand in her hair.

"God, I love licking you." She buried her face between Elin's legs to do just that. Eyes closed, she savored the taste and smell of Elin, the way she rolled her hips in shameless need.

"Fuck, Elin." Kael's voice came from somewhere above Anna. She continued to lick and suck at Elin even as her heartbeat picked up at Kael's return. "Does that feel good, baby?"

"Incredible," Elin murmured. "God, Kael, she's so good at this."

Anna sucked swollen flesh into her mouth, laving Elin with her tongue. Her heart swelled with pride at Elin's words, and she felt some of her lingering shyness ease. Emboldened, she slid her hand up over Elin's stomach to cup her firm breast and tug at her nipple, drawing a breathless cry.

"Anna...you're gonna make me—" Elin's words were lost as she arched her back and cried out in pleasure.

Anna pulled away before she could release Elin, gazing up at her with a crooked smile. *I'm not sure I'm supposed to make her come so fast.* She raised a questioning eyebrow at Kael.

Elin whimpered in disappointment. "What? You're just going to...you can't just...just *do* that and—"

Kael turned stern eyes on Elin. "Oh, don't worry, baby. We're going to take care of you."

"But I—"

"I mean it," Kael murmured in a low voice. "I hope you're ready for us, Elin. Between Anna and me, I have a feeling that you're going to be exhausted tomorrow. Sore, too."

Kael turned intense indigo eyes to Anna, smiling wide. "Come here," she murmured and threaded strong fingers through Anna's dark hair. She pulled Anna's face to hers and captured her lips in a hungry kiss.

Anna moaned at the realization that her mouth was still covered with Elin's juices, and that Kael's tongue sampled the sweetness in lazy pleasure. Kael licked at the sides of her mouth and her chin, then parted her own lips in silent invitation. Anna slipped inside, groaning when Kael sucked on her tongue to draw Elin's flavor into an eager mouth.

Kael pulled back with her fingers still tangled in Anna's hair. "Elin," she murmured, never taking her eyes from Anna's face. "You taste amazing on Anna's lips."

Elin released a long-suffering whimper. "You guys, this is so unfair." She bucked her hips into the air, exposing flushed, pink flesh shiny with arousal. "Please, I was so fucking close."

"What do you want?" Kael asked.

"I want to come in Anna's mouth."

Anna swallowed, exhaling as she tried to contend with deep, aching desire that left her weak in the knees. Kael's hand caressed the back of Anna's head, blunt fingernails scraping over her scalp in a soothing rhythm.

"I'd like to watch you come in Anna's mouth," Kael said. "You two...I never thought I would see something so beautiful as the two of you giving pleasure to one another." She guided Anna's head down between Elin's thighs once again. "Lick her, then. Slowly at first."

Anna turned her face to nibble on Elin's inner thigh. "I get to start the teasing part over again?"

Elin groaned in frustration, bringing her arm up to cover her eyes. "Please, no. Please. I need to come."

Powerless to resist the quiet pleading, Anna traced the tip of her tongue around Elin's opening, then pressed inside, penetrating Elin with her stiff tongue. Kael's hand stayed tangled in her hair, providing silent encouragement as Anna slid her tongue up to play with Elin's clit. It was hard and swollen, literally throbbing beneath Anna's touch. Elin's quiet moaning grew louder and more demanding, until finally she chanted one word over and over again in a mindless incantation.

"Anna," she whispered. "Anna." She lifted her hips, rolling them to force contact with the flat of Anna's tongue. "Anna." She rubbed her wetness over Anna's nose, lips, and chin. "Fuck, Anna, please."

Anna sucked Elin's clit into her mouth, narrowing her lips and sliding them up and down the distended shaft. She kept her movements precise, controlled, the gentle suckling she sensed would bring Elin release.

"That's right, Anna," Kael urged softly. "Make her come in your mouth. You're doing so good."

Anna's eyes slipped shut. She kissed Elin for all she was worth, sliding her tongue up and down and around and inside, desperate to explore every inch of her. She pinned Elin to the sleeping bags with her weight in an effort to keep her from wiggling away from her increasingly demanding mouth.

"Come for us, Elin," Kael murmured, then Elin did just that.

Pale thighs trembled next to Anna's head; a breathless moan exploded from Elin's mouth as a flood of wetness soaked Anna's face and tongue. Anna answered Elin's moan, circling her tongue around her swollen clit in an unrelenting assault. Elin rode out the pleasure for long moments before tightening her fingers on Anna's face, pushing her away with shaky hands.

"Please stop," she gasped. "Oh God, I need...I need to rest for a minute."

Kael's hand fell away from Anna's head, and she sat up, slightly disoriented.

Near her, Kael sat cross-legged, still wearing her boxer shorts. Her gaze was glassy with desire. Her nipples were rock hard, and Anna fought the urge to reach out and rub the palm of her hand over one of them. She wasn't certain what kind of contact Kael would permit.

Nobody spoke for a moment, until Elin caught Anna to her and licked her wet cheeks and chin with her tongue. "That was wonderful, baby," she murmured against Anna's lips. She bent her knee, easing her thigh between Anna's legs. "So strong."

Anna ground her wetness into Elin's thigh. "You tasted so good I didn't want to stop." She left Elin with one last kiss and sat up beside Kael again. "Of course, I had to make sure Kael got his turn."

Kael relaxed into a wide smile and stroked her fingers over the small of Anna's back, drawing a shiver of pleasure that left her gasping. "Oh, Kael's going to get his turn, all right." She turned playful eyes to Elin. "Aren't I?"

Elin nodded, still breathing heavy. "Are you wearing your cock, baby?"

Kael tipped her head with a self-assured grin. "Of course I am. And I'm going to fuck you with it. Aren't I?"

Elin rubbed her hand over Kael's boxer shorts, curling slim fingers around the bulge between Kael's legs. "I can't wait to feel you inside of me."

Anna looked over to Kael with tentative eyes. This was an entirely new aspect of lovemaking for her, as was the dynamic that she was witnessing between Kael and Elin. Where Elin was always assertive and in control when they were together, with Kael she seemed submissive. *I wonder where I fit into all of this.* Her gaze dropped between Kael's legs. "Kael?"

"Yeah, sweetheart?"

"May I...may I see it?"

Kael gave Elin a crooked smirk. "You want to help me show her?"

Without a word, Elin got to her knees and grasped the waistband of Kael's boxers with both hands. She lowered them, leaning in to kiss Kael as she did.

Anna stared in fascination as a series of black leather straps were revealed, secured around Kael's hips to create a kind of harness. A flesh-colored phallus jutted out from between her legs, long and slender and slightly ominous. Anna stared at it nervously.

Elin curled her hand around the phallus, stroking it with gentle fingers. "It's okay." She gave Anna a tender smile. "This isn't something you need to experience if you don't want it. Kael knows how much I enjoy it, though."

"I know it looks a little intimidating," Kael said. "Do you want to watch me use it on Elin?"

Anna nodded, unable to tear her eyes away. She risked a soft question. "Does it feel good to you, too?"

"It feels very good. I enjoy knowing that I'm inside of Elin, giving her pleasure. I love feeling her body against mine as I fuck her." She paused, then gripped the phallus close to where it sat against her body. "The base presses into me as I move. That brings me pleasure, too."

Nodding, Anna tried to imagine what it might be like to make love to Elin in that way. "Do you usually wear it when you make love to Elin?"

"Usually," Kael said. "I also use my fingers and my mouth, of course. We like to try a lot of different things. But I don't enjoy being penetrated, myself."

Anna tipped her head in understanding. *I don't think I do, either.* Elin hadn't pushed the topic, and Anna hadn't offered, so far. While she was increasingly tempted to ask Elin to try it, she was certain she didn't want to experience it with Kael's impressive toy.

"I love it." Elin's seductive tone drew Anna's attention over to her flushed face. "Kael really knows how to make a girl feel good with that thing. Just like you really know how to make me feel good with your fingers, Anna." She lay down and directed a lazy smile up at the two of them. "I'm such a lucky woman to have two such talented lovers."

Kael placed a hand on Anna's arm. "Want me to show you something that Elin really loves?"

Anna met Kael's hungry stare, feeling her desire rise again after her brief case of nerves. "Of course."

Kael smirked down at Elin, and gripped her hips in firm hands. She rolled Elin onto her stomach, chuckling at the breathy whimper the forceful action elicited. "That's right, sweet girl. On your tummy."

Anna's stomach flip-flopped at Elin's submissive position. Watching her confident lover take Kael's handling stoked the flames of her arousal, sending her headlong into dizzy awe.

Elin looked over her shoulder at Kael, who cupped her buttocks in both hands. "Kael, honey, you're gonna kill Anna."

"Breathe, Anna," Kael murmured. "You look gorgeous right now, you know that?"

She leaned over to press a soft kiss to Anna's lips, before returning her attention to Elin's pale bottom. She gripped Elin with large hands and spread her wide, leaning down to blow a gentle stream of air over Elin's anus. Anna stared down at puckered flesh, unable to suppress an excited moan when the tight ring of muscle contracted then relaxed. A shocked gasp escaped her when Kael lapped at Elin with her tongue. Elin's gasp was filled with pleasure.

Kael drew back, tossing a murmured question over to Anna. "Has she ever asked you to take her ass before?"

Anna shook her head. Her mouth hung open in dazed excitement. "No. I've never —"

"I'll show you. She goes crazy when I slip a finger or two into her ass."

Anna ran distracted fingers through Elin's auburn hair. "It feels good?" she asked Elin in a quiet voice.

"Oh, baby, it feels wonderful." Elin thrust her bottom higher into the air. "If you go nice and slow —"

"And get her nice and wet —" Kael squeezed her buttocks with her hands, keeping her open and exposed. She smiled at Anna. "Want me to teach you?"

Anna blinked. "To...to —" She blushed, unable to produce the words.

"To fuck Elin in the ass? Yes."

Anna didn't even hesitate. "Okay. Yeah. Please."

"Oh, God," Elin mumbled into the arms that were folded beneath her head.

"The first thing we need to do is get her wet and open and relaxed. This takes time, if you do it right. And doing it right is necessary so that it feels good. Her anus is a lot tighter than her pussy and not as naturally accommodating. How are your fingernails?" Anna held her hand out and allowed Kael to inspect her short, blunt nails. "Perfect."

"How do we relax her?" Anna asked, easily falling into the role of eager student to Kael's teacher.

Kael's lips twitched with mischief. "Well, my favorite way..." She leaned down and dropped a kiss on Elin's right buttock before sliding her tongue down to probe at her anus.

Elin gasped, pushing back against Kael's face. "My favorite way, too."

Anna watched as Kael stroked Elin with her tongue, alternating between lapping gently at the puckered opening and dipping inside. Kael moaned and tightened her fingers on her lover's bottom. Just as Elin's quiet noises of pleasure began to grow loud and uncontrolled, Kael pulled away.

"Do you want to try?" she murmured to Anna.

With a nod, she placed her hands on Elin's bottom. She pulled her open and lowered her face for a tentative first taste. Anna snaked her tongue out and slid over familiar wetness before dragging the tip up to tease at territory she had never before explored. Elin whimpered as she circled the tight ring, and Anna's eyes closed as she sampled this new delicacy.

Once again, when Elin's moaning grew too loud and her body began to tremble beneath Anna's touch, the teasing stopped. Anna pulled back with a wide smile. *That was fun.* "Think she's relaxed now?"

"If feeling desperate to come again is relaxed, then yes," Elin said, her voice muffled by her arms. "Very fucking relaxed."

Kael and Anna both burst into laughter, and Kael delivered a sympathetic pat to Elin's rear end. "Are you saying you want me inside, baby?"

Elin thrust her bottom higher into the air. "Please."

Kael turned to Anna with a slow smile. "All right. Watch me, okay?"

"Okay."

Kael brought her hand between Elin's legs. "One of the most important things to remember is to make sure she's well-lubricated. Lucky for us, Elin is very good at producing natural lubricant."

Kael pushed two fingers to Elin's center, thrusting within, before withdrawing and holding shiny fingers up for Anna's gaze.

She then moved to Elin's anus. "Start with one finger. You aren't going to just push inside. You need to get her to open up and accept you. This is all up to her. You just need to rub, stroke...press the tip inside just a little to get her nice and ready for you." Kael did just as she instructed, teasing and probing Elin's anus with a slippery finger. "It's easiest if you just let her decide when she's ready for you. Let her push back on your finger and take you inside."

As if following a command, Elin took a deep breath and pushed back against Kael. One long finger slipped inside the tight opening, wrenching a breathless moan from Elin's throat. Kael's eyes fell shut, and she released a shaky sigh.

"How does that feel, baby?" she murmured.

"Really good. You can...you can move."

Given permission, Kael began a slow thrusting into Elin's anus. She pulled the length of her finger out until only the tip remained inside, then pressed into Elin again. Elin gasped, setting her legs farther apart on the sleeping bags.

Anna stared at Kael's hand, fascinated, then after a moment crawled up to lie beside Elin so that their faces were only inches apart. "You're so sexy," Anna whispered to her lover. She reached out and fingered auburn locks. "It makes me so hot to watch Kael touch you like this."

Elin bit her lip, whimpering. "It makes me so hot knowing you're watching." All of a sudden her mouth fell open, and her eyes widened in panic. "What? No..." She looked back over her shoulder to a smirking Kael. "You can't stop now!"

Kael delivered a gentle slap to Elin's bottom. "Sure I can. It's Anna's turn."

Anna sat up, slightly nervous. Kael leaned over and captured her mouth in a slow kiss. The reconnection soothed her nerves and left her feeling emboldened. Kael drew back, took Anna's hand in her own, and murmured, "Let me help."

While Anna watched, Kael guided her hand between Elin's legs and pressed Anna's fingers into Elin's wetness.

Anna groaned at the hot slickness that covered her skin. "God, Elin, you feel so good."

"Just wait until you're inside her ass." Kael pulled Anna's hand up so that her fingers were poised at the puckered ring of muscle she had so recently explored with her mouth. "So tight and hot," Kael purred to a whimpering Elin. Her wolfish smile told Anna that she knew exactly how her words affected their lover. "One finger, okay?"

Anna started a slow probing of Elin's anus with her wet finger. She massaged the slick flesh gently, then gasped when Elin pushed back against her almost immediately. Anna held her finger steady, amazed as Elin took in her full length.

Kael's right. This feels amazing. Anna allowed Elin to set the pace, taking her cue from the movement of Elin's hips and the soft noises that fell from her lips. She stared wide-eyed at the wetness that poured from Elin, which was so abundant that she could see the juices literally trickle down the inside of Elin's thigh. She fucked Elin slowly and gently, transfixed by the sight of her own finger buried in the pale, trembling flesh.

"Are you ready to come for us again, baby?" Kael asked. She

worked her hand back and forth between Elin's legs. "We want you to come for us."

"Yeah," Anna joined in. *If Elin likes talking, I can do talking.* "I want to feel you come when my finger is fucking your ass like this."

Elin stopped moving at Anna's statement, and her body stiffened in sudden pleasure. She cried out, loud, incoherent words that were lost when she pressed her face hard into the pillow. Kael and Anna grinned at one another in goofy triumph, sharing their pride at bringing their lover to screaming release.

When Elin collapsed onto the sleeping bag with a muffled sigh, Kael said, "Go slow pulling out, Anna. Try and let her kind of...expel you."

Anna opened her mouth to answer, only to feel Elin's muscles gripping her finger and forcing her out. "Oh," she whispered, giving Kael a shy smile. "Wow."

Kael beamed at Anna. "You liked that?"

"I loved it. It made me feel...so close to her."

"Trusted," Kael murmured.

Unable to suppress a blissful grin, Anna said, "Yes."

Elin rolled over and brought the back of her hand up to rest on her forehead. "You two are going to have to give me some time to recover." A light sheen of sweat covered her pale skin. "I'm useless for at least a few minutes."

Kael gave her a seductive smile. "And then I'm fucking you. With my cock."

Elin shivered at the low words. "I know. I just need to catch my breath."

"Of course, baby." Kael gave Anna a smirk. "We can wait."

Anna nodded in agreement, shifting where she knelt. Her body thrummed with desire, and her breath came in short bursts. She was on fire.

"Anna, how are you doing, sweetheart?" Elin traced languid fingers along Anna's thigh.

"About to explode. I...I'm really having fun tonight. Thank you two for sharing this with me."

Elin's eyes shone with emotion, and she gazed up to Kael with a watery grin. "I'm having fun, too," Kael said. "I love watching you, Anna. I'm honored that you're allowing me to share in your love for Elin."

Anna looked down at the blankets, tracing her finger over the zipper at the edge of the sleeping bag. "My love isn't just for Elin, Kael." She looked up when Kael didn't answer and blinked in surprise at tear-filled indigo eyes.

Elin cleared her throat, breaking the silence. "This has been a very nice evening, and I thank you both so much for loving me."

"We can't help it," Anna murmured, still looking at Kael. She dropped her gaze to Elin's stomach and tickled around her belly button with a fingertip. "You're just too cute."

Elin beamed up at Anna, then tossed Kael a careful grin. "Could you two...could I watch you kiss a little more? While I'm recovering, you know."

Anna snickered at Elin's attempt to move them past the moment. "Pervert."

Elin folded her arms behind her head and raised a mischievous eyebrow. "So?"

"So that's another reason we can't help loving you," Kael said, speaking for the first time since Anna's sincere words. She moved forward and reached for Anna with tentative arms. "And I'm not inclined to deny your request."

Anna moved into Kael's embrace without hesitation. "Anything to make you happy, Elin."

Kael's passionate kiss took Anna by surprise, as did the strength of her embrace. She wrapped her arms around Kael and splayed her fingers over broad shoulders. She groaned into Kael's mouth, meeting her stroke-for-stroke in her unspoken expression of desire. Kael pressed her hips into Anna, brushing the toy that was strapped between her legs against Anna's stomach.

"Please don't be afraid," Kael said as Anna stiffened a little. "I'm not going to go inside of you."

She pressed Anna down on the sleeping bags and slid her mouth over Anna's collarbones. Anna turned her head to the side and grinned over to Elin.

Elin reached out and played with Anna's hair. "Kael has a wonderful mouth, doesn't he? Does that feel good?"

Anna crinkled her nose in pleasure. "Really good." She whimpered when Kael's lips latched on to her erect nipple. Looking down on Kael's shaven head, she groaned when Kael's hand found her other breast.

Elin rolled onto her side and trailed a string of kisses along Anna's jaw until she reached her lips. Anna's legs fell open at the pleasure of having Elin's tongue in her mouth as Kael suckled at her breast. She felt Kael's hips settle between her thighs, felt the hard length of Kael's cock press against her, and surprised herself by grinding her hips into the solid pressure.

Kael looked to Elin with a crooked grin. "I think Anna is ready to come, baby."

"I think so, too," Elin said.

Kael traced a line down the center of Anna's chest with her

finger. "Why don't you go sit up on that couch for me, sweetheart?"

Anna obeyed the quiet request, unable to do anything else. She got to her knees and crawled onto the leather couch next to them. Kael shuffled over to Anna on her knees and gripped Anna's hips in firm hands.

"On the edge," Kael said with a playful smile. "Spread your legs."

Anna hesitated a moment, biting her lip, then did as Kael requested. *I trust him.* Indigo eyes dropped to take in Anna's arousal, then Kael moved away and urged Elin to take her place.

"Hey, baby." Kael wrapped strong arms around Elin from behind. Elin knelt between Anna's spread thighs and closed her eyes when Kael pulled her back into a tender embrace. "I want you to use your mouth on Anna while I'm inside of you, okay?"

Nodding, Elin pressed her bottom back against Kael. "I'm gonna come without either of you touching me, I swear it."

Kael latched hungrily onto Elin's throat, sucking hard enough to leave a light red mark. Pulling away, she pressed a firm hand against Elin's upper back and pushed her down close to the dark curls between Anna's legs. "Maybe...but Anna's going to need some attention, I think. Lick her for me, baby?"

Anna's eyelids grew heavy when Elin nodded and bent to drop a kiss on the soft skin of her inner thigh. Nibbling her way up to the tender juncture of hip and thigh, Elin snaked her tongue out and traced nonsense designs with the tip. Trembling, Anna lifted her hips to try to force Elin's tongue against her swollen clit.

"Are you being mean to her, Elin?"

Anna watched as Kael gripped Elin's hips with both hands and moved to position her body behind where Elin rested on her knees.

"No," Elin mumbled into Anna. She kissed the damp curls above Anna's clit and pressed down with her lips. "I think I'm being pretty nice, actually."

Kael raised her eyes to meet Anna in a heated stare. She dropped one hand to grip her toy at the base, then glanced down to guide herself to Elin's opening. Once again, Kael raised her eyes to Anna as she pushed forward and guided her length into Elin with agonizing slowness.

As Kael entered her, Elin's mouth fell open against Anna's flesh, washing hot breath over her wetness. She turned her head and pressed her cheek against Anna's thigh, biting her lip in pleasure.

Anna was fascinated by the look of tender concentration on Kael's face and the way that Elin cried out at every forceful stroke. She curled Elin's hair around her fingers, tightening her grip as her need rose. Elin lifted her face, spread Anna wide open with her hands, and bent her head to cover Anna's clit with her hot mouth.

Anna's head fell back at Elin's deliberate sucking. She cupped Elin's cheek in her hand and raised glazed eyes to stare at Kael's deliberate fucking of their lover. Kael bit her lip, eyes hooded and dark with desire. She pounded into Elin, staring at Anna with naked lust.

Elin pulled her mouth away from Anna, crying out at Kael's skillful thrusting. Then she returned to Anna and swirled her tongue over hot, swollen flesh. Anna's thighs began to tremble as she neared release.

All at once, Anna was struck by an unfamiliar desire, a need that came on so strongly that it took her breath away. She ached deep inside, desperate for something she knew only Elin could give her. Swallowing, Anna pushed past her lingering fears so she could ask for what she craved so badly.

"Elin?" Anna tightened her grip on Elin's red hair.

Elin stopped her tongue and raised concerned hazel eyes. "Yes, baby?" She whimpered as Kael continued to move inside of her.

"Could you...try going inside of me?"

Elin blinked up at her, suddenly still. Behind Elin, Kael slowed her thrusting to a stop as if aware of the significance of Anna's nervous request. Elin bent to kiss Anna's hip, then stared at her with unveiled tenderness. "Are you sure, sweetheart?"

"Yes," Anna whispered. She flicked her gaze to Kael's face, seeing only gentle compassion there. "I...need more."

Elin's face shone with delight. "I'm going to make it feel so good for you."

Anna nodded at the familiar promise. "I know you will."

Elin slid her finger through Anna's abundant wetness. Circling her throbbing clit gently, she gave Anna a beatific smile. "You're going to love it. It's wonderful to have someone you love inside of you." She tossed a quick look back over her shoulder at Kael, who rested motionless inside of Elin, then looked back to Anna. "And I do love you. Very much."

"I know." Anna welcomed Elin's reassurance. "I want to feel you."

Elin brought her hand down so her finger was poised at Anna's entrance. She held Anna's gaze as she slowly and gently pressed inside. Anna closed her eyes at the unexpected pleasure of the feeling and lifted her hips to encourage Elin's motion. When Elin came to rest deep inside, Anna felt another gentle kiss on her inner thigh.

"Are you okay, baby?" Elin whispered.

Anna nodded to her lover with a relieved grin. "Yeah. Please make me come, Elin."

Kael groaned at Anna's words, starting narrow hips thrusting once more. "I'm sorry. I can't wait any—"

"Don't be sorry," Anna cried out as Elin slid her finger out then pushed back inside again. "Make her come, Kael. I want to hear her come."

Kael gritted her teeth in concentration. She pulled pale hips back against her, forcing Elin to meet her deep strokes. Elin continued to move her hand, her own thrusts becoming harder, more demanding. Anna whimpered as Elin rubbed her inside, then closed her eyes when Elin's tongue found her clit once again.

"Christ—" Anna's mouth dropped open as she was overwhelmed by breathless, gasping pleasure. She cried out and her thighs trembled as Elin continued to lap at her clit and work her finger deep inside. She watched Kael through half-closed eyes, rapt at the look of naked bliss on her face.

Elin tumbled over the edge only moments after Anna, her own noises of release muffled against Anna's wetness. She continued to lick and suck as she rode out her orgasm, stilling her finger when Anna collapsed, limp, against the back of the couch. Elin fell onto Anna's lap immediately thereafter, panting hard in the aftermath of her third orgasm.

Elin eased her finger out of Anna with a quiet apology, her words lost in the tortured groan that escaped her mouth when Kael pulled out of her. She left Anna with a final kiss on sweat-slicked brown skin and turned to Kael.

"Do you need me to take care of you, baby?" she whispered.

Anna gazed at Kael, noticing for the first time the trembling of strong thighs, the shaking of large hands. Indigo eyes were stormy with unfulfilled arousal; her chest heaved with her heavy breathing. Without a word, Kael rose to her feet and stood in front of Elin.

Eager hands reached up and unbuckled the straps that were secured to Kael's hips, freeing her from the harness. Elin dropped the toy to the ground and slid her hands up the back of Kael's thighs. On her knees, she waited for Kael to set her feet apart. Then, without hesitation, Elin spread Kael with her hands to expose her wet, swollen need. Anna watched in fascination as Elin leaned forward and sucked Kael into her mouth, loosing a growl of pleasure from Kael's throat.

It appeared to take only three or four strokes of Elin's

tongue before Kael stiffened, threw back her head, and shuddered in quiet release. Her hands dropped to hold Elin's face between her legs, keeping her lover close until she recovered from her silent orgasm. When Kael came back to herself, she quickly dropped to her knees and wrapped Elin in a strong embrace.

"Thank you," Kael murmured into Elin's hair. "I love you."

"I love you, too, baby." Elin rubbed her hands up and down Kael's back. "That was so nice."

Kael pulled back to give Anna a shy smile. "Come here," she said, beckoning Anna closer. Anna obeyed, slipping from the couch and crawling over to where Kael and Elin sat. Kael pulled Anna into a tender hug as soon as she was within reach. "Thank you, too."

"It was my pleasure." Anna shot a playful smile over Kael's shoulder to Elin.

Elin moved forward and wrapped her arms around Kael and Anna. "You're both going to hold me tonight, right? When we go to sleep?" She yawned in Anna's ear, drawing a quiet chuckle from Kael.

"Tonight and the rest of our lives, baby." Kael kissed Elin slowly and deeply. Drawing back, she leaned over and gave Anna a shyer kiss.

"Absolutely," Anna confirmed, holding Kael's gaze. "Forever."

Chapter
Ten

"SO YOU THINK we're near a town?" Anna called to her lovers, who walked side by side ahead of her. After two relaxing days in their little cabin in the woods, they were on the road again.

"Yeah," Kael drawled without turning around. "Unfortunately."

"Oh, come on." Elin bumped into Kael with her shoulder. Her body language was relaxed, as was Kael's. "You know you want to go shopping again. Maybe we could find some cute stuff for Anna and me to wear."

"I have to admit, I'm curious about towns," Anna said. "I haven't been to very many since the sickness. Even after Garrett and I were on our own, we mostly found in nature what we needed to survive."

"It's not a bad philosophy," Kael muttered.

"But think of everything you're missing!" Elin said. "I'm not saying I want to *settle* in a town or anything, but I happen to enjoy some modern comforts from time to time. My dad always had music in the house—we used car batteries, solar panels—he always found a way to let me experience some of the things from his past. Just having a house full of books and magazines—"

"Baby, you know I don't mind taking you into town every once in a while," Kael said. "I know you love exploring. And I know you love your books, and I'd never deny you those. It's just that I don't understand the big deal about that stuff. I lived with full electricity, music—even movies—from the time I was fourteen years old. I'm happier now, in nature, than I ever was with any of that."

"Electricity?" Anna had heard stories about the wonders electricity could provide, but she had never actually seen it for herself.

Kael gave her a short nod. "I guess they had an engineer or three join the Procreation Movement. A couple of years after we settled there, they figured out how to generate power. They used to play classical music through the speakers in my room every evening. On Sundays I was allowed to have a 'night off' in my room with a television and DVD player. They showed me old movies all the time."

"Wow," Anna murmured.

"Yeah, fantastic. Didn't make my life any better."

Elin grabbed Kael's hand. A moment later, she found Anna's slightly curled fingers and entangled them with her own. "It's not the important stuff in life, I'll admit, but it can give you a lot of pleasure." Elin glanced over to Kael. "In otherwise pleasurable circumstances."

Anna gave Elin's hand a gentle squeeze. "Uncle Roberto used to tell me that technology never did anybody any good. That it was all that technology that led to the wars and the sickness. The people in my tribe believed in living without all that stuff. We stuck to the forests. We learned to hunt. My uncle would always say that eventually all that stuff that was left behind will be depleted or expired or just...dead. If I depended on it now, where would I be?"

"I can respect that," Kael said.

"It may take a while," Elin mused, "but I don't think those things are gone for good. Maybe it won't happen within our lifetime, but it's not like people won't eventually start it all over again. Look at where you lived, Kael. When the population becomes less dispersed and people start forming communities again, all that stuff will follow."

"We're better off without it," Kael said. "What good has it ever done anyone?"

"Oh, come on!" Elin cried out. "Think about what you lose by turning away from our past like that. There's a whole world of knowledge and music and beauty out there, just waiting for us to discover it in every town we walk through."

"I...want to explore that stuff, too," Anna admitted. "I want to know about the things you love."

"I'd like that," Elin said.

Still chatting lightly, they made their way across a bare trickle of river nestled in the middle of towering trees and leafy bushes. No longer did they see the odd cabin or vehicle as they walked; all that surrounded them was falling leaves, buzzing insects, and the warm bond between them that grew stronger every day.

Suddenly, Kael stifled them with a hand held up to shoulder level. Anna stood in silence with Elin, wondering what she had seen or felt that prompted her sudden change in demeanor. Her easy gait, the relaxed smile on her face, disappeared as familiar tension settled in.

"This way," Kael murmured. She walked them down a grassy trail that led through a stand of maples, then they stopped cold.

The body sat slumped forward at the base of a large sycamore tree. Dried blood stained the dirt around him, and his hand lay open at his side, empty. He was wounded in the head and chest, and Anna guessed that he might have been dead for at least a week. With a quick glance at Kael, she went and knelt at the corpse's feet.

"I don't like this," Kael said. "At all."

"Neither do I." It turned her stomach, but Anna lay her baseball bat down and slipped a hand into the front pocket of the dead man's jeans. She came up empty, though she hadn't been sure what she thought she might find.

"We need to keep our eyes peeled," Kael said from behind her. "And we need to be quiet until we know that whoever killed this guy isn't still hanging around."

"He looks like he's been dead for a little while." Elin spoke in a quiet voice that hinted at her own unease. "I can't imagine that his killer has bothered to stick around."

"Even still, stay close."

Anna rose to her feet with her bat clutched tight. "It looks like whoever did this picked him over pretty good. No supplies, nothing in his pockets."

Kael's eyes stayed locked on the ground as she made a slow circle of the immediate area. "There was a hell of a fight. He didn't go down easy." She pivoted where she stood between the trunks of two tall trees. "There was more than one of them."

Anna caught sight of something in the bushes. When she walked over, she found a scrap of silky white fabric caught there, and she disentangled it carefully before lifting it to her nose. It held a light, almost flowery, scent. "I don't think this is from him."

"From a woman?" Kael sounded like a positive answer would confirm her worst fears.

"Yes, I think so," Anna said.

Elin shuddered. "Do you think we could get going, you guys? This is really creeping me out."

Kael stepped over and rested a hand on Elin's shoulder. "Yeah, we'll go, sweet girl. I want to put some distance between us and whatever happened here, for sure."

Anna took Elin's hand and gave it a reassuring squeeze. "Why don't you tell me more about Led Zeppelin, baby? I'm interested in what you were saying."

She accepted a look of quiet gratitude from Kael before turning her back on the dead man. Though she would never have admitted it out loud, Anna was just as creeped out as her innocent lover and just as eager to escape from the ominous air of the stranger's final resting place.

Behind them, Kael sighed deeply. "Let's be extra careful today, okay, girls?"

ELIN'S SCREAM ECHOED throughout the forest.

"Kael! Help me! Anna, please!"

Anna scrambled to her feet, unsheathing her hunting knife, and immediately took off in a fast run. *Something is really wrong.* She wondered why Elin wasn't using the distress whistle. Where was Kael? She was out practicing with the bow and arrow, but she had to be within earshot. That was the cardinal rule when they enjoyed time alone.

Anna broke through the trees into the clearing where they'd set up camp for the night. She gasped as a large black bear lunged toward Elin, who stood in front of the fire, her hands raised in feeble supplication. The bear grunted and swiped at her. Elin stumbled backwards over the flames where their rabbits were spitted and came down hard in the embers, one hand trying to brace her fall.

"Elin!" Anna raised her knife intending to release it in a deadly arc toward the bear, but at the last moment she froze in fear. *What if I hurt her? What if I just make that thing more aggressive?*

Elin scrabbled backwards out of the fire and continued crawling away on her hands and knees. The bear followed and seized her lower leg in its powerful jaw. Elin threw her head back and released a bone-chilling scream.

Without a second thought, Anna raised both hands high in the air so she'd look larger than she was and released an enraged noise as she stomped through the clearing in an attempt to intimidate the animal. "Get the fuck away from her, you piece of shit!"

The bear released Elin and backed up a few steps, growling and baring its teeth. Whimpering, Elin crawled cautiously away. Hands still held high, Anna started a slow advance toward the bear. "Get outta here!" she yelled, furious at the dark blood that stained the torn denim at Elin's calf.

With a loud growl, the bear reared up and stood on its hind legs. Anna steeled her nerve and willed her feet to stay planted on the ground. *If you run, it's all over.*

As she tried to weigh her dwindling options, a fast-moving object whistled through the air from her left. An arrow struck home deep in the center of the bear's throat. Twisting away, it made a strange whining noise of pain and fell to the ground. Anna swiveled to see Kael among the trees at the far side of the campsite, her face pale and drawn, compound bow with a fresh arrow nocked still held in front of her body.

Anna dropped to her knees beside Elin's prone body, gasping at the sight of Elin's mangled leg, visible through her ripped and bloody jeans.

"Fucking piece of—" Kael stalked across the campsite toward the fallen bear. The steel of her blade hummed as she dropped the bow and pulled her sword from its sheath. She advanced on the bear and finished him off quickly and cleanly.

Anna looked into Elin's frightened hazel eyes. "Baby, you're going to be okay," she said, even before she had a chance to examine the extent of the injuries. Her gaze dropped to the reddened hand that Elin clutched to her stomach. "Do you think you're badly burned?"

Fat tears rolled down her pale face. "I really fucked up. I can't believe he bit me!" Elin rolled onto her back, sobbing and writhing in pain.

As Anna cut away Elin's torn jeans, Kael ran to them and dropped to her knees.

"Oh my God. Oh my God."

At the panicked horror of Kael's words, Elin looked up through her tears. "I'm sorry, Kael. He just came at me. I...I never—"

"It's okay," Anna said as calmly as she could. "It wasn't your fault. I've never seen a black bear so aggressive before." She took Elin's ankle in gentle hands and met Kael's eyes, willing her to re-focus. "Kael. She's going to be okay, but we need to stop the bleeding and make sure that nothing is broken. Bring me some cold water. I want to rinse off my hands before I touch this bite. Get Elin's bag, too. We need bandages and something for burns. I think she has aloe."

They worked in silence, their breathing the only sound beyond the occasional chirp of a distant bird and the buzzing of nearby mosquitoes. Anna was so intent on stopping the flow of blood from Elin's wounds that she barely noticed an insect landing on her ear. Elin lay deathly still on the ground, except for shallow, anxious breaths.

Anna studied her face as she kept pressure on the leg wound. Elin's lips were bluish, and her forehead shone with sweat. "I'm afraid she's going into shock," she murmured to Kael.

Kael grew even paler, if possible. "What can we do about that?"

Anna chewed on her lip. *Beg whoever's listening that she'll be okay.* "We need to treat these injuries and keep her warm and comfortable. I'm not sure that there's much more we can do out here."

Kael gently probed at Elin's wrist and winced when Elin cried out in pain. "Besides the burn, I think it's sprained. It doesn't feel broken, but if it's hairline..."

Elin's breathing grew more labored, and she brought her uninjured hand to her stomach. "I feel sick. I almost wish I could pass out—" Her whole body tensed as Anna began wrapping the injured leg in bandages. "Am I gonna lose it?"

Anna managed to smile even as she worried about the fogginess of Elin's gaze. "You're going to be fine, sweet girl. It's going to hurt like hell for a while, I won't lie to you, but we're going to get you back to as good as new."

Kael placed Elin's gauze-wrapped hand on her stomach with care. "I want to elevate that wrist as much as possible. Let me just—" She leaned her backpack against Elin's. When she had a suitable arrangement, she helped Elin rest her bandaged hand on top. "I'm sorry I can't do more."

"Elin, do you have something to help you sleep?" Anna finished bandaging Elin's calf and pulled back, disgusted by the dried blood that stuck to her hands. "In your bag?"

Elin's forehead crinkled in deep thought. "Um..." She blinked, looking confused. "Melatonin? I think. Green bottle." Her words were soft, slurred. "I don't know if I'll need it."

Anna took Elin's uninjured hand and gave it a gentle squeeze. "Just in case you do. I don't want to move you very much, but maybe we can get you to a sleeping bag."

Kael pulled a green bottle from Elin's bag and gave Anna a brief nod. "I'll lay out her sleeping bag on the closest level spot, then help you move her over."

"Thanks, Kael."

Elin gazed up at Anna in distress. "I'm sorry."

Winding silky auburn hair around her fingers, Anna murmured, "Baby, don't be. You didn't ask for that bear to attack you. This isn't your fault."

"But how am I going to travel? How are you—"

Anna leaned over and, with excruciating care, planted a loving kiss on Elin's lips. "Hush, baby. Let me and Kael worry about that, okay? You just worry about resting and healing."

Kael crouched beside Elin's prone body. "You listen to her,

sweet girl. Don't worry about a thing. We're going to take care of this, and you're going to be just fine."

Elin nodded. "Okay. I love you."

"I love you, too," Anna and Kael replied, almost in unison.

With incredible caution they positioned themselves so they could lift Elin's body one foot or so from the ground. They carried her to the sleeping bag Kael had laid out, settling her as gently as possible. Still, Elin groaned in pain.

"Sorry, little one," Kael murmured.

"Elin, do we have anything for pain?" Anna asked.

Elin shook her head, and fresh tears leaked from her eyes. "Not really."

Anna stroked Elin's forehead tenderly. "Close your eyes, baby girl. Kael and I will take care of you. Just try to sleep now."

Elin turned her head to the side and squeezed her eyes shut. She continued to sweat, and Anna watched her chest rise and fall in rapid motion. "So much for...those rabbits," Elin muttered.

Anna glanced over at the disturbed fire that still smoldered. The spitted rabbits were blackened, charred shapes lying in the embers. "That's okay." Anna stroked a cool hand over Elin's clammy forehead. "I was getting sick of rabbit, anyway."

Elin grinned, then sighed deeply. Then her mouth lolled open as she fell into uneasy sleep.

"I was too far away." Kael's voice was rough with self-loathing. "Goddamn it, I'm always going too far away."

Anna pulled Kael into a gentle embrace and ran a soothing hand over her shaven head. "You only got back a moment after me, and at least you were able to stop it. I'm the one who watched her fall into the fire and get attacked by that thing. I couldn't even throw my knife. I was halfway through the motion when I realized I'd only make it madder. I—"

Kael pressed her fingers to Anna's lips, stopping her words. "You're good at healing. Thank you for reacting like you did. I just saw that blood and—"

"I know." Anna blinked back stinging tears and watched her pale lover toss in fitful sleep. "I couldn't believe it when I saw that thing attacking her. It was crazy."

Kael's eyes swam with anguish. "I don't like seeing her in pain. It tears my heart out. I feel paralyzed by it."

Anna thought hard. "Didn't we pass a cannabis field not too far back? I almost suggested we stop and pick a few heads, but—" *Enough. No more "should haves,"* she thought. "I'll hike back and get some."

"I don't like you going off alone."

"We can't leave Elin. And it'll help with the pain."

"Be careful," Kael said, her voice hoarse with emotion. "How far back is it?"

"A couple of miles."

Kael looked up at the gray sky. "It'll be dark before you get back."

"There's a full moon. I'll take matches and a candle, just in case."

"We need supplies. We need more bandages, and vitamin E, and antibiotics for that bite, and a roof over our heads. While Elin heals." Rubbing her hands over her scalp in frustration, Kael finished with a resigned sigh. "All right. Get the cannabis. I'm going to study our maps and figure out where we can go. And I'll figure out dinner, too. We have a whole bear to choose from."

"It really will be okay, Kael," Anna said.

Kael stared down at Elin's pale face. "I know," she whispered. "It has to be."

Chapter
Eleven

TWO CITY BLOCKS from the looming brick hospital in downtown Owensboro, Kentucky, Kael took an abrupt turn into the entryway of a large office building. The building looked long abandoned, as had every other part of the city they'd seen, but Kael, a silent Elin cradled in her arms, stopped their progress.

"Let me go in first." She turned to Anna. "Put down your bags and take her from me, will you?"

Anna surveyed Elin with anxiety. While the cannabis did seem to ease her pain, she had spent most of the two-day walk to the city pale and whimpering. Infection was settling into the bite wound, and she was increasingly feverish and sluggish. They couldn't have arrived in Owensboro at a better time.

"Do you want me to go back to the hospital for supplies?" Anna murmured as Kael worked on the door. "You must be exhausted. I know you haven't been sleeping."

Kael opened the door to the office building and poked her head inside. "I'm fine. I'm going to the hospital, and you'll stay here with Elin."

Anna wished she could reach out and touch Kael, but even if she had a free hand, the emotional distance between them since Elin's injury would have stopped her.

"Fine. Remember, though...bandages, any antiseptics you can find, antibiotics, of course—"

"Anna." Kael stared at her. "I know what to get. We've talked about nothing else for the past forty-eight hours. Trust me, okay?"

Like you trust me? Anna shook off the niggling thought, instead giving Kael an agreeable nod. She lowered her eyes to Elin again and cradled her closer.

"Wait just inside the door," Kael whispered. "If you hear anything suspicious, I want you to run with Elin and hide. No hesitation, okay? And if anyone approaches—"

"I'll come get you," Anna finished. "Don't worry. I know the drill."

Grunting in acknowledgement, Kael slipped inside the office building. Anna hung back in the open doorway with Elin securely in her arms. She stared out at the empty city street in front of them, keeping one ear attuned to the interior of the office building.

Kael is right about one thing. Cities are a hell of a lot creepier than the forest. Anna shifted on her feet, gazing at the few abandoned vehicles that were parked along the street. Parking meters lined the sidewalks like silent sentries, and large yellow traffic signals hung, dead, over the intersection to her immediate right. The sounds she was accustomed to hearing — the chirping of birds, the rustling of forest animals — were absent.

Anna dropped her gaze to Elin's face. "My poor girl," she whispered close to Elin's ear. "Once Kael gets back from the hospital, we'll be able to take care of you the right way."

They were out of bandages as of yesterday. The vitamin E had run out the first morning of their trip, and the aloe wouldn't have lasted through another evening of travel. Cannabis was the only thing they had plenty of, because Anna had gathered enough to ensure that Elin wouldn't have to suffer any more pain than necessary. It was one of the few things she could do for her lover until they gathered more supplies in Owensboro.

"I love you." Anna touched her lips to Elin's damp forehead. "I can't wait to hear you laughing again."

"Hey, Anna?" Kael tromped down a staircase behind Anna, drawing her attention into the office with her soft words. "I found a great room upstairs. There's even a couch where she can sleep."

"Fantastic." Anna stepped inside and let the door close behind her. "Lead the way."

Anna pressed her nose into Elin's hair, inhaling the scent of her lover as Kael went outside for their bags. Shortly after, Kael walked back in carrying the backpacks, sleeping bags, and medical bag with nonchalant ease, her cool gaze fixed over Anna's shoulder.

Somehow they made it up the two flights of stairs without waking Elin. Kael led the way through a maze of hallways to a large office. There was an overstuffed leather couch in the corner, obviously dusted off by Kael, and Anna deposited Elin on the cushions with care. Kael set the bags down and came over to plant a soft kiss on Elin's forehead.

"I'll be back in a little while." She straightened with a friendly nod to Anna. "I'll also look for some water."

Before she could stop to think about it, Anna reached out and gripped Kael's muscular bicep. "Be careful."

For the first time since the night of Elin's injury, Kael met her gaze with eyes full of naked emotion. Anna could see the bone-deep weariness, the guilt, the fear; she could see a struggle to maintain the distance that had been killing Anna, and for a moment, she thought that the stoic façade might crumble.

Instead, Kael raised one shoulder in a half-shrug. "Take good care of Elin."

Anna let her hand slide down the length of Kael's arm, briefly entangling their fingers. "Of course."

Without another word, Kael left the room and closed the door behind her.

The office was one of the most luxurious places Anna had ever seen. An enormous wood desk sat in front of the windows in the center of the room, a layer of dust obscuring the heavy polish. The couch where Elin rested was positioned at one side, and two bookcases full of binders and various hardcover books flanked walls hung with framed artworks. Between them sat two comfortable-looking leather chairs. Anna got the medical bag and brought it to Elin. She settled on the plushly carpeted floor and dug through Elin's bag until she found the aloe. She contemplated removing the bandages from Elin's hand so that she could apply more of the soothing fluid to her burn. *I could let it air out for a while. Before Kael gets back.* Still, she was loath to wake Elin.

Anna leaned back against the couch, resting her head on the arm with a tired sigh. Closing her eyes for just a moment, she allowed her mind to wander.

That's a computer on the desk. I wonder what it looks like inside. Maybe I'll take it apart tonight after Kael gets back. Or maybe I'll wait until Elin can help me. I bet she'd have a good time with that.

"Anna?"

Anna opened her eyes and gave Elin a surprised smile. "Elin. Baby. How are you feeling?"

"I've been better." Elin blinked at the surroundings. "Where are we?"

"Downtown Owensboro. We got here just a little while ago. Kael went out to the hospital down the road for supplies. He should be back soon, and then I can change your bandages again."

Elin sat up, alarmed. "The hospital?"

Anna also sat up and faced Elin with a puzzled frown. "Yeah. The hospital. We need more bandages, and antiseptic, and we want to try some antibiotics to deal with the infection in your leg—"

"Anna." Elin's breathing hitched, and she brought her

uninjured hand to her throat.

Anna laid a soothing hand on Elin's shoulder and pushed her back against the cushions. "It's not a big deal. It's maybe two blocks away. Kael will be fine."

Elin shook her head and tears rolled down her cheeks. "No, he's terrified of hospitals. Most of his nightmares...the Eve Institute was housed in an old hospital. He's so scared of them—"

Anna swallowed. "Goddamn it. I could have gone."

"Just make sure he's okay when he gets back."

"I can try, but...it's not like Kael is talking to me much these days." She couldn't meet Elin's gaze, embarrassed by the admission. "Or looking for me to comfort him. I'll wake you up, though, if you're sleeping when he gets back. You can talk to him."

"Sweetheart, what do you mean Kael isn't talking to you?"

Anna leaned her head against the cushion, sighing when Elin rolled closer to drop a gentle kiss on her hair. "He's just...distant. He's upset. He...I don't know."

"Upset about me?" At Anna's nod, she said, "He's scared."

Anna didn't even have to think before agreeing. "Yes." *Terrified. I can see it in his eyes every time he can bring himself to look at me.*

"He's scared of caring about something that could be taken away from him."

"I know. But everyone's scared of that, right?" Anna packed some cannabis into the bowl of their pipe. It was about time to top up Elin's pain relief.

"Yeah. Different people just have different ways of dealing with it, I suppose."

"Well, Kael's way sucks. You really need to work on him with that."

"We'll work on him together, sweetheart." Elin took the pipe gratefully. "I'll just give him a kick in the right direction to start."

"I want to unwrap your hand, put more aloe on it, and let it breathe for a while."

"I hate seeing it. It's ugly." Elin lay back against the pillows and offered her injured hand to Anna. "I just hurt and feel disgusting and horrifying—"

"You're beautiful." Anna carefully unwrapped the bandage. "You're always beautiful, Elin."

"Just a little banged up right now." Elin's eyes were foggy again, though the tight grimace of pain that she had worn after waking was gone. "And cold."

"You've got a bit of a fever. We're hoping that Kael can find something to help bring that down. Are you hungry?"

Elin blinked and watched Anna uncover her hand. She stuck out her tongue in disgust as the raw flesh was revealed. "I was until I saw that."

Snickering, Anna gathered some aloe on her fingertips, then began the painstaking process of spreading it over Elin's sensitive skin. "Then don't look. I'm going to try to get some food in you once I finish with this."

In the end, Anna managed to feed Elin half an apple and some dried meat before she succumbed to exhaustion. Listening to her lover breathe, Anna lay back and soon slipped off into sleep with her. She had no idea how much time had passed when she jerked awake later. She hissed at the stiffness of her neck as she looked out the office window with bleary eyes and studied the overcast sky. Elin was still sleeping. Her mouth hung open and she snored softly.

Anna got to her feet with a low groan. *Not the most comfortable nap I've ever had, but I'll take it.* She placed her hands on her lower back and stretched. On the large wooden desk, a silver picture frame caught her attention. She picked it up and smiled at the sight of a young man who had his arms wrapped around two sandy-haired children. After a moment of silent scrutiny, she put the picture down and looked out the window again.

Kael, where the fuck are you? You expect me to just sit here and get worried sick about you?

It took only five minutes of internal debate before Anna decided to venture outside of the office, if only down the hallway, in an attempt to divine when the hell Kael would return. Hiding out was going to drive her crazy. As soon as she opened the door, she spotted Kael only fifteen feet down the hallway, facing the wall, forehead pressed against the cool surface. An overstuffed plastic bag sat at her feet, and her backpack lay behind her.

"Kael?" Anna could see the controlled rise and fall of Kael's chest, and the way her fists were clenched tight at her sides.

"Get back inside, Anna. I'll be there in a minute." She turned to stare at Anna with hard eyes. "Where were you going, anyway? You weren't going to leave Elin alone, were you?"

"She's sleeping. I wasn't going to leave the building or anything." Biting her lip in indecision, she approached Kael and touched her shoulder. "I was just worried about you."

Kael shrugged and pulled away with a quiet snort.

"You're barely talking to me. You're exhausted. You're...you're scared of hospitals, and you didn't even fucking tell me." Anna's voice rose as she spoke, all of the anger and frustration of the past few days finally crashing over her. "I thought you were my lover, too, Kael. I thought you were my *friend*."

With an uncomfortable look, Kael shifted, then shoved her hands in the pockets of her jeans. "I am your friend. Please, just get back in the office. I'll be right in, I swear."

Releasing an exasperated sigh, Anna wrapped her arms around Kael's tense shoulders. "Stop it, please."

Kael pressed both hands against Anna's shoulders in a half-hearted shove. "I'm fine."

Anna tightened her embrace. "Stop it. Kael, I know about the nightmares. I know what going into that hospital must have done to you. And I promised Elin that I would make sure you were okay when you got back. Just let me be your friend, okay?"

Kael released a defeated sigh. "I threw up...at the hospital. But I got everything we need."

Anna brought her hand up to cradle the back of Kael's head. "Thank you for going." *And for telling me, and for letting me hold you for even just a minute.*

"I've got about twenty-five bottles of water, and the Ohio River is just a few blocks away. I figured maybe we could try washing her at some point soon. I'm sure she's craving a bath."

"Yeah, she'll enjoy that."

Kael leaned into Anna, accepting more comfort than she had in days. "I forgot how nice this feels."

"That's why I'm reminding you," Anna said. "Just remember that no matter what, I'm here. And so is Elin. And we both need you right now, okay?"

"Okay." Kael leaned forward to take Anna's mouth in a brief kiss then picked up the bags and left, saying, "I understand."

Anna sighed. *I hope so.*

THE CITY WAS deathly still.

Anna trailed her fingertips along the back bumper of a car as she reached it, then tossed a nervous look back at the office building where her lovers slept. *I really shouldn't go more than a block or two away.* If she got lucky, Kael and Elin wouldn't completely flip out when they woke up and found the note she left. If she were even luckier, she would make it back before they missed her at all.

Two weeks trapped inside, and she felt like a prisoner. She needed to breathe fresh air and see the sky above her head. Kael insisted on running all their errands in the city, but it was time

she learned that Anna could take care of herself. She couldn't
spend the rest of her life stuck in the role of defenseless girl who
takes orders without protest.

Anna looked up and down the deserted street. An orange
leaf skittered down the sidewalk on a cool breeze that also blew
her hair into her face. After a moment of hesitation, she turned
right, toward a blue truck that was parked at the end of the
block. She swung the baseball bat casually at her side, attuned to
the streets and buildings around her, ready to strike any threat
that appeared.

Listening in the city was different from listening in the
forest, but she was confident that nobody was within the
immediate area. Her fingers relaxed on her weapon, and she
started to pay attention to the vacant businesses she passed.

There was a bakery that had the meager remnants of old,
desiccated cakes and cookies on display. Anna wrinkled her nose
at the twenty-plus-year-old delicacies and looked across the
street at a shop that advertised various electronics. Television
sets sat in the front window, a dozen blank screens staring out at
Anna as she passed by and headed for a sporting goods store at
the corner of the block.

Though she had been to more sporting goods stores than any
other kind, she thought maybe she could find a present for Kael.
Not that it would keep her from being pissed at Anna when she
got back. The front door lock had been torn off long ago, and
Anna entered the store and made her way along aisles that were
still well stocked with various sporting equipment. She perused
the baseball bats, but decided to keep her current weapon. There
was no reason to trade up. Bored with the same old stock, she
wandered up to a glass display case that at some point had been
smashed and ransacked.

A slingshot!

She grabbed it with a satisfied grin. The body was black,
with a tan rubber sling, and it had a decent heft to it. Kael would
love it. She was surprised he didn't have one already. Garrett
had sure loved his. She was opening a box of steel pellets when
the hairs on the back of her neck stood up in sudden awareness.
Her head snapped up, eyes immediately drawn to the front door.
The flesh of her upper arms pebbled and her stomach flipped in
uneasy anticipation. Shivering, certain she was being watched,
she scanned the street outside. Everything was as quiet as it had
been when she walked in, and then she hadn't felt anything more
than her typical guardedness.

*I'm just feeling guilty about sneaking out. After all, Kael has
gone out almost once a day for the past week and a half and he hasn't*

seen a damn thing. If he had, we would've been out of here days ago.

Anna gave the front window one last suspicious glance before finding a large paper bag with cord handles behind the counter. She stuffed the slingshot and pellets into it, then set off to look for a bookstore. Elin was tired of reading the same few books she carried with her, and Anna could imagine how thrilled she'd be with some new ones.

She looked both ways when she exited the sporting goods store, taking in the length of the city block. The long-abandoned buildings stared back at her; the traffic signals and parked cars bore silent witness to her disquiet. Anna continued down the street the way she had been going, scowling at the storefronts as she passed from one block to the next. The fresh air was nice, but she was feeling more creeped out than she'd expected.

By the time she found what she was looking for, she was more than two blocks away from the office building. The sign said Barnes and Noble, and inside the smashed front windows, faded posters advertising books from twenty years earlier fluttered from overturned display stands. Books littered every surface. From the size of the store, there could be thousands of them.

Shaking off her lingering nervousness, Anna tiptoed her way through broken shards, wincing at the crunching noises beneath her feet. Inside the massive store, nothing stirred. It took a few moments for her eyes to adjust to the dim light. Row after row of books, categorized by subject, surrounded her. To her left was a long wooden counter lined with computer monitors. Old racks of candy and bookmarks sat at each station of the checkout.

For a moment Anna imagined what it must have been like in the days when a store like this would have been filled with people. She smiled at small tables that sat in front of a section of the store that sold coffee and baked goods. Elin would have loved a place like this. Anna could almost visualize her sitting at one of the tables with a hot drink and a stack of books by her side. *Maybe I'll ask Kael if we can stop in before we leave the city. I'd love to watch Elin exploring in here.*

She made a slow circuit of the store, reading section names. She lingered at the gay and lesbian literature section, reading the backs of various paperbacks and wondering if Elin had ever read a lesbian novel. Hoping to find one she'd like, Anna rested her bat against her leg and flipped through the pages of several stories, pausing when a few sexual words caught her attention. She read the entire page of a rather graphic sex scene, then, with rosy cheeks, tucked the book into her bag with Kael's slingshot.

This one is a definite keeper.

Pleased to have found the ideal gift, she ambled through the general fiction and picked out a couple more novels, one by Virginia Woolf and another by Stephen King, then she hurried toward the front door. Enough time had passed. She didn't want Kael and Elin worried sick as well as angry.

She turned a corner and looked up at the front door, then stopped dead, paralyzed by the sight of a gray-haired man standing just inside. *Oh, fuck.* She tightened her fingers on her baseball bat and kept a firm grip on the bag she carried. She trained her face to remain calm even as her heart started thumping in her chest. *Of course I had to run into trouble. As if Kael wasn't going to be mad enough.* His body was wiry-thin, but the bare arms exposed by a sleeveless T-shirt were defined and lined with corded muscle. He wore a trimmed mustache, and his stringy hair came to his shoulders. His baggy cargo pants were tattered and stained with age.

"Hello," Anna said, to break the silence. "How are you?"

He studied her with a wild gaze, looking her up and down. "You sick?" His voice rasped as if he hadn't spoken in years. "I don't want no sick people 'round here."

Anna shifted under his scrutiny, forcing herself to affect a casual air she didn't feel. *He might be friendly, you never know.* "No, sir. I'm not sick."

"So you say." He took a step closer, shoes crunching in the broken glass just inside the doorway. "What are you doing here?"

Anna held her ground, raising her bat so that the end rested on her shoulder. "Shopping."

"You lie," the old man growled, and his volume rose until he was nearly shouting. "You're all sick, and I don't want you 'round here."

Anna flinched and glanced over his shoulder to the empty street behind him in pure nervous reflex. *Well, he's not worried about anyone hearing us.* His face twitched with his agitation, and he dripped sweat. *Then again, I'm willing to bet that he's a few arrows short of a full quiver.*

Anna gave him a respectful nod. "Well, I'll just be getting out of here, then, and I'll leave you to your...bookstore."

"You think so? You think I'm just going to let you waltz out of here to spread your sickness around?"

Anna lowered her bat from her shoulder, holding it out in front of her in a protective stance. "Listen, friend, step aside and let me leave."

"Oh, I'm not your friend, you diseased little whore," the man ranted. "You wouldn't believe the death I've seen, and all because of your sickness." He reached into the back pocket of his pants and withdrew a black object.

Raising it into the air, he pointed it directly at Anna's face. After only a moment, it registered.

Gun. That's a gun.

Anna's mouth dropped open, and she stumbled backwards, still holding the bat that now felt so ineffectual. She hadn't seen a gun since the soldiers raided their house only days after her father died, seizing the weapons he kept locked in a closet. The government had sent the military to confiscate all civilian firearms during the sickness and the ensuing riots, and while they surely hadn't found them all, enough had been hidden away or destroyed so that she had spent the past fifteen years without ever seeing one. The sight of the pistol clutched in this man's hand turned her knees to water. *Where did he get it? Does it work? Does he even have bullets?*

"Are you alone?"

"Listen, guy...just calm down." Anna held up her hands, bat in one and paper bag in the other. "If you let me go right now, I promise to walk right out of this city and never come back. You can have it."

The old man waved the gun back and forth in the air, apparently lost in his own paranoia. "You lie. They all lie."

Fuck this. If I get shot, Kael will never let me live it down...if I live through it.

Not allowing herself the luxury of a second thought, Anna struck out at the man's gun arm. The blow from her bat landed with a solid thwack, and her would-be assailant screamed in pain as his weapon tumbled to the floor. Anna kicked out at the gun, sending it skittering beneath the front counter nearly twenty feet away. As the man tried to scramble after it, she threw a hard punch to the side of his head with the hand that still held the paper bag. Then she took off running, out the front door and straight into the solid chest of a lean man.

She gasped, then cried out in relief when she realized that it wasn't a man at all. It was Kael.

"Anna, what the fuck—"

"Quick, let's go!" Anna looked frantically over her shoulder, half-expecting to see the gray-haired man with crazed eyes stumble out of the bookstore waving his pistol. "He's got a gun. A man in there."

Kael blinked at that, then shoved Anna aside with an impatient hand. Drawing her sword, she rushed into the bookstore. "To your left," Anna shouted. "I kicked it under the counter."

She gulped a breath as she heard a quiet groan followed by the unmistakable sound of a body hitting the floor. The absence of a gunshot meant that Kael was the victor in their confrontation, but Anna could only draw comfort from that for a few seconds. *Now he's going to stroll back out here and finish the job that lunatic started.* She contemplated making a run for it back to the office. *Elin wouldn't let him kill me.*

When Kael emerged from the bookstore, it was with steely eyes and a grim face. The blade of her sword dripped red blood; her entire body trembled with quiet tension. "He's dead."

"I could have gotten away," Anna said. "He wasn't going to catch me."

"He wouldn't have had to catch you, not with a gun."

"If he even had bullets," Anna whispered, and lowered her eyes to the bag she held, a glimpse of the cover of the Virginia Woolf novel inside.

"That's irrelevant," Kael snapped. "He had a gun, Anna. What the fuck is wrong with you? Can't you follow simple instructions? I told you not to go out."

Kael's condescending tone raised her hackles, and Anna demanded, "Did he have bullets?" *I had that asshole beaten. I took care of myself, but Kael will never admit that.* "I know you must have checked the gun."

"The gun wasn't loaded. That's not the point. You aren't supposed to be out here alone, and you know it. I don't understand. Are you stupid or just suicidal?"

"What I *am* is an adult. I'm perfectly capable of taking care of myself. I did it for over a year before I met you, and I can do it now." Exhausted despair overwhelmed her anger. "Please, Kael. Just leave it alone. I don't need the lecture."

"We can't have this discussion here." Kael scanned the upper-story windows in the apartment building across from them and started walking. "I left Elin alone to come find you."

Well, I knew he would be mad. Anna's feet felt heavy as she trudged along behind Kael in dutiful silence. *Maybe it was a stupid idea, but what does he expect when he treats me like a child?*

"I'm sorry that you had to leave Elin to come find me." She spoke to Kael's unforgiving back as they approached the office building. "But I've still got to live my life. Just like you never hesitate to live yours. If I want to go out, I'll go out, whether it's dangerous or not."

Kael didn't even glance backwards. "Inside," she ground out, and pulled the office door open, stepping aside to let Anna pass.

As soon as they were safely indoors, Anna protested, "Kael, I'm sick and tired of feeling like you think I'm just some stupid girl you can order around."

Kael's lip curled into an angry snarl. "You think I'm just trying to exert control over you? For no reason at all? Elin was worried sick about you when she realized you'd left this morning, Anna. You think that's okay? Is that part of living your life?"

Anna hurried to keep pace with Kael, who was walking like she wanted to get away from her. *I wasn't thinking about Elin as much as I was thinking about me.* "You can't use that to blackmail me. This is not about Elin."

"Well, excuse me. I thought you loved her more than that, but maybe I was wrong."

Anna could not suppress her fury. "Fuck you, Kael. You know I love Elin. Don't you dare ever question that."

"I'm questioning a lot of things." Kael gave her a dark look.

Anna dropped the paper bag on the floor and took a step away. "What the fuck does that mean?"

"Let's just get upstairs, okay?"

"No. I want an answer."

Kael stopped walking and turned to face her. "Come upstairs with me right now. This conversation is over."

"No." Anna held her ground, desolate inside at the sudden turn of the conversation. *Kael loves Elin, right? That's what it boils down to, in the end. Kael loves Elin, and he just tolerates me. Barely. I wish I had just slept in this morning.* "You go on. I'm not—"

"Goddamn it." Kael's voice rose in renewed anger. Anna winced as a strong hand latched onto her upper arm. "We're going upstairs. Don't argue with me right now, or I swear—"

"What? You don't scare me, *boy*. You never have." Anna tried to wrench her arm from Kael's cruel grip. "Let go of me!"

Kael picked up the bag Anna had dropped. "What's this?" she asked, holding it up in front of Anna's face.

Helpless tears leaked from Anna's eyes. "I wanted to get Elin some new books."

Kael stared at her for a moment, then pulled her sharply toward the staircase. "Let's go give them to her, then."

"Kael, please don't—"

"Just walk." Kael kept her face forward as she led them up the stairs.

Anna tightened her fingers on the narrow end of the baseball bat she still carried in her free hand. Some part of her twitched with the desire to bring it crashing down on Kael's arm to force her release, but she couldn't bring herself to strike out at the woman whom she both loved and despised in that moment. Infuriated by her own impotence, she shouted, "You're hurting me!"

Kael ignored the angry protest and marched her ruthlessly down the third-floor hallway toward their office home, only faltering when they were within feet of the door.

Anna took advantage of her brief hesitation, finally tugging herself free. Wanting to put an end to their fight, she mumbled, "I'm sorry, okay?"

Kael's hand froze on the door handle, and Anna's heart stuttered as she waited for her response.

"Kael? Anna? Are you two okay out there?"

Elin's tentative voice sounded from behind the closed door. Kael hesitated a moment, then reached back to grab Anna's hand. "Look who I found," she said, pulling her inside.

Chapter
Twelve

ELIN SAT UP on the couch. "Anna, God. I'm so glad you two
are back."

All of Anna's reluctance to come upstairs with Kael
disappeared at Elin's soft words. Managing a smile, she wiped at
her tear-dampened cheeks. She dropped her bat on the floor and
jammed both hands into the pockets of her jeans. "I'm glad to be
back."

Kael snorted. "I'm sure she is." She crossed the room and
leaned one hip against the desk in the center of the office, the
shopping bag dangling from her careless hand. "Guess who
managed to find some trouble this morning."

"It wasn't that big a deal," Anna said, sensing Elin's anxiety.
"I had already handled it when Kael showed up."

"What happened?" Elin sat forward on the couch. "Are you
all right?"

"It was just this crazy old man who thought I had the
sickness." Anna offered an embarrassed shrug. "I knocked him
down, and I'd already escaped when Kael found me."

"He had a gun," Kael said.

Elin gasped at the revelation, but before she could speak,
Anna hastily shot back, "And no bullets."

"You didn't know that," Kael pointed out coolly.

Anna turned imploring eyes on Elin. "Look, I know it wasn't
the smartest thing to go out like that—"

"That's an understatement," Kael said.

"I just wanted some fresh air." Anna's cheeks colored at the
shame of being made to explain herself to her friends. "I'm sorry.
I'm not used to being confined inside, and I hate being told what
to do. I wanted to see the sky over my head."

Elin gave Anna a warm smile. "Sweetheart, it's okay. I love
you. I just worry...Kael worries—"

"Yeah, Kael worries. He made sure to let me know exactly
how upset my leaving had made you."

"Here." Kael tossed the paper bag onto the couch next to
Elin. "Why don't we see what Anna brought back for you, baby?
After all, she nearly got killed for it."

Anna swiveled around where she stood and exploded in
anger. "Why don't you just shut the fuck up, Kael? You've barely
spoken to me all week, and now you give a damn?"

Kael recoiled as if struck. For a moment, her face was
startlingly vulnerable. "I always give a damn about you, Anna.
You know that."

Anna fought back her rising emotion. "You give a damn
about whether or not I'm upsetting Elin. You give a damn if I'm
disobeying you. But me, Kael? Sometimes I think you'd rather I
wasn't around, so you wouldn't have to deal with someone who
isn't willing to let you dictate her every action."

"That's what you think, huh?" Kael pushed off the desk to
tower over Anna. "After everything we've been through,
everything I've told you? You think I wish you weren't around?"

*What about everything you've never told me? What about all the
things I feel for you that I'm starting to doubt you'll ever really feel
for me?* Anna looked at Elin, and for a brief, startling instant, she
was envious of her lover. She and Kael had grown close, that was
certain, but there was still something between Elin and Kael that
Anna had never felt with Kael. It was a gaping hole in their
family, an incompleteness that tore at Anna's soul.

Anna wondered if Kael had ever even noticed.

"Forget it," Anna said, wishing she could take back the
words, no matter how true they were. "I'm sorry, okay?"

"What's this?" On the couch, Elin held the slingshot in her
hand. Her attempt to defuse the situation was obvious. "This is
for me?"

Anna blushed. "No, that...was for Kael."

Nobody spoke. Anna felt the weight of the silent exchange
she knew was happening between Kael and Elin, but she stayed
outside of that intimacy. It was a place she felt she would never
be invited.

"Thank you for the books." Elin held up the Stephen King
novel. "I've always wanted to read this one."

"You're welcome. You should have seen the bookstore. It
was really cool."

Kael picked up the slingshot and held it in both hands, all of
her attention riveted on the gift. "This wasn't worth getting hurt
over."

"Kael," Elin said quietly, "can't you just say what you
mean?"

Kael's throat worked, as if she were struggling with

something deep inside. "That is what I mean. I understand that Anna was feeling claustrophobic, and I understand that she felt capable of going out, no matter what I said, but none of it is worth getting hurt over."

"I didn't get hurt." Anna met Kael's challenging stare. "I took care of that guy, and I got away. Goddamn it, Kael. What is it going to take for you to give me just a little trust?"

"Maybe you could start by acting trustworthy. I'm supposed to trust you when you sneak out of here when we're sleeping, like some kind of criminal?"

"Maybe if I wasn't kept fucking prisoner—"

"Anna!" The strength of Elin's voice snapped them both to attention. "Listen, both of you. Things can't continue like this. I know you're frustrated, but please calm down."

Anna took a step backwards, exhaling harshly. "Why do you always take his side?"

Elin held up both hands. The left one was still wrapped in a bright white bandage. The burn beneath grew less painful and ugly every day, but it didn't yet allow for Elin to effectively defend herself. Thus, they remained in the city. She gave Anna a pleading look. "I'm not taking his side."

"Like hell—"

"I'm not taking his side." Her face darkened. "I'm not taking your side, either. What you did was dangerous. And more than that, it showed a real lack of respect for both Kael and me. I *was* scared when Kael woke me up this morning and showed me that note. I had no idea how long you'd even been out. I also get scared every time Kael leaves, but at least then I know what's going on."

"I'm sorry," Anna said, chastened. "I screwed up. I told Kael, I'm telling you, I'm sorry."

"I know. I forgive you." To Kael, she said, "And as for you—"

"What?" Kael asked gruffly. "I told her it was dangerous to go outside, and I was right."

"Kael, you can't go on like this. You can't keep holding back from Anna like you have been."

Kael blinked. Her cheeks flushed red, and she lowered her eyes to the slingshot once again. "I don't know what you're talking about." Obviously tense, she spoke in a clipped tone.

"You're taking out all your fears about me—about losing me—on Anna. And it's not fair, baby. You know it's not fair."

"I've been trying to be better," Kael muttered. She tossed the slingshot on the desk and strode toward the office door. "I don't understand what you expect me to do. I can't just—"

"For better or worse, this is the situation," Elin called after

her. "The three of us together. We have to find a way to make
this work. Keeping Anna at a distance isn't going to help
anything."

Kael stopped as she reached the door, but didn't turn
around. "I don't."

"You do. We both know how you feel about Anna. But does
she know?"

Anna held her breath at the question that hung in the air,
waiting to see some confirmation in the movement of Kael's
body. Strong shoulders stretched the thin cotton of her T-shirt,
stock still at Elin's quiet question.

"Anna knows I care about her," Kael said to the door. "I've
told her that."

"You more than care about her," Elin declared. "I think
maybe she even knows that, but sometimes it's hard for her to
believe when—" Elin sighed helplessly. "Stop holding so much of
yourself back from her. Please. You know she deserves more
than that."

Anna stood by, uncertain. On the one hand she felt the need
to go to Elin and seek the comfort that she was always willing to
give; on the other, she prayed that Kael would offer her even a
glimpse of what she always saw between her companions. When
Kael turned and found her with a fearful gaze, Anna managed a
brave smile.

"I'm not holding back." Kael lowered her eyes as she
whispered the weak denial.

"Kael, you know there's a piece of you that you've never
shared with Anna. It's a piece that I love very much. I know
Anna would love it, too. Anna loves you, baby. Why can't you let
her know you feel the same way?"

Kael's face screwed up, then she regained her stoic mask.
Weakly, she asked, "How did this become a discussion about
me?"

"Because this is about more than just Anna sneaking out this
morning," Elin said. "It's about the way Anna feels in this
relationship. It's about the fact that the only times you ever
really let go with Anna is when you're angry or frustrated." Kael
started to speak then stopped, frowning. "It's not enough for you
to be honest with me anymore. I'm asking you to be honest with
Anna, too. For all of us."

Kael seemed to shrink a little, and her broad shoulders
bowed inward like she wanted to disappear where she stood. At
length, she shifted her attention to Anna. Her full lower lip
quivered, making Anna's chest ache as she watched the struggle
playing out on Kael's face.

"Do you really believe that I wish you weren't around?" Kael's voice radiated hurt.

"No," Anna said. "Well, not usually." She gave Kael an embarrassed shrug as their eyes finally met. "I do know that you care about me, Kael. I know I don't act like it sometimes, but...I know."

"But I don't tell you all of it." Kael cocked her head. "Do I?"

"I don't know," Anna said quietly. "Do you?"

Kael hesitated only a moment before crossing to Anna. Reaching out with a shaking hand, she brought her fingertips inches from Anna's cheek, but stopped before she made contact. Then she drew away.

"I just keep screwing things up, don't I?" Kael rubbed the palm of her hand over her head, exhaling shakily. "I don't know what's wrong with me. It never seemed this hard with Elin."

Anna lifted one shoulder in a half-hearted shrug. "I understand." After all, it was Elin.

Strong fingers gripped her chin. "It's not because I don't love you," Kael said. "I promise you that. If anything, it's because I love you so much it seems unreal to me. I feel so much for you, Anna. It scares the hell out of me."

She never thought she would actually hear those words from Kael's lips. Her chin trembled in Kael's hand. "Even when I'm being a stubborn bitch?"

"Especially when you're stubborn." Kael's voice was full of affectionate exasperation. "Goddamn it."

She gave Kael a tentative smile. "Hug?"

Kael pulled Anna into a tight embrace. "I think I need one." Pressing her face into Anna's hair, she mumbled, "I really was scared this morning, Anna-baby. I'm sorry if I hurt your arm."

Anna exhaled at the silly nickname that fell from Kael's lips as though she'd uttered it countless times. "I'm okay. I'm sorry I scared you. And I'm sorry I snuck out."

"I wouldn't like being kept inside, either," Kael said. "In fact, I don't like being inside. I apologize for that. We'll figure something out."

Anna shot Elin a quick grin. "You'll trust me to do some stuff on my own?"

Kael's nose wrinkled as she scowled playfully. "But I don't have to like it."

"I don't expect you to like it." Anna raised up on her tiptoes and kissed the corner of Kael's mouth. "And I appreciate it. Thank you."

Kael brought her hand up to cradle the side of Anna's face. She tangled her fingers in Anna's hair, then curled them into a loose fist to draw her nearer. "I really do just want to make you happy. Both of you. In the end, that's all that matters."

"I know." Anna looked deep into her eyes. "I don't want you to think that I don't know that everything you do comes from caring about us. As for what I said...when I get mad, sometimes I say things I don't mean."

"Tell me about it." Kael held Anna's gaze a moment longer, then pulled her into a tight hug. "God, I can't believe how much I love you. I'm sorry I've been trying so hard not to feel it. I never thought I could love like this again."

Anna burrowed into the circle of her arms. "I never thought I'd see you looking at me the way you are right now."

Kael dropped a trail of kisses along Anna's jawbone. "Sweetheart, I've been looking at you like this for weeks now. I've just been doing a pretty good job of hiding it."

Behind them, Elin giggled. "Not from everyone."

Kael tipped her face and pressed her forehead against Anna's, splaying her hands across the small of Anna's back. "I have a hell of a time hiding things from Elin."

Anna smiled in appreciation of their lover. "I know what you mean. I kinda hope you'll say the same of me someday."

Kael captured her mouth in a slow kiss. Anna parted her lips and allowed her inside with a low moan. She sucked on Kael's tongue, following her eventual retreat, desperate not to lose her taste. They kissed until Anna couldn't breathe anymore, Kael's arms so tightly around her the embrace was almost painful.

Pausing for air, Kael said, "Someday may be sooner than you think," then kissed her again. Deep. Soulful. Consisting of a thousand words, all in one kiss.

Anna closed her eyes and celebrated her first true, unhindered connection with Kael. It was so shattering, it nearly knocked her off her feet. She rocked backwards, unsteady, when Kael pulled away. Dazed, she looked to Elin, who beamed at her, then at a similarly speechless Kael.

"It may take you guys forever to work up to things, but you always make it worth my while," Elin said. "You have no idea how good it makes me feel, seeing you two like this."

Anna thought of all the other times she thought she had broken through Kael's barriers, only to discover that the walls remained. In the wake of that kiss, she searched her indigo eyes for any sign that this was another of those times.

"It makes me feel good, too," Kael mumbled. "Scared out of my mind, but good." She tucked a lock of hair behind Anna's ear. "I guess I'd rather be terrified than think that you truly don't know what you mean to me. I'm tired of protecting myself if it means hurting you. I don't want to risk chasing you away. And I think I would, eventually."

"I don't think you could." *What would I do without both of you?*

"Even still. I think it's time for me to try to be brave."

Tipping her head, Anna said, "Thank you. I promise to try to do what I can to spare you the fear. No more sneaking out. I promise."

"But you still have to live your life." Swallowing, Kael turned shining eyes away. "I do understand that."

Anna found Kael's bicep and gave it a squeeze. "We'll take that part slow, okay?"

"I'd appreciate that."

Anna soaked up the warmth of Kael's embrace. She leaned in, breasts pressed against Kael's chest, and stole another quick kiss. For a moment, they just stared at one another with goofy smiles. Kael made no move to release her, nuzzling her neck. Exhaling, Anna let her eyes slip shut at the way Kael's touch made her tremble with desire. Reluctantly, she pulled away from Kael and drew a line down the center of her chest with one fingertip, delighting in the shivers that consumed her lean frame.

"You've got to get better soon, baby." She looked past Kael to Elin. "I've got all kinds of pent-up energy and no outlet."

Elin gave her a sly smile and shifted to rest against the couch cushions. "A few weeks without sex, and you're dying, huh? Trust me, I know the feeling."

Kael poked her lower lip out sympathetically. "My poor girl."

Elin raised an eyebrow. "Tell me you're not feeling the same way."

Kael's dark eyes found Anna. "I'm feeling the same way."

"Well, you two look able-bodied." Elin lay back and raised her injured hand above her head. The other she let rest on her stomach. "Don't let me stop you."

Anna coughed in surprise. Kael looked just as unbalanced by the suggestion. Until this moment, Elin had always been the focal point of their shared sexual activity.

"But..." Anna darted her eyes back to Kael's face.

"Elin, we should —"

"Frankly, I don't know how you've managed to keep from making love with one another," Elin said with a smirk. "Don't worry about me. I can take care of myself."

Anna felt her face go hot. To her surprise, Kael's face grew pink, too. They traded nervous smiles before breaking eye contact.

Elin sighed deeply. "Cowards."

Kael snorted, then bit her lip. "Why haven't we made love?" she asked Anna.

"I'm not sure." In her chest, her heart beat in rapid staccato. "I, um...I—"

Kael ran her hands down Anna's sides, so gentle. "I've wanted to touch you. I love watching you with Elin, but—"

But something has been holding us back. Anna rested her arms on Kael's shoulders and interlaced her fingers behind her head. "I know."

A smile crept across Kael's face. Hesitating only a moment, she asked, "May I touch you, Anna?"

Her legs gave out a little at the quiet question, and Kael chuckled, kissing the top of her head. "Is that a yes?" she whispered.

"Yes." Anna noted Elin's shit-eating grin with some amusement, but struggled to remain focused. "You're sure you're okay?"

"I'm great," Elin said. She slid her uninjured hand into the boxer shorts she had borrowed from Kael, settling it between her legs. "Excited."

Anna's mouth went dry as she stared at the place she hadn't visited in far too long. Checking Kael, she smiled at the way her eyes grew hooded. For a moment they both watched Elin, until their lover shot them an admonishing frown.

"Right." Turning to Anna, Kael brought her hands to the hem of her T-shirt. "May I?"

Anna raised her arms and allowed Kael to undress her. As soon as Anna's T-shirt hit the floor, Kael's mouth was all over her neck and shoulders. She moaned at the sudden fierceness of Kael's arousal.

Somehow they made it onto the sleeping bags. Anna didn't even know what was happening. She was hot, panting. Kael ended up on top of her, lips blazing a frantic path over her upper body.

She cupped the back of Kael's head with her hand. Arching her back, she murmured, "I love you." She held her breath as she waited for an answer.

Kael moved up to kiss her lips. "I love you, too, baby. So, so much."

Anna cried out her joy at the declaration. When deft hands moved to unhook her bra, it was all she could do to keep from climaxing simply from the sensation of being the center of Kael's world for even one moment. She had known it would feel wonderful, and she was right.

Kael removed the bra and tossed it to Elin, who giggled when it landed on her stomach, hanging half off her arm. "Thanks," Elin said.

Anna tipped her head back to smile at Elin. "Lucky you."

Kael pressed her face into the valley between Anna's bare breasts. "Lucky me," she murmured. "You can have the bra, Elin. I want these." She brought both hands up to cup Anna's breasts and press them together, nuzzling into her skin.

"I think I'm the lucky one." Anna ran her fingers over Kael's head, marveling at the softness of the short hair growing in.

Kael spent a lot of time on her breasts, kissing and licking and biting at the erect tips. She worshiped them with the kind of full-blown intensity with which she pursued her bow and arrow and her sword, as if she sought to conquer Anna's flesh with her fingers and mouth. Overcome by the emotions of the day, Anna writhed against her. She didn't speak as Kael undressed her and kissed the skin she revealed.

Naked, Anna felt a sudden flash of vulnerability. "I want to feel your skin, too." She looked into Kael's eyes, where she saw a subtle shift, a discomfort, at her request. "Please, Kael. I want to feel your whole body on mine."

Kael's nostrils flared, and for the first time, Anna noticed the way her entire frame vibrated with tense energy. Battle-lust, maybe. She knew that adrenaline was surging through her own body, and she hadn't actually killed today.

She put her hand on the wrist Kael had planted next to her head, stroked up her muscular forearm and bicep, and looked deep into her dark eyes. "I want you, Kael."

Kael leaned back on her knees and tore her T-shirt over her head. She seemed to gather her courage momentarily, then pulled off her sports bra as well. She knelt astride Anna's hips for long moments, breathing heavily, then stood and shed her jeans. The boxer shorts stayed on. Kael clasped her hands over her crotch with an entreating look.

Anna reached for Kael with a tender smile. "Come here and let me feel you, baby."

Kael lowered her body between Anna's spread thighs. She settled in with a wiggle of her hips, loosing a quiet groan from Anna. Kael eased into a crooked smile as she regained confidence and control.

Anna's eyelids grew heavy at the feel of Kael's bare breasts pressed against her own. Her thighs fell open completely, as wide as she could spread them, desperate to accommodate her lover. Her stomach flipped at the wantonness of her actions, still such a new thing. For an instant she felt the cold tendrils of fear deep in her belly, but it was chased away when Kael bent and whispered into her ear.

"Let me taste you."

Anna's clit pulsed at the mere suggestion of feeling Kael's tongue, and her whole body jerked in reaction. Kael chuckled, then licked over Anna's collarbone, and pinched her nipple gently. Anna pushed her hips into Kael's stomach.

"Yes," Anna said. She stared down at her dark breast cupped in Kael's pale hand. Kael rubbed her thumb over her nipple, drawing her gaze upwards. "Please."

"I love you, Anna." Kael took Anna's lower lip between her teeth. She stroked it with her tongue, then pushed inside of her mouth with a soft growl.

Anna ran her hands up and down the soft skin of Kael's back as she returned the kiss. Her fingertips brushed over the sides of Kael's small breasts, but she was careful not to linger there. She knew that Kael felt less confident during sex without her cock, and she didn't want to do anything that would threaten her. She threw one arm over her eyes as Kael's lips blazed a hot trail down over her breasts, her stomach, her abdomen, her thighs, then covered the damp curls between her legs with wet, lingering kisses.

"Yes." She found Kael's head with her hands, gripping at her scalp with frantic fingers. She tried to pull Kael closer and whimpered when she refused to budge.

Kael moved back just enough to pin Anna's thighs to the sleeping bag with her arms. Gentle fingers pulled her open, exposing her, making her squirm in anticipation. When Kael bent and touched her tongue to her wetness, Anna cried out. Kael performed oral sex like she approached every other task at which she was gifted, with a focused intensity that took Anna's breath away. Her mouth dropped open, and her head tipped back as she felt Kael's tongue drag up the length of her. She watched Elin watching them, touching herself beneath her boxer shorts.

Elin met her dazed stare with a smile full of playful understanding. *Amazing, right?* she mouthed.

Anna could only manage a weak nod, gasping as Kael traced her entrance with the stiff tip of her tongue. Looking down into Kael's eyes, she telegraphed silent permission for her to continue, never hesitating to give her that trust.

Kael pushed her tongue inside, just the tip, drawing a keening moan from deep in Anna's chest. She raised her hips, and Kael grabbed one leg and hauled it over her broad shoulder, pressing deeper inside, tongue firm and pointed. Anna surprised herself by lifting her hips even higher to draw Kael farther inside.

It was one of the most intimate things she had ever felt.

Kael pulled out and slid her mouth up over slick folds until she found Anna's swollen clit. Sucking, licking, tugging at the throbbing flesh, she drove Anna into an absolute frenzy. Soon Anna was pumping her hips against Kael's mouth, demanding everything. Kael matched her movements, in control of their dance even as Anna grew frantic with need.

"I want to come," Anna breathed at last, unable to hold back any longer. She had the idea that she should ask permission from Kael for that release; Elin always asked, and Anna found that unspeakably erotic. "Please, Kael, I want to come. I want to come." She continued to move her hips as she chanted her plea.

When Kael paused to answer, she nearly cried out in despair. "Come, sweetheart," Kael mumbled against her labia. "You taste so good. I want to feel you come...right now."

Kael sucked up and down the length of her distended clit, flicked the tip of her tongue over it, until Anna's thighs began an uncontrollable trembling. The weakening of her muscle control, the inability to keep still, preceded the loud, screaming orgasm that shook her to the core and left her a weak, quivering mess beneath Kael's ministrations.

Boneless and panting, she pushed at the top of Kael's head with limp hands. "Oh my God." She sighed in relief when Kael pulled away. "Oh my God."

Kael surged upwards and captured her mouth in a hard kiss. Anna closed her eyes and shared her juices, groaning in contentment as her cheeks and chin grew wet from Kael's face.

Kael kissed down her cheek and murmured, "Raise your thigh, baby."

Anna did so, and moaned when Kael straddled it. She was hot beneath her boxer shorts, and the material was wet from her arousal. Kael rocked into her, settling into a steady rhythm with her hips. Anna kept her thigh firm and wrapped her arms around Kael's back. Finding Kael's mouth, she initiated another wet kiss as Kael humped her way to a quick, trembling orgasm. She barely made a sound, but her strong body shook and stiffened as she came. Anna kept her hands on Kael's shoulders, closing her eyes at her lover's quiet pleasure.

Kael held herself on shaking arms after she came, then collapsed on top of Anna's body with a quiet groan. She found Anna's throat and trailed worshipful kisses over her sweaty skin. "Thank you."

Anna laughed. "No. Thank you."

After a moment of silent reverence, they both smiled up at Elin, who released a sigh of blissful contentment.

"Thank both of you." Removing her hand from her boxer shorts, Elin licked her fingers clean. "That was incredible."

Kael lifted her head from Anna's shoulder with a dazed grin. "It was."

"Incredible," Anna echoed. She kept her hand pressed on the center of Kael's back, holding her close.

Kael made no move to leave. Her eyes on Elin, she asked, "Feeling pretty satisfied, huh?"

"Yes, sir." Elin leaned over the edge of the couch and extended her uninjured hand to stroke the back of Kael's head and then the side of Anna's face. "Think I could have some cannabis now? That took a lot out of me."

Kael chuckled. "You know you can have anything."

Elin traced a little circle on Anna's forehead with her fingertip and asked, "Smoke with me, sweetheart?"

Anna relaxed into a lazy smile. She felt too good to refuse.

Chapter
Thirteen

AS MUCH AS she had wanted to explore cities, Anna was ready to leave this one. It was not a moment too soon, she decided as they took a much-needed break on their second morning outside of Owensboro. They were perhaps twelve miles from the city; not a bad pace for Elin, who was still limping from her injuries. She was uneasily aware of an additional weight in her backpack and still couldn't believe Kael had entrusted her with the gun she'd taken from the old man in the bookstore. It had no bullets, but the mere sight of it would probably keep a threat away. Anna wondered how Elin would feel about it if she knew.

Kael hadn't wanted to tell her.

Wincing from an upset stomach she'd had all morning, she buttoned her jeans and stared at the woods around her. The brilliant purples and reds of autumn had only another week or so to flourish before the dogwoods would start losing their leaves. Beyond the trees lay a clearing of grass and weeds. Elin and Kael had said they would wait for her there, allowing her some privacy to do what she needed to do. Anna swiped the back of her hand across her sweaty forehead, picked up her bat and her gear, and started walking. It must have been breakfast. *That just...wasn't natural.*

Her head snapped up as a loud distress whistle broke the silence of the day. Her blood froze at the sound. *What the fuck?*

She stumbled forward on trembling legs, only making a few steps when a second whistle sounded. This was one she had only heard once before, when Kael and Elin had taught her their alarm system during her first full day of traveling with them. Instantly, she dropped her pack and reached inside for the gun. As she fumbled, she heard a distinctive low, loud whistle and her stomach hollowed. The final whistle contradicted the distress call before it, signaling her not to come.

They're in danger. One of them wants me to come help, but the other wants me to save myself. Or maybe at first they thought they could handle the situation, and then something happened... She left her bags behind, and started to run to them, her mind racing with the possibilities. *They're in danger. I can't just ignore that.*

She tore into the clearing without thought, running in a low crouch, scanning the area for Elin and Kael, though she suspected that they must have reached the forest at the other side. There were trees, gravel paths, and picnic tables scattered intermittently across the entirety of the clearing. She saw nothing to raise her alarm. But if her lovers were facing a threat serious enough that one of them had whistled for her to run and hide, she needed to be careful.

Slipping into the trees, Anna stealthily moved toward some muffled sounds she could just make out. As she drew closer, she could hear shouting, the clanging of weapons. A woman sobbing. Then, a roar of triumph.

Men. Her blood froze. Winded from her sprint across the field and terrified about what she might find as she drew closer to the commotion, she darted from tree to tree, and the volume of the voices rose.

When she found them, she dropped to her knees in horror. Ahead, through the trees and lush vegetation, in a clearing in the woods, stood a group of at least twenty-five men. They formed a semicircle around two still forms on the ground. Elin sat, clutching her injured leg. Tears streamed down her face as she gazed down on Kael, who lay immobile on the dirt and plants. Red blood covered her closely shaven head. Her sword lay in the dirt beside her outstretched hand.

One of the men kicked the weapon away. Another, who stood directly behind Elin, held Elin's steel baton in an upraised hand. Anna's stomach dropped as he moved his arm as if to bring it down on Elin from above.

The older man next to him stopped the descent of the baton with a firm hand and said, "Enough. She's beaten. Enough." He looked like he was in his mid-thirties, and his hair was almost as blond as Garrett's had been, but it was cut close to his scalp.

Spitting down onto Elin's head, her attacker snarled at the man who restrained him. "The bitch hit me with her stick."

The blond man glared at his angry compatriot. "You could kill her by doing something stupid like that. What good would that do us?"

"It'd do me a lot of good," the younger man muttered, but he fell into line.

From her hiding place, Anna stared at Kael's motionless body, willing her to move. There were two other bodies on the ground, one behind the semicircle of men, the other surrounded by a group of his buddies to Kael's right.

"He's dead, sir." One of the group addressed the blond man Anna figured must be their leader.

Another of the men glared down at Kael's unconscious form. "He killed Derek and Sue, sir." He retrieved Kael's sword from the ground and placed the tip against Kael's throat. "I say we finish him off on general principle."

Anna's shaky inhalation echoed Elin's cry of stark horror.

"No!" Elin screamed. "No, please! Just...just take me. Leave him alone. You've hurt him enough."

The man with the sword yanked Elin to her feet. "Not as much as he hurt those two poor souls." He gestured at the dead bodies. The second, Anna now saw, was a woman.

"Leave him," their leader ordered. "He's as good as dead anyway, with that head injury. You know we don't kill unless it's in self-defense. He's no longer a threat to us." Glancing around at his men, he asked, "How many of you are injured?"

A chorus of grumpy voices resounded.

"All right. Search the area, then we'll head back to camp and have the medic take a look at any injured. Dex wants us to move out, anyway. We've got enough."

"What are we supposed to be searching for?" asked a man Anna couldn't see.

"Those two weren't whistling for their health," the blond man answered. "There must be someone around here that they thought would hear them. If it's another woman, it's worth looking."

Anna felt frozen in place. Her hand twitched on her baseball bat as she weighed her options. *I can't just let them take her. But Kael...he could still be alive. And if he is, he needs my help a lot more than Elin does at the moment.* Anna took in the sheer size of the group with dismay. *I have the gun, but I really don't think it's going to help me against more than twenty of them. If I go in there, I'll most likely be killed or captured...and then I won't be able to help either one of them.*

"It's my brother." Elin wept within the grip of one of the men. "He was traveling on ahead of us. Please, leave him alone. Just take me, and let's go wherever you want to go. Please."

The leader turned to his men. "Go. Don't bother spreading out more than about a mile away. If we can't find this girl's...*brother*...then so be it. We leave."

Anna stared at Elin in agony. As though her fear and rage were palpable, frightened hazel eyes suddenly darted over and found Anna through the dense foliage, widening in subtle panic.

She held Anna's gaze for only an instant before turning away as though fearful that the men would notice where her attention had focused.

In that moment, Anna understood her silent plea. *Hide. Help Kael. I love you.*

It made her sick to her stomach, but Elin was right. There was nothing she could do right now that wouldn't get one or all of them killed. She needed to hide, even if it meant letting these men take Elin away.

Elin. Anna wanted to vomit when she imagined, for an instant, what could happen to Elin in a group of men. She had seen the hungry looks a few were already casting in her direction. She struggled over what to do. Most of the men carried a weapon of some sort, the majority of them blunt. A few carried blades, and a couple wielded wicked-looking knives. She surveyed the scene for clues, for any advantage she could press. The leader of the men pivoted, sweeping cold eyes in her direction, and Anna saw the one thing she absolutely could not fight.

He had a handgun tucked into the waistband of his jeans.

And I bet he has bullets.

Without another thought, she crawled backwards until she could stand without being seen. She tucked in her T-shirt and shoved the baseball bat down the back. Taking a running start, she leapt up and grabbed the trunk of a large sycamore tree. She scurried desperately up the trunk, managing to reach the weaker upper branches in relative silence. She stopped when she could climb no farther.

Below, the men began their efficient search. Careful to keep quiet, Anna peered down through the foliage, spotting the tops of two heads heading in opposite directions just beneath her perch. After they passed, she strained hard to see down into the clearing where her lovers had fallen.

She spotted the blond leader first, then the angry young man who had threatened to hit Elin. A third man was securing Elin's hands behind her back.

"I thought it was an eye for an eye," the angry man said. "This faggot killed two of us. He killed a woman, for Christ's sake! His little bitch—"

"Brian," the leader warned, "watch your mouth."

"She smacked a bunch of us real good. At the very least, let's kill him so we know he won't come after us."

"Come after us and do what? He did a pretty poor job of defending his woman when he was in good shape. With that head injury, he's not going anywhere."

"Then why shouldn't we put him out of his misery?"

"Because we're not common criminals." The blond put a hand on Brian's shoulder. "We're good men with a righteous cause. Killing people isn't a part of that. You know that. All life is sacred."

Anna frowned as she listened to the rhetoric. It made no sense coming from a man who led a small army around with the apparent purpose of abducting young women. *I wonder how he feels about rape.*

Brian shot a look of pure hatred down at Kael, who remained inert. With an even more venomous look toward Elin, he stalked off into the forest. Even from her height, Anna could see Elin visibly relax when he left.

The leader of the men approached Elin, and stroked a hand over her cheek. "I really am sorry for the way this happened. My name is Trey. We don't intend to harm or mistreat you, as long as you obey and do what you're told."

"Where are you taking me?" Elin asked.

In the tree, Anna cheered at the question. *Tell me, because I'll go...whether Kael is able to come with me or not.*

"Pennsylvania," Trey said. "We have a whole city full of people. You'll find a home there, and a purpose."

"What purpose is that?" Elin's voice radiated quiet rage.

"Don't worry about it, my darling. For now, we're going back to camp. We've got men waiting for this scouting party to return. Soon we'll start moving north. Before winter settles in."

"Where—"

"Enough questions." Trey cut her off. "You'll need to learn to speak only when spoken to."

"But—"

This time he delivered a light slap across Elin's face. It didn't appear to be serious enough to have hurt her, but it stopped her protest and got her attention. "Quiet now," he said, almost too low for Anna to hear. "Just because we're not going to kill your lover, that doesn't mean we're weak."

Elin stared at him without saying a word. Anna was too far away to see the fire that she knew was burning in her eyes.

"Understand?"

Elin held Trey's gaze for a full twenty seconds before lowering her head in reluctant deference. "Yes."

Fast as lightning, Trey grabbed Elin's shoulder and spun her around to face away from him. He raised the steel baton and delivered a sharp blow to the fleshy part of her bottom. Elin howled in pain.

"I never want to see you hit or otherwise attack one of my

men again," he growled. "I understand that you did what you thought you had to do, but that's over now. You're ours. And you'll do what I say."

Elin's sobbing began anew. "Yes, I understand."

"Sir."

"Sir," Elin repeated in a whimper. "I understand."

"Good," Trey said. "I promise you that none of my men will touch you unless it's to deliver physical punishment for disobeying an order. That should be lashes, nothing else. If anyone does anything inappropriate, you tell me. Understand that?"

"Yes."

"All right, then." He stepped away from Elin as his men began wandering back into the clearing.

"Nothing to report, sir," one said. "We didn't find anything."

Trey nodded. "Fair enough. Keep an eye on the girl...and her man. If he wakes up, make sure he's not a threat. Make sure that she doesn't get any more ideas of defiance, however slight."

"Yes, sir," the small group of men replied as one.

Trey dismissed them with a brief nod, then leaned against a tree trunk not far from the one where Anna hid. He gave Elin a blank smile. "And now we wait," he told her.

So Anna waited.

IT FELT LIKE hours before the men left, and their voices disappeared in the general direction in which she had been traveling with her lovers. Anna remained in the tree for as long as she could, extending her senses out into the silence. When she'd heard nothing for several minutes, she descended at an almost dangerous speed, finally dropping from a low-hanging branch to fall forward on her hands and knees in the dirt.

Without pausing to regain her balance, she released a grunt of rage and got to her feet, making it all the way back to the clearing before dropping to her knees next to Kael's body.

Anna didn't know which injury to examine first. There was the scalp wound that bled fiercely and the fine slice on her muscular left arm, also bleeding. Anna cringed at the thought of what cuts and bruises might be hidden under Kael's clothing. With a trembling hand, she pressed her fingers to Kael's throat, searching for terrifying moments before she located the pulse — weak, thready, but there. *He's alive.*

Anna looked around. The bodies of the people Kael had slain were gone. She couldn't see Elin or Kael's bags and could only assume that the men had stolen their gear. Anna's bag and

Elin's second, smaller bag, were across the grassy clearing where Anna had left them. Moving her hand to the long, ugly cut on the front of Kael's head, she pressed down with her fingers in a frantic effort to stop the bleeding.

She needed her bag and the extra bandages inside it. Kael had been slowly bleeding for at least an hour, and if Anna didn't do something, blood loss could kill her faster than any brain injury she might have from the blow that had knocked her unconscious.

"Baby, you're going to be okay," she whispered. "We'll just stop this bleeding and then you'll be okay."

Hot tears streamed down her face as she pressed hard against the head wound, keeping her other hand clapped over a wicked cut on Kael's arm. Warm blood oozed between her fingers. The only sound she could hear was her own frantic breathing, filling her with panic. Every moment that ticked by felt like an eternity. The sun hung lower in the sky, and the temperature began to fall. She tried hard not to think about what could be happening to Elin that very second. *What are they doing to her? Where will she sleep tonight?* Her heart felt like it was rent in two.

"I can't think like that," she mumbled under her breath. "Kael is going to be okay, and we're going to find Elin."

Stifling a quiet sob, she tentatively lifted her hand from Kael's scalp. The blood had finally clotted. She checked the arm wound and felt a rush of relief followed by new anxiety that she might have missed something. Hastily, she lifted Kael's shirt to her chin and inspected her body for any other injuries. There was an ugly scrape over her ribs on the left side and a purpling bruise high on her chest. Anna could see it peeking out from beneath her tight sports bra.

Forcing herself to leave the injured woman for a few minutes, she retrieved her bag, then she washed and dressed the scrape on Kael's side. All the while, Kael remained limp and cold. Anna ran her hands down the denim of Kael's blue jeans, examining her thighs and legs for injury. Finding nothing obvious, she debated the wisdom of moving her to examine her back. If she had a neck injury, rolling her over could be a horrible idea.

Feeling as helpless and frightened as she ever had in her life, Anna sat back on her heels, tears rolling down her cheeks. "Wake up, Kael. Please."

Her lover remained unconscious, and Anna's entire body felt chilled by a profound feeling of loss.

Elin is gone, and I don't even know if Kael will ever wake up.

There was no other choice; she would have to wait some

more.

Chapter
Fourteen

"ELIN!"

ANNA JERKED awake at Kael's frantic scream, and her heart jack-hammered in her chest. She sat against a fallen log near the smoldering fire in the middle of their impromptu campsite. Kael rested only a couple of feet away, close enough so that Anna could hear her if she needed anything.

From Kael's screaming re-entry into waking life, it was clear what she needed—she needed the same thing that Anna's soul had been missing for the past half day.

"Oh God, Elin!"

Anna scrambled to her knees and crawled over to Kael's writhing body. Kael struggled against some unseen force as she tore into consciousness, bruised limbs striking out in a weak attack. Anna was relieved to hear Kael's voice, her words, to know that she was still capable of speech.

And that he remembers something.

"Kael, honey, calm down." The sky she glimpsed through the trees was dark, and she wondered just how late it had gotten. "You're okay, but you were knocked out. You need to keep still so we can figure out how hurt you really are."

"Oh God, Anna. Oh God," Kael sobbed. "Elin—" She struggled to sit, and Anna reached out to steady her as she slumped to the side.

"Please, honey, you've got to keep still." She wrapped her arms around Kael's torso and tried to guide her back to the ground. Kael lurched forward and vomited onto the dirt next to them. Anna cringed but held on tight, afraid that Kael would hurt herself in her panicked state. "Try to calm down, baby, please. Take deep breaths."

Kael sobbed uncontrollably, broad shoulders shaking within Anna's embrace. "Anna...Elin..." She vomited again, face twisted in agony. When she could retch no more, she grew limp in Anna's arms. "My fucking head hurts so much. There were men—"

"I know," Anna said in a soothing tone. She rubbed a gentle hand over the back of Kael's torn and dirty T-shirt. "I know."

Kael released a piteous moan and collapsed within Anna's embrace. "I failed her...I failed her. God, what are they doing to—" She retched once more.

Anna felt utterly helpless. She needed Kael back, mentally, even though she knew it was asking a lot. She didn't know how to help Elin alone. "Baby, please try to breathe. Please. I need you to calm down. If we're going to get Elin back, we need to start thinking about what to do next."

At once Kael grew so calm, so still, it was almost eerie. The change was instant and startling. She withdrew from Anna silently, putting distance between them. When she spoke again, after some time, her voice was flat, emotionless.

"They won't rape her tonight."

Anna had to fight the urge to recoil at the matter-of-factness of Kael's statement. "If what the leader told Elin was true, I think you're right. They won't."

"They're Procreationists. They don't believe in rape. Or at least they think they don't. If a man forces himself on a woman who is not his wife or who is not in service to him, he's punished. Imprisoned."

"In service?" Anna folded her arms over her stomach, sick from the implication.

"That's what they called what they did to me—to all the unmarried women or orphaned girls. Marry by sixteen or go into service. When I got there...well, I was damaged goods by that point. I didn't get to wait until I was sixteen. Young girls who find their way into the community often don't."

"That's so evil." Anna's stomach flip-flopped at the despair that radiated from her lover. "You're sure these are the people who took Elin?"

"When the first two surprised us, they acted friendly at first. A man and a woman, so I thought—" Kael shook her head, then winced. "They asked us where we were going, why we were traveling. Where were we from? Asked us what we thought about Procreation, had we ever thought about making it our life's goal, they have a great community we could join."

"I heard that guy Trey tell her she would have a purpose in Pennsylvania." Anna stood to gather their gear so they could move fast as soon as Kael was able. "Did you know they were the same people who had you?"

"No, but they were spouting the same rhetoric, and I got upset...I told them to go fuck themselves. I shoved the woman out of the way, and we tried to get past them. The man grabbed Elin's hand...her burned hand, and I just saw red—"

Anna was trembling, imagining the scene before she had stumbled upon it. "There were just the two of them?"

"At first." Kael brought shaking fingers to her face and gave her bandaged head an experimental once-over. "But then there were more. It's hard to remember. I think there were a lot more."

"I counted at least twenty-five," Anna said quietly. "Maybe thirty."

"I guess the odds weren't in my favor."

Anna nodded at the truth of that statement. "The leader said that they would go back to their base camp so a medic could look at the men you and Elin injured. Then he said they'd leave. He said they...had enough."

"Base camp." Kael struggled to stand. "We need to find her. We've got to get her back before they make it to Philadelphia."

Anna placed a steadying hand on Kael's arm as she rose to her full height. As much as Kael would kill herself trying, she wasn't going anywhere tonight. Her skin was sallow, her breathing shaky and erratic, and her speech remained slightly slurred. She was pouring sweat in the cool breeze of the evening. She had lost so much blood—not to mention taken quite a blow to her head—that Anna was shocked she was on her feet at all.

Kael tore her arm away from Anna's gentle grasp. "We've got to get her!" She took a step away, then grabbed her head and let out a soft groan. "And if you're not willing to go, then I'll have to do it alone."

Anna blinked at the angry words. *I'll cut you some slack here, tough guy, but watch what you're implying.* "I agree, baby, we need to get her back. But not tonight."

"Goddamn it, right now!" Kael growled. "We start walking this-fucking-minute, and we don't stop until we kill every single one of those assholes." Without waiting for a reply, she grunted in disgust and turned as though to walk away, only to double over as pain consumed her.

"Kael, what can you do tonight?" Anna kept her voice neutral, not wanting to further provoke her fury. "Look at you, honey. You just got knocked unconscious for hours. You probably have a concussion. At the very least, you've lost a lot of blood."

"I'm fine," Kael snarled, still bent low at the belly. Only a moment passed before she turned her head to vomit one more time. When she was done, she spat on the ground in anger. "I'm *fine.*"

Anna finally stood and placed a hand on Kael's uninjured

arm. "What would happen if you found her tonight? If you tried to rescue her feeling like you do right now? Do you think we'd get her back? Or do you think we'd just get ourselves killed, and Elin would be hurt even more?"

Kael's lower lip trembled. "But—"

"I don't like it, either. Trust me. The odds will be against us anyway, but I just want half a chance to succeed. So we can live with Elin, rather than die for her. Because I don't think our dying for her would make her very happy. Do you?"

The corner of Kael's mouth twitched as she no doubt relived some memory of Elin. "No. I don't think it would."

"So we rest tonight. And then we get up tomorrow, and we go find her."

A tear leaked from Kael's left eye and snaked a lazy trail down her cheek. "All right." She shifted a little, then leaned heavily on Anna. "But only because I'm pretty sure I'll pass out if I don't sit down right now."

Anna helped her to an undisturbed spot next to the campfire she'd just started to build. *I need to go kick some dirt over quite a few patches where Kael was sick before I go to bed. And hope that we don't run out of real estate before the night is through.*

"I only have my sleeping bag," she said. "They took most of your stuff."

"Great."

"They left your bow and arrow. But they took your sword."

Kael managed a weak nod. "We'll try to find another on the way. If not, well, I'll figure something out."

Anna bit her lip as she remembered one last piece of information. "Oh...and the leader had a gun."

Kael sighed. "You're right. We're going to need our rest."

THEY WALKED IN silence for most of the next morning, Anna following Kael as they discerned the trail together. Twenty-five men couldn't move through the forest without leaving evidence of their passage. Anna allowed Kael to guide them, but covertly watched her for signs of illness or pain.

She had a sudden, startling thought. "You said they went through your bag? Do you think they found your...dildo?" Anna couldn't imagine what those men would think of something like that. *How much trouble might Elin be in?*

Kael cracked a smile, doubtless over Anna's tentative use of the word. "No, thank God." Her cheeks turned light pink.

"You don't think they saw it?"

"I know they didn't. If they had, they'd have checked me out more thoroughly before they left. Two women would have been a lot more valuable to them than one."

"Jesus, Kael."

"I know. I'm goddamn lucky I had it on me instead of in the bag."

Anna raised an eyebrow.

"I had plans."

"I see."

"Don't worry. It's in Elin's other bag, now. The one you're carrying. I put it away this morning."

"Thanks for the warning." Anna tried for a smile, but she knew her face was as tense as Kael's.

They climbed a gentle hill that ended on a wide, paved highway. As Kael examined the gravel on the other side, Anna stepped out onto the road, taking in the broken yellow line in the center of the asphalt that seemed to go on forever. Autumn colors framed a path she hoped they wouldn't have to take.

"Fuck!" Kael cussed.

"Trail doesn't continue on the other side?" Anna already knew the answer, but she felt her stomach clench in anticipation as the implications hit her.

"No. I'm guessing they're traveling along the highway."

"Well, we can assume they're heading northeast."

"Yeah." Kael checked the compass she carried in her pocket. She pointed to Anna's right. "That means we go this way."

Anna stared off into the distance where the road curved, wondering what lay beyond the terrain she could see. A lone billboard stood fifty feet in front of them, the faded advertisement for Dr. Pepper tattered from years of weather. Next to it, a car sat abandoned with the front doors standing open.

"You should walk on one side of the road, and I'll walk on the other," Kael said. "We'll keep our eyes open for where they may have left the highway."

"You're doing okay?" Anna asked.

"Lay off, all right?" Kael snapped in response. When Anna drew away from her side, Kael turned with a tired sigh. "Listen, I'm sorry. I'm sorry."

They didn't speak as they continued to walk.

It was at least three o'clock in the afternoon before Anna had to force Kael to take a break. For nearly an hour, her lover had been stumbling every few steps. It was painful to watch and impossible to ignore.

Kind of like how much I have to pee right now.

"Kael." Anna stopped walking on her side of the highway.

"It's time for a break."

"No chance." Kael kept walking. "We're not making good time as it is. If we ever want to catch up to them, we need to keep going."

Anna could allow Kael a lot of things, but on this she would be firm. "We need to keep up our strength, and you know it. We need to eat."

"We can eat as we walk," Kael called back over her shoulder.

Huffing in exasperation, Anna jogged to catch up with her. At no time did she stop searching her side of the road for clues as to the movement of the men who had taken Elin. "Goddamn it, Kael, *I* need to rest for a minute. I'm about to piss myself here. You can bet that those guys who took Elin are taking breaks. If we don't, how long do you think we're gonna last? Even if we caught up to them — "

"All right!" Kael exploded. "I get it. Fine, we'll take a break. You go piss, and I'll make some lunch."

Anna blinked at Kael's fury. Unwilling to be intimidated by her lover, she resisted the urge to overreact. "I'm not the bad guy here, Kael, and you know it."

Kael's eyes softened. "I'm trying. I swear I'm trying."

"So am I." Anna touched Kael's shoulder, then looked up sharply as a weak whining sound filtered through the trees around them. Puzzled, she tipped her head. There was something oddly familiar about the sound. "Did you hear that?"

"Yes, but I don't know what the hell it is."

"I think it's a dog." She'd only ever heard one dog, back in her tribe, and this brought back the memory of Lucky immediately. Anna stepped off the highway, intent on heading toward the mewling sound.

Kael drew her knife and lumbered reluctantly across the highway with her, calling, "Anna, we don't have time for this."

They had ventured only a few yards into the forest, when Anna saw a dog lying at the base of a tree, its golden hair matted with blood. She dropped to her knees next to it, knowing they were too late.

"The poor thing," she mourned, stroking its plush coat.

This dog looked nothing like Lucky, who had been sleek and black. This one had longer hair and a more earnest face. Anna felt truly sad that they had not been here to save her.

"Looks like wolves," Kael said, grimly surveying the wounds to the dog's back legs and throat. "Let's go. They could be hanging around."

Anna stood up, and they started back toward the road when she heard another mewling whimper and halted. The noise from the forest just barely tickled her senses, and she tried hard to pinpoint the source, quickly forging a path through the trees.

"We don't have time for this," Kael hissed. "What the hell are you doing?"

"I hear something. Hurt...or maybe...Kael, it sounds like a baby."

"Just great."

Anna dropped her gaze to the forest floor. The little noises of distress grew louder, and she stooped low to search through the vegetation.

"I hear it, too." Curiosity tempered the frustration in Kael's tone.

Anna pushed back the thick, leafy branches of a squat bush and gasped at what she found. Three tiny, still forms were scattered on the ground. Baby dogs — puppies. *I think momma was protecting her babies.*

From her left, beyond a large oak tree, a small squeal demanded her attention, and she pushed the undergrowth aside urgently until she saw a small pale shape. He was tiny. Stumbling. His eyes were open and alert, but he seemed confused. Anna's mouth dropped open, and she bent to scoop the puppy up, bringing him close to her chest to warm him. She pressed her lips to silky golden fur and chuckled as the puppy licked her face with a tiny pink tongue.

"Absolutely not."

Anna looked up at Kael with a goofy smile. "I think he's the only one who survived."

"Good for him," Kael said dryly. "Wish him luck on his journeys."

Anna cooed into the puppy's floppy little ear. "Don't listen to him. Kael's just grumpy."

For the first time in days, a genuine smile tugged at Kael's mouth. "He'll slow us down."

Anna held the puppy away from her chest, wrinkling her nose as he began to squirm. "He won't. I'll carry him until he can keep up."

"He'll need more bathroom breaks than even you."

"It'll slow us down maybe, what...twenty, thirty seconds every few hours? Think of what Elin will say when we get her back."

Kael's face softened. "She'd love a puppy, wouldn't she?"

"Of course she would." She held the puppy up to Kael. "When's the last time you even saw something like this? A puppy?"

"I've never seen one that small. I remember a few bigger

dogs, when I was a kid."

"Elin would be furious if she thought that we just left this little guy out here to fend for himself." Anna maintained a straight face even as Kael's eyes flashed with mild panic. "Don't you think?"

"How would she find out?"

"We're bringing her this puppy. End of discussion." Anna handed the puppy to Kael, who accepted it awkwardly. "It's my decision, and I'll take care of him, I promise."

"Anna—"

"Besides, he's a good omen. I can feel it."

Kael lifted the puppy into the air, staring intensely into his tiny face. The puppy squirmed and panted in her hands, staring back. At length, she rolled her eyes and thrust him back into Anna's hands. "We should name him Zep," she said as she started the short walk back to the highway.

"Zep?" Anna stared into the puppy's blue eyes, trying to see whatever Kael had seen.

"Short for Led Zeppelin," Kael called back over her shoulder. In a quieter voice, she added, "Elin will love that. She says they're the best rock band ever."

Chapter
Fifteen

HIGHWAY 65-NORTH WAS much wider than the Wendell H. Ford West Kentucky Parkway they'd left behind. Kael was dragging, and Anna wondered how she was still walking at all. They'd been traveling for days, and Kael was barely sleeping. As usual, her gaze was fixed on the side of the road in a desperate, never-ending quest for clues. Her shoulders were slumped, and she walked with mindless determination. Anna knew that her days and nights were spent worrying about Elin and agonizing over their helplessness, which was more fully realized with every step they took not even sure they were going in the right direction.

Two days ago, they'd made a decision at an interchange for Interstate 65. Going north was the natural guess, but Anna couldn't say for certain that they were still on the right trail. It was impossible to track someone on a concrete highway. Fucking bastards.

Anna wondered how much longer they could go on. Zep squirmed within her arms. Taking him was silly, and he did slow them down a little, but Anna had to believe in Elin's potential wrath over leaving a tiny thing like Zep alone in the woods. It kept Elin alive for her, a guiding presence, even as she felt the lover who walked next to her slipping farther and farther away.

"Somebody's coming," Kael hissed.

Anna looked up, snapped out of her distraction by the knowledge that, yes, someone was approaching from the north. She strained to see into the distance, but the road curved and she couldn't make out the source of the noises she barely heard.

Kael tugged on her arm with exhausted impatience. "We'll hide until they pass."

Anna shook her head and stood on her tiptoes so she could study the road ahead. "Do you think you could defend yourself if you needed to?"

"Of course I can." Kael shot her a dark look, full of increasingly familiar short-tempered irritation. Anna worried that the blow to the head and Kael's quickness to anger were related, but hoped it was simply a temporary reaction to the pain and lack of sleep. If it was permanent, they could be in trouble. "But we don't look for trouble unless there's no other choice, remember?"

"I remember, but maybe whoever this is has seen the Procreationists. They're coming from that direction. Maybe they've passed them and can tell us something about where they're heading. Maybe they even have some idea of where they've camped."

"Maybe they won't have any idea. Maybe they're just assholes who would love to run across a couple of victims today."

"Maybe. But we're running out of options, Kael. Without talking to people, we're just guessing. What happens when we get to the next interchange? It may not be so easy as north and south."

Kael reached out, but stopped short of taking Anna's arm again. She stared at Anna with tired, bloodshot eyes. "I'm scared." The words escaped in a rough whisper. "I'm scared of something happening to you. I'm scared of not being able to make it to Elin."

Anna pulled Kael into an awkward one-armed hug, making sure to shift Zep so he wouldn't be crushed. She understood Kael's fear, but she was more afraid of taking even one step in the wrong direction, away from Elin. She needed her family back. They both did. "I know, baby. But we need to take a chance right now. If these people know something—"

With a defeated smile, Kael stepped away. "I know you're right. I just...hate people."

"I know you do. But I'll protect you."

"Thanks." Kael released a humorless snort and stepped to the middle of the road, her hands on her hips. "Let's meet them head-on."

"I agree. Will you put Zep on my back for me?" She turned so that Kael could tuck the small puppy into the sling they had fashioned for him, which Anna wore over her shoulders.

"He's all set." Kael let her hand rest on Anna's hip, startling her into remaining still to soak up the unexpected caress. Then Kael pressed a quick kiss to the side of Anna's neck. "Let's do this."

"Thank you."

Kael shrugged, then continued walking. "Well, you're right.

We need something to go on. Following this fucking highway is driving me crazy."

They met the two young men at the curve in the road. Anna felt Kael tense at the sight of the healthy men who eyed them with obvious surprise, but kept approaching with confidence. The taller man, perhaps in his late twenties, dismissed Kael with a brief gaze, but stared at Anna hungrily. The other one, a boy of perhaps sixteen, glanced back and forth between them with innocent curiosity.

"Hey there," Kael called out as they approached, her voice deep and powerful. It was so convincing that Anna almost forgot she had been worrying only minutes earlier about whether Kael could stay on her feet. "Good afternoon."

The strangers closed the distance between them, coming to a stop about six feet away. Four pairs of eyes examined and evaluated in practiced wariness, then accepted with tentative caution. The older of the men nodded at Kael, then gave Anna a cocky grin. He had an unshaven face and dark hair that reached his shoulders. "Good afternoon. I'm Robby."

Kael wrapped a possessive arm around Anna's waist, and Anna leaned into her, grateful for the contact. It was more affection than she'd experienced in days. "I'm Kael, and this is Anna."

Robby licked his lips. "She yours?" he asked Kael.

Kael pulled Anna closer. "That's a hell of a question." With her free hand, she touched the bow that was strapped to her back.

The boy stepped forward and offered Kael his hand. Upon closer inspection, Anna guessed him to be in his late teens. His blond hair was even lighter than Garrett's had been. "I'm Matt. Robby didn't mean nothing by it. We're coming from Ohio. It's nice to meet you."

Kael released Anna to shake the boy's hand, shooting Robby a cold look as she affirmed, "She's mine."

Anna repressed the urge to sigh. Privately, she raged at being talked about as though she weren't there, but she understood the reality of the situation. Trying to look her most confident, she shook Matt's hand and asked, "Have you been traveling on this highway long?"

The boy gave her a shy smile. "Since Louisville. Before that we were traveling alongside Interstate 71."

Anna nodded, though it meant nothing to her. "Seen anyone else traveling along this road the last couple days?"

The boy opened his mouth to answer, but Robby stopped him with a hand on his chest. "Why do you want to know?

Looking for trouble?"

"What, only you can ask the questions?" Kael stepped forward, getting in Robby's face. "Let the kid answer."

Robby dropped his hand from Matt's chest and shoved it against Kael's shoulder. "Back off, man. You don't want to start something here."

"Kael." Anna laid a calming hand on her arm. *Please just control your temper until we get the information we need.* "You saw something?" she asked Matt.

"Yes. A group of men, yesterday afternoon." He glanced nervously at a fuming Robby. "They were traveling north. We passed them just after lunch."

Anna's heart began to pound. *That has to be them.*

"How many men?" Kael asked.

Matt shrugged. "Twenty, maybe?"

"Nah," Robby interrupted. "I'd say more like twenty-five, maybe thirty."

Anna's tongue felt glued to the roof of her mouth. She knew the next question to ask, but she struggled to tamp down her rising emotion. This was something—real, solid information— just when she thought they might never know where Elin had been taken.

"Did they have any women with them?" Kael's voice cracked, betraying her anxiety.

"One that I saw," Matt said, with a vague look of embarrassment. "They were leading her along with her hands tied."

"Do you know the prisoner or something?" Robby asked. His eyes softened a bit, but his posture remained ramrod straight. "What's it to you?"

"Depends." Kael kept a straight face, but Anna could feel the barely perceptible quaking of her lean frame pressed against her side. "What did she look like?"

"Redhead," Matt said. "I didn't get a good look because we were kind of lying low until they passed, but...she was definitely a redhead."

"She was hot," Robby said. All traces of sympathy were gone as he eased into a nonchalant half-smile. "I bet she won't be when those guys are finished with her."

Kael's arm shot out, and she gathered the front of Robby's T-shirt in her fist, pulling his face close to hers. Her lips curled, and she growled at him in wordless rage. Seeing the quick flash of violence in Robby's eyes, Anna stepped between them and pushed Kael away. She shot Kael a pleading look before turning to Robby with hard eyes.

"She's my sister," she lied. *I don't want to get into the particulars of our relationship right now.* "Don't say anything like that again, okay?"

Robby looked her up and down, obviously dubious that she could have a pale-skinned, red-haired sister. But he backed down slightly and said, "I'm just being realistic. What...are you planning on catching up to them and staging some heroic rescue? Two against twenty-five?"

She hoped there were only twenty-five. "How did she seem?" Anna asked.

"She looked healthy enough. One of her hands was bandaged, I think."

"She was limping, too," Matt offered in a helpful voice. "I'm sorry about your sister, miss. When we saw them I wished I could save her, but—"

"But even a punk kid like him knows when a girl is beyond help." Robby's gaze was almost apologetic, then his eyes went blank. He nodded at the gash on Kael's head, which was slowly healing but still ugly. "That from them?"

Kael held Robby's gaze. "It's nothing."

"Looks like something to me."

"It's nothing," Anna repeated. Turning to Matt, her stomach flip-flopping with sudden urgency, she asked, "Where were you when you saw them? Can you tell us anything about where they're heading?"

Matt's face colored under her attention. "Well, I guess we saw them just before we got on 65, so...yeah, they were heading north on Interstate 71. We passed them just north of Louisville."

"Thank you," Anna breathed. Despite the fact that nothing had changed, her spirits lightened. "Matt, thank you so much."

"It's no problem."

Zep chose that moment to release a little yelp, startling everyone into gaping at one another with identical looks of surprise. After a moment Anna laughed, then half-turned to show Matt and Robby her precious bundle.

"Puppy," she explained. "His mother and littermates were killed by wolves." Matt took an excited step forward then stopped short, meeting Anna's eyes. She nodded. "Go ahead and pet him. He loves attention."

"Cool." Drawing a brief look of disapproval from Kael, Matt reached out to stroke the tiny puppy. "What's his name?"

"Zep."

"We should get going." Robby turned dismissive eyes from Kael. "I'm sorry to interrupt your wet dream here—a hot girl *and* a puppy, you fuckin' loser—but we're burning daylight."

Matt shot Robby a red-faced scowl. "Fuck you, man. Why do *you* always decide when we break?"

Anna had to suppress a giggle at the all-too-familiar argument. Kael stood silent and tight-lipped. From the way she held her body, Anna guessed that it took every ounce of her will not to pummel Robby.

"Tell you what, kid. I'm going to go take a piss while you say goodbye to your new friends here. Then we leave." Robby stalked off in the direction of a large billboard at the side of the highway.

When he was out of earshot, Kael murmured, "No offense, Matt, but your buddy's a real asshole."

"I know." Matt stroked Zep's head. "But it's better than traveling alone. He's not so bad, most of the time."

"Go ahead and take him out of the sling," Anna offered. "You can hold him, if you want."

Matt positively beamed. "Really?" His voice cracked a little on the word.

"Sure." She stood still as he extracted the puppy from the sling and brought him close to his chest.

With his eyes shining and his nose crinkled with the force of his smile, for a brief moment he reminded her of Elin. His innocence, the light in his eyes, all of it recalled what Anna adored most about her red-haired lover. She blinked back tears and checked Kael's reaction.

Bitter melancholy immediately crept into her heart. Kael was silent and expressionless.

As if sensing Kael's mood, Matt again tried to buy some slack for his rude traveling companion. "Robby's had a hard life. He doesn't mean half the shit he says. He just...doesn't know how to be any other way."

"Robby's had a hard life," Kael muttered. "Haven't we all?"

Matt looked so uncomfortable, Anna sought to reassure him. "You handle Zep like a pro. You ever had a puppy before?"

"I've never even seen one." He scratched Zep's head and laughed when the puppy's leg began to twitch in synchrony with his fingers. "This is a good day."

"I'm glad." And she was. Watching Matt's happiness made her feel as good as she had in days.

Matt's smile faded, replaced with a stricken look. "I really am sorry about your sister. I hope you find her and get her back. I'd love to help, if I thought Robby would ever go for that."

"Somehow I don't see your friend engaging in acts of heroism," Kael said cynically.

"I just don't understand..." Matt seemed to be speaking his

thoughts out loud. "I mean, I want a girlfriend as much as the next guy, but I can't understand just taking—" He lowered his gaze to the ground. "I hope you get her back."

"Thanks," Anna said. "The information you just gave us helps a lot."

Matt ruffled Zep's fur before returning the puppy to Anna. "Your sister will love him. Thanks for letting me hold him."

"You're welcome. How old are you, by the way?"

"Sixteen." Matt grinned and raised shy blue eyes. "Seventeen next month."

"Cool." Anna imagined Matt filled out with age and with curly hair. *He could be Garrett's baby brother.* "You remind me a little of a friend I used to have."

"Ready to go, kid?" Robby returned and cut off any response the boy might have managed.

Matt gave a disappointed nod. "Yeah, man. I'm ready." He held out his hand to Anna. "It was great to meet you, Anna."

Anna shook his hand. "Likewise, Matt. Thanks for everything."

Matt nodded, then looked at Kael with almost fearful eyes. "Good luck. I know you'll get her back." He offered his hand.

Kael took it, and glared at Robby when the older man snickered under his breath. "Thanks, kid."

Eager to cut off a possible confrontation, Anna waved at Robby. "Thanks for your time."

Robby nodded at her, then, after a hesitation, at Kael. "Travel safe."

Kael secured Zep in the sling as they watched Robby and Matt walk away. "I didn't like that guy," she grumbled. "Asking if you were mine. What a fucking asshole," she said. "I thought he was going to come in his pants just talking to you."

"Shut up." Anna kept pace with Kael at the center of the road. Now that they knew which route they needed to take, there was no need to scour the shoulders. "Matt seemed like a good kid."

"He did. I hope he stays that way, with the company he keeps."

Anna frowned at the thought of the fresh earnestness in blue eyes being wiped away by his surly companion. Or by anything else. The sudden surge of protectiveness startled her and reminded her again of how she felt about Elin.

"Then again," Kael continued, "I suppose nothing stays that way forever."

Anna's eyes filled with tears at the naked disillusionment in Kael's voice. For a moment it felt as though Kael was giving up—

not only on Matt, but also on Elin—and it took everything Anna
had not to strike out at her lover in anger.

Anna jerked in surprise when Kael took her hand. She gazed
at Kael, too tired to hide her volatile emotion.

"Except Elin," Kael told her in a soft voice, her indigo eyes
radiating quiet empathy. "We'll make sure that Elin stays that
way."

Anna managed a tremulous smile at that. She had no choice
but to believe it was true.

THE SKY WAS black and fuzzy with stars that looked
distorted through Anna's watery eyes. She'd awakened with the
sweet strains of a dream about Elin still floating through her
mind, and she felt her delicate control slipping.

She sensed Kael stretched out beside her, but she didn't turn
to look at her lover. *My lover. My lover whom I hardly recognize
anymore.* Kael seemed to grow weaker every day, but she
remained stubborn about keeping their pace. It tore Anna apart
to watch her struggle through every step they took. She felt as
though Kael were dying right in front of her eyes.

They'd agreed on a new travel strategy as they passed
through the town of Shepherdsville a couple of hours before they
set up camp. Anna glanced across at the bicycles they'd found.
They would help, but everything depended upon whether they
could find Elin if the trail grew cold, and beyond that, whether
they could defeat at least thirty-odd men even if they did. Every
day Anna grew less hopeful, but she struggled to maintain a
confident façade for Kael. Kael was determined to be strong by
refusing to stop no matter how battered she felt, but Anna knew
that her emotional state was more fragile than her body at this
point. For days Anna had worried that if she cracked, Kael
would surely follow.

And if Kael cracked, Anna was afraid of what might happen.

In the daylight, she wouldn't let herself cry. Not for Elin, not
for Kael, and certainly not for herself. But at night, she felt the
sadness, fear, and exhaustion weigh down upon her and she
lacked the will to fight it off. She looked over to Kael.
Amazingly, she slept, with Zep curled up next to her head. Anna
experienced a feeling of pure relief at the sight, then the release
of knowing that for the first time in days, she could think about
something else.

After a moment of brief struggle, she began to cry.

*Anna lay in Elin's arms, naked and sweating slightly. Kael was
off hunting, as usual, so they had stolen some private time together.*

Since becoming lovers only a week earlier, Anna had devoted herself to making Elin feel good.

"That was amazing." Elin pulled Anna up for a long kiss. "I love everything about you, sweetheart."

"I love everything about you, too." Grinning, Anna buried her face between Elin's breasts, inhaling the scent of her freckled skin. "Especially the way you look when I'm touching you."

Elin ran gentle fingers through Anna's hair, and after some time, Anna whispered, "When I was growing up, I never, ever thought I would find someone who would love me like this." The confession made her feel vulnerable and strong at the same time. "I thought I was a freak because I liked girls."

"Did you ever tell anyone?"

"Only Garrett. And only after he told me that he liked boys. I was so embarrassed to think of anyone finding out."

"You knew people would think it was wrong?"

"How could I not? All everyone talked about was when I would get married and start having babies. I think it was pretty much assumed that I would marry Garrett. I would have, too, though we would have had a hard time with the babies."

"You never thought about trying to find someone to love?"

Anna shook her head and kissed the slope of Elin's breast. "I never thought it would be possible."

Elin caressed the back of Anna's head. "I always dreamed of growing up and finding my true love. I just never imagined I would find two."

"I don't know where I'd be if I hadn't found you," Anna whispered. "It scares me to think about it. If I'd been traveling any slower, if I'd taken even one step in a different direction...I may have never known what loving you was like."

"But you do know." Elin cupped Anna's face in her hand. "And you'll never have to be alone again."

Anna choked back a loud sob. She closed her eyes and tried to hold on to the memory of Elin: her smell, the softness of her skin, the feeling of her hands. Cold tears slid down her face. She struggled to get a grip, to bring her emotions under control, but she felt terrifyingly empty. Without thinking, she slid her hand into her panties, moving between her legs and stroking herself with tentative fingertips. She replayed the memories she had over and over again. Making love to Elin. Talking with her. Sharing every aspect of her soul with the first woman to ever kiss her.

She wasn't wet, but the steady rhythm of her fingertips circling her clit brought a sense of comfort that she hadn't felt since Elin had been taken. She continued to touch herself, still crying, and wishing for sleep. If she were lucky, Elin would be there waiting.

When Kael touched her thigh, Anna's eyes flew open and she gasped in surprise.

"Shh." Kael put a hand over her mouth to prevent her scream. "I'm sorry, sweetheart. I didn't mean to startle you."

"I thought you were asleep." Red-faced, Anna pulled her hand from her panties. *Does he know what I was doing? Does he think I'm a terrible person for it?*

"I was. I think I got more sleep tonight than I have in days, actually."

"Good." Anna wiped the tears from her face. "I'm sorry if I woke you up."

"You didn't." Kael traced her thumb along Anna's cheekbone. "You're crying."

"I'm sorry."

"Don't be." She pulled Anna into a strong embrace. "Bad dream?"

The sudden move took Anna by surprise, but she melted into Kael's arms. "Good dream."

Kael kissed the top of her head. "I understand."

Anna didn't respond, still unsure if Kael knew what she had been doing when she had awoken. *I don't know that he would understand that.* Anna felt ashamed, but not so much that she didn't crave the comfort of human touch. She burrowed into Kael's arms, soaking up the warmth of her lover's body.

"I'm sorry," Kael whispered after some time. "I'm so sorry I lost her."

"It's not your fault. I saw what you were up against. And with Elin being hurt—" She sighed deeply. "*I'm* sorry. I'm the one who stayed behind. If I'd been with you—"

"They'd have taken you, too." Kael tightened her arms, holding her in a possessive bear hug. "No, I'm glad you stayed behind. I just...we shouldn't have left Owensboro so soon. We weren't ready."

"We're both to blame for that. And I'm sorry. I'm sorry for every time I disregarded your fears—"

"And I'm sorry for every time I hurt your feelings. I know I keep doing it."

Anna exhaled tiredly. "We're a couple of sorry-ass fools, aren't we?"

Kael actually laughed. "I guess we are. At least I know I am."

Anna grinned, ear pressed against the rumbling of Kael's broad chest. "But I love you anyway," she chanced to say.

At first Kael was silent, then she squeezed Anna so hard that she had to gasp for air. "I love you, too."

"And I don't think we should blame ourselves anymore. This isn't our fault. It's their fault."

"I know." Kael eased her hold on Anna and touched her hip. "I just don't know what to do with everything I'm feeling right now. I don't know what I'll do if she's not okay."

It was the first time they had spoken of that possibility. "I'll do whatever it takes to make sure that you never have to find out," Anna said. "One way or another, I'm here for you."

Kael pulled back, hovering over her with dark, sad eyes. "I know I haven't said it lately, but I really am glad you're here with me."

"Me, too."

For a moment they just stared at one another. Then Kael blinked and leaned forward to press her lips unexpectedly against Anna's, pushing her tongue inside of Anna's mouth. Anna accepted the invasion with a grateful moan, resting careful hands on Kael's shoulders. Her breathing grew ragged as she tried to keep up with the fierce kiss.

When Kael's hand slid between her legs, cupping her through her panties, Anna pulled back with a gasp.

"Did you finish earlier?" Kael whispered hotly into Anna's ear.

Anna closed her eyes, face burning. She considered denying it. "What—"

"You were touching yourself when I woke up." When Anna opened her mouth to protest, Kael continued, "It's okay, sweetheart. But if you didn't finish, I want to help you."

Anna released a shaky sigh. *God, I'd love to be touched right now.* But she shook her head. "You don't have to do that."

"I know I don't have to do it." Kael traced one blunt fingernail along the elastic waistband of Anna's panties, then slipped her hand inside. "I want to."

Kael's soft words and strong fingers snapped Anna's control. "Okay." She felt guilty about accepting pleasure while Elin was still lost, but her mind and body craved the comfort of intimacy and the few moments peace after release. She let her thighs fall open. "I'm sorry, I just need—"

Kael's fingers found the sensitive flesh between Anna's legs. "I understand. I think I need it, too."

Now Anna was wet. Kael gathered her arousal from the source, then rubbed at Anna's swollen clit. Anna hooked an arm around Kael's neck and stared up into her eyes, breathing hard as she worked her hand in silence.

"Come on my hand, baby," Kael whispered.

Anna lifted her hips, thighs trembling, and closed her eyes. She imagined Elin lying beside them and quickly reached a gasping, shattering orgasm. Kael lay on her when the aftershocks subsided, face pressed into her neck.

Anna felt renewed tears slide down her cheeks. She brought her hand up to cradle the back of Kael's head, careful of the healing gash on her dark scalp.

"I want to be inside of you," Kael whispered against Anna's throat.

Anna stiffened, feeling Kael's hand trapped between her legs, held hostage by thighs pressed tightly closed. Before she could respond to the husky request, Kael lifted her head and stared to her left. They had slept beneath a small cluster of large trees, and in the distance was the highway. Anna looked, but she didn't understand what had drawn Kael's attention.

Kael lowered her head until her lips were pressed against Anna's ear. "Don't move, do you hear me? There's someone watching us."

Anna shuddered. Knowing that someone had just witnessed her conflicted pleasure, she felt almost claustrophobic beneath Kael's bulk. A flashback threatened to overtake her, and she struggled to remain calm.

"What are you going to do?" Her chest rose and fell with her panicked breathing. She hoped that Kael would answer; she needed to hear her lover's voice, to be reassured.

So fast that it left her gasping, Kael sprang to her feet and sprinted toward the road. Anna could make out a dark shape tumbling from the bushes a moment later, landing on the ground with a loud grunt. In shock, she watched Kael struggle with the stranger, then after pinning him down, Kael cursed out loud.

"Goddamn it, kid, you almost just got killed!"

At that, Anna found her blue jeans and tugged them on, then jogged to where Kael lay panting on the ground with the intruder. Anna saw blond hair reflected by dim moonlight.

"Matt?" She folded her arms over her breasts, all too aware that she wasn't wearing a bra beneath her thin T-shirt.

The boy looked at her with wide, scared eyes. "Uh...hey, uh...Anna. How are you?"

"What the fuck are you doing here?" Kael stood and yanked Matt to his feet. "Why the fuck are you spying on us?"

"I wasn't spying, I swear! I just didn't expect to catch up with you guys in the middle of the night, and I didn't know how to approach—"

"Matt, it's okay," Anna said. Despite her embarrassment at what he may have observed, she wasn't altogether unhappy to see him. "Why did you want to catch up with us?"

"I, uh...I'm, uh — "

"You like hiding in the bushes and watching people sleep?" Kael took a step toward the boy, who looked as if he were one wrong word away from pissing himself.

Matt swallowed hard, then glanced from Anna to Kael and back again. "I came to help."

Chapteen
Sixteen

"WE DON'T NEED him," Kael muttered to Anna while Matt tested several new bicycles they had taken from the Sports Authority store that loomed, massive and quiet, behind them. "How can a kid like him help us? How do we even know he *really* wants to help?"

Mildly exasperated, Anna asked, "Why would he be here unless it's to help?" She reached around to the sling on her back, and Zep squirmed playfully at her touch.

"That's a great question." Kael watched Matt race on a bike around the perimeter of the lot. "Why would he leave his companion just like that? I don't buy it."

"You're the one who thought Robby was such an insufferable asshole. Why do you find it so hard to believe that Matt would leave him?"

Kael shrugged, silent as Matt pedaled over to them and swapped to another bike, saying, "It was okay, but I want to try the blue one again and then we can leave."

"Make it fast," Kael growled.

Matt hesitated, obviously unsettled by Kael's tone. "It's okay, I can just—"

"Go ahead and take it for a spin." Anna gave him a gentle smile. "Another couple minutes of rest won't kill us." As the kid pedaled away, she took Kael's hand and asked, "What is it about him that upsets you so much?"

"I don't know. I just...don't want him around."

"But he's offering to help us. How can we refuse? I think we need to accept any help we can get."

Kael dropped her gaze to their joined hands with a half-smile. "He doesn't look like a fighter to me. I doubt he can use that knife he carries."

Anna smiled at the truth of that statement. Matt probably wasn't the fiercest of warriors, but she hoped that he would be capable of holding his own. "No, he doesn't seem like the violent type."

"I'm serious, Anna." Kael's jaw was tense, all traces of good humor gone from her lean face. "How can he help us?"

"I don't know yet. Aren't you the one who told me not to think ahead of myself? That's not a question to be answered now. I say we keep him with us until we find out."

Kael released Anna and mashed the heels of her hands into her closed eyes, exhaling harshly. "What if he gets hurt? He's just a kid." Her voice cracked on that last word. "He's only a little older than my firstborn."

Anna didn't like thinking about the danger Matt would surely be in, but the threat of it wasn't enough to sway her to turn him away. "I don't know, but I think we'd be stupid not to take any advantage we can."

"Fine. He stays. But you take care of him, too." Kael flashed Anna a reluctant smile. "Him and the puppy."

Anna smirked. "Got it."

As though sensing that the time was right, Matt coasted back over to them on the blue bicycle. "I'm taking this one. We can leave now."

"Great." Kael hopped onto her bike and walked it forward a few steps before tilting dangerously to one side. She planted her foot to stop the fall, shooting Anna a self-conscious look. "We've got a long ride ahead of us."

"DOES KAEL HATE me?" Matt pedaled his bicycle next to Anna, the two of them straddling the center line of the road leading to Interstate 65. They were about thirty-five miles south of Louisville, now heading north at a healthy pace. The topic of their conversation pedaled briskly in front, far enough ahead that she couldn't hear Matt's question.

"He doesn't hate you." She bit her lip as she struggled to explain Kael to a relative stranger. *Now I know how Elin felt.* "He just has a hard time trusting people."

"What does he think I'm going to do?" Matt sounded truly perplexed. "I told him I want to help. Doesn't he believe me?"

"He's upset about Elin. It's been a hard week or two. Give him some time. He's a good guy — he'll warm up to you."

Matt nodded. "I'm going to prove myself to him. I swear I will."

Anna smiled at his strong-willed determination. "I believe you."

"Is Kael very close with your sister?"

"We're a family." Anna felt no need to elaborate; that was enough to make him understand. Curious, she asked, "Why did you really leave Robby?"

Matt cruised for a moment, then pedaled to maintain his speed. He shrugged. "Like Kael said, he's an asshole. I left him while he was sleeping."

"But why now? Why all of a sudden?"

Matt looked away from her. "He was just ragging on me pretty bad, that's all. I got sick of it, and I thought—" He glanced at Anna, then settled his gaze on Kael's form ahead of them. "I thought you were really nice, and I thought that trying to help you and Kael was better than staying with him."

"Why was he ragging on you?" She watched Matt's cheeks redden and wondered if she was asking something too personal. "You guys were friends, right?"

"I guess. He was my father's friend. I grew up around him, like an older brother."

"But you weren't close?"

"Nah. Robby wasn't really close to anyone except my father."

"Your dad's not around anymore?"

"He passed away about three months ago." Matt's voice was so quiet that Anna had to strain to hear him. "I don't know what was wrong. His stomach hurt, and it just kept getting worse until one day he didn't wake up."

"I'm sorry." That was a shame. He was a post-sickness baby, after all.

"Your parents died in the sickness, right?"

"Yes. And my older sister Marina. I'm twenty-five."

"My mom died during childbirth," Matt said. "Not me. My little brother. He died, too. That was about six years ago."

"Again, I'm sorry."

Ahead of them, Kael called back over her shoulder, "We're coming up on the highway."

"Understood," Anna shouted. She looked back at Matt to find him watching her intensely. She smiled at him, causing a fierce blush to arise on his tanned face. "So Robby doesn't know where you went?"

"He might guess." Matt looked back to the road. "I talked about you and your sister after we met you. He knows I felt bad about what happened to her."

Anna had a sudden flash of understanding. "Is that what he was ragging on you about?"

Matt shrugged, then gave her a shy nod. "He's always giving me a hard time about something. It's going to be great not to have to listen to him anymore."

"You don't think he'll come after you?" She wasn't sure if Robby could catch up to them, or if he was capable of tracking their movements, but the thought made her uneasy.

Matt laughed. "No. Robby loved my father, but he and I have never had a lot in common. It wasn't so bad when dad was around, but ever since he died, I think Robby's been taking it out on me."

"Well, we're glad to have you. And I thank you for your help, Matt, from the bottom of my heart. You have no idea how much it means to me."

Matt's face turned an even deeper shade of red. "Well, I just...I hope I can really help." He chewed on his lip, then blurted out, "I should tell you that I'm not the best at fighting. I've never really been very good at it."

Anna's suspicion was confirmed. "What are you good at?" she asked in a gentle voice.

Looking emboldened, Matt said, "Tracking. Hunting." After some hesitation, he muttered, "Writing."

"Really?" Anna had never met someone who liked to write. "Like stories?"

"And poetry."

Anna raised her eyebrows in surprise. *A sweet boy who doesn't like fighting, blushes when he talks to me, and writes poetry. He may be as rare a find as Zep.*

"That's very cool." She gave him an encouraging smile.

Matt shrugged, not meeting her eyes as they steered onto the highway. "I guess. I don't think my father ever understood it. And Robby...well, sometimes Robby called me a faggot because of it." Matt blinked hard, obviously upset by the confession. "I'm not a faggot."

Anna gave Matt a brief nod. "It wouldn't matter if you were gay."

Matt's face darkened. "Just because I like to write doesn't mean I'm not normal."

Frowning, Anna tried to decide how best to approach this rather sensitive topic. After only a split second of internal debate, she said, "And just because someone's gay, that doesn't mean they're not normal." When Matt swung defensive eyes in her direction, she said, "I believe that you're not gay, Matt. I just want you to know that even though Robby thought that calling you a faggot was a good way to be mean to you, that doesn't mean that gay people are bad."

"But homosexuality is wrong." He gazed at her with innocent eyes, no doubt repeating exactly what he had been taught. "It serves no purpose, and so it's wrong."

"My very best friend when I was growing up was named Garrett. He was like a brother to me. He was gay."

Matt blinked rapidly at that. Anna suspected that he had likely never known of a gay person, and so she gave him time to adjust to the idea. "Just think about it, okay?" she said. "No matter what Robby made you think, there are worse things than being a faggot. Like being an asshole."

"Robby gave me a hard time, you know, because I never wanted to go out and find women. I just...if I'm going to be with somebody, I want it to be someone who really wants me." Matt coughed, face even redder, and stopped speaking as though afraid that Anna would mock him.

"I think that's very honorable," Anna said. "Some woman will be very lucky to find you."

Matt looked almost painfully sunburned by this point, cheeks rosy-red with his embarrassment. Anna did the kid a favor and stared up at Kael's back, careful not to look at him while he struggled to regain his cool.

"Do you think I'm pathetic?" he finally asked.

"No," she said. "I think you're one of the best men I've ever met."

INTERSTATE 65 TOOK them up to Louisville, through the surrounding communities, and finally to 71, the road where Matt and Robby had seen Elin. Riding through the silent remains of the once-bustling metropolis was unnerving, and Anna felt uncomfortable at times talking with Matt, too aware of the way their voices seemed to echo off the concrete and steel that surrounded them. Twice they saw people.

The first time it was a group of three men and two women who glared at them suspiciously from the parking lot of an old shopping mall that was visible from the highway. They'd been far enough away that Anna could barely make out their features, and while she was unsettled by their presence, she hadn't felt threatened.

The second time it was a lone man who walked along the side of the highway. He wore an oversized backpack, and his brown hair was shaggy and wild around his head. As they rode past him, he leered at Anna and blew her a kiss. Shuddering, she pedaled harder with her desire to leave him behind. Kael, who had fallen back at the sight of the stranger, glanced at her, protective indigo eyes reassuring her in an instant.

Kael was down, but she wasn't out. And she would kill to protect what was hers. Her eyes told Anna that and so much more.

The sun went down shortly after they left metro Louisville, and they continued northbound on Interstate 71 for a few miles until Kael pulled over to the shoulder of the road.

When Anna and Matt caught up, she asked, "Matt, how far north do you think you were when you saw Elin?"

"Not far at all. In fact, we better start checking for their trail anytime now. It couldn't have been more than two miles from here."

With a nod, Kael climbed off her bike. "We stop for the night then. We'll start out again as soon as there's enough light to see tracks if they've left any."

Anna gave Kael a grateful smile. "Sounds good. I don't know about you guys, but my ass is killing me."

Kael laughed, and when Anna followed the direction of Matt's gaze, she realized that their young companion was staring at the sore body part in question.

"Mine, too," Matt said quickly. Looking well and truly busted, he tore his gaze from her bottom and said, "And I've gotta piss. I'll be right back."

Kael smirked as Matt stumbled off the road and disappeared behind a large billboard far out of earshot. "It's kind of cute, but if that kid puts one hand on you—"

"He's harmless," Anna said. *Though I've got to admit that getting checked out is kind of freaky.* "How are you feeling?"

"Tired. My ass hurts, too."

"We covered a lot of ground today." Her fingers twitched to grab Kael's hand, but she remained still, afraid of being rebuffed if she tried to initiate more intimate contact.

Hesitating for a beat, Kael stared at her, then invited, "Come here."

Anna fell into her embrace with a sigh of relief. Kael's lean frame felt thinner than she could ever remember; Anna was sure she could feel her ribs, but she ignored that and concentrated on her scent and the softness of her neck. She didn't realize she was crying until Kael pulled back and looked down on her in concern.

"What's wrong, sweetheart?"

Anna shook her head and wiped the tears from her face. "It just feels good to be held, that's all."

"It feels good to hold you. I'm sorry I've been neglecting you."

"Don't be sorry. I think you've got a good excuse for being distracted."

Kael kissed the top of Anna's head. "Maybe. But Elin would

kick my ass if she knew how I've been acting. She's always telling me not to bottle things up inside. To talk about stuff."

Anna ran one hand over the back of Kael's head. She eyed Kael's scalp wound, which was actually starting to heal. "I don't expect you to be good at it right away. And not with me, certainly."

Kael frowned at the quiet comment. "Why not? I really do love you." She traced the backs of her fingers over Anna's cheek, then leaned in and brushed her lips across Anna's. Groaning in relief, Anna parted her lips and tasted Kael until strong hands settled on her upper arms and gently pushed her away.

"Our friend is returning," Kael murmured.

Dazed, Anna stared at Kael's mouth for long moments before she realized what her lover was saying. She looked over her shoulder and blushed, knowing what Matt had just witnessed. *Then again, he probably saw Kael with his hand between my legs last night. I shouldn't get bent out of shape about a little kiss.*

Kael jerked her head to her left, toward a grouping of trees. "Let's get away from the road. We'll scout out that area and set up camp, then I'll catch some dinner."

The threesome walked their bikes off the highway and across gravel and grass toward the trees. This would be their first full night together. Anna hoped that Kael would warm up to Matt.

"You know, I could catch dinner." Matt gave Kael an eager smile. "I'm a good hunter, I swear."

Kael hesitated, and for a moment, Anna thought she would turn down Matt's well-intentioned offer. Instead she thanked him, adding, "That'd be great."

Anna bumped Kael with her hip. "Hey, maybe we could take a bath in the river." It had been at least two weeks since she'd had the time and the means to give herself more than a cursory cleaning, and despite the slightly chilly air, the idea of a swim was intoxicating.

Kael bit her lip, and Anna could see how her eyes darted nervously to Matt. "I don't know—"

Matt interrupted, eager to please. "I'll totally give you guys some privacy. You can bathe, and I'll catch and clean dinner. I'll even cook, if you want."

Kael chuckled. "You know, kid, maybe I could get used to having you around."

Matt's beaming grin cut through the darkness. "Yeah?" His voice, as it often did, broke in excitement.

"Sure." Kael bumped Anna back. "Anna really does need a bath, after all."

Anna laughed in surprise at the unexpected return of Kael's humor. Like her unbridled rage, it came in flashes, unpredictable and usually short-lived. Anna's chest grew heavy with pleasure at the prospect of spending time with Kael during this moment of respite.

"Shut up," Anna scolded. "Dickhead."

Matt giggled, a surprisingly childlike sound. He stopped abruptly when Kael shot him a look of admonishment. "Sorry," he muttered.

"I'm not *that* used to you yet," Kael said.

Despite the tone, Anna knew that Kael was being playful, and that brought a smile to her face. Things were looking up.

Chapter
Seventeen

IT TOOK ANNA a day and a half to work up the nerve to say the words. When she did, they came out as tense as she felt. "Matt, I want to talk to you about something."

He looked up from peering at the side of the road and squinted into the setting sun. "Yeah? What's up?"

Anna flushed as she contemplated how to actually start this conversation. She glanced at Kael, who wheeled her bike ahead of them, out of earshot, studying the road. They had decided to walk for a while because they had to be drawing closer to their quarry. Kael was far enough away from them to encourage a private conversation, but close enough to react in case something happened. Anna suspected that this proximity was intentional.

"Is everything okay?" Matt asked. "Did I do something wrong?"

"Of course not." Anna took a step closer to the middle of the road and the boy she was really beginning to like. Her stomach flip-flopped in uneasy anticipation.

"I'm sorry dinner was a little dry last night."

Anna held up her hand in protest. "Seriously, dinner was great. If you think that was dry, you should taste Kael's cooking."

"I don't know. I'm sure Kael's great at cooking. He seems like the kind of guy who's pretty much great at everything he does."

Anna suppressed a giggle at that. Still, Matt's hero worship was strangely endearing. "Cooking isn't one of his biggest talents."

Matt gave her a shy smile. "But you love him, anyway."

"I do."

"I hope that one day I can find a woman who looks at me like you look at him."

Anna took in the wistful expression on Matt's face. "You

will. You're a good guy, Matt. I knew that as soon as I met you. Some lucky girl is going to see it, too."

He gave a dubious snort. "Yeah, well..." Obviously embarrassed, he moved the conversation along. "You wanted to talk to me about something?"

Anna blinked as she remembered why she was speaking to Matt in the first place. She stared down at the broken yellow line at the center of the highway. "I wanted to talk to you about Elin. And Kael. And me."

"Yeah?" Matt sounded curious.

"It's just that, before I knew you, when we met you and Robby on the road that first time—"

"What is it?" Matt's expression grew more earnest. "Anna, you can tell me anything. We're friends, right?"

Anna smiled at his attempt to put her at ease. "Yeah, we are. I'm just...nervous because now that we are friends, I want to be honest with you. But I need you to know I trust you, and I never wanted to mislead you."

"I get it." Matt pushed shaggy blond hair back with a casual hand. "You didn't know us, and it's not like Robby made a good first impression. There are a lot of bad guys out there, and you didn't know that I wasn't one of them. I understand, I swear. But you know me now."

"I do," Anna agreed. She took a deep breath. "Elin isn't my sister." That was the easy part. "It was easier to tell you that she was, but she's not."

"Oh." Matt regarded her with innocent blue eyes. "Who is she, then?"

"She's my best friend." Anna held Matt's gaze. "Our best friend." Glancing ahead at Kael, who still plodded along, she murmured, "And she...she's Kael's lover."

It seemed easiest to start with that admission. She'd work up to the rest.

Matt's eyes grew wide. He gaped at Kael, then looked back to Anna, mouth still hanging open. "Kael has two girlfriends?"

Anna couldn't help smiling at Matt's awestruck reaction. Encouraged by his apparent lack of negativity about the idea, she pressed on. "He does. Does that...bother you?"

Matt stared at Kael, confusion written plainly on his face. He shook his head. "No, but...does it bother *you*? You don't get jealous? I mean, are you both...you and Elin, are you...do you both—"

Anna honed in on Matt's question, sensing that she had the opportunity to get out the rest of what she needed to say. "I have no reason to be jealous of Elin. It's not like—" She cleared her throat, heat rising in her face. "Elin and I both love Kael, but we love each other just as much. She's...she's my lover, too."

Matt came to a sudden stop, practically stumbling over his bike. Anna also stopped walking and waited for the reaction she couldn't quite predict. Matt opened and closed his mouth a couple of times, then looked at her in complete shock.

"You're—"

"We're a family." Anna squinted to see Kael cresting a hill some distance in front of them. "Come on, Matt, we've got to catch up."

"You love..." Matt shook his head vigorously from side to side. "What do you mean?"

"I have a relationship with Kael," Anna said, watching her lover disappear over the hill. "And I have a relationship with Elin. They have a relationship with one another, and together, we're a family. I know it's different. I just hope you can try to understand."

Matt remained unmoving. "So you...sleep with both of them?" He wrinkled his nose as he said the words, and Anna felt her heart rate increase at his expression.

He's disgusted, Anna worried, but she forced her confidence to the front. *I can't act like I'm ashamed or embarrassed about this. If I act like there's something wrong about our love, why should Matt think any different?* Anna stepped over to the boy and placed a gentle hand on his arm. Matt didn't flinch.

"I do." Anna gestured at the road ahead. "We'll talk about this while we walk, okay? I don't want to let Kael get too far ahead of us."

Matt stared at her for a moment longer, then started walking again. "I really wasn't expecting that," he said in a shaky voice.

"I'm sure you weren't." Anna squeezed his arm, pleased that he didn't recoil. "I wasn't either, for the record. When I met them, I mean. We all just...clicked."

"Did Kael want you to be with Elin?" Matt asked. He didn't meet her eyes. "I mean...is that why you—"

"I love women. I always have." She gazed at him until he returned her look. "Kael came as a surprise to me. Elin didn't."

Matt blushed and looked away. "But why? I mean, you're so beautiful. I know you could find a man who would love you. Only you."

Anna flushed at the boy's compliment. "I have two people who love me. And I love those two people with all my heart. It's the most wonderful feeling in the world, and there's nothing I want more than what I have with them."

"This is a really fucked up thing to hear. You know that,

right?"

"I know. But I'm still the same person I was a half hour ago."

Matt frowned. "I'm sorry, I'm just not used to the idea of...two women being together. My father and Robby always said that it was wrong for two people of the same sex to...do that. Even women."

"Wrong for us to love one another?" Anna gave Matt a careful smile. "You seem like a romantic to me. Do you really think that love could ever be wrong? We're all adults, and nobody is doing anything they don't want to do."

Matt's cheeks turned light pink. "No, I don't think love is wrong."

"Hey, Matt." Anna reached out to take the boy's arm. "We're still friends, right? What I told you doesn't change that, does it?"

Matt shrugged, pulling away from Anna's touch with a sad smile. "We're still friends. I just...need a chance to get used to the idea. Is that okay?"

Anna nodded. *You can't expect him to accept it just like that.* "That's more than okay, Matt. I understand. Take all the time you need."

When they reached the top of the hill, Anna stopped and stared at the sight that greeted them. Kael stood ten feet in front of them, her bike propped against a highway sign, her hands on her hips. She stared at a smattering of glittering lights that shone in the distance.

"The lights." Anna squinted, puzzled by what she was seeing. The source of such a display eluded her. "What are the lights?"

"I think that's what some might call progress. Unless I'm mistaken," Kael said, "this city has inhabitants. And electricity."

KAEL WALKED THEM around the perimeter of town, staying close to the trees as they passed dark storefronts, abandoned gas stations, and dilapidated homes. Electricity wasn't evident in that part of the city, and Kael led them on a cautious route between those buildings and along deserted streets until they saw a light over the front door of a large brick house. At Kael's signal, they left their bikes behind the fence of an adjoining property. They were sidling along the decayed wood screen this provided, when a figure stepped out from the side of the house and knelt down next to a well-tended garden.

After a few minutes, the figure rose with a fistful of something in one hand, and they were looking at a relatively short woman with a rounded frame. The bright light shining at the front of the house illuminated her face, and Anna was struck by the beauty of her skin. It was dark brown, even darker than her own, and the woman walked with an air of casual confidence.

Anna felt bad that they would probably scare this poor woman to death with their approach. If she was an innocent, unaffiliated with the Procreationists, she didn't deserve even a moment of uncertainty about their intentions. But if she was with the men who had taken Elin, Anna didn't want her to have the slightest opportunity to raise an alarm before they could question her.

Anna saw Kael's approach long before the woman did. Her lover stepped out of the shadows and loped up behind the woman in a stealthy, silent run. She held her new sword in one hand, and with the other she reached around the dark-skinned woman's face and clapped her palm over her mouth, stifling a panicked yelp. Pulling the woman back against her, Kael whispered into her ear. The woman nodded and stared wide-eyed at the far edge of the property. Anna's chest tightened. She could almost feel the thoughts racing through the woman's mind. Taking a deep breath, she stepped out of the trees, hoping that the sight of her might prove reassuring.

"We're not going to hurt you," Anna said. "We just want to ask you a few questions, but we don't want you to panic and get the whole town running here until we know that they're not going to want to hurt us."

The woman, suddenly calm and still, stared at Anna with compassionate eyes. She was significantly older, perhaps in her fifties. Her dark hair was streaked with gray, lending her a quiet dignity that remained intact even as Kael restrained her from behind. Anna fought the uneasy notion that her most intimate thoughts and emotions were being carefully examined and evaluated by this woman.

"If I uncover your mouth, you'll keep quiet. Right?" Kael murmured. Without hesitation, the woman nodded. Kael's eyes met Anna's, then she removed her hand.

The woman raised a dark eyebrow at Anna. "Well, that was certainly dramatic," she said. "You scared the hell out of me."

"I'm sorry." Anna found herself smiling with relief at the woman's dry humor. "We're normally more civilized than that."

The woman's attention seemed to shift, and following her gaze, Anna saw Matt standing a few feet away wearing an expression of childlike sheepishness.

"I'm sorry, too," he piped up.

The woman chuckled and shook her head. "Don't you worry,

son. The minute you stepped out I knew everything was okay. You looked far more nervous than I felt." She offered Anna her hand. "Let's do this right. It's nice to meet you. I'm Dr. Kate Woodard."

Anna introduced herself, then said, "Dr. Woodard? Like a medical doctor?" She raised hopeful eyes to the healing gash on Kael's head. This could be too good to be true.

"Call me Kate. And yes, a medical doctor." She gave her hand to Kael. "You look like you could use some help. Maybe after you ask me your questions?"

"It's nothing. Thank you for offering, though." Kael scowled, but shook her hand politely, adding, "I'm sorry for grabbing you like that. My name's Kael, and he's Matt."

Kate shook Matt's hand, then said, "So, these urgent questions?"

"We're looking for a friend," Anna said. "She was traveling with us, and—"

"Our friend was taken," Kael said, picking up the story. "She and I were approached by a man and a woman who wanted us to join their community. Luckily, Anna was separated from us at the time. After we refused, about twenty men showed up and...I couldn't stop them."

"I understand," Kate murmured. "Do you know who these men were?"

"There's a group up in Pennsylvania, and they believe—"

"The Procreationists," Kate interrupted. "Tell me, what does your friend look like?"

Anna's heart began to pound. "Red hair. Pale skin. Beautiful. Her name is Elin."

Kate's eyes darted to the trees and shadows that surrounded them. She seemed anxious, all of a sudden, and grabbed Anna's arm, urging, "Come on inside."

"Is everything okay?" Kael gestured Matt forward. "Is there someone out there?"

"Not now, I don't think," Kate whispered. "We just need to get inside. We need to talk and not be overheard. I know who took your friend."

"You know where she is?" Kael gripped Kate's arm.

"I've been to their camp. It's not more than two miles outside of town." Kate locked the front door and ushered them into the cozy interior of her house. In her left hand, Anna noticed for the first time, she clutched various herbs.

Kael pressed her fingers to her temple, wincing in that familiar way that told Anna that her head was pounding. "Please tell us, have you seen her?"

"She's okay. I examined her myself. She had a rather nasty bear bite, or so she told me, on one calf. And a healing burn on her hand."

"That's her." Kael sagged against the wall. "We found her."

Anna stepped forward into her waiting arms. "We found her," she repeated. "Baby, she's going to be okay. We found her."

Kael turned to Kate. "Why you? Why did you examine her?"

Anna flinched at the slight accusation in Kael's voice. Still, she was interested in the answer. "I think what he means, Kate, is just how are you involved with the Procreationists?"

Kate nodded at the sword Kael still clutched in her hand. "Why don't you put that thing away and come sit down so we can talk?" She gestured to a door farther inside the house, which Anna assumed led to the kitchen. Matt leaned on the doorframe, watching them in silence.

"I'm sorry." Kael sheathed her sword. "We've been going on so little for so long, I'm just overwhelmed that you know where she is."

"I understand." Kate pushed the kitchen door open and beckoned them. "Who wants water?"

There was a large white refrigerator and freezer. Anna could hear the slight hum that emanated from them, which confused her for a few moments before she realized what it meant. The kitchen also contained a full-sized oven, a microwave oven, and various appliances that looked familiar, but that she couldn't name. Kate took a glass to the refrigerator and pressed it against something that made a low, grinding noise. Anna hurried over to see the refrigerator spit something into the first glass.

"Ice?" she murmured, awestruck.

Kate smiled. "A luxury I'm afraid I take for granted again."

Anna blinked as Kate filled another glass with ice. "Wow."

"So about Elin," Kael said from a seat at the kitchen table. Her leg bobbed up and down, impatient. Matt sat next to her, leaning away from her nervous energy. "Did you talk to her?"

Anna took the chair next to Kael's and held her hand. It was cold and trembling, betraying her turbulent emotion.

"I wasn't able to talk to her alone," Kate said. "Trey — one of their leaders — told me she was too dangerous for me to see without a guard."

"Too dangerous?" Kael asked in an incredulous voice.

Kate shrugged and handed out glasses of water. "He said she resisted them. That she knew how to fight. In fact, the only reason they sent a messenger here to request a doctor was because she and her partner had beaten so many of his men so badly. The camp medic was overwhelmed." She gestured to

Kael's head wound. "I assume that was you."

"Kael killed two of them," Anna said. "They seemed pretty angry about the fight he and Elin put up."

"Yes, I got that. Trey seemed concerned about keeping Elin separated from his men."

Kael released a shaky sigh. "How long ago did you see her?"

"Three days ago."

"And she was okay?" Anna asked.

"Physically, she was healthy. I noticed the healing injuries I mentioned earlier, but other than that there was just the black eye—"

Kael stiffened. "A black eye? What else?"

Kate gave Kael a look of tender sympathy. "Nothing, really. I asked her if she was injured in any other way, and she told me she wasn't."

"How did she seem?" Anna asked.

Kate's mouth twitched into a smile. "Mad as hell. I think they were a little intimidated by her, honestly. I could tell she was trying hard to rein in her anger."

"The last time she saw Kael, he was unconscious and bleeding on the ground," Anna said. "I'm sure she's very upset."

"How do these men treat their women prisoners?" Kael asked, eyes glued to the tabletop. "Their *breeders*," she said in a contemptuous voice.

"From what I could tell, relatively well. But to be honest with you, I just don't know. They've never summoned me before this year. They've camped just outside of town for almost five years, but until now they've mostly left us alone."

"Mostly?" Anna asked.

"The first year, they marched right into the center of town. Tried to recruit some of the young women who lived here. When the girls refused, the men just...took them." Kate cast ashamed eyes down to the table. "Some of the men in town, my husband Walter included, went after them. All but one came back after a week or so, bruised and battered. I had to amputate a leg and an arm. These men—Procreationists, they told us—beat them to within an inch of their lives, but didn't finish them off. They let them come back and show us what would happen if we resisted."

"They don't believe in killing," Kael whispered.

Kate gave Kael a sad smile. "Right. The second year, they came to town to re-supply. And that's all they've asked since then. Once a year, around October, they camp outside town and ask us for supplies. We give them whatever they need. I guess we hope that's all they'll take."

Kael looked around. "You say you have a husband?"

"Yes," Kate answered. "But Walter's away for a few days. Perhaps you'll get a chance to meet him later."

Kael returned to the topic at hand. "How many men did you see when you were there?"

Kate's warm brown eyes flashed with worry. "Almost fifty, all told. When I was out there on Monday, there were only about thirty of them. A second contingent was out 'recruiting,' Trey called it. They're expecting them back this weekend. He said they're planning to leave for Philadelphia as soon as the other contingent returns."

Kael sighed. "So we've got maybe two days to come up with a plan and rescue Elin before their force nearly doubles."

Kate reached across the table and placed a gentle hand on Kael's arm. "Young man, I'll tell you where to find them. I'll tell you everything I know, everything I saw. God knows, I don't like those men anymore than you do. But I have to tell you, just for my own conscience...I don't know how the three of you, especially looking as worn-down as you do, are ever going to pull off what six men tried and failed to do just a few years ago. Trey had fewer men then, and I'm certain they weren't as well-trained."

"I don't know how, either, but we will," Kael said. "We don't have any choice."

Anna gave Kael a serious nod. "We will." She gazed at Matt, who tipped his head in agreement. "Please, Kate," Anna said as she took the older woman's hand. "Tell us everything you know."

Chapter
Eighteen

WHEN ANNA WOKE up in Dr. Kate Woodard's guest bedroom, it was with the fuzzy remnants of another dream of Elin still lingering in her mind. Visions of red hair and pale skin refused to leave her, and Anna retreated under the fluffy down comforter and closed her eyes against the pleasure and pain of it all.

"Wake up, sleepyhead." Kael sat down on the mattress beside her. "Kate is making us breakfast."

Anna inhaled deeply, grinning as she caught a whiff of the delicious smells coming from downstairs. Something about it tickled at her memories of her mother and big family breakfasts before the sickness had come.

"You talked me into it." Anna giggled as Kael pulled the comforter from her body and exposed her naked skin.

"Kate also wanted me to let you know that you're welcome to use the shower." Kael traced her fingers over the swell of Anna's breast. "I highly recommend it. I feel like a new man."

Anna studied Kael carefully. Her eyes, dim and red-rimmed with exhaustion only the day before, were bright and clear. The ugly scalp wound was looking better. All in all, it appeared as though new life had been breathed into Kael.

And all from one decent night's sleep. Imagine what a good breakfast could do. Anna curled her fingers around the back of Kael's neck and drew her into a soft kiss. *Maybe we will have a fighting chance, after all.*

Kael pulled back and murmured, "We're heading for their camp as soon as we eat. Kate has already given me directions."

"What's the plan?"

"At first, we watch. We watch and wait for our opportunity."

"What if one doesn't present itself?" Anna whispered. It was her greatest fear. *What if there's no way to do this without getting ourselves killed?*

"That's not an option. There's always an opportunity. Some are just more desirable than others." She ran her hand over Anna's belly, then her bare side. "I've got Zep downstairs eating. He'll stay with Kate while we're gone today."

"Okay." Anna sat up, and the comforter fell around her waist. "I'll go take that shower now." She looked over her shoulder as she retreated into the bathroom, and blushed at the way Kael's eyes followed her naked progress. In the shower a few minutes later, she thought of Elin.

"I loved being inside of you last night."

Anna turned her head at the sound of Elin's soft, throaty voice and gave her lover a shy smile. Kael was out fishing while they spent a lazy morning in bed. "Yeah?"

Elin curled even closer into Anna's naked body. "It was one of the most amazing things I've ever felt." She must have looked doubtful at that, because Elin said, "Really, sweetheart. I could feel your heartbeat around my fingers. It was incredible."

Anna blushed. "It was. I never thought it would feel that good, I guess."

"I thought it might feel that good being inside a woman." At Anna's quizzical look, she explained, "That was the first time for me, too, you know."

Anna's mouth dropped open in sudden understanding. Kael would never have allowed that privilege. "Oh. I suppose it would have been."

"And it was perfect." Elin planted a gentle kiss on Anna's mouth and murmured, "Like you."

Tears stung Anna's eyes. "It was perfect. I felt so close to you. I never wanted you to leave."

Elin nipped at Anna's earlobe. Whispering, she promised, "I never will."

Anna turned off the shower and dried her tears. They needed to get Elin back.

ANNA CARRIED HER baseball bat, though she hoped she wouldn't need it before the three of them had a chance to observe and to plan. The unloaded handgun that Kael had taken from the crazy old man in Owensboro was tucked into the waist of her blue jeans, pressed against her back. That was a last resort, something for when she had no other choices.

I definitely hope I won't need that.

Kael walked in front, sword strapped to her back. Outside of Kate's house, they had debated taking her bow and arrows, but had finally decided that if they got into a situation during this reconnaissance mission that required a weapon, a sword would probably be more useful. Carrying both could hinder their stealth. In her pocket, Kael had a hand-drawn sketch that Kate had prepared from memory, detailing the layout of tents and sentries.

Matt walked next to Anna. He had his hunting knife strapped to his belt, and he carried a wooden bat similar to Anna's. Neither Kael nor Anna was comfortable allowing him to face possible danger without something more than such a close-range weapon as a knife.

Anna struggled with her guilt over letting such a young kid risk his life for their cause. She gave him a brief, sidelong glance, covertly studying his face. He had been quiet since Anna's confession the day before, but she hadn't sensed any animosity. Instead, he seemed introspective. Anna wondered what was going on behind his blue eyes.

"Matt?"

The boy turned his head. "Yeah?" He kept his voice low, though they were more than a mile from the Procreationist camp.

"I'm just wondering how you're feeling about all this. What we're doing."

Matt shrugged. "Nervous, a little. Anxious, really. I guess I don't know what to expect."

"Are you sorry you ever offered to help?" Anna kept her voice light, but she was worried. She needed to know.

Matt shook his head without hesitation. "No. These guys have no right to just take women like that. Someone has to stand up to them."

"It's going to be dangerous."

"I always knew that."

"And your feelings about me?" Anna asked. "After what I told you about yesterday? We haven't had much of a chance to talk since then."

"I know." Matt stared at the ground. "I guess I'm not sure what to say."

"That's okay. You don't have to say anything."

"I'm not judging you. Or Kael, or Elin. You love him. And you love her. Nobody has a right to judge that." He glanced over at her with a shy smile. "Just as long as they love you, too, with all of their hearts."

Anna's lips twitched at Matt's protectiveness and the bit of a lingering crush she could hear in his voice. "You really are a good guy, Matt. You know that?"

Matt blushed. "Just remember to tell that to any pretty girls you meet."

"Will do."

They fell silent after that, observant as they drew nearer to the Procreationist camp. Anna kept her senses alert, unwilling to be surprised. She heard the quiet crunching of Matt's feet on the leaves; she could hear the buzzing of insects in the vegetation around them. From Kael, she heard nothing. Her lover moved in the forest as though she were a ghost.

Kael stopped and waited for Anna to catch up. "Quiet," she breathed in Anna's ear. "I think we're within a half mile of their camp. Tell Matt to follow close behind me."

Anna's stomach churned. *Please*, she prayed to a God she didn't believe in. *Let a plan become clear to us.*

Kael led them to the Procreationist camp like she had been walking there every day for a month. No missteps, no hesitation, she just took Matt and Anna to a hill overlooking the camp, and they concealed themselves behind a cluster of trees about twenty yards above the site. Immediately below, a small river, lined with trees, ran along the bottom of the ridge they occupied. Spread out beyond the trees was a ring of tents with a group of smaller tents placed in the center. According to Kate, the men held their female prisoners in those center tents.

Anna crouched next to Kael, and Matt hunkered down to her right. The camp was teeming with men. A dozen or so tossed around a football some distance away from the tents. Four more stood at various positions around the perimeter, presumably standing guard. Another three men sat talking next to one of the tents closest to them, and while Anna couldn't make out their words, she could tell by the grins on their faces that they were feeling pretty good about life.

Anna followed Kael's line of sight, taking in a figure emerging from a blue tent at the far side of camp.

"That's Trey," she told Kael. "He's the one who told the others not to finish you off." *The one who hit Elin.* She didn't dare say it out loud. Turning to Matt, she said, "The blond over there? That's Trey, the guy I was telling you about."

"Looks like he's got something on his mind," Matt remarked.

Trey walked to a prisoner tent, then put his hands on his hips and looked up at the sky. "Dan, Randy, come over here," he shouted and two men hurried from a stand of trees on the far side.

One man was young and well-built, clean-shaven, maybe a couple of years older than Matt. The other was shorter than his companion, with ginger-colored hair. After some discussion, the ginger-haired man, addressed by Trey as "Dan," turned to his young partner and gripped his shoulder with his hand. With that, Trey drew away and returned to his tent. Anna memorized its location before resuming her surveillance of the two men instructed by Trey, eager to see what they would do next.

Dan bent and scratched at the front of a little red tent, then he unzipped the door and said something to the occupants inside. A minute later, two young women stepped out into the open and regarded the men warily. Dan spoke, and Anna could tell from the body language of the women that they didn't like what they were hearing. But they followed the two men away from their tent all the same.

The four figures moved around a line of trees to Anna's left and took a path down to the narrow river that ran along the bottom of the rocky wall, twenty yards below. The women walked with bent heads and heavy feet, as though being led to their execution.

When they reached the water, ginger-haired Dan gave some instructions and both women stepped backwards, the fear on their faces unmistakable even from Anna's vantage point. The stockier of them, a blonde, said something that made their captor frown. Anna wished she could hear them. She snuck a quick look at Kael. Her lover's face was dark. *I wonder which tent Elin is in.*

Anna let her eyes stray to the cluster of center tents, straining for some sign of movement inside any of them. She was desperate for a glimpse of red hair, for the sight of pale skin, for anything that would confirm that Elin was imprisoned at this place. Matt's sharply indrawn breath drew her attention back to the river, where the blonde woman had stripped off her T-shirt to reveal a dingy white bra. She hesitated for a moment, then unhooked the bra and tossed it to the ground, folding her arms over her chest.

"At least turn around, you fucking perverts!" she shouted and snaked one arm around her friend's waist. "Can't you see she's upset?"

Kael growled in the back of her throat. Anna put a hand on her shoulder, trying to calm her seething anger. Her own stomach churned. The only thing that kept her from vomiting in the dirt was the unfaltering dignity of the blonde. Her friend, a lanky brunette, looked how Anna felt inside.

The ginger-haired man reached out to touch the brunette's arm but the blonde woman intercepted him, slapping him away. The man frowned, but with a curt nod, he retreated and half-turned away from his prisoners. He then grabbed his partner's arm and encouraged him to stop looking directly at the women as they completed undressing.

Anna leaned forward and murmured in Kael's ear, "I don't like this."

Kael shook her head. "Neither do I."

The women eased into the river, naked, and began washing with hurried, nervous motions. Dan kept his eyes mostly averted, paying only enough attention to ensure that his prisoners weren't going to make a run for freedom. But his partner, Randy, snuck surreptitious glances, looking away every time the angry blonde met his eyes.

When they were finished, the men let them get dressed, then led them back to their tent. The blonde kept her arm around the brunette the entire time and stared down the men who leered and called out to them.

And so it went. The men led pair after pair of women to the river, forcing them to undress and bathe. Dan seemed respectful, given the circumstances, and none of the women were touched or threatened, but Anna's gut refused to unclench. She was on edge the entire time. Every single one of the women looked terrified.

By the time they got to the last tent, a small green one at the far edge of the inner tents, Anna's stomach was in knots. If Elin wasn't in that one, she was going to lose it. Her heart pounded as the ginger-haired man held the tent flap open, and when Elin emerged, neither Anna nor Kael could stop their whisper-soft noises of relief. She still wore the blue jeans and pale yellow T-shirt she had been wearing the day she was taken, and she looked dirty, as if she hadn't been allowed to clean up since.

Matt leaned in. "That's Elin, right?" When Anna nodded, he whispered, "Why do you think she's wearing handcuffs? None of the others were."

Next to Anna, Kael's whole body trembled. "Because they're scared. And they should be."

The men seemed to be having a problem, peering into the tent and gesticulating, plainly frustrated.

Finally Elin spoke to whoever was in the tent, and a tiny, thin arm appeared around the flap. Kael's trembling grew uncontrollable as a dark-haired girl, perhaps nine or ten years old, emerged from the tent. She ran to Elin's side and wrapped suntanned arms around her waist.

Dan grabbed Elin's upper arm and practically dragged her along behind him. He treated her far more roughly than he had any of the other women. The girl clung to Elin's middle, jogging to keep up, and staring around with huge, terrified eyes.

Anna flinched when a shaggy-haired man left the football game underway at the edge of the camp and loped toward the

men and their prisoners. There was something familiar about
him. When he glanced back at the football field, and Anna had a
decent view of his face, she gasped.

Brian. Running toward Elin was the man who had
threatened to strike her with a steel baton because she had hit
him during the attack. Anna whimpered at her sudden
realization.

"What?" Kael asked. "Anna, what's wrong?"

"That man." She pointed a shaking finger to Brian. "He
threatened to hit Elin with her own weapon after she was on the
ground. Trey had to forcibly stop him. His name is Brian." Kael's
eyes flashed. She leaned forward and stared as Brian intercepted
the small group only a few yards from the river. Elin lowered her
head in immediate deference. Seeing this uncharacteristic
response, Anna knew her own fears were warranted. Elin judged
this man to be a threat, as well.

She wished like hell she could hear what was being said.
Brian clapped the other guard on the back and pointed to the far
side of camp where some men were beginning preparations for
the afternoon meal. Dan gestured in the direction of Trey's tent,
but Brian dismissed him with an impatient wave. As the ginger-
haired man handed him something then walked back to camp,
Brian watched him go, a slow grin overtaking his face.

"No," Anna whispered. Sweat trickled down her spine, and
tiny hairs rose on the back of her neck. "No."

Kael grabbed Anna's hand. Her palm was damp and sweaty.
She looked at Anna with terrified eyes, then helplessly, they
both returned their attention to Elin.

Brian and Randy joked and laughed together, occasionally
turning to direct a comment to Elin. Brian dragged Elin along the
path by her wrists, much as the ginger-haired man had, but Anna
could see that he was much rougher by the way she stumbled
and struggled to stay upright. Still, Elin walked with her head
held high, not meeting Brian's eyes, but refusing to be beaten.

When they reached the river, Brian said something to Elin,
then to the cowering child. Elin shook her head, and the little
girl moved to hide behind her.

Without hesitation, Brian drew back and delivered a hard
backhanded slap across Elin's face. When Elin barely moved, he
hit her again. The child began crying so hard that Anna could
hear the keening, frightened sound from her position atop the
hill.

Kael's fingers were clamped around Anna's hand so tight
that she winced, fearful that her bones might break. She felt
utterly helpless, scared to expose their hiding place in broad

daylight when they had no plan whatsoever to take on these men who sorely outnumbered them. Watching Elin being mistreated nearly made her throw caution to the wind and leap to the rescue, but she held on to Kael, not only to keep her lover still, but also to stop herself from doing something stupid.

Brian turned to the other guard and growled something at him. Then he pulled Elin hard against his body, setting her off balance, while his companion swept in to grab the little girl and cover her mouth with one meaty hand.

"Please! Stop!" Elin cried out.

Brian's face was only inches from hers, and Anna was filled with crawling disgust when he leaned in, obviously sniffing Elin's hair. He must have said something because Elin nodded, and after a moment's hesitation, he stepped back and fiddled with her cuffs. All at once her hands were free, and she rubbed at her wrists. Then, with a look of intense discomfort, she brought her hands to the hem of her T-shirt.

Both men stared with unabashed interest as she removed it.

"I'll fucking kill them," Kael breathed, so quiet that Anna almost wasn't sure she had said anything. One look at the murderous rage in her expression, and Anna knew she had heard correctly. Kael was fast approaching her breaking point.

"And I'll help, when the time is right," Anna murmured. "We can't afford to reveal ourselves now."

"I know. But if they hurt her—"

Anna didn't say anything. She didn't know what she would do if that happened. She didn't think she could just watch.

Elin undressed, revealing the bandage on her calf. The one on her hand was gone; Anna was too far away to assess the damage, but she supposed that if Kate had visited, her wounds were being cared for. She tried to keep her thoughts clinical, desperate to ignore the ugly memories that tickled the edges of her mind at the way the men devoured Elin's naked skin with their gazes.

Nude, Elin held her hands out to Brian in unspoken obedience and allowed him to secure her wrists again. Anna swallowed as Elin was rendered almost completely helpless once more. She glanced over to Matt, who was averting his eyes from the scene with a look of pure shame.

The other guard released his captive after a signal from Brian, and the little girl ran to Elin and flung her arms around Elin's bare stomach. When Elin moved to stand in front of the child, she turned her back toward Anna and Kael. They gasped simultaneously as they saw previously smooth, pale skin now criss-crossed with ugly red marks that looked at least a couple of days old.

Kael growled again, louder this time, and Anna was so startled by the noise that she spent a few frantic moments scanning the camp to make sure none of the men had heard it. Anger surged through her veins, and she struggled with her own urge to growl. *Why are they so afraid of her? Has she been resisting them? Has she tried to escape? Or is this just about what happened when they attacked her?* She watched as Elin helped the little girl undress, shielding her from the men's eyes.

To Anna's surprise, Brian and Randy lost interest as soon as Elin led the girl into the river for her bath and got into conversation with her. Elin was careful to keep her body between the men and her little charge, and she knelt and talked cheerfully to the scared child as she washed with her cuffed hands. The girl even returned a few playful splashes, giggling and gazing at Elin with a look of adoration on her face. Anna broke into an unconscious smile at the sight. *I always knew she would be good with kids.* She lost her smile when Brian shouted something that made Elin look over her shoulder at him.

Elin nodded, then helped the child out of the river. The girl followed her, keeping her slim body behind Elin's, shivering in the cool air. Elin found the girl's clothes on the shore and bent awkwardly to gather them with her cuffed hands. Anna felt bile rise in her throat at the way Brian and his friend craned their necks to ogle her.

Elin formed a protective barrier between the naked child and the men as the girl got dressed. She didn't make a move for her own clothing, not that it would do her much good; it was obvious that Brian would need to release her hands to allow her to dress.

Anna shifted, uneasy about the way the men stared at Elin while her back was turned. Brian elbowed his friend in the side and whispered in his ear. His hand strayed to his crotch, and he stroked himself casually before pulling away with a laugh.

Anna moved slightly away from the tree she knelt behind and sat back on her feet, releasing Kael's hand so she could fold her arms over her stomach. Then she surged forward and planted both hands on the ground, shaken by the swift and sudden certainty that she was going to throw up.

Matt eased a tentative arm around her middle and whispered into her ear, "Anna, it's going to be okay."

Anna shook her head, watching fat tears fall into the dirt below her face. *It won't be okay.* She couldn't bring herself to say the words out loud. *If they do something to her, it won't be okay, because Kael and I will both get ourselves killed running down there.*

Or worse.

Matt moved his hand to press against Anna's back, keeping his touch light and non-threatening. "I promise, all right? I promise."

Somehow, the boy's earnest words helped, and Anna was able to fight back her nausea and sit up. Kael gave her a brief sidelong glance. She was deathly pale, sweating, and her eyes glittered with murderous intent. *I love you,* she mouthed.

I love you, too, Anna mouthed back. As much as she felt the relief of not watching what was happening to Elin, she also felt like a coward, when Elin was having to suffer without hope or knowledge of rescue. She shuffled back next to Kael, and they shifted a little to maintain their line of sight. Naked, Elin stood in front of Brian and held her wrists up in a silent request to be released from her bonds. He put his hands on his hips and shook his head as he told her something that made her take a step backwards. She gestured at the child, then glanced over her shoulder back in the direction of the camp.

Brian reached out and gripped Elin's shoulder where the lash marks had to be highly sensitive. Her cry of pain was quickly silenced by a lightning-fast slap across the face, and Brian shoved her cruelly toward the river, standing over her when she fell to the ground on her side. He gave her a light kick to the ribs, and she curled her body inward to protect herself.

The little girl took a few steps backwards when Elin fell, then started to run toward the camp with a panicky yelp. She made it only a few feet when Brian shouted to the well-built Randy, "Grab the kid!"

For a tense moment both Brian and Randy stared at the area where the tree line ended, waiting to see whether the child's cries had alerted any of their comrades. Elin also raised her head, opening her mouth as though she might scream as well, but Brian stopped her with a few harsh words and a swift kick to her stomach. When nobody came to interrupt their fun, Brian hauled Elin to her feet and summoned the other man, whose hand was clamped over the child's mouth. He brought the girl over, and Brian twisted a few strands of her dark hair around his fingers, saying something to Elin.

Without hesitation, she turned and strode into the river until she was submerged to her upper thighs, then she swiveled to face the men. She held her bound hands up and spoke to them. Brian leaned against a tree, folded his arms over his chest, and tilted his head to say something to his buddy. Randy laughed and called out to Elin.

Even from this distance, Anna recognized Elin's discomfort

at whatever the men said. Her shoulders stiffened, and she stood completely still. Anna imagined Elin's fists tightening, though she was too far away to see that. She could see Elin's chest expand and contract as she took a deep breath then exhaled, and then she saw Elin dip her hands into the water and bring them up to stroke her own breasts.

Horrified, Anna dug her fingers into the rough bark of the tree. She wasn't sure whether the men planned to rape Elin, but they sure as hell intended to degrade her. She dared a glance at Kael and found her weeping openly at the sight.

Brian called out to Elin, who stood still and pointedly gestured at the little girl. Brian said something to his friend, who removed the arm he had around the girl's middle so that he could clap his fingers over her eyes, rendering the child both mute and blind with the placement of his hands.

Anna just watched helplessly as Brian continued to call out instructions, and Elin moved her body as told, occasionally sliding her bound hands over her skin or twisting and turning to suit his demands. Anna kept hoping that Brian and his friend would tire of the game, especially as Elin began shivering violently in the cold water, but they seemed happy to keep suggesting new and embarrassing ways for her to pose and touch her own body.

Finally, Brian held up his hand and Elin stopped what she was doing, which had been to stroke between her legs for the sick amusement of the men. Brian waved her forward, out of the water. He met her halfway between the river and where he had been standing. He gestured at the ground and gave a command that had Elin shaking her head in immediate refusal.

Brian hit her again, and this time, red blood trickled down her chin. Elin shook her head once more, and Brian captured one of her breasts in his hand. As she winced in pain, he pointed to the girl, still held by his friend, then used the same finger to poke hard against Elin's collarbone, saying something Anna couldn't make out.

When Elin gave him a vigorous nod, he released her and once again pointed to the ground. Clumsily, and with obvious fear, Elin dropped to her knees in the grass. She stared straight ahead as Brian unzipped his pants.

"No!" Kael hissed. She backed away from the trees and stood, rubbing the palm of her hand across her scalp. "No, I can't let him do that. I've got to—"

So fast that Anna didn't know what was happening, Matt surged forward and tackled Kael onto the dirt. Kael grunted as she landed, grabbed for Matt, but the boy was already on his feet and running.

What the – ? Sick to her stomach again, Anna let her eyes flit back to the river, where Brian had exposed himself. Elin's face was turned to the side in disgust as he spoke and brutally grabbed at her red hair.

Anna realized what Matt was doing just as she reached Kael. She leaned in close, hissing, "Matt's going down there."

"So am I," Kael gasped. It was clear that Matt had knocked the wind out of her, and she struggled to regain her breath.

Anna was torn between following Kael blindly and preserving their rescue plans. "If we go down, it's over. Even if we kill ten of them, we'll never defeat thirty. Not like this."

"Stupid kid forgot to take his bat," Kael protested.

Anna looked over and saw Matt's weapon still lying in the dirt. Fuck. The boy was never going to win this fight.

Anna tipped her head back and released the loudest hawk call she could manage. It was something from teenaged days with Garrett, practiced in the summer under the tutelage of his adoptive father. She knew it would get somebody's attention. She would give Matt's rescue attempt a chance, but she needed to help in any way she could without getting herself killed.

Just as Brian looked up at the sound she made, faltering for a moment in his effort to force Elin's head closer to his erection, Matt burst from the trees. He stumbled down the relatively steep incline that led to the edge of the water. He didn't hesitate to dash across the river, splashing in a frantic attempt to reach Elin on the other side. He slipped once, twice, but kept going. Brian turned his head at the sound of the boy's approach and released Elin's hair.

Anna glanced back at camp, hoping and praying that someone heard the hawk cry. The camp guard closest to the trees looked around in mild interest, then tilted his head when Matt shouted at Brian as he emerged from the river.

"Leave her alone! What the fuck is wrong with you, man?"

Brian took a step backwards and frowned hard at the blond teenager storming toward him. Behind Brian, Randy released the little girl, apparently shocked by the sudden appearance of a stranger. The girl took one last, terrified look at Elin, then set off running and sobbing. It took the second man almost a full ten seconds to start after her.

By that point, Brian had swatted Elin aside, tucked himself back into his pants, and zipped up. He stepped up to Matt, meeting his challenge. Angry words were exchanged, then Brian swung at Matt, catching the boy hard in the jaw with his fist.

Anna moved her eyes back to the camp. Elin's little friend

had made it to the tree line when she ran smack into the front of the guard who had been standing closest to the river. Randy was hot on her heels, and he skidded to a stop when he saw his comrade. For a moment he stood, stunned, then he said something to the guard and pointed back at the river. The new guard, a man with a bushy mustache, swept up the child and jogged with Brian's companion back to the riverside.

Anna swept her gaze ahead of them, just in time to see Matt land a blow to Brian's face. Matt shook out his hand, wincing, as Brian's head snapped backwards from the impact. It took Brian only a moment to recover, and when he did, he lunged and tackled Matt to the ground. He drew back to deliver another punch to Matt's face but never had the chance to strike. The guard with the mustache set the little girl down and rushed to break up the fight.

"Come on." Kael grabbed Anna's arm and pulled her to her feet. "We're moving closer."

Anna let Kael tug her along by the hand. They jogged over the path that Matt had taken, to a better position. Anna knew they weren't being as quiet and cautious as they should as they tore through the trees, but she counted on the men being too distracted to notice them.

"Here," Kael hissed, and they dropped down against the trunk of a thick tree. Now only thirty feet from the scene of the fight, they peered through the foliage that obscured them from view.

"Brian, that's enough!" The guard with the mustache wrapped both arms around Brian's chest, restraining him from lunging at Matt again. Matt scrabbled backwards on his hands and feet, then struggled to stand. He turned his head and wiped at his nose with his arm. It came away red with blood.

"Fucking little bastard attacked me!" Brian roared. "I'll fucking kill you, you little prick!"

Matt stepped backwards as another guard ran into the clearing and joined the man with the mustache in restraining Brian. This guard looked to be only a year or two older than Matt.

The man with the mustache glared at Randy, who hovered to the side in awkward silence. "Go get Trey," he ordered.

At first, Randy stared down at where Elin sat naked in the grass, shaking, and didn't respond to the command. Then, after a sharp bellow from the mustached man, he said, "Sure thing, Doc."

Doc gave him a short nod, then tugged Brian's arm behind his back. "Calm down! Stop fighting me and calm the hell down so you can tell me what's going on here!"

"I'll tell you what's going on." Brian jerked his head at Matt, who held his T-shirt bunched to his face to soak up the blood that poured from his nose. "That little motherfucker there decided to try to take the woman and the girl. He tried to jump me, and you got here just as I was beating his ass—"

"He was...he was abusing this woman!" Matt's voice cracked on the words, but he stood his ground, straightening his shoulders. "I saw him trying to *force* her to...to—"

"That's bullshit!" Brian snarled. "And I'll kill you for even saying it."

Anna watched the two guards holding Brian look at each other behind his head. Doc raised an eyebrow, and the younger one gave him a slight nod in return.

Silently, Matt stepped over to Elin's discarded clothing, strewn across the grass in front of him. He bent and gathered the items with shaking hands, then walked to where Elin sat. Without a word, not looking at her body, he crouched down beside her and offered her his arm. Elin grabbed onto him with her cuffed hands and allowed the boy to pull her to her feet.

Meanwhile, Brian was going crazy. "Why the fuck are you holding on to *me*? I'm the one who's in this army. He's the one who doesn't belong here! Whose word are you going to take?"

Matt handed Elin her clothing, and she hurried to cover her naked body as two more men entered the scene. One was Randy, who looked as though he wanted to disappear into the trees. The other man was blond-haired Trey, who stormed over to Brian.

Matt turned and, in a show of quiet authority that left Anna breathless, said, "Will someone please uncuff this woman so she can get dressed?"

Trey stepped between Brian and Matt, glancing first at the teenager then at his red-faced subordinate. "What are you doing, Brian?"

"I was taking her to bathe, sir," Brian said, calming in the presence of his leader. He shook off the men who restrained him and ran a hand down the front of his T-shirt. "As you ordered."

"I ordered Dan and Randy to bathe the women," Trey said. "Not you. What are *you* doing here?"

"I took over for Dan, sir," Brian said. "He needed to take a trip to the woods, and he asked me to take the last pair to the river."

Trey looked over his shoulder at Randy, who immediately dropped his gaze to the grass. "Is that true, Randy?"

Randy's silence was indictment enough.

"What the fuck?" Brian cried out. "This guy jumps out of

fucking nowhere and attacks us, probably to take *our* girls, and *I'm* being questioned?"

Trey glanced at Brian, then turned to regard Matt seriously. He looked the boy up and down. His eyes flitted over to Elin, who still held her soiled clothing in front of her naked body, then back to Matt.

"What's your name?" he asked.

"Matt. And I wasn't trying to kidnap anyone. Do you really think a guy like me would take on these two guys? He was trying to hurt this woman. And I wanted to stop him."

"How was he hurting her?"

"He was...he was trying to..." Matt stuttered.

"He was trying to have intercourse with her?" Trey's face was expressionless, his eyes cold.

Matt started to shake his head, then stopped with an embarrassed shrug. "He was trying...he was making her do things, and then he tried...he wanted her to use her mouth..." He shifted in discomfort and shot Elin a nervous look. Elin lowered her eyes to the ground.

Trey swiveled on his feet, took two steps toward Brian, then drew back to deliver a hard punch to his face. "Stupid fucking *wasteful* bastard. You were going to traumatize her, and for what? A fucking *blow job*?"

Brian turned back to Trey, spitting out a mouthful of blood. His eyes burned with fury. "So you're taking his word over mine?"

"You've been dying to hurt her from the second we got her."

Anna blinked in surprise. There was something unsettling in Trey's tone of voice.

Brian opened his mouth, but Trey kept talking. "Don't you dare deny it. You can't get over the fact that she managed to land a few blows on you. That her lover killed Sue. Yes, I believe him. He's got no reason to lie, as far as I know, but you've got every reason. I don't know why Dan allowed you to take his assignment—I'll deal with him later—but I do know that you didn't volunteer so you could be a good guy."

Brian shook his head and muttered under his breath, but he kept his gaze to the ground, refusing to meet Trey's challenging stare.

"You'll report to me after lunch." Trey nodded to Doc, who put his hand on Brian's shoulder and encouraged him to turn in the direction of camp. "Collect the key for Elin's cuffs from him, Doc. I want you to hold on to those for now." Trey glanced over at Randy. "You, too. Report to me after lunch. I'll determine what to do with you then."

As Doc and the other guard led Brian and Randy away, Trey turned to Elin. "It happened like the boy said?"

Elin nodded, eyes downcast. "Yes, sir." She shifted the T-shirt in front of her chest, tugging on the cotton material to try to cover her upper thighs.

Anna's lip curled in disgust as Trey moved to Elin and wrapped his arms around her, pulling her into a close embrace. "You're okay now," he told her.

Elin nodded. She didn't pull away, nor did she accept the comfort Trey obviously thought he was offering. "Yes, sir."

Trey ran a gentle hand down the length of Elin's naked back, then stepped away to fish around in the pocket of his blue jeans. Clearly he carried a set of handcuff keys of his own. "Let me see your wrists."

Elin had to pull the T-shirt away from her bare breasts in order to obey the command. She held out her hands and waited patiently as Trey unlocked the cuffs. After he removed them, he captured Elin's wrists and rubbed them, asking softly, "How does that feel?"

Something about the tender nature of his voice and actions made Anna's stomach turn. She looked at Kael and caught the unabated anger in her indigo eyes.

"Better." Elin met Trey's eyes for a moment, flinched, then added, "Sir."

"Good." Trey planted a soft kiss on Elin's forehead. "Get dressed, darling. It's nearly lunchtime."

Matt looked away as Elin dressed, but Trey watched until she tugged her T-shirt back on, then he turned his attention to Matt.

"I'll talk to you in my tent first. I think we have a few things to discuss."

"All right." If Matt was afraid, he was doing an excellent job keeping that fear out of his voice.

"Do me a favor and grab the little girl, okay?" Trey said. "Let's get these two settled down for lunch, and then we can talk."

Matt nodded. He approached the dark-haired girl slowly and crouched in front of her so that he was at eye level. "Hey there. What's your name?"

When the girl didn't answer and kicked at the grass shyly, Elin said, "Her name is Lana."

"Lana. That's a pretty name." The girl wouldn't meet his eyes. "Do you want to come with me so you can eat lunch?"

"Go ahead, Lana," Elin said. "Matt's not going to hurt you."

Lana raised her eyes and assessed Matt, uncertain. Matt

smiled at her until, after only thirty seconds or so, Lana lifted her arms into the air in silent consent.

"Thanks, Lana," Matt scooped her into his arms. "I'll just follow you," he told Trey, and Anna sent a silent thank-you to him for not leaving Elin alone with the leader.

There was something about the way Trey treated Elin—however solicitous it seemed—that made Anna uneasy. From Kael's quiet sigh beside her, Anna knew she felt the same way.

"You're wonderful with children," Trey commented to Elin. From his tone, it was clear that he considered this a high compliment. "Somehow I knew you would be."

Anna shuddered.

"Thank you, sir," Elin mumbled.

"All right, then. You want to stay uncuffed for lunch?"

Elin didn't hesitate to nod vigorously. Anna wondered how often Elin got to be free from her restraints. From the brief flash of light in Elin's eyes at the suggestion, she guessed that it was relatively rare.

"You're going to behave?" Trey took Elin's upper arm, pulling her to his side.

"Yes, sir."

"That's all I need to hear." Trey gestured to Matt. "Come on. I imagine the food's almost ready."

Kael pulled away from the tree and sat back on her heels. She covered her face with both hands and exhaled shakily. "That was...too close."

Anna didn't want to think about it. She was having enough trouble maintaining her relative calm as it was. Her cheeks burned as though Elin's humiliation had been her own. "I guess now we know how Matt can help us," she whispered. *Thank God we found the boy. We would have been killed on the spot, but Matt...I think Matt might just be accepted into the fold for that one.*

"Come on." Kael grabbed her hand. "We're going back to our original position. I want to see the camp."

Anna allowed Kael to drag her through the trees once more. They were stealthy and sure-footed this time, careful not to attract attention now that the excitement had died down. They found the place where they had originally crouched, and they resumed their positions looking out over the camp.

Near the center, women sat in a large circle on the ground. Elin and the little girl, Lana, were led to a gap in the circle and encouraged to sit. Trey waved his hand at a subordinate, who immediately shackled Elin's left foot to the right foot of the woman sitting beside her in the circle, Elin's right foot to Lana's left foot, and Lana's right foot to the left foot of the woman to her right. Once finished, the men had all of their prisoners ready to eat lunch without risk of escape.

Anna gazed at Elin's profile. Her lover was too far away for Anna to easily read her face, but what she did see was troubling. Elin's shoulders were slumped in a kind of defeat that Anna was certain hadn't been there before Brian's attack. She looked lost and forlorn and barely responded even as Lana laid her dark head on her lap. Elin stroked the girl's hair with a heedless hand.

Trey retreated toward his tent, gesturing for Matt to follow. Matt hesitated a moment, then, while Trey's back was turned, quickly leaned down and whispered something into Elin's ear. Just as quickly, he stood up and hurried to follow Trey back to his tent at the upper edge of the circle of the camp.

For a long moment Elin didn't react. Anna stared at her lover, desperate for some clue as to Matt's words, and after a number of heartbeats, she saw it.

Elin lifted her face and looked into the blue sky overhead. She sat up straighter and threw her shoulders back in quiet determination. Then, so subtly that nobody around her seemed to notice, she turned her head to glance in the direction of the trees where Anna and Kael were hidden.

Anna swore she could see the slight, hopeful smile on Elin's face despite the distance between them. She knew without a doubt that Elin was aware she and Kael were out there, waiting and watching and utterly determined to rescue her. Anna closed her eyes and thanked Matt for restoring Elin's hope. To see her lose it for even a moment had been terrifying.

Kael gave her a nudge. "That asshole is on the move."

Anna opened her eyes and scanned the camp until she saw what Kael meant. Brian, having been released from the watch of his fellow guards, was stalking angrily away from the tents. He passed the field where the football game was breaking up and made it into the trees not far from where Kael and Anna were hiding. Nobody followed him. Anna assumed that he was either deserting or looking to blow off some steam before Trey meted out his punishment.

"I want to go talk to him," Kael growled. The tone of her voice left no doubt that talking wasn't all she wanted to do.

Anna felt her heart stutter in anticipation. Nodding, she squeezed Kael's hand with her own. "Then let's go find him."

Chapter
Nineteen

THEY FOLLOWED BRIAN'S trail almost a half mile through dense forest, snaking onto higher ground far above the river. Anna couldn't imagine that this encounter would end any way but in bloodshed. She felt as though they were stalking an animal, waiting for the first glimpse of their prey. A dark energy radiated from Kael's lean body, her desire to kill almost palpable in the cool afternoon air. Anna felt her own murderous rage, though she wasn't sure she could follow through with it.

If she killed Brian, it wouldn't be the first time she'd taken a life. After losing Garrett, she'd sworn that unless it was in true self-defense, her blind retribution for his murder would be the last time. She hadn't liked how lost she'd felt when she gave into her violent desires.

She didn't want to kill Brian. But she wouldn't necessarily mind if Kael did.

She understood the concept of vengeance, and more important, she was unwilling to direct Kael's actions in whatever came next. Anna saw that Kael was struggling with her own demons, and she would allow her to exorcise them however she needed. Hearing something, she signaled Kael and they both stopped walking and listened keenly. Anna gestured to a cluster of maples to their left. *He's there,* she mouthed, hearing angry muttering and harsh breathing.

When they caught sight of Brian, his back was to them. He was leaning against the broad trunk of a tree, forehead pressed to his forearm, his other hand busy in front of his body.

He remained oblivious as they approached from behind, panting in time with his aggressive strokes. "Fucking little redheaded bitch. When I'm fucking done with you — "

Brian's curses were cut short when his body slammed up against the tree as Kael tackled him. He grunted loud and struggled in an effort to turn and face his attacker. Kael wrapped one arm around Brian's neck while she produced a wicked-looking knife from the back of her jeans with the other. Anna hadn't even realized she was carrying it.

"Make one sound, and I'll slit your throat," she growled into Brian's ear and pressed the blade against his neck. She eased her free arm from his throat to make room for the knife and pinned him in place with a rough hand on his back. She kept him pressed hard against the trunk, face smashed to the side against the bark. "*After* I cut your dick off. Do you understand?"

Brian hesitated, then he gave Kael a fast nod.

"We're going to take a walk." Kael pressed the edge of the blade against his throat, drawing a thin red line of blood to the surface. With a glance at Anna, she said, "Get out the gun and keep it pointed at his head. If he so much as breathes wrong, put a bullet in his brain."

"No problem." Anna forced false confidence into her voice as she pulled the unloaded handgun from the back of her jeans. She made a show of cocking the gun, then pointed it at Brian's head. "My pleasure."

Kael clapped Brian on the back. "All right, asshole. When I step back, you move away from the tree and put your hands on your head. If you try anything, my partner here will blow your head off. Do you think anyone will come after you?"

Brian managed to shrug. "Eventually."

Kael stepped back and Brian immediately turned to look at Anna, who kept her gun pointed at his face. She met his stare, unwilling to be intimidated by the hatred in his cold eyes. *This man hurt Elin.* She was glad she didn't have any bullets in her gun.

Brian reached down to tuck his flaccid penis back into his blue jeans. Anna jerked her gun at the movement, and Kael's blade returned to Brian's throat before either Anna or Brian could react.

"What are you doing?" Kael hissed.

Despite his predicament, the loud-mouthed defiance they had seen at the river returned to the surface. "I'm just zipping up, faggot. Or did you want to do it for me?"

Kael delivered a sharp punch to Brian's kidney. "Shut up and walk."

Kael steered them farther away from the Procreationist camp, back toward where they'd stayed with Dr. Kate. Brian set the pace, with only a little additional urging from Kael with the tip of her knife against the small of his back.

About a half mile from Kate's home, they came upon a run-down old barn that had obviously been abandoned for years. Kael poked Brian in the back.

"In there," she told him. "We need to have a conversation."

Brian changed direction without a word. He pushed open the large front door, half-rotted off its hinges, and stepped inside. When he reached the middle of the barn, he turned to face Kael squarely for the first time.

"Wait, you're—" Brian's eyes widened in surprise. He dropped his hands from his head. "You're the faggot who was with the redhead. You killed Sue and Derek."

"I wish I could say it was nice to see you again." Kael gestured with her knife. "Get your hands back on your head."

Brian looked over to Anna. His expression betrayed his genuine confusion. "So who is she? Christ, faggot, you were fucking the redhead a week and a half ago. It didn't take you long to find a new one."

"Shut the fuck up," Kael snapped. Anna watched a vein pulse in the side of Kael's neck. Brian was trying hard to upset her, and it looked like he was doing a good job of it. "It's none of your business who she is. Stop looking at her. And stop calling me faggot."

Brian's lips curled into a defiant smile as he slowly dragged his eyes back over to Kael. "What's wrong, fag? Hit a little too close to home?" He laced his hands casually on top of his head. "You look like you're probably just as good at sucking cock as that little bitch we took from you. Elin, isn't it?"

Kael's eyes flashed with pure rage, and she came at Brian with the knife, slicing him across the chest. Brian's hands dropped from his head, and he moved as though to strike back at Kael, but Kael delivered a hard punch to his stomach that doubled him over. She followed up with a blow to his face, knocking him onto his ass on the dusty floor.

"Say anything disrespectful about her again, and I'll cut your tongue out." Kael stood over Brian, heaving in anger.

Kael was deadly close to losing control. Anna didn't understand why Brian insisted on pushing Kael's buttons like this. Didn't he see that Kael was dangerous?

On the floor, Brian shook with laughter. His T-shirt was stained with blood from the gash on his chest. "Man, the look on your face," he guffawed and pointed at Kael, who loomed over him. "You need to calm down. Don't worry, she loved everything we did to her."

Anna went hot at Brian's crude insinuation. She aimed the gun at his forehead. "What the fuck is wrong with you? Keep going and I'll kill you myself."

Brian released helpless laughter. "Your boyfriend is going to kill me, anyway." He raised hard eyes to Kael. "You think I don't realize that?"

"But you get to decide how you want to die," Kael said. "And how long you want it to take."

Brian's grin faded. "So, what do you want to talk about?"

"Anna," Kael said, "keep the gun on him while I find something to bind his hands."

"Do I look like I'm resisting?" Brian asked.

Just looking at him turned Anna's stomach. His cruel eyes reminded her of the first man who'd attacked her almost a year and a half ago. She'd had to stare into those empty green eyes for almost twenty minutes while he moved on top and inside of her. Anna struggled to keep the gun trained on Brian as her hand began to tremble. She took in the damage Kael had inflicted when she'd smashed him into the tree. Two of his fingers were bent at an awkward angle, obviously broken. His forehead was scraped raw, and blood trickled from his nostrils and mouth.

"Anna, huh?" Brian spit out blood and gave her a toothy, red-stained smile. "Pretty name. The faggot sure does find pretty girls."

Anna didn't respond. She couldn't find words that wouldn't betray her anger and fear, and so she didn't say anything. She tried to steady her hand, gritting her teeth to stop the gun from trembling.

"Are you scared of me? That's so sweet." Brian grinned up at Anna, feinting an attack. When Anna didn't flinch, he stuck out his tongue and waggled it crudely. "Are you as good as your friend? She's a real squirmer. I love that."

Just as Anna felt like she had no choice but to turn and flee from Brian's taunting or simply kill him on the spot, Kael saved her. She jogged up to Brian, drew back her foot, and delivered a sharp kick to his ribs. Leaning down, she pressed her blade to his throat again. "Hands behind your back."

Brian glared as though tempted to try to attack Kael, but when Anna kept the gun and her eyes pinned to him in silent warning, he allowed Kael to tie his hands with a worn length of rope.

"They'll be wondering where I am by this point," he commented in a casual voice. "I'm sure we left a trail."

"They'll think you deserted," Kael said. "And I doubt they'll bother coming after you. It didn't look like Trey was all that concerned about whether or not you were around after what happened at the river."

"Yeah, well he just wants that redheaded bitch to himself, that's all." When Kael didn't answer, he added, "If you think you're going to swoop in there and rescue your girl, you'd better think again. Trey's got her earmarked. He's not giving that little piece up."

Kael dragged him to a pillar and propped him against the wood. His hands, secured behind his back, rested on the floor between his ass and the wooden pillar.

"What are you talking about?" Kael asked.

"Trey gets to take a wife just as soon as we get home from this tour. He's done seven years with the army, and that's the deal."

"And he wants Elin?"

"He's been drooling over her since day one. Guess he must like the idea of a challenge."

"She's that important to him, yet you still tried to hurt her today?" Kael said. "I don't believe it. Why would you take that kind of risk?"

Brian shrugged and cast a dark look toward Anna. "You don't understand, man. They expect us to take these women, but we're not allowed to fuck them. We're out on the hunt months at a time, then we have to take them back for the guys who're allowed to marry. Or they just go into service—what a fucking waste that is. And what do we get? If we make it through seven lousy years—if we manage to avoid getting killed by some faggot like you for *seven years*—then we get to fuck again."

"Is this story supposed to make me feel bad for you?" Knife in hand, Kael knelt in front of Brian, resting her blade against his cheek. "Because I really can't feel bad for a rapist who isn't allowed to rape."

"It's all a bunch of bullshit, anyway," Brian muttered. "That fucking hypocrite. He thinks we're different somehow, him and me. But guess what? She doesn't want him either, but she won't have any choice. Know what I'm saying here? Just because I don't dress it up as being in the interest of the human race and all part of God's plan, I'm the bad guy."

Anna blinked in surprise at Brian's clear-headed critique of the moral distinction the Procreationists used to justify their actions. It told her that he understood the difference between right and wrong. He just didn't care. He understood perfectly what rape meant, and he yearned to commit it.

"Does Elin know that Trey plans to take her as his wife?" Kael played the tip of her blade over Brian's face, every so often pressing into his skin to raise a few drops of blood. "Has he told her?"

"He hasn't told anyone. But it's obvious. She'd have to be stupid not to notice he's paying a whole lot of attention to her. For all I know, he's already proposed."

"Proposed," Kael scoffed.

"I know," Brian said. "Hypocritical bullshit."

"Who's the kid?" Kael asked in a quiet voice. "The little girl with Elin."

"Fuck, man," Brian said with a tired laugh. "I don't know. Lacy? Lauri? We just picked her up along the way."

"What about her mother? Where is she?"

"We've got her, too."

"Then why is the girl with Elin?" Kael ran the point of the knife down the middle of Brian's lips, over his chin, down to the center of his neck.

"Because it's easier to keep her under control. That was Trey's idea. That cunt won't be trying to escape anymore now that she's got the kid to think about."

Kael nicked Brian's throat with a flick of her wrist. The blade moved so quickly that Anna didn't realize what had happened until a new line of blood appeared. "Don't use that word again," Kael said.

Brian stared past Kael, stiff and unmoving under the knife she still held against his throat. "What word?"

"You know the one." Kael moved her face in front of his, forcing him to meet hate-filled indigo eyes. "Her name is *Elin*. That's what you'll call her, understand? Nothing else."

Anna cleared her throat. They needed to get back on topic before Kael snapped and killed him. She thought about the ugly marks she'd seen on Elin's back. "Is that why she was beaten? Because she tried to escape?"

"The first time." Brian tore his eyes away from Kael's fierce stare to look at Anna. "Then it was because she was disrespectful to Trey. He wanted her broken as soon as possible, but she hasn't made it easy."

"I'm sure she hasn't," Kael said, a faint note of pride in her voice. "When does your second contingent return to camp?"

Brian rolled his eyes. "You think I'm the leader or something? I'm supposed to know everything? You jumped the wrong guy. Trey's the one with the radio."

"We heard it was tomorrow or the next day," Kael said. "Does that sound right to you?"

Brian stared hard at his feet. After a tense silence, he lifted his face and looked at Anna. "Your tits are bigger than Elin's."

Kael's punch knocked the back of Brian's head hard against the wooden pillar. Brian, one eye now swelling shut, managed a hysterical laugh almost as soon as Kael pulled away.

"Well, they are!" Brian said, giggling hoarsely. "Whose tits do you like?" He grinned at Kael. "I'd have a better idea if she took her shirt off, but I think I like Anna's."

Kael dropped down, placing her weight on Brian's knees to force his legs flat. Anna watched in horror as Kael unzipped their prisoner's jeans. Brian released an involuntary shriek when the blade touched his penis.

"Do you think I'm fucking joking around here?" Kael grasped Brian's penis with her free hand, angling the knife between the organ and Brian's testicles. "Do you want to lose this for the rest of the questions?"

"No!"

"Then talk. When does the second contingent return?"

"Tomorrow or the next day," Brian gasped out.

"Who guards the women at night?" Kael kept the knife pressed against Brian's exposed penis and stared directly into his eyes.

"I don't know, man. I haven't been doing guard duty lately."

Kael moved her arm slightly, and Brian yelped in pain. "Why the fuck do you insist on making this so difficult? Do you know how happy it would make me to cut you to pieces right now?"

"So do it," Brian snarled. "Stop talking about it, and do it already."

"Tell me about the guards instead," Kael said. "How many guards at night?"

"Six. Four around the perimeter and two standing guard with the prisoners."

"Do you communicate?" Kael asked. "Do you keep voice contact, have radios?"

"We've got walkie-talkies," Brian said. "We don't use them all the time. Nobody has ever really bothered us much. You'd have to be crazy to attack a force our size."

"I guess it's a good thing I'm crazy." Kael waggled dark eyebrows at Brian. "When do you usually wake up in the mornings? Who's the first person awake?"

"Trey doesn't take guard duty anymore, but he's always the first one awake. He likes to be the one to get the women up in the morning, check on them—"

"What time is that?"

Brian shrugged unhappily. "I don't know. Sunrise? Fuck, man, I'm usually asleep."

"Is Elin restrained in any way at night?" Anna asked Brian.

Brian snickered. "Yeah. She pretty much always wears the wrist cuffs. I think Trey stopped cuffing her ankles at night after he put the kid in her tent." He fell silent, apparently adding two and two. "You're really thinking about trying to get her back?"

"We really are," Kael said. "Any words of wisdom to help us on our way?"

Brian shook his head. "You'll never do it. There are too many of us. You're a hell of a fighter, but that didn't stop us from taking your woman the first time." He glanced at Anna, then back to Kael, as if genuinely mystified. "You should just take what you have and forget about the other one. Otherwise you'll lose them both, I guarantee it. And you'll die."

"You underestimate how much we want her back."

"He does," Anna said.

"Look, whatever." Brian's eyes were glued to the knife between his legs. "I'll make you an offer. If you let me go, I'll help you get Elin back."

"Bullshit," Kael said. "Why would we trust you to do anything like that?"

"Because I wouldn't mind walking away from this, you know?" Brian said. "Think you could find it in your heart to accept my help so you can get your woman back?"

"No," Kael said. "No fucking way. What would make you keep your word? It would be just as easy for you to stroll right back in there and tell them that we're coming as it would to actually do anything to help."

"I'm your only chance," Brian said.

"That would be the saddest thing in the world if it were true," Kael said. "But it's not. There's no fucking way I'm going to trust anything you say. You've lied to me before, and I'm sure you're lying to me now."

"What do you think I lied about?"

"You never touched Elin," Kael growled. "Tell me you didn't."

"Oh, I touched her. You saw me touch her today, didn't you?"

"You know what I'm talking about," Kael said. "You want me to lose control and kill you quickly. That's why you're pushing me. I'm not impressed."

"If I'm going to die anyway, as you say, I may as well have a little fun before I go," Brian said. "I just want you to know how your woman will remember me."

The longer Anna had to look at the man, the more her stomach churned. They'd gotten all they were going to get from him. He'd known Kael was going to kill him from the start; Anna didn't trust a single word that he said. "Are we about done here, Kael?"

"Yeah," Kael muttered. "I think we are." She turned to Anna. "Do you want to do this?"

Anna sputtered in shock. "Do I want to—"

Kael held out the knife. "You have just as much right as I do."

Anna shook her head and backed away. "No, thank you. I...he's all yours."

Brian's eyelids fluttered as Kael knelt beside him. He scooted away from Kael on his butt. "Listen man, for real. I never fucked her. I swear it."

"I know you didn't." Kael grasped Brian's bare penis and squeezed. "But I also know you wanted to."

Something about the timbre of Kael's voice told Anna that her lover was entering a very dark place. She took another step away from Brian and Kael. She kept the gun on Brian, unable to look away. She wanted Kael to hurt him, but she was almost afraid to watch.

Brian began to sweat. "Listen, man, I told you what you wanted to know. Why don't you just have your woman there put a bullet in my head and leave it at that?"

"No, I don't think that'll do it." Kael moved her knife so that one swift upward stroke would sever Brian's flaccid member. "You really seemed to enjoy making Elin suffer today. I think I'll enjoy doing the same to you."

Brian snapped. His face turned red, and he screamed up at Kael. "Fine! You know what? I *was* lying. You really think I didn't get at that little bitch before today? We've had her for days, faggot. We took turns—"

A flick of Kael's wrist and Brian released a bloodcurdling scream. Anna turned away, unable to stomach the sight of Kael's sloppy surgery. She could hear Kael chuckle, then the sound of a hard blow that stopped Brian's blubbering screams. There was a wet, gasping sound from Brian that suggested Kael had caused some serious damage. Anna stared at the wall of the barn and jerked in surprise when Brian managed another hoarse cry moments later.

Kael placed a gentle hand on Anna's shoulder. "Come on. We should get going."

Anna looked over her shoulder, catching a glimpse of red blood and Brian's pain-wracked body. She didn't focus on his face. She turned back to stare at the barn wall again. "You're not going to finish him off?"

Kael shook her head. "Slower this way."

"But what if they find him? He could tell them—"

"He'll bleed to death within an hour." Kael encircled Anna's waist with her muscular arm and pulled her close. "Besides, he's not going to be talking to anyone. I made sure of that."

"Good." Anna became aware of the guttural, grunting noises behind her and felt a sense of perverse justice at what Kael had taken from the man who had threatened to take Elin's innocence.

Kael interlaced her fingers with Anna's. "I understand, you know. Why you didn't want to kill him. I respect that."

"Thank you."

"Do..." Kael paused and swallowed. "Do you understand why I did what I did?"

A sad smile tugged at the corners of Anna's mouth. *I imagine Elin wouldn't, but...* "Yes," she said. "I do." She squeezed Kael's hand. "You acted for both of us." *And I've never felt safer in my life.*

Chapter
Twenty

"I THINK WE should go tonight," Kael said, moving restlessly against Anna on the bed in Kate's spare room. The planes of her lean face seemed starker than ever, cast into relief by the late afternoon sun that streamed through the flowing white curtains of the open bedroom window. They'd showered the moment they got back from the barn and were lounging naked on the bed, taking some time alone to plan their course of action.

"Shouldn't we try to contact Matt and coordinate something with him from the inside?" Anna's eyes flitted over Kael's body, all of a sudden aware of how much skin Kael was allowing her to see. Even littered with cuts and bruises, her lover was sleek and gorgeous.

"I don't want to wait. We can't take the chance that Trey's partner and the extra men might show up tomorrow."

"So how are we going to do this? It's time to worry about the plan, right?"

"Two plans, I think. The plan for a perfect world, and then the plan if things don't go exactly as we hope."

Anna rested her head on Kael's shoulder and melted into her embrace. "What's our perfect world plan?"

"We sneak in there late tonight, take out the six guards Brian told us about without alerting any of the others, then we get the women out of there as quickly and quietly as possible. If we're lucky, we can do it without waking anyone up."

"That does sound like a plan for a perfect world." *But what are the chances that we'll be able to poke our heads into the tents of fourteen frightened women and quietly inform them that we're the good guys, without creating at least a little noise?* Running a fingertip around the smooth skin of Kael's belly button, she asked quietly, "What's the back-up plan?"

"Explosives. Kate says her husband Walter knows how to make some. We could use them to create confusion while you're getting the women out of there. If Elin can help the other women escape by that point, maybe you can take care of the men with me." Kael cupped the side of her face. "I plan on killing them, Anna. One way or the other, I think I have to kill them all."

"Even if they don't wake up?"

Kael's eyes flashed. "We won't be able to just steal fourteen women from them without having them come after us. I want this mission to be stealthy for as long as possible, but it's not going to end that way. I can't leave Trey alive, at the very least. Not if he really does want Elin as a wife."

"You're right, he has to die," Anna whispered. "I'm not as...excited...about killing them as you are, but I'll do what needs to be done."

"I *am* excited about killing them." Kael's dark eyes shone with a danger Anna had only sensed before that day.

Seeing Kael's fierce protectiveness, unrestrained and unapologetic, bolstered Anna's confidence. "So we sneak in, take out the six guards, and get the women out. Then we go after Trey first?"

"Yeah. If we're lucky, we can kill him in his sleep."

"God, I hope I don't have to show that gun to anybody. And on that note, what are we going to do about Trey's gun? I know he has one. For all we know, so do some of the others."

"Call it a hunch, but I think Trey will be the only one with a gun. Nobody pulled one today at the river. If there had ever been a time, I'm thinking that would have been it."

That's probably true. Still, all it'll take is for Trey to wake up with that gun... "At least Elin knows that we're coming for her." Anna called to mind that moment when she saw Elin's defeated posture transformed as hope returned. "Did you see Matt tell her?"

"Yeah," Kael said in a hoarse voice. "Remind me to give that kid a big hug when we see him next."

Anna studied Kael's face. A fire flared deep in her belly, and she blinked in surprise. The adrenaline that had her shaking ever since they'd captured Brian suddenly left her, and she found herself weak with arousal. Immediately, she felt guilty that she could even think about making love with Kael when the woman they both loved was in such danger. Yet the darkness she saw in Kael excited her, and Anna was certain she was the only one to experience it this way. She was the first person to see this side of Kael and to accept it.

Kael's strength in dealing with Brian had renewed Anna's hope and at the same time had thrilled her in a way she couldn't have predicted. Bearing witness to that passion, that power, had struck something deep inside of her. Kael was utterly, wholly determined to get their lover back, and nothing was going to stop her. That intensity of focus gave her an energy Anna could feel and see, and she found it irresistibly attractive.

Kael lowered her eyes to Anna's bare breasts, then shrugged. "You know, I'm more alive right now than I have been since they took Elin."

Brutal torture helps, huh? Well, I won't question what works for Kael in this case. Anna drew her closer and said, "I want to feel you."

She curled into Kael's body and pinned her narrow hips to the bed by slinging her leg over Kael's thighs. Naked Kael was a rare treat and Anna intended to enjoy it as much as possible. Rather than answer, Kael eased her thigh between Anna's and kissed her slowly. Anna kissed back, then groaned when her thigh found the warm heat between Kael's legs.

Kael ground her center against Anna's thigh, squeezing her hips with strong fingers. She pushed her tongue into Anna's mouth with a hungry moan and rode Anna's thigh. For a long, exquisite instant, Anna could think of nothing but the heat and force of her lover, then she came back to the moment. There would be time to express how she felt later. Their mouths lost contact, and they drew back slowly from one another.

Anna caught her breath. "I know what you mean about feeling alive. That's why we're...like this, I guess."

"I guess." Kael stroked the curly hair between her legs.

"I feel...like we can do this," Anna said.

Tenderly, Kael placed a delicate kiss on her forehead. "Thank you. It makes a difference—that you believe that." She gave a small sigh, tinted with regret, and ceased her sensual caresses, rolling onto her back. "I think a couple of hours before dawn would be best for the rescue. We'll go back tonight just before dark for one last reconnaissance mission. We can try to get a message to Matt then, but we won't actually infiltrate their camp until the early hours of morning. That's when their sleep will be the deepest. If they wake up, it'll still be dark enough to really take advantage of their disorientation."

Three loud knocks on the bedroom door cut off Kael's words and sent them both scrambling under the comforter. Anna stared up at the ceiling, amazed at how quickly Kael had managed to roll off and hide her nakedness. "Anna? Kael?" Kate called from the hall. "I'm sorry to bother you kids, but—"

"That's all right." Anna sat up in bed, folding her arms over her naked chest. "Come in."

Kate poked her head around the door. "You two need to

come downstairs. Right now. Matt is here." She drew back, giving them privacy.

"Matt?" Kael sat up next to Anna, bringing the comforter with her. "Is he okay?"

"He's fine." Kate's voice was anxious. "He needs to talk to both of you. They're expecting him back soon, so—"

"Of course," Kael said. "Just give us a few minutes. We definitely want to talk to him."

"I'll make you some hot tea," Kate said. "We'll be in the kitchen."

As soon as the door had closed, Kael jumped out of bed and stumbled across the room for her clothing. "I guess I should tell her I'm not a guy," she said as she dressed.

"I think she's guessed that already." Anna dug in her bag for some fresh clothes, amused when she caught Kael's faint look of surprise.

"What makes you say that?"

Anna shrugged. "Just a feeling." Unable to help herself, she broke into a face-splitting grin. "I can't believe the kid made it back here so soon."

"I know," Kael said. "I want to have a nice, long talk with him. We may be able to modify our plans a bit with his help."

"What do you have in mind?"

Kael gave her a dangerous smile. "Just something to tip the odds in our favor a little more, that's all." She buttoned her jeans, rubbed a hand over her shaven head, and turned intense eyes on Anna. "We're going to have Elin back by tomorrow, you know."

"Yes, we will." Now dressed, Anna stepped over to pull Kael into a hard hug, which was returned full force. There was no longer a question in her mind. One way or the other, Elin was coming home that night.

MATT STOOD UP from the table when Anna and Kael burst into the kitchen. His upper lip was cut and swollen, so his reassuring smile was painful to watch. There was an ugly, purple bruise under his left eye, and his favorite blue T-shirt was torn and bloody.

"She's okay," he blurted. "She's had a rough time, but she's okay."

Anna stepped over to Matt and pulled the boy into a tight hug. "Thank you, Matt," she whispered into his ear and pressed her nose into blond hair. "Thank you so much for today."

Matt gave her a shy squeeze. "Don't thank me. It was the only thing to do."

"Are you okay?" Anna touched Matt's cheek, wincing in sympathy when he inhaled sharply. "That guy really beat the shit out of you."

Matt gave Kael a sheepish look. "Yeah. Some hero I am, right? If the other guards hadn't come running, I'm not sure what would have happened."

Kael shook her head. "Don't say that. You were a hero today. I'll never be able to thank you enough for stopping that asshole before he...before he hurt Elin." To Anna's surprise, Kael closed the distance between her and Matt and pulled him into a brief one-armed hug. She slapped him on the back, then pulled away, averting shining eyes from his awed gaze. "I owe you, man."

Matt shrugged. "I'm sorry I knocked you down. I was afraid they would recognize you."

Kael gestured at the table. "How about we sit down and talk before you have to leave?"

With an eager grin, Matt dropped into his chair for a quick sip of Kate's tea. Anna sat down and lifted Zep onto her knee, stroking the hot little body as she waited for her own tea to cool.

"Have you spoken with Elin?" Kael asked. "I know you wouldn't have had much privacy, but..."

Matt gave them a nervous nod. "I delivered some water to her tent. She said to tell you that she's all right. I told her we'd all seen the marks on her back, and she got upset about that. She says to tell you...she swears they haven't touched her. What happened today at the river, that was the farthest things have gone."

"You think she was telling the truth?" Anna's throat felt parched, and she took a sip of tea. "Or do you think she's afraid for us to know?"

"I think it's the truth. She swore it was. And...I think that Trey would have been all over it if that had happened."

"Well, it's sure a great thing he's such an ethical guy," Kael snarled.

Matt chuckled, a hollow sound. "Isn't it?"

"So Trey recruited you?" Kael asked.

Matt darted shy eyes over to Kate. She nodded and he replied nervously, "I let him think so. He sent me into town to pick up supplies so that I can leave with them the day after tomorrow."

Kael gave Anna a sidelong glance. "So we've got two days."

Matt shook his head. "No, Dex gets back with the other guys tomorrow night at the latest. We'll need to do something before then...probably tonight, to be safe."

Kael exhaled. "Well, that was our plan, anyway. Probably a

few hours before dawn."

"They've got guards," Matt warned.

"Six of them," Kael said. "Brian told us. Four around the perimeter and two guarding the women at the center."

Matt blinked in surprise. "Brian? Do you know where he went? Trey was freaking out when he didn't come back after lunch."

Kael's eyes flashed dark satisfaction. "Brian won't be coming back."

"Oh." Matt cleared his throat. "Well, I don't know much about the guards. I just know that Trey told me not to worry about pulling guard duty until I've been trained."

"Damn," Kael swore under her breath. To Anna, she said, "It would have been nice if Matt had been one of the six."

"What tent are you in?" Anna asked. *We need to know who not to kill.*

Matt gestured to a pile of supplies on the floor. "I just picked it out. It'll be the only green and purple tent out there."

"Okay," Kael said. "So what have you learned?"

Matt leaned back in his chair. "Trey has a radio in his tent. Dex called him on it while we were talking. He said he would be returning with one additional female prisoner, probably after noon tomorrow. Maybe not until dark." Matt paused, then said, "Trey told Dex about what happened with Brian today. With Elin. Trey was really pissed."

"Was he?" Kael asked, voice strained.

"Yeah. Dex thought Trey should flog Brian as an example to the other men. Seems like they struggle with controlling them sometimes, especially the new recruits. Trey grilled me about how I would treat a woman prisoner. To be honest, I think he really wanted to recruit me because I helped Elin. So, he figures I'm not just a rapist looking for women."

Kael released a disgusted snort. "Funny. I thought that was the movement's big draw—the perfect place for a rapist looking for an opportunity."

"With God's blessing." Matt cast shamed eyes to the table. "I felt awful telling Trey just what he wanted to hear from me, agreeing with the things he said. The guy's a piece of shit. We can't let him take those women."

"We're not going to," Kael said.

Kate gazed around the table at each of them. "You're talking about a wide-scale rescue? I hope the three of you have one hell of a plan."

"We kind of have two," Anna said.

Kael gave her a smoldering look that was meant for her

alone, full of heat and need and deep, abiding love. Anna felt that look between her legs.

"I'm not sure either is very impressive," Kael drawled. "We're hoping one will work."

"So what's the plan?" Matt asked. "Are you bringing weapons? Will you come to my tent when you get there?"

"The plan is to conduct a rescue mission as quietly as possible for as long as possible," Kael said. "I don't want to start fighting any sooner than absolutely necessary. There's too much chance that the women will get hurt. Not to mention the fact that the men could use them against us."

"How are we going to get to the women's tents without anyone noticing?" Matt asked.

"First, Anna and I are going to take out the guards. If we do it well, we won't even wake anyone up. Then we'll start getting the women out of there. Elin first, so she can help us with the rest. Anna and Elin will have to tell them what's going on. If you or I stick our heads into their tents in the middle of the night, we'll be asking for a scream or two."

"Maybe Matt can get a message to Elin, and she can spread the word ahead of time," Kate suggested. "If the women know to expect something, it'll make things easier for you."

"No good," Kael said. "I don't want people talking about what's going to happen. All it would take is one of those guys catching wind of the plan...Trey's not an idiot. He could even guess it's about Elin. Then what? He'd probably beat the truth out of her."

Anna shuddered. To Kate, she said, "I wish we could risk it, but I agree with Kael."

"I know it's a dangerous plan." Kael took Anna's hand without looking and stroked the length of her fingers. "I expect that we'll be forced to fight at some point. In fact, even if we got every last woman out without disturbing a soul, I'd still need to go back to kill Trey."

Matt's head snapped up from his serious contemplation of his now-empty tea mug. "You're killing Trey?"

"I have no choice. Brian told us that he wants Elin for himself. I can't take the chance that he'll come after us."

"But any of the men could come after you," Matt argued. "A lot of them are very devout about their beliefs. They're not all just assholes hoping to take advantage of their prisoners."

"I understand that." Kael gave Matt a hard look. "That's why I'll have to kill as many of them as possible. Maybe all of them."

Kate gasped. "Oh, honey..."

"Kate, they want to take those women back with them and

force them to bear children. They want to take that little girl we saw today and take her innocence away as soon as she's able to reproduce. These are evil, soulless people. I refuse to apologize for wanting them dead." Her eyes darkened, and she threw her shoulders back. "Every single one of them. For every woman they've ever hurt."

Blinking in surprise at the impassioned words, Kate touched Kael's free hand. "I'm not judging you, young man. I'm just reacting to the scope of your plans."

Kael fell briefly silent, apparently calming herself down, then she said, "I was hoping your husband could show me how to make some explosives. I figure that in the worst-case scenario, if the men start waking up, we'll have something to distract them with."

Kate nodded. "I've sent word to Walter that we need him to return home right away. He should be back soon, and I know he'll help you with the explosives. He owes that group a payback." Kate's smile was grim. "I'm sure he'd love to go with you, but he's the one who lost a leg. Afraid he wouldn't be much help against their numbers."

"There are twenty-five guys, not including Brian," Matt said to Kael. "All they have to do is start climbing out of their tents, and you're surrounded."

Anna's heart rate picked up as she thought of something. "We could zip-tie their tents closed. It wouldn't keep them from getting out, but it would slow them down."

Kael's eyes lit up. "That's a great idea. Matt and I could handle it while you and Elin get the women out."

"I still think you're being extremely optimistic," Kate said. "All you need is one light sleeper to ruin your plan before you even begin."

"That's why we'll need explosives. We have to be prepared to wage one hell of a war if need be, but we'll try to avoid it, if we can." Kael pressed her fingertips to her temple. The tightening of her lips was almost unnoticeable, but not to Anna.

Anna reached out to stroke the soft, dark hairs on Kael's arm. She felt Kael's muscles twitch beneath her touch and could sense her rising frustration. "Does anyone have any other ideas?"

Kate snapped her fingers and pointed at Matt. "If I were to give you a couple of bottles of wine, do you think you could share them with the men?"

"Maybe. I mean, I'm not sure that Trey would drink any, but very light drinking is allowed. Some of the guys were saying we'd be celebrating when we get back to Philadelphia. But I don't think they'd let anyone get drunk. That would ruin their security."

Kate grinned. "We don't have to get them drunk. All we need is to put something in there that will make them sleep. That could really help this rescue mission of yours."

"That's a great idea," Kael said. "But what if they can tell it's drugged? That would tip them off."

Kate pulled a small glass bottle of clear liquid from the cupboard. "Not a problem. This stuff is tasteless and odorless. You won't have to give each man very much to put him out in just an hour or two. Sometimes I use large dosages of this stuff on my patients when I'm doing surgery."

"How long will they sleep?" Kael examined the bottle carefully.

"Right through the night."

Anna stroked Zep, who'd fallen asleep in her lap. "And if the guards sneak a little bit, they'll be drowsy."

"You could give me the drugged wine and maybe some extra that I could slip into the water." Matt sounded excited. "That way it won't matter if some of them don't drink the wine."

Kael shook her head. "No way, man. I don't think you should be carrying around something like that. If they catch wind of the fact that you were trying to drug them, we're fucked. I don't want to take any unnecessary risks. Even if we can drug even half the men, it'll help."

"So how will I know when you're there?" Matt asked.

"We'll take out the guards, then come to your tent. Anna will go get Elin while you and I start zip-tying the tents closed."

"A few hours before dawn?"

"Yeah."

Matt laid his head down on his arms. "I'm going to have a heart attack before then, just thinking about this."

Kael glanced to Anna, then, after a moment of hesitation, reached out and ran her fingers through Matt's hair, ruffling the blond locks affectionately. "You're a brave man, Matt. And you're my brother forever for all your help."

Matt gazed at Kael with humble eyes. "Thanks, Kael. That means a lot."

Anna rose from her chair and gathered Matt in a warm embrace, Zep squirming between them. "I love you, Matt. Be safe tonight."

He planted a kiss on Anna's cheek. "I will. The same goes for you." He returned Kael's playful scowl with a toothy grin. "Both of you."

Chapter
Twenty-one

THE SOFT STRAINS of Jimmy Page's guitar filled the bedroom when Kael returned that evening. Judging by the smile on her face, explosives-making had been a success.

Anna reclined on the bed, having said goodbye to Matt hours ago. In one hand she held a snapshot of Elin, and in the other, a rope toy that she used to wrestle with Zep absentmindedly. The picture was old; Elin as an infant, cradled in her mother's arms. Her mother was smiling, cradled in her father's arms. They looked like such a happy family.

Kael shut the bedroom door with a tired sigh and nodded at the small stereo on the oak dresser. "What's this?"

Anna raised stinging eyes to Kael, welcoming the warm rush of affection that flooded her body at the sight of her lover. "Led Zeppelin." She surrendered Zep's toy and picked up the case to Elin's favorite CD. "'Ten Years Gone,' it's called." She smiled at the case, a familiar treasure. "I was just looking through Elin's bag I was carrying that day. I didn't even realize we still had this."

Kael hesitated only a moment before she sat on the end of the bed. Zep scrambled over to her, whimpering excitedly, and she managed an affectionate smile as she stroked his head. "It's pretty. I'm glad she didn't lose her CD. I know we could have always picked up another copy, but—"

"I know. She doesn't have much from her dad, and I'd be really upset if she had to lose any of it." She showed Elin's beloved photograph to Kael. "Especially this."

Kael took the picture and studied it with a wistful expression. "I guess you were carrying the right bag, huh?"

"I guess so."

Kael set the photograph and CD on the nightstand, then stretched out beside Anna, lacing her hands behind her head. "So you've just been sitting up here thinking about Elin?"

"Yeah. I guess after seeing her today, I can't really stop thinking about her."

Kael pressed a kiss to Anna's temple. "I've been thinking about her, too. For days now I'd been trying not to think of her at all. It hurt too much. But after today..."

Anna turned and focused on Kael's face, so close to hers. "After today?"

"After today I know we're going to get her back." Kael's jaw tensed, then relaxed when Zep sprawled on his back between them. "I'm utterly fucking determined to go in there tonight and kill anyone who tries to stop us." Her eyes met Anna's. "I mean it. She's *ours*."

"She is." Anna rested her head on Kael's shoulder and entangled their fingers. "And I thank you for that, by the way."

Kael stroked her thumb over Anna's hand. "For what?"

"For being okay about sharing her heart with me."

"Elin wasn't going to abandon me because of you," Kael said. "She would never do that. She told me, after the first time we made love, that she would never stop loving me. And Elin...never lies. I probably wouldn't have believed any of a million people who could have told me that, but I believed her."

"So do I," Anna said.

Kael dropped a tender kiss on her head. "Once I stopped being stubborn and started giving you a chance, I just...knew you felt right. You really fit. And you made Elin so happy."

"I couldn't believe it when she told me how she felt," Anna whispered. "That morning, when we..." She smiled, blushing at the memory. "I was so worried about how you would feel, but you were so sweet to me that day."

"Aw, hell," Kael muttered. "I already had a crush on you by then. Elin had been teasing me for days about how wonderful you were."

"Really?" She shook her head, overcome. "I never thought I was ever going to be with anybody. I can't believe I found both of you."

"I know exactly what you mean. Until I met Elin, I had no idea what love even was. I had no idea that sex wasn't just some disgusting thing that other people did to you."

Elin had reinvented the world for both of them, it seemed. "Tell me about when you met Elin. Tell me about falling in love with her."

Kael's toothy grin took Anna by surprise, as did the pink hue that rose in her cheeks. "Oh, God. I was clueless."

"Tell me."

Kael sighed and pulled Anna closer. "Well, I think I was in love with her from the moment I found her sneaking around my campsite. She was just so...beautiful. Gorgeous. And her eyes...they were so bright, you know? She was so untouched."

"She thought you were a man," Anna said, eager to hear Kael's side of this story.

Kael snorted. "I don't know, maybe for a little while. I'm pretty sure she saw through me right from the start."

"Really? I find that hard to believe. You're very convincing."

Kael's chest swelled with pride, and Anna giggled. "She was the first person who ever made me feel understood. Accepted."

"Did you know that she was attracted to you, too?"

Kael groaned. "That was part of being clueless. Looking back, she was *awfully* flirtatious. At the time, I thought she was just being sweet. I didn't figure it out right up until the second she kissed me. That was about a week and a half after we met."

"So?" Anna grinned. "Tell me how that happened."

Kael's face turned a lovely shade of red. "This is all a little embarrassing, you know."

Anna slapped Kael's shoulder with a gentle hand. "You want to talk about embarrassing? I couldn't stop shaking the first time Elin and I made love. And I burst into tears right after my first orgasm."

Kael gave her a brief, sidelong glance. "Elin gave you your first orgasm?" There was a hint of quiet wonder in her voice.

"Yeah." Anna blushed and grinned down at Zep's golden fur.

"Don't be embarrassed." Kael stroked the side of Anna's face with her fingertips. "I think that's wonderful."

"It was wonderful." The sadness in Kael's gaze kept her silent, unwilling to ask the obvious question and bring up a painful memory. "So tell me about that first kiss." She pressed her lips to Kael's. "Please."

Kael traced her tongue over Anna's lower lip. "*She* kissed *me.*"

Anna pulled back with a chuckle. "I kind of figured that much."

"It was her birthday. She was bathing in the lake we'd camped near, while I cleaned up after breakfast," Kael said. "I was trying to keep my distance at first, but I heard her crying and I went to check on her. That was the first time I'd ever been able to really look at a naked woman. In real life, I mean. I couldn't help staring, but I felt so dirty for wanting—"

"And as far as you knew, she still thought you were male."

"Yes," Kael said. "It was ridiculous, the way she trusted me. When I found her crying, she didn't even try to hide her body. I could see her nipples just below the surface of the water. She was breathtaking. I hated myself for thinking the things I did, for what I wanted to do to her." Anna felt Kael's heartbeat pick up beneath her hand. "I really thought that she should be more scared of me. I was scared of me, back then."

"What did she say?"

"That she missed her dad. It was her twentieth birthday, the first he hadn't been around to celebrate. I told her I was sorry and left her to finish her bath. Then I started planning how to make her birthday a happy one. Even if her father couldn't be there."

"What did you do?" Anna asked. Kael was a romantic and didn't even know it.

"We were camped near a city, so I took her to a bookstore. She'd told me how much she enjoyed reading, so I had her pick out a few, told her I would carry the extras so she could take more. She found this book by Virginia Woolf, *Orlando*, that she told me she loved. I asked her to read it aloud in the evenings after dinner." Kael released a quiet snort. "I couldn't believe how happy that made her, the idea of reading to me. After the smile I got for that, well, I decided my new purpose in life was to make Elin happy. I was addicted to her smile."

"So is that when she kissed you?" Anna grinned, eager to get to that moment.

Kael gave her a patient smile. "No. It was after dinner that night. I'd caught a rabbit—that's when I found out it was her favorite—and for dessert we had some berries I'd picked earlier. She read the first chapter of *Orlando* to me, then we sat by the fire, just talking, for hours. I'd never talked to anyone like I talked to her that night. It made me feel so good. I was so content there with her. And then she was telling me about a kitten she used to have...I guess I was staring at her lips as she spoke. The next thing I knew, she leaned over and kissed me."

"And?"

"I pulled away." Embarrassment colored her voice. "Our mouths barely touched. She scared me so badly."

"Was it terribly awkward?"

Kael shook her head. "No. Elin handled it so well. She apologized if she offended me. I told her she hadn't, so she apologized for taking me by surprise. She thanked me for making her birthday so special. And she told me that she...thought I was sexy. That it had taken her a week and a half to work up the nerve for that kiss. She asked me if I'd rather she not kiss me again."

Anna chuckled in sympathy. "And you told her no, I imagine."

"Of course I told her no," Kael said. "When she kissed me, I was so excited, but I was also terrified. I was having all these feelings, all these desires I wasn't used to. And I felt...embarrassed. A little ashamed. But I wanted her. I loved her already, and I wanted to feel her love me."

"Did you make love that night?"

"Oh, no. We didn't even kiss again. I was too raw. But that was the night we started sleeping next to each other. Elin asked me if we could zip our sleeping bags together. She wanted to be close to me, she said. I was afraid I wouldn't like sleeping with someone so near, but...with Elin, it was great."

"She *is* amazing at cuddling," Anna murmured.

"When I woke up the next morning, I was practically wrapped around her. She was sound asleep and holding me like she never wanted to let go. It felt so natural...and my fear just disappeared. I couldn't be afraid. Not with her. To this day, I can't explain how she got past my defenses so quickly. She was just—"

"Elin."

"Yeah." Exhaling slowly, Kael said, "The whole next day I really noticed how I felt when I was with her. Safe. Happy. I hadn't felt happy like that since I was a child. Being with her filled up the emptiness I had inside of me. I kissed her that next night. I felt so clumsy about it at first. I'd never actually tried to kiss someone back before. I think I was all tongue."

Anna grinned as she imagined a younger, fumbling Kael. "Well, you've certainly perfected your technique since then."

"I've made it a point to practice a lot." Kael nuzzled Anna's hair. "Elin was so patient with me. That night after I first kissed her, well, we must have spent hours kissing. Nothing more than that. Just kissing. I learned a lot."

"Did she know you were a woman by then?" Anna asked.

"Yes," Kael said. "But I didn't know she did. I wouldn't let her touch my chest, even though I had my breasts bound. That night of kissing, it was more than I'd ever hoped to experience, but I ended it feeling guilty. I felt like I was taking advantage of her. Here was this beautiful girl who thought I was something I wasn't, and I was letting things escalate because she was making me feel so good."

"When did you tell her?"

"The next night. We were kissing again, and she put my hand on her breast." Rumbling with quiet laughter, Kael said, "I nearly passed out when she did. I wanted to touch her everywhere, but I felt so dirty and guilty. I felt no better than any of the men."

When Kael trailed off, Anna asked, "What did you say?"

"I told her that we needed to stop. That I needed to tell her something. And she..." Kael snorted. "That sweet girl, she told me not to worry. She told me that she knew who I was. She knew I was worried about showing her my body because I thought she was expecting something else. She leaned in really close to me and whispered, 'I know you're a woman. I also know that I'm in love with you.' My heart almost stopped."

Anna grinned at the story. She could picture her lovers in her head: Kael shy and frightened, Elin brave and determined. She tilted her face so she could kiss Kael's jaw. "That must have been a relief."

Kael laughed out loud. "Relief doesn't even begin to describe...I was walking on air. I was invincible. If Elin hadn't been genuine, if she'd turned around and hurt me...I think it would have destroyed me. I gave my heart to her that night, completely. She took a piece of me that I'm never getting back."

"Elin told me she was nervous her first time with you. Could you tell?"

"A little bit, maybe. I was a lot more nervous than she was, that's for sure. But I knew it was her first time, and that she wasn't quite sure what we were doing, either, so that made me feel better."

Anna pulled back so she could look at Kael's face. "So?" she asked with a goofy smile. "How was it?"

Kael's face was red, but she couldn't stop her shy grin. "Amazing, of course. I was clumsy and nervous and shaking, but I made her come." She flexed her fingers where they curled around Anna's shoulder. "I felt it on my hand. It was fucking incredible. At first, when she told me what she wanted me to do to her, I couldn't believe it. I'd thought about those things, of course, but...I don't know, I thought it was sick, in a way. That I should feel horrible for even thinking it. Watching how it made Elin feel, how much she enjoyed it, I realized that it wasn't. It wasn't disgusting at all."

For a moment, Anna was lost in a memory of making love with Elin. "No, it sure isn't."

"I didn't know that before Elin." Kael's voice was hushed. "I didn't know a lot of things. She's taught me so much."

"Me, too. My life changed completely, and it started with Elin."

Kael beamed. "Exactly." Grin fading, she traced Anna's eyebrow gently. "She made it possible for me to love you the way I do."

"And how is that?" Anna trailed her fingers over Kael's shaven scalp.

"Wholly," Kael murmured and took Anna's mouth in a deep kiss. She stayed close when she broke away, pressing her forehead against Anna's. "I know I don't tell you enough, but the love I feel for you...consumes me. What I've found in you, it's just as important as what I found in Elin, but it's different. It's something all its own, and it means so much to me."

Anna blinked at Kael's eloquent words. Tears fell from her eyes, surprising her. "I feel the same. I love you so much it hurts me sometimes."

Kael captured one of Anna's tears with her thumb. "That doesn't sound pleasant."

Anna caught Kael's hand in her own and pressed her lips against the strong palm. "And yet it is." She guided Kael's hand to rest against the swell of her hip. "I want to make love with you before we go tonight."

"I want that, too," Kael murmured. She closed the distance between their faces, and gave Anna a brief kiss. "How about we make this little guy a bed somewhere?"

Anna grinned at the puppy, who wrestled with his toy on Kael's lap. She scooped Zep into her arms, then carried him and the knotted rope to the far corner of the bedroom. After settling him down with one of her old T-shirts, she returned to bed smiling.

"He just asks that you give him extra attention tomorrow." Anna kept the smile on her face.

"That can be arranged." Kael beckoned her closer. "But tonight...is for you. Elin can help us love on Zep tomorrow."

Anna straddled Kael's hips and eyed the closed bedroom door. "You think Walter and Kate have gone to bed yet?"

"I don't know." Kael settled her hands on Anna's hips. "Probably not. But I can be quiet. I promise." Waggling dark eyebrows, she added, "Though I guess I can't promise the same for you. I know that you can be pretty...vocal."

Anna slapped at Kael's chest. "I can be quiet."

"We'll see." Kael ran both hands up Anna's sides, then palmed her breasts. "I've been wanting you all day."

Anna rocked against Kael's stomach. "I want you. I want to feel all of you."

"You will," Kael said and tugged at the hem of Anna's T-shirt.

Anna didn't move to help. "Kael," she said in a hesitant voice, "I want..."

Kael stopped her hands and pressed them against Anna's stomach. "What, baby? Anything."

Anna raised onto her knees and slipped her hand between

their bodies. She pressed her palm against the crotch of Kael's blue jeans. "I want you to wear...I want to try—"

Kael's eyes flashed with unmistakable hunger, but her words were quiet and restrained. "Sweetheart, are you sure?"

Blushing, Anna managed a shy nod. "I'm nervous about it, but I've thought about...well, I wondered—"

"You don't have to do that for my sake." Kael pulled her down against her body. "You know that, right?"

"I know." Anna nervously toyed with the collar of Kael's T-shirt. "That's not why I'm asking."

"Then why are you asking?" Kael didn't break their tender gaze.

"Because I want to be with you like that. And I know how much you enjoy it."

"I enjoy it because Elin enjoys it."

"Yeah." Anna gave Kael a shy smile. "But you enjoy it, too."

Kael waited a beat, then said, "Yes. I love feeling her body against mine when I'm inside of her. I love being inside of her. But you know, even if I never made love to Elin again, I wouldn't want to be with you that way unless you really wanted it. I don't need that from you. Knowing that she wants me like that, that's what satisfies me."

"I want you inside of me." Anna traced the hard line of Kael's bicep with her fingertip, and lowered her eyes. "I'm a little afraid, but I know how much I love Elin's fingers. I know how much Elin loves being with you like that. I want to be that close to you."

Kael tangled her fingers in her hair and waited until Anna met her eyes before she spoke. "Okay, sweetheart. But we go slow, okay? You're in control."

"I'm in control?" Anna started a deliberate grinding with her hips and smiled cautiously. "That's a little different than you're used to, isn't it?"

Kael blushed, then pulled Anna down into a firm hug, pressing their upper bodies together. "I like being in control, yes," she whispered. "I could never completely give up control. But the only reason I take control with Elin like I do is because she enjoys surrendering it to me. I don't need it to be that way, especially when we're trying something new like this."

"Okay." Anna rolled off of her lover and watched Kael rise from the bed and kneel down by their bags. "I trust you."

"I know you do. It's a gift I treasure with everything that I am." Kael pulled her flesh-colored dildo from the bag, along with the black leather harness. "Let me just get ready, okay?"

"Okay." Anna placed one hand behind her head and laid the

other on her belly. "Hurry."

"Yes, ma'am."

When Kael disappeared into the bathroom, Anna exhaled shakily. She slipped her hand beneath her T-shirt, fingers cold against the heated flesh of her stomach. Sliding her hand up, she touched her right breast through her bra. Her nipple was tight with arousal. She pinched it between her fingertips, then reached up to touch the slope of her breast, enjoying the simple eroticism of caressing her own soft skin.

"You're so beautiful, you know." Anna turned to find Kael leaning against the bathroom doorframe. She was naked except for a pair of dark green boxer shorts. Hard pink nipples topped small breasts, and lean muscles flexed under Anna's gaze. "I could watch you all day."

Anna's eyes locked onto Kael's shorts. Voice shaking, she asked, "You're...ready?"

Kael pushed away from the door and crossed the room to stand beside the bed. "Baby, I want you to relax. We're going to work up to that part. First, I just want to love you."

"I'm not sure that relaxing is an option right now." Anna's heart thumped at the heat in Kael's gaze. "Not with the way you're looking at me."

"I can't help it." Kael removed Anna's T-shirt and bra and pressed her back against the bed. "You have wonderful breasts." She trailed licking, sucking kisses across brown skin until her mouth covered an erect nipple.

Anna gasped and fell back against the pillows. Kael followed, licking and worrying at the hard nub with gentle teeth. The room fell quiet as Elin's CD ended and the stereo stopped; contented murmurs and heavy breathing were the only sounds that remained.

Thoughts of the mission ahead receded to the back of Anna's mind. Her body still hummed with an acute sense of danger, a knowledge that this could quite possibly be her last chance to touch Kael, but rather than mute her desire, it drove her arousal to breath-stealing heights. She arched her back as Kael switched breasts, licking a trail from the left to the right, then dragging her tongue in lazy circles around Anna's right nipple, now painfully hard.

Anna groaned at the way Kael's mouth was making her throb and ache. Wetness trickled out of her, soaking her panties, and she squirmed beneath Kael in excitement. "Take my jeans off," she gasped.

Kael released Anna's nipple with an audible pop. She pulled back and worked on the button of Anna's blue jeans with steady hands. "Fine idea."

Anna studied the strong lines of Kael's body. Her arms were muscled and smooth, her collarbones well-defined. Her stomach was flat, almost concave after the events of recent weeks, but a healthy glow had returned to her skin since they'd arrived at Kate's house. In fact, Kael looked better than she had in weeks.

He's gorgeous.

"Lift up," Kael said, urging Anna's hips into the air. She took off Anna's jeans and panties and inhaled deeply. "I can smell you, baby. You're excited."

Anna allowed Kael to press her thighs apart on the mattress. "After the way you kissed me earlier? Of course I'm excited."

"I've been wanting you all day." Kael slid her lips up over Anna's ankle, her calf, her knee, her thigh. "May I kiss you here?" She trailed a fingertip through Anna's wetness.

"I may go crazy if you don't." Anna lifted her hips. "Use your tongue." She grinned when Kael looked up at her with a wry smile.

"You seem pretty comfortable giving orders." Kael eased her hands beneath Anna and cupped her buttocks, bringing her close. "Don't you?" She dipped her head and dragged the flat of her tongue up over slick folds. When she pulled back, Anna could see a shiny string of wetness connecting Kael's lower lip to her center.

"Yes." Groaning in pleasure, she urged Kael nearer. "Lick me, baby. Please."

Kael allowed Anna to guide her face to her wetness, this time covering Anna's swollen clit with her whole mouth. She swirled her tongue over and around the sensitive, distended flesh. Anna bit her lip to stop the loud moan that threatened to explode from her mouth when Kael gripped her buttocks and flattened her tongue over Anna's clit and across her labia. Anna stared down, entranced by the sight of the shaven head moving between her legs.

Kael pulled back, face shiny with wetness. "I love how you taste." She licked her lips, then bent so she could drag her tongue up the length of Anna's sex once again. Closing her eyes, she asked, "May I make you come?"

Anna's breathing picked up at the question. *He's really letting me have control.* She squirmed when Kael's fingers flexed on her buttocks. "I want to come in your mouth." Her clit twitched as she gave the command.

Kael lowered her head, and Anna's eyes slid shut as she concentrated solely on Kael's lovemaking. She thrust her hips against Kael's face, though her movement was largely restricted by the fierce grip Kael kept on her bottom. Still, she felt a heady rush of power, and it pushed her close to the edge.

"Don't stop." She kept her voice low, afraid of being overheard. "Don't stop, baby, don't stop what you're—" Her words died in her throat, and she clapped one hand over her mouth to stifle the cry that nearly burst out when Kael's tongue drew a quivering, shaking orgasm from her body. Whimpering, she squirmed away from Kael's relentless mouth as she struggled to recover from the shattering pleasure. Her thighs trembled next to Kael's head. "Stop, baby," she pleaded. "Oh, baby...please, I can't...stop, baby, stop."

Immediately Kael pulled back and ran her wet tongue along her shining upper lip. "Enough?"

Anna gasped. "Give me a few seconds to catch my breath."

Kael rested the side of her face against Anna's warm inner thigh. "That was nice." She stroked lightly over her slippery labia. "You're so pretty down here."

Anna flushed in pleasure at the compliment. Thighs spread, she caressed Kael's head as her lover traced patient designs over her slick folds with reverent fingertips. "Thanks. I kind of like having you look at me."

Kael's eyes flitted up to meet hers. "I love looking."

"How about touching?" Anna groaned as Kael's fingers increased their pressure.

"I love touching, too," Kael husked. She eased her left hand from beneath Anna's body, then slid it up over her abdomen until her fingers grazed the underside of Anna's breast. "You're so soft."

"Do you want to be inside of me?" Anna felt a surge of wetness at her own cautious words.

From the way Kael sucked in a breath, stilled her fingers, and glanced up at her, it was clear that she felt the same thing.

"One finger first?" Kael's nostrils flared as she waited for Anna's answer.

"Sure." She kept her body relaxed, eyes locked onto Kael's. "I know you won't hurt me."

Kael slid her fingertip down to play at Anna's entrance. "Never." She pressed into Anna slightly, then drew back, holding her gaze. "I want to make you feel good."

"You do." Anna ran her fingers over Kael's head and down her cheek. She eased her lover's face against her inner thigh. "I want you inside."

Kael pressed the length of her index finger inside in one slow, deliberate movement. Anna's mouth fell open as she accepted Kael into her body, and a soundless cry of pleasure fell from her lips. She was so wet that she barely felt the penetration and was able to concentrate entirely on the pleasant fullness she felt with Kael's finger resting within her.

"Does that feel good, baby?" Kael held her finger steady, not moving. The effort of her restraint was palpable. "Do you like that?"

"Yes." She squirmed on Kael's finger. "So good."

Kael withdrew her finger only to press it back inside again. "You feel like Elin," she whispered. "But different." She angled her finger and stroked Anna inside, finding a spot that made her gasp in muted surprise. "There you are."

"Oh," Anna panted. She'd never felt anything like what Kael was doing to her; the pleasure never ebbed, just flared up more intensely at every pass of Kael's finger over the spot she rubbed. "Oh, Kael, I...what are you—"

"You like that?" Kael lifted her head from Anna's thigh, grinning.

Anna moved her hips to meet Kael's thrusts. "I...I...love..."

"That's what I like to hear." Kael withdrew her finger, and Anna whimpered. "I'm coming back with two, okay?"

Anna granted permission with a quiet nod, exhaling steadily. She bit her lip as Kael pushed back inside, surprised at the pleasure she felt in being fuller. Then she smiled, awed by her body's response at being touched that way.

"That feels amazing." Anna ran her fingers along the edge of Kael's ear. "Come up here and kiss me while you touch me, baby. I want to taste your mouth."

Kael surged up Anna's body, two fingers buried deep between her thighs. She wiggled her fingers gently, and her mouth met Anna's in a slow, lazy kiss. "I love you," she murmured.

Anna felt herself contract around Kael's fingers, and Kael groaned quietly. Brushing her lips against Kael's, she murmured, "I love you, too." She lay back and watched Kael's eyes as her lover moved within her, as waves of pleasure rippled through her heavy-limbed body. Before long, she was rocking her hips to meet Kael's gentle thrusts. "Baby, I...think I'm ready for more."

Kael stilled her fingers, but kept them tucked snugly inside. Her heart pounded against Anna's chest. "You're sure?"

"I'm sure." She lifted her hips, drawing Kael's fingers deeper. "Everything feels so good right now."

"Okay." To Anna's surprise, Kael withdrew her fingers and rolled off. She lay on her back and gave Anna a cautious look. "I want you on top of me, baby, at first. That way you can...control things."

Anna's body warmed at the tender concern in Kael's voice. She sat up and ran her hand down a muscular arm. Kael stroked Anna's bare back with her fingers.

"May I take off your shorts?" Anna stared down at the dark cotton, stomach flip-flopping at the thought of what lay beneath. She was as excited as she was timid.

"Of course." Kael lifted her hips with a patient grin.

Anna's cheeks flushed as she hooked her thumbs in the waistband of Kael's boxers and pulled them off. Her eyes locked onto the dildo that was strapped to Kael's hips, jutting out away from her body. She tossed the shorts aside and settled her hands on Kael's thighs.

Kael shifted beneath Anna's touch. "You okay, sweetheart?"

Anna swallowed. "It seems a little...big."

"We don't have to do this." Kael laced her hands behind her head and gave Anna a crooked grin. "I would be perfectly happy to put my fingers back inside of you."

"No." Anna ran her fingers down the length of the dildo, then wrapped her hand around the base and met Kael's eyes. "I want your cock inside of me."

She settled on top of Kael, gasping at the way the dildo pressed into her belly.

Kael pulled her down into a tight hug. "Do you know how much I love you?"

Anna closed her eyes. "Yes."

"Good." Kael slid her hands down to cup Anna's bottom, squeezing gently. "As long as you know."

Anna nodded. She got onto her knees and planted one on either side of Kael's narrow hips. "And do you know how much I love you?"

Kael gave her a happy nod. "Yes."

With a pleased grin, Anna repeated, "Good." Meeting Kael's eyes, she reached down between their bodies and grasped the dildo in her hand. She bit her lip and guided the head to her entrance.

"Go slow," Kael said. She squeezed Anna's hip when she winced at the effort of trying to penetrate herself. "Baby, go slow."

Anna was determined to take Kael inside. Sweat beaded on her forehead as the head of the dildo stretched her open and she pressed the first inch into her body. She exhaled, wishing that her body would yield to the invasion.

"Don't tense up," Kael murmured. She rubbed her thumb over Anna's clitoris, still swollen and wet. "Just relax, baby."

Anna stopped concentrating on the slightly uncomfortable

sensation of the dildo, now fixated solely on the bliss Kael was creating between her legs. She breathed deep and watched Kael's thumb swirl through her wetness. "You're so hard," Kael said. "So swollen."

Anna stared into Kael's eyes. "Yes." She realized that her hips were rocking against Kael's hand and that the dildo that sat poised at her entrance was sliding deeper inside of her body. She gasped as she was entered, all of a sudden open and ready for Kael. Kael pulled Anna down against her chest again.

"Give yourself a minute to get used to it," Kael murmured. She kissed Anna's face and rubbed their cheeks together.

Anna nodded and pressed her lips against Kael's temple. She brought her hands up and curled her fingers around Kael's shoulders. Releasing a shaky breath, she willed her body to relax. Then she whimpered into Kael's ear, surprised at a sudden revelation. "It feels good."

Kael chuckled at Anna's awed whisper. "That's kind of what I was hoping would happen." Anna sat up fully. Kael was buried deep inside of her, and Anna loved the way she stared at their joining with inflamed indigo eyes. Instinctively, she rocked her hips, swaying against Kael's abdomen. She could feel the length of Kael moving inside of her in time with her lazy rhythm.

Anna tipped her head back and moaned. "Oh, Kael."

"Shh, baby," Kael cautioned with a silly grin. "You were going to be quiet, remember?"

Anna blushed but never stopped moving. Having Kael inside of her lit fires deep in her belly, driving her to rock harder against her lover in desperation. Kael's strong hands stayed busy, one pinching and tugging on Anna's nipple, while the other snuck around to stroke Anna's clit again. Anna's mouth dropped open in pleasure.

"It feels...so..." she whispered under her breath, then gasped as Kael hit a rhythm that made her hips buck and jerk in reaction. "Oh, God...Kael, I'm gonna —"

"That's right, sweetheart." Kael thrust her hips upward, meeting Anna stroke for stroke. "Ride me, baby. Does that feel good?"

Anna nodded, not trusting herself to speak. If she opened her mouth, she would scream.

"Are you going to come for me?"

Anna nodded again, then arched her back as Kael rubbed tiny circles around her aching clit, delivering a breath-stealing orgasm that Anna felt in places she hadn't even known existed. Her muscles contracted around Kael's cock, gripping and releasing. Baring her teeth, she rode it out in silence, grateful that Kael's strong hands supported her trembling body.

When she recovered, she found herself cradled in Kael's muscular arms. "That was amazing," she said and sighed in contentment.

"Absolutely amazing," Kael agreed. She moved her hands down to Anna's bottom and pulled her closer. "I can't believe how sexy you are."

Only Elin had ever made her feel as safe as she did in that moment. "I can't believe I was ever afraid of you," Anna said. "When I first met you...but now that I know—" Her head was spinning.

"You were afraid of me?"

Anna couldn't decide if Kael sounded confused or hurt. "Just a little. And not for very long." Pulling back, she stared down at Kael solemnly. "I trust you with my life."

Kael touched the side of Anna's face. "I trust you with mine."

"I want you on top of me now."

Kael blinked at the quiet request. "Are you sure?"

"Very," Anna said. "Do you think you could come that way?"

"Yes," Kael said, and smiled shyly.

"Then do it. I want to feel your body on mine."

Without a word, Kael engulfed Anna in her arms and rolled them over, still buried inside of her. The sudden change in position took Anna by surprise, and she needed a moment to adjust, fighting off a brief brush of panic at the vaguely familiar scenario. *But it's Kael,* she reminded herself, and reached up to touch her lover's lean face.

"Make love to me, tough guy."

Kael grinned hard at the nickname and pressed her lips to Anna's. Anna pushed her tongue inside of Kael's mouth, groaning loud. Kael moved tentative hips, withdrawing from Anna, then pushing inside again.

Kael pulled back from their kiss. "Does that feel good?" She was panting, but she stopped at that single stroke.

"So good," Anna whispered, full of wonder. She never knew it could be that good, that her entire body could feel so sensitized and alive. "Don't stop."

Kael began moving again, establishing a gentle cadence with her thrusts. She kept Anna's mouth busy with kisses and moaned into the joining of their lips. Anna hugged Kael and spread her legs wide, eager for the pleasure that Kael's body gave her. The base of the dildo bumped against Anna's clit on every stroke, and she could tell from the way Kael ground against her that she was feeling the same sensations.

Kael picked up her pace. She broke a frantic, wet kiss, and gasped, "Still good?" Sweat dripped from her forehead and splashed onto Anna's cheek.

"God, yes." Her earlier climaxes had left her nerves singing and ready for more. "I think I could..."

Kael sucked at Anna's throat as her hips continued to pound against her. "I'm going to come, baby. I'm gonna...baby, I—" Kael stopped speaking and gasped, bringing her mouth down to cover Anna's. She cried out into their kiss, and that noise was what pushed Anna over the edge again a moment later.

Kael buried her face in Anna's neck. She groaned, as if in pain. "I'm throbbing."

"I'm done," Anna said. She shifted beneath Kael, frowning at the dildo that still rested inside of her exhausted body. That last climax had been her limit for the night. "Out," she instructed.

Kael laughed out loud and started a slow withdrawal with her hips. "That's exactly what Elin always says. One minute I'm a god, the next I'm an unwelcome guest."

Anna groaned as Kael pulled out, then she closed her legs. "I still love you. I'm just...spent."

"I understand." Kael tugged her into a warm hug, then took her mouth in a languorous kiss.

When Anna pulled back, she took note of Kael's flushed face and chest, her erratic breathing. "You're not done, though, are you?"

"I'm okay." Kael managed a weak smile.

"You need to come again."

Chuckling, Kael said, "Busted." She struggled out of the harness that was strapped to her hips. "Do you mind if I...I mean, if you'd just let me..." Kael blushed. "You could just raise your thigh..."

Anna curled her hand around the back of Kael's neck and propped herself up on her elbow. "I watched Elin use her mouth on you once." It was something she had wanted for so long, but had been afraid to ask. She didn't know how Kael would react.

Kael's cheeks turned a rosy shade of pink. "You want to do that?"

Anna gave her an enthusiastic nod. "You can't imagine how much."

Kael seemed to consider a moment, then said, "All right."

"But only if you enjoy it," Anna hastened to add. "I don't want to do anything unless you're going to like it."

"I like it. It's just..."

"What?"

"I don't want to be on my back," Kael muttered.

"That's okay." Anna stood, groaning as sore muscles began to announce themselves, then knelt on the carpeted floor. She lifted her eyes to Kael. "How about if I'm on my knees?"

It was the position she had seen Elin use to pleasure Kael. It was exactly how she had fantasized about tasting Kael herself.

Kael relaxed into an easy grin and climbed off the bed. "I'd like that a lot, sweetheart."

Anna's heart stuttered when Kael came to stand in front of her. She was eye level with neatly trimmed dark curls coated with sticky wetness, betraying her fierce excitement. On her knees, Anna could see Kael's body as she never had before; dark pink labia that peeked out when Kael planted her feet apart on the floor, and when she reached down with one hand and spread herself open, a rosy, swollen clit that protruded from its hood in unashamed arousal.

Anna inhaled and licked her lips. She wondered how Kael would taste.

"You want it?" Kael threaded the fingers of her free hand through Anna's hair.

"Yes."

Kael urged her forward. "Taste me."

Dipping her head between Kael's thighs, Anna snaked out her tongue and took a long swipe up the length of slick, pink folds. Kael was coated with juices, fragrant with them. She tasted like Elin, but different. She was saltier, muskier. Delicious. Anna groaned when Kael pulled her face forward and forced her tongue deep into her wetness.

"That's right, sweetheart," Kael groaned. "Suck me."

Anna obeyed, pulling engorged flesh into her mouth and sucking gently. Kael moaned and shook at her action, and so Anna sucked harder. Kael's fingers tightened in her hair and held her in place.

"You're so good, honey." Kael's voice broke on the compliment. Thrusting her hips forward, sliding her wetness over Anna's lips, nose, and chin, she settled into a mindless rhythm as she sought release. "I'm so close already."

Anna was in heaven. Kael tasted incredible, and the noises she made had Anna almost frantic to send her over the edge. She angled her neck so she could attack Kael's center with renewed vigor, sliding her lips and tongue over the hot, wet flesh.

"Anna. Oh, Anna, Anna-baby —" Kael's entire body stiffened and jerked as she came and released a rush of salty-sweet liquid into Anna's mouth.

Anna moaned and lapped up Kael's juices, ecstatic at what she had just unleashed. *I did that.* She licked at Kael's hot, contracting flesh, and delighted in the way she could feel the orgasm with her lips, her tongue, her whole face.

"I'm about to fall down." Kael staggered backwards and did just that, collapsing onto the bed with a shaky sigh. "I can't believe my legs didn't give out on me."

Anna licked her lips, enjoying one last taste of her lover. "That was fantastic."

Kael lifted her head with a dazed smile. "You took the words right out of my mouth."

Anna climbed into bed, basking in the afterglow of their joining. With some coaxing, she was able to maneuver Kael so that her head rested on the pillows. She looked sated but alert, and Anna wondered if there would be any real rest for her lover that night. "We need some sleep," she murmured. "We've got a long morning ahead of us."

"Thank you for tonight," Kael held out her arms and sighed when Anna moved into her embrace. "This was just what I needed. I feel...renewed."

"Me, too." Smiling, Anna yawned and cuddled closer to warm, naked skin. "I have a clock set to go off about four hours before dawn."

"Okay." Kael gave Anna a lingering kiss, then whispered, "Until tomorrow."

"Until tomorrow. When we get Elin back." *At last.*

In a quiet, determined voice, Kael repeated, "When we get Elin back." It was a statement of fact.

Chapter
Twenty-two

FOR THE FIRST time since she was a little girl, Anna felt nervous and unsure in the inky blackness of night. She followed Kael along an invisible, determined path, straining hard to keep her black-clad lover in sight. They wore matching outfits — loose black cotton pants that granted them ease of movement, long-sleeved T-shirts, and heavy boots that felt a lot more comfortable than they looked. Kael had even gone so far as to smear black grease paint on Anna's face before they set out.

Kael was loaded down with weapons. Her sword, strapped to her back. The bow and arrows, gripped in her left hand. Her backpack was full of explosives. Most of the small bombs would be detonated by igniting a fuse, and for that they each carried a fancy silver butane lighter from Walter. They had a handful of smoke bombs, which they would use to cause confusion in the event that men started waking up during their rescue attempt. Walter had also slaved to create several explosives that could be detonated remotely, via radio. They intended to place those in key locations a safe distance from the center circle of tents before they entered the camp.

Those would be used only in the most dire of emergencies.

Anna's empty gun was tucked into her waistband, handle pressed against the small of her back. In her right hand, she carried her baseball bat. Her left hand was clenched into a tight fist. She kept part of her mind on their surroundings while the other was consumed by doubts and worries.

Did anyone drink the wine? Does Elin know we're coming? What if we can't take the guards out silently? Will we be able to get all the women out of there without waking even one man up?

Her head felt like it would crack open from the pressure inside.

Ahead of her, Kael stopped near a familiar patch of trees. She motioned Anna to her side. Below them, the Procreationist camp lay still and quiet in the night.

Well, not entirely still.

Almost immediately, Anna spotted a guard leaning against a tree at the east side of camp, over near the men's playing field. As she watched, he pushed away from the tree, took a step forward, and spit onto the ground. That accomplished, he returned to his post.

There's one. And he doesn't look tired to me.

Anna tapped Kael and gestured to the guard. Kael nodded, then directed Anna's attention to the opposite side of the camp. For a moment Anna saw nothing, then she recognized the dark form of a man, slumped against the base of a tree. He wasn't moving, and Anna assumed that he was asleep.

And there's number two.

One after the other, they found and pointed out the guards to one another, silently analyzing the situation as they found it. Anna could practically hear Kael's mind working, until finally she leaned over and whispered, "We start with the guy on the far right. He's the most awake, I think. After that, clockwise until we finish with that guy who's snoring at the other side of camp, next to the first. After that, we move to the center. If we can't isolate the one farthest from us right now so that the other doesn't see, we may have to coordinate attacking the last two." Kael's soft words were clipped and precise. There wasn't a trace of hesitation in her voice. "I'm going to volunteer to be the one to take down each of them, while you stand by in case I need help, but if you have another idea, tell me."

Anna was surprised that Kael was giving her the chance to suggest an alternate plan. *But he's right. That's the way we should do it.* She shook her head. "No, I'll stay behind you. I'll keep an eye out for other guards while you strike. If you need help, I'll come. Otherwise, I'll stay put."

Kael pressed her lips against Anna's cheek, smearing the black grease painted there. "I love you, Anna-baby." Anna heard the first hint of vulnerability in her stoic lover's voice. "Be safe."

"You too, love." Anna's hands were shaking. "What about the bombs?"

"I'll plant some along the way. Don't worry. I'm hoping we won't need any of them."

Anna nodded. "I'm ready."

"Let's go."

Kael took Anna's hand, and they worked their way through the trees and down a gradual slope that led to a clearing adjacent to the playing field. Crouched low, senses attuned to the surroundings, Anna was determined to hear any threat long before it could surprise them.

The first guard still leaned against the same tree where they'd spotted him earlier. He hummed softly, under his breath, and Anna was grateful for the noise to cover their approach in the trees behind him. She took up a position behind the trunk of a solid oak and nodded at Kael.

Kael bent to lay her bow and arrows on the ground, rolled her neck from side to side, and then she was moving.

She struck so quickly that even Anna was taken by surprise, and she had known what was going to happen. She heard only the soft crack of the man's neck breaking. He fell limp in Kael's arms, and she stepped back into the shadows, taking his body with her.

One down. Anna breathed a sigh of relief. The butterflies in her stomach calmed as she considered the ease and cold efficiency with which Kael had dispatched the first guard. *Kael's right. He really is good at killing.*

Kael knelt down beside the body, then fiddled with something from her half-opened backpack before setting it on the dead man's lap. Anna's eyes widened when she realized that this was one of Kael's remote bombs.

The second guard was even easier. This one wasn't sleeping, but he sat against a tree, staring blankly at the tents. He looked exhausted, and Anna wondered if he'd accepted a drink from Matt earlier and was struggling to stay awake. He slumped to the side after Kael broke his neck, his death no more dramatic than a candle being snuffed out by the wind. Kael dragged his body into the trees.

There were two men left around the perimeter, two in the center. So far, nobody seemed to have noticed that the guards were being picked off one by one.

Kael ushered Anna past the trees that bisected the river from the camp, around to the guard who stood closest to Trey's tent. Anna's stomach fluttered uneasily as they worked their way into position well behind him, a grouping of trees their only cover. Once again, Kael set down her bow and arrows. But this time she produced a wicked-looking knife from her belt. She lowered herself to the grass and started a slow, stealthy crawl on her belly toward the guard, knife held between white teeth that stood out in stark contrast to the black clothing and makeup she wore. Watching Kael's glacial progress through the grass was torturous, and Anna's heart pounded so loudly that she was afraid the statue-still guard would hear it.

When Kael was only ten feet from their target, the guard raised his arms, took a step backwards, and sighed tiredly. Kael froze, immobile in the grass.

Oh, fuck. Anna's hand ached from holding her baseball bat so tightly. She stared at the back of the guard's head, willing him not to turn around. The guard lowered his arms so he could plant his hands on his hips. He twisted back and forth, then bent at the waist and stretched down to touch his toes.

I wonder if he's bored or just trying to stay awake. He seems awfully active for someone who might be drugged. Anna shifted, ready to bolt from her hiding spot if Kael needed her.

All of a sudden Kael was moving. To Anna's left, through the grass, beating a silent path to a fallen tree only feet away. Anna breathed a sigh of relief when she made it behind the thick trunk undetected.

As she was wondering what they should do, the guard turned, striding with purpose toward the tree where Anna hid. He walked directly over the spot where Kael had lain on the ground barely twenty feet away, making Anna profoundly grateful for Kael's intuition. When Kael sat up fast, the thin moonlight revealing panicked eyes, the reality of the situation dawned on her.

He's coming right at me.

Anna bit back a gasp and retreated fully behind the trunk, trying to make her body as narrow as possible. The sound of footsteps in the soft grass grew louder. Only the thick trunk of the tree and the darkness of the moonlit night separated her from the enemy.

We may not be able to take this guy quietly. What if he sees me? I don't think he drank the wine. Fuck it all.

For the span of what felt like a hundred hushed, measured breaths, there was silence. Anna didn't move a muscle, one hand clenched into a fist and the other going numb from gripping her baseball bat so tightly. She wondered what Kael was doing. *Is he sneaking up behind this guy even at this moment?* She closed her eyes for an instant, then opened them for fear that she wouldn't react in time if the guard realized she was there.

The sound of a wet stream hitting the opposite side of the tree jolted Anna, and she jerked in surprise and released a quiet, involuntary gasp. Before she could worry about whether the guard heard her over his urination, she heard the man grunt and utter something, then a frantic gurgling cut off the exclamation. That, too, was silenced after another instant, and then Kael hustled around the back of the tree dragging the man's heavy bulk in her arms. *Help me,* she mouthed.

Anna grabbed the man's feet and hefted his lower half. She and Kael lumbered a few yards farther away from the camp and dumped the body in some undergrowth. They returned stealthily to their vantage point and scanned the distant tents for any sign that the guard's aborted cry had alerted someone.

When nothing stirred for several minutes, they shared a brief, joyful grin at the danger they'd just faced and defeated, and Kael mouthed, *Let's go.* The final perimeter guard was ridiculously easy. The guard sat on the hard ground with his long legs stretched in front of him and his back against a fallen log. Head tipped back, he snored open-mouthed at the sky. Kael cut his throat without waking him, and Anna tucked the second remote bomb beneath his lifeless arm.

They took their time working their way to the middle of the loose ring of tents. Starting from the far side of camp in relation to their observation point, they dropped into crouches so they could ease their way between tents occupied by sleeping Procreationists. As they passed one green tent, Anna heard a loud snore emanate from inside, then a series of muttering grunts and murmurs. She pressed her hand over her mouth to stop the hysterical laughter that threatened to escape, an irrational impulse, and saw Kael glance backwards at her with bright-eyed sympathy.

Crouched behind a small red tent, the first in the back row of prisoner tents, Kael peeked her head around the side, then drew back immediately. She didn't move, didn't turn to look at Anna, but Anna knew what Kael's caution meant. She had spotted the two inner guards they needed to dispatch.

"They're within sight of each other," Kael whispered. "We'll have to take them both at once."

Anna nodded. Her stomach turned at the knowledge of what she would have to do. *That means one of these guys is mine.*

Kael's serious pantomime of the motion required to break a man's neck was almost enough to send her into panicked, frantic laughter. She breathed deeply in an effort to stay calm. *This is no way to be a ruthless killer.*

Anna had never been a ruthless killer, and she hated the necessity of what she was going to do. But she was prepared to do whatever it took. If it meant killing every last man here, she was just as determined as Kael to get Elin back.

Kael shot her a compassionate smile and offered the hunting knife that she carried. The blade was still smeared red with blood from the third guard's throat, the handle sticky with it. Anna accepted the knife with a grateful smile. *Any little edge I can get.* On edge, she smirked at her own pun.

The guard closest to her was a mere ten feet away. He stood with his back to her, and as she watched, he scratched at his ass with a distracted hand. Anna rolled her eyes and turned her attention to the other man. This one stood with his back to Kael, staring into the distance. He opened his mouth in a wide yawn. Anna smiled in satisfaction and retreated behind the tent to await Kael's signal. She stuck the knife in the front of her waistband and set her baseball bat in the grass, having no need for the blunt weapon in this situation. As she watched Kael counting down on her fingers, she cleared her mind of all doubt, all worry, and focused solely on the task at hand. These two men were quite likely the last obstacle standing between them and Elin. She could not afford to blow it.

On Kael's signal, Anna rose to her feet and did not allow herself the chance to hesitate as she ran full throttle at her guard. She could see Kael's mirroring movement from the corner of her eye. Unthinking, unfeeling, she advanced upon the man and grabbed him from behind.

It was both easier and more difficult to snap his neck than she had thought it would be. Easier, in that she did it without hesitation and without remorse, only experiencing a dim flicker of dismay as she committed the fifth murder of her life. More difficult, in that it took slightly more effort than she had anticipated, and for a brief, startling moment, she feared that she wouldn't be able to do it. She felt him grow agitated, and she tensed in anticipation of a cry for help. Then his neck cracked, and he dropped.

She caught the guard in her arms and looked up at Kael, who cradled the second guard, also dead. Anna couldn't help but grin along with Kael, in relief and delayed horror, as they dragged the bodies to the edge of the camp and dumped them unceremoniously in a patch of lush vegetation that sat close to a brown tent.

"Matt's tent is at the other side of camp," Kael said softly. "I'll go get him, and we'll start zip-tying tents while you and Elin get the women out. I'm going to send Matt with them back to Kate's. I'll have...business to finish here."

"I'm staying with you," Anna murmured into Kael's ear. "You'll probably need help."

"I've got a bolt cutter for you to use on Elin's handcuffs." Kael handed Anna the hefty tool from her backpack, then two smoke bombs, which Anna stuffed into one of the large cargo pockets on her black pants. "It could be loud, so you may want to take her away from the center of camp to do it."

"Understood. I'm keeping your knife. It'll be faster and quieter to cut my way into the women's tents than to unzip them."

"Good call." Kael gave her a brief hug. "Be safe. Kiss Elin for me."

Anna smiled. "Only until you can kiss her yourself."

KNEELING IN THE grass just outside of Elin's small tent was one of the hardest things Anna could ever remember doing. Separated from her lover by only a thin layer of nylon, knowing that a quick slice with the knife she clutched in her hand was all it would take to touch Elin again, Anna didn't know how she managed to wait as Kael stalked, wraithlike, through the maze of tents until she reached a small green and purple enclosure on the other side of the prisoners. Anna couldn't see her features, didn't know whether she gave any kind of signal that it was time to move, but somehow she could sense the time was right. Raising her knife, she quietly drew the sharp blade down the length of the zippered door of Elin's tent, cutting through it with ease. She moved fast, aware that the moment she breached the tent, she ran the risk that one or both of its occupants would notice and, in panicked confusion, start yelling.

Anna poked her head inside just in time to see the young dark-haired girl from the river open her mouth and inhale as if preparing to let loose a mighty scream. Anna's heart stuttered in her chest, at once sympathetic to the child's terror and terrified herself that their game might be up so quickly. She started to lunge forward in an effort to clap a frantic hand over the child's mouth, only to have someone else beat her to the punch.

Elin turned on her side to press a gentle hand over the girl's mouth, her other hand twisted awkwardly where her wrists were cuffed together. The girl—Lana, Elin had called her by the river—breathed hard and stared at Anna with wide, fearful eyes. Anna was captured for a moment by her lover's bright gaze and the sweet curve of her neck as she bent to whisper soft words into the little girl's ear.

At Elin's reassurance, Lana visibly relaxed and Elin lifted her hand from the child's mouth and crawled to Anna.

Holding her close and tight, Anna whispered, "Kael's gone to get Matt." There was no time for the words of love she wanted to utter; in this, they needed to be efficient. Reconnecting would come later. "We need to get the women out of here as quietly as we can. Matt drugged the men's wine. We've already killed the six guards on duty, and we're hoping we can get the women out while the rest sleep."

"I understand," Elin breathed. She was unable to return Anna's embrace, but she rubbed her bound hands back and forth over Anna's T-shirt-covered chest as though making sure she was real. "My hands—"

"I have a bolt cutter, but we have to wait until we're farther away from camp. I don't know how loud it will be."

"Okay. I love you."

Anna's heart swelled at everything she heard behind the three simple words. "I love you, too. I want to get a couple of other women up right away. Someone can take Lana into the forest to wait, the other can lead the women back to that place as we take them out of their tents."

"I know who to get."

Before they parted, Anna caught her in a brief, heartfelt kiss that Elin returned with equal passion. More than a kiss, Anna knew, it was a promise: that they would enjoy many more kisses in the future, that nothing and no one could ever tear them apart, that they would make it out of this camp alive, together.

Filled with renewed confidence, Anna slipped out of the tent, looking left and right as she emerged into the night. The camp was still quiet, and for several seconds, she didn't see anything stir. Just as her throat grew dry with anticipation, she spotted Kael and Matt at the far side of camp. Kael turned her head to meet Anna's gaze just as Elin crawled out of the tent.

Elin turned to see what had Anna's attention as she stood, and Anna felt the physical impact of Elin's first glimpse of Kael, of Kael's intense regard of their lover. Their shared look lasted for only an instant, then Kael was back to work with Matt and Elin helped little Lana to her feet.

Anna's heart threatened to pound out of her chest. *This is working.*

Gesturing for Lana to keep still, Elin led Anna over to a familiar red tent. Anna remembered its occupants: a lanky, frightened brunette and her companion, the healthy blonde who had demonstrated a quiet defiance that stirred Anna's pride.

Anna sliced down the length of the door with her knife and pulled the nylon open so that she and Elin could ease inside. Blinking as she adjusted to the darkness, Anna was surprised to find the stocky blonde woman already awake, staring with glittering eyes. Her brunette companion slept soundly beside her, cradled within the blonde's strong arms.

"Jen, she's with me," Elin whispered.

Immediately, the blonde woman brought her mouth close to her companion's face, which looked peaceful in slumber. "Sweetheart." The voice was so quiet that Anna almost didn't hear it, and achingly tender. "Wake up, Caroline, and don't say anything. Everything is okay."

She placed a gentle finger over Caroline's lips.

Elin hurriedly told Jen the plan and said, "Caroline can stay with Lana in the forest. We'll show you where."

The two women dressed with obvious apprehension, but their excitement was equally clear. Anna led the small group to the edge of the camp, then up the slight incline into the forest. She found the path she and Kael had taken from Kate and Walter's house then turned to Elin and produced the bolt cutters with a tender smile.

"I bet you want those off," she whispered.

Elin raised her hands into the air, eyes flashing with turbulent emotion. "Please."

Anna tamped down on the surge of anger she felt at Elin's captors for the pain she read in Elin's gaze. She clipped the handcuffs off with a *snap* that made her glad she had waited until they were far enough away from the sleeping men.

Elin shook her hands as they were released and cast embarrassed eyes at the ground. "Thanks."

Without thinking, Anna reached out and captured Elin's wrists in her hands. She rubbed her thumbs over the skin rubbed raw by the cuffs. As she did, she had a flash of Trey doing the very same thing at the river the day before. Startled, she dropped Elin's wrists, all at once awkward and uncertain about how to behave. She was vaguely aware of three pairs of eyes watching them, though Jen, Caroline, and the child remained silent.

As if sensing her hesitation, Elin wrapped her arms around Anna's shoulders and buried her face in Anna's neck, hugging hard. "Kael is really okay?"

"He's okay. Pissed, but okay." Anna continued to hold Elin close, unable to release her quite yet. "Did they hurt you?"

Elin's body trembled for a moment. "Yes." When Anna stiffened, Elin tightened her arms. "But not like that."

Anna's body flooded with relief. Despite what Matt told them, she needed to hear the words from Elin's mouth. "We'll help you heal," she swore.

When they moved apart, she quickly organized the others, hoping the next stage of the plan would be as smooth as the first.

"Jen, come with us. You'll lead small groups back here." Looking to Caroline, she said, "If something happens, we're staying with a doctor—Kate Woodard—in the city about two miles due west. She lives in a large brick house on the northeast edge of town. The address is 427 Vaughn."

Caroline took Lana's small hand in her own and, gazing at Jen with slightly unfocused eyes, murmured, "Come back to me, you understand?"

Jen gave her a gentle smile, before turning to Anna and Elin.

"Let's go. I don't know how they haven't woken up yet, but I don't trust it to last."

Remembering one last detail, Anna dug around in the largest pocket of her cargo pants. She retrieved a thin black tool and offered it to Elin.

"My steel baton," Elin whispered. It wasn't the same one she'd had when she was taken, of course, but Kael and Anna had been able to find one remarkably similar to her confiscated weapon. She took it, eyes flashing. "Thank you."

"Our friend Matt drugged some wine," Anna told Jen. "But we don't know how many of them drank. Hopefully it'll keep most of them in a deep sleep. Our friends are securing tents closed right now to slow down anyone who might wake."

Jen nodded. "Then we shouldn't waste another second."

JEN DID A good job moving through the tents quickly and quietly, assembling the women in small groups. Anna's stomach churned, and she knew that she wouldn't be able to relax until everyone had made it to the trees without rousing any of the sleeping men.

Anna stood guard while the last few women prepared to leave, the knot of worry in her stomach twisting as she scanned the tents around her. Thickening fog swirled around her ankles, a testament to the damp approaching dawn. She was unable to suppress a growing sense of foreboding deep inside. *This is going too smoothly.*

She approached the last tent, a small orange enclosure that lay at the western side of the camp, only feet away from a larger blue tent that housed sleeping Procreationists. Anna had saved it for last on purpose; it was the riskiest extraction and she had wanted all the other tents cleared first.

Elin joined her and cut the tent open, then pushed her way inside. Anna followed closely behind.

Almost immediately, a dark-haired woman sat up and leaned forward to grip Elin's arms, her attractive face lined in worry. "Is it Lana? What's wrong?" she whispered.

Elin touched the woman's face with a reassuring hand. "She's fine. We've got her away from here already. Hurry and we'll take you to her."

The woman — Lana's mother, Anna surmised — glanced over at her groggy tent-mate, a blonde girl who looked as though she couldn't be more than twenty. "But what if they catch us?"

"We need to go," Anna urged. "Taking your chance at escape is better than condemning Lana to this life. Come on."

Lana's mother hesitated only a moment before she released Elin's arms and gathered her shoes from the end of her sleeping bag.

That's when Anna heard it—at first a soft indistinct muttering, increasing in intensity until Anna could hear the confusion in the voice. Startled, she scrambled out of the tent and leapt to her feet, leaving Elin to deal with the women. She picked up her baseball bat and swung her gaze around, trying to identify the source of the noise. Next to her, two other women huddled together in front of their tent, looking as though they were struggling not to dive back inside their nylon prison.

"What the fuck?"

The words, slightly slurred, came from somewhere ahead of her, on the opposite side of camp from Trey's tent. Anna started forward, baseball bat in hand, just as she spotted Kael's sprint across the camp. Kael withdrew a large knife from her waist as she approached a green tent where a confused man could be heard wrestling with the zipper from inside. He clawed at the material when he couldn't get out, his curses growing louder. Anna heard what she assumed was his tent-mate joining the struggle, just as Kael reached them.

Kael sliced at the tent with her right hand, then immediately reversed direction and plunged her knife into the form of a man who struggled beneath the green nylon. Reaching through the material where she'd cut it open, Kael pulled her opponent out by the neck and cut his throat with lightning-quick precision.

Elin scrambled out of the last prisoner tent, closely followed by Lana's mother and her blonde companion. "Fuck," she breathed as she spotted Kael dropping the second man.

"Yeah. They're waking up." Anna swept her eyes along the other tents, already spotting movement in two more. "I've got to get you guys out of here."

Elin frowned. "I won't leave you two."

"Elin, you're the only one I trust to help those women escape," Anna said in a harsh whisper. "Please don't make this whole thing have been in vain. Please just do this."

The blonde woman grabbed Anna's arm. "They're going to kill us."

"They won't," Anna said. "You're too valuable." Herding the women together, she told Elin, deadly serious, "Take them to the others. I want you to go find Dr. Kate Woodard's house, okay? She's expecting you."

Before Elin could say a word, they both heard the sound of material being rent apart not far from where they stood. The noise level in camp was growing exponentially, and Anna gave up all hope that they could turn back the tide on this one. Reaching into her pocket, she grabbed a smoke bomb and the lighter. She watched Kael fight with two new men, still across the camp from Trey's tent. She couldn't see Matt in the growing chaos.

Tears spilled from Elin's eyes, and even as Anna agonized over the sight, she realized that one of the men who had escaped his tent was running over to them. Without conscious thought, Anna dropped the smoke bomb to grip her weapon with both hands. She drew back and swung her wooden baseball bat at the man's head as he approached.

Thunk. And he was down.

Anna's heart broke at the shock on Elin's face. *Goddamn it, Elin, I never wanted you to see that.* "Go!" she urged. "Get them out of here." She picked up the smoke bomb from the grass with shaking hands.

"I love you," Elin whispered, in tears. "Get Kael and find me as soon as you can."

"I will," Anna swore. "And I love you." She lit the smoke bomb and tossed it onto the ground between her and a small group of groggy-looking men who advanced on them. She retrieved the other smoke bomb and paused for a split second to survey the camp as Elin hurried the women away.

Kael was fighting hard, already surrounded by motionless bodies lying at her feet. As Anna watched, she struck down two enemies in succession, then reached into her pocket to withdraw a bulky object. Anna barely had time to wonder what she was holding before the relative quiet of the night was broken by the most incredible sound she had ever heard.

An impressive explosion rocked the south side of camp, then the northeast. Anna pivoted on her feet, momentarily disoriented by the noise of the detonation. As she surveyed the north side of camp, she noticed that a third explosion had also occurred; the source of the smoke and flames was in the general vicinity of Trey's tent.

Anna lit her last smoke bomb. She tossed it to her left, judging the northern side of camp as the most dangerous to Elin's escape. *The last thing we need is for Trey to see Elin making a run for it. If he's still alive after that blast.* She strained hard to see through the thickening smoke, unable to do anything until she saw Elin disappear. Then she turned back to the escalating fight.

Anna didn't take the time to count the bodies of the slain, whose blood stained the grass around Kael's feet, but it was clear that the Procreationist ranks were rapidly decreasing. It was also clear that Kael wasn't in need of her immediate help.

So where's Matt?

Anna sprinted toward the northern portion of the camp, where she had last seen Matt and Kael tying the tent flaps. Running through a cloud of thick, white smoke, she was startled when two solid forms appeared in front of her. Acting on instinct and pure adrenaline, she lashed out and swung her bat at the knees of the man on the left, then brought it up to crash into the face of the man on the right. Both dropped to the ground and howled in agony.

Not wanting to finish them off — but needing them incapacitated — she took another hard swing at the knees of the man who held his bashed face, rivulets of blood running through his fingers. The man screamed again and curled into a tight little ball.

"Stay there," Anna told them. The one on the left took a clumsy swing at her with his sword, easily avoided, and Anna brought her baseball bat down on his arm. He dropped the sword with a pained grunt. "Be nice," she growled.

When she emerged from the smoke, Anna spotted the ruins of Trey's tent ahead to her left. The canvas was black and still smoldering from the explosion; an impressive radio lay in pieces on the grass outside. A tiny smile tugged on Anna's lips at the sight.

The smile faded only moments later when Anna heard something that chilled her blood. To her left, at the northwest side of camp, a boy cried out in fear. Even having never heard that particular sound from that particular boy, Anna knew in an instant.

Matt.

She took off running, feet pounding against the damp grass, eyes desperately scanning her surroundings for her blond friend. Droplets of sweat rolled down her face, evidence of the cold terror that seized her at the sound of that cry in the damp, pre-dawn hours.

When she found him, she also found something else. The explosion at Trey's tent hadn't killed the man, as she had fervently hoped. His hair looked singed, and he was bleeding from the forehead, but he was alive.

And pointing a very real gun at a kneeling Matt's head.

Chapter
Twenty-three

"YOU KNOW WHAT I do to traitors, you little fuck?" Cold words, delivered with pure malice. Trey drew back and kicked Matt in the ribs, then shoved the barrel of his pistol hard against Matt's forehead.

Anna pulled her unloaded gun from the back of her pants and pointed it at Trey with a panicked scream. "No! Put the gun down."

Trey snapped his head up and pinned Anna with cold, dark eyes. If he was surprised at her presence, he hid it well. "Who the fuck are you? And what the fuck do you think you're pointing at me?"

"Put yours down and I'll put mine down." The palm of Anna's hand was damp with sweat, making it difficult to keep a grip on her empty gun. She concentrated on not letting her hand shake. "Don't take this out on the boy."

Bright red blood dripped down the side of Trey's face. His skin looked red and raw, and his T-shirt was charred and torn. Looking down at Matt, he drew back and kicked him in the stomach again. Matt lurched forward, gasping in pain. "Why? He belongs to you, doesn't he?"

"It's over, man." She didn't use Trey's name, not wanting him to realize just how much she knew about him and his men. "Most of your men are dead. The rest will join them soon. And the women are already gone."

Trey curled his lip into an ugly sneer. "You'd better be lying, you little bitch."

"I'm not. Put the gun down and let the boy go. I'm not afraid to pull the trigger."

Trey studied her for long moments, as if evaluating her sincerity, then snorted. "You don't have any bullets in that gun." His voice betrayed not even a hint of doubt about that statement.

Anna tilted her head to the side. "Funny," she remarked in a voice devoid of humor. "That's almost exactly what your man

Brian said to me. Right before I blew his brains out."

Trey flinched. "You're lying." The look of restrained rage in his eyes set Anna's heart thumping. For long moments they stared one another down, Anna's gun trained on Trey's head, the barrel of Trey's hovering inches from Matt's forehead. "You're not going to shoot me. You can't."

Matt kept his eyes on the ground. Anna could see him shaking in fear. *Goddamn it. I will not let him hurt Matt.*

She steeled her nerve. "Want to bet?"

"Sure." Trey turned to point his gun at her.

Anna was aware of the noise first. Ungodly loud, it made her ears ring in protest, accented by the flash of the muzzle as Trey's gun fired. Then she felt the impact. The bullet jerked her off her feet and sent her tumbling backwards before she even registered what was happening. She landed hard on her back in the grass with a muffled grunt, as the air was forced from her lungs. Her vision blurred and darkened for long, crazy moments.

The pain was the last thing to register, and when it did, it took Anna's breath away.

Dimly, through her shock, Anna mourned yet another failure in what felt like a lifetime of them. *I couldn't save Matt.* She blinked, wincing at the burning, throbbing pain in her shoulder. *And I'm going to break my promise to Elin. And Kael.* Tears welled up in her eyes. The emotion stung, so badly that she had no choice but to give it free rein. Holding it inside seemed so much more agonizing.

Somewhere close to Anna, there was a soft *thump* as a solid body hit the ground near her. Anna battled a moment of confusion and struggled to twist around so that she could see what was happening. She hadn't heard a second gunshot. When she found Trey's cold eyes staring back at her, blinking with his own shock, her confusion grew.

Her confusion was dispelled only a moment later when she dragged her gaze from his singed, bloody face down to the steel shaft of an arrow protruding from the upper right of his chest. Trey seemed to notice it at exactly the same time she did. He reached up and gripped it with a weak hand.

Kael.

Anna lost consciousness with a smile on her lips.

"ANNA."

SHE HEARD Kael's voice, frantic with worry. Then a groan, which might have come from her own mouth. She blinked her eyes open and stared up into Kael's tense face.

"Anna, hold on for me, baby."

"Matt—" Anna said, but her mouth was dry and she couldn't manage more than a pathetic croak. Hazy, she realized that she was cradled in Kael's arms and her lover was practically jogging through the darkness. The movement jarred Anna's body, leaving her aware of pain she was certain would be excruciating if only she could wrap her mind around it.

"I'm right here, Anna."

Matt's blond head entered Anna's peripheral vision. She tried to twist in Kael's arms to look at his face as she struggled to piece together what had happened, and what was happening now.

"He's fine, baby," Kael murmured.

"You saved my life." Matt was pale and wide-eyed. "I owe you my life."

Anna's head swam. *But I didn't save Matt.* She gritted her teeth as the pain registered again, taking her by surprise and pushing the tender voices of her lover and her friend to the background. *And Elin's going to be so mad at me.*

"Anna-baby..." Orders from Kael. "Hang on."

She managed a half smile. It was good to hear Kael. And Matt again, especially when she knew he must be dead. She wondered if she would hear Garrett, too. Anna closed her eyes and let herself drift away, imagining a sunny afternoon spent with Kael, Elin, and Matt, all of them happy and alive.

It was a nice dream, anyway.

THE NEXT TIME Anna woke, it was quiet. She could hear the sound of breathing, the subtle ticking of a clock, and the muted chirping of birds. Her foot itched.

And the rest of me doesn't feel so great, either.

Floating back into awareness, she took a mental inventory. Her throat felt like it was glued shut. Her shoulder throbbed, and she had to pee. A soft warmth pressed up against her side, bringing her unthinking comfort. Sunlight filtered through her eyelids, all red-gold heat and light, lending to her sense of displacement. Her body rested on something yielding, but she couldn't remember where she was.

With a wounded groan, she opened her eyes and almost immediately recognized the guest bedroom at Kate's house, as well as the tender hazel eyes that stared back at her. Elin's face was pale, making her hair look even more vibrant with color. When she saw that Anna was awake, she leaned forward where she sat perched on the edge of the bed.

"Welcome back." Her eyes sparkled with tears, and she brought a trembling hand to cover her mouth. "Oh, baby, I've never been so happy to see those beautiful brown eyes."

She picked up a tall glass from the nightstand and maneuvered the white drinking straw between Anna's parched lips. Anna took a grateful sip, then another when she realized how good it felt.

"Go slow," Elin murmured. "Take it easy, sweetheart."

"What happened?" Anna asked, propping herself up by slipping an arm heavily over Elin's shoulder, clinging to her soft warmth. She turned her head and noticed for the first time that Kael was lying on the bed beside her. Kael's mouth hung open slightly, and amazingly, she slept despite Anna's distress. "Is Kael okay?"

Elin encouraged Anna back against the pillows and tugged the thick comforter up over her chest. "He's fine. As for what happened...if I understand it correctly, you saved Matt's life. You got shot in the shoulder doing it." Elin's voice faltered, and she looked away from Anna with shining eyes. "Kael carried you back to the house. And then I helped Kate remove the bullet and repair your wound." Elin's voice hinted at so much unsaid.

"Some rescue attempt, huh?" Anna could hear the self-recrimination in her voice. "I end up pointing an empty gun at someone who sees right through my bluff. Such a hero." She lowered her eyes to Kael, who continued to sleep. Anna fought down a niggle of worry that her lover was injured, sure that Elin would tell her if that were the case.

"Hey." Elin took her hand. "Kael told me that your bluff bought everyone enough time to let him take down Trey before he could kill Matt. And Matt's told me more than once that you saved his life." Elin's mouth twitched, and she squeezed Anna's hand. "In fact, I think the kid has a little crush on you."

Anna looked down at their enjoined hands with a sheepish smile. "I already told him I was taken."

Elin gave her a humorless snort. "Well, if he didn't know it before, he does now. Kael and I have been frantic over you."

"I'm sure I must have looked horrible." Anna gazed down at Kael again, unnerved by her sound sleep. "Kael's okay, though, right?"

Elin joined in her study of their lover. "He's okay. He's exhausted. I finally got him to agree to have some of Kate's tea just this morning, and that's the only reason he's out like he is. I convinced him that it was for his own good. He...hasn't been sleeping much since you were shot."

"When was that?"

"Three nights ago."

Anna blinked in surprise. *I've been out for over forty-eight hours?* She said the first thing that came to mind. "The camp. Did all the women make it?"

"Every one. Next to you, the worst injury was a sprained ankle."

"What about all the bodies?"

"Kael, Jen, and Matt cleaned everything up. Even if they send more men to search for the ones that were killed, they'll never find anything."

Chances are they won't realize anything's wrong for some time. It could take months for anyone to come looking for them. Another thought occurred to Anna. *Except...* "The second contingent, did they —"

"We took care of them. Well, Kael took care of most of them. Matt helped, and Jen, and two of the women you helped rescue, Leah and Heidi."

"How?"

"It's a lot easier to fight outnumbered when you have the luxury of setting up an ambush. We were waiting for them. There were only twelve men in that group, and Kael didn't have much of a problem handling most from a distance. We even managed to rescue the girl they had with them. Seventeen years old, poor thing."

"Nobody was hurt?"

"Kael has a new bruise or two, and Jen took an elbow to the face, but everybody is fine." Elin traced her fingers over the side of Anna's face. "I'm very relieved, Anna."

Tears stung Anna's eyes. She touched Elin's cheek, returning the tender caress. "So am I. I missed you, baby. We both did, so much."

"I know. You can't even imagine how I missed you two. I knew you would come for me, but after how they left Kael...I tried not to lose faith, but —"

Anna let her fingers linger over the curve of Elin's jaw. "I won't lie. Kael was in pretty bad shape. But he was determined. He's so strong."

The corner of Elin's mouth curled. "I know he is." She lifted her eyes to Anna's face. "God, Anna, I've never seen him so upset as he was carrying you back here to the house. He managed to hold it in until after we dealt with the rest of the Procreationists the next day, but afterwards...with you still unconscious...he fell apart. I've never seen him like that before."

Anna stared at Elin in wonder. "I imagine it was a lot like he reacted when you were taken."

"I imagine it was."

Anna exhaled slowly and tried to get more comfortable. Her whole body ached. "My head is pounding. Are you sure I didn't get shot there?"

"Kate said that you hit your head on the ground when you went down. She said a headache would be perfectly normal with that kind of injury."

Anna cracked a smile. "Well, as long as I'm normal."

Snorting, Elin murmured, "Hardly."

"But you love me, anyway."

"Forever." Elin closed the distance between their faces. "Think you feel well enough for a kiss, baby? I'm having a hard time holding back here."

"I always feel well enough for a kiss."

Elin pressed her lips to Anna's and gave her the gentlest, most tender of kisses.

"It's gonna take a lot more of that to get me well again," Anna mumbled, her nose in Elin's hair.

Elin shook with quiet laugher. "Same here."

Kael released a low snore, drawing their attention down to her slack face.

"We should wake him up," Anna said.

"I think he'd never forgive me if I didn't." Elin stroked the back of her hand over Kael's cheek. "It might not be that easy, though. He's really out."

Anna shifted closer to her sleeping lover and rested her cheek against the pillow, watching Elin's knuckles caress Kael's pale skin. "Kiss him," she suggested in a quiet voice and grinned. "That'd make everyone feel better, too."

Elin chuckled and leaned over Anna, careful not to put any weight on her body. She brought her face close to Kael's and gave Anna a brief sidelong glance. "If you insist."

"I do." Anna settled back and watched with satisfied eyes as Elin let her lips just barely touch Kael's. She increased the contact so slowly that Anna held her breath in anticipation, exhaling only when her sore body required it. As she gazed at her lovers, Kael murmured sleepily and returned the kiss, caressing Elin's lips with a lazy tongue.

"You're right, Anna. I think that worked," Elin murmured.

Kael's eyes flew open. When she turned her head to find Anna smiling back at her, her jaw dropped, and momentarily, she was speechless.

"Hi," Anna said.

"Hi." Kael's lower lip trembled, and she moved to bury her

face in Anna's neck, against her uninjured shoulder. "Are you okay?"

"I will be."

Kael wrapped a careful arm around Anna's middle and hugged her as though she were almost too delicate to touch. She said nothing, but Anna felt every word.

"I told you we missed you," Elin said, joining their embrace.

Careful not to jostle Anna's wound, she wrapped an arm around Kael's shoulders. Though she appreciated the caution with which her lovers handled her, Anna was beyond caring. She closed her eyes and savored their touch.

She felt completed.

A quiet knock distracted them from their reunion, and Anna and Kael wiped at their damp eyes with the backs of their hands. Elin turned toward the bedroom door with tears rolling down her cheeks.

"Look who's awake," she said, gesturing for Matt to come in.

He managed a shy grin as he approached the bed. "Hey, Anna."

Inexplicably, Anna blushed. "Hey. I'm so glad you're okay."

Matt grinned even harder. "I'm very okay."

Anna ran her eyes over the boy's face and body, taking note of the bruise below his eye, the cut above his lip, the stiffness with which he held himself. He looked battered, but alive. "I've been having some really bad dreams the last couple of days," she said. "I admit, at times I wasn't sure you made it."

"I almost didn't. If you hadn't come along at just the right moment—"

"Kael saved your life. Not me."

"Don't even," Kael protested. "You were a goddamn action hero out there. Not many people would have been brave enough to step up in that situation, but you did. For your friend."

Anna met Matt's eyes, humbled by the deep love she saw in them. "I'm just glad it worked out."

Matt leaned over and planted a gentle kiss on Anna's mouth. "Anyway...thanks. I'll never be able to tell you...I don't know how to say—"

"I love you, too," Anna said. "I'm proud to call you friend. And besides, it was the least I could do to repay you for all your help."

Blushing, Matt cast his gaze down to the ground.

"Yeah, man," Kael piped up. "Thank you."

Elin stood and wrapped her arms around Matt in a warm hug. "Thank you."

Matt shrugged, but returned Elin's hug. "It wasn't a big

deal." He looked at Kael, eyebrow upraised. "Is this a good time for the surprise?"

Anna's heart warmed at the way Kael's face was suddenly aglow with the same excitement as Matt's. "Oh, yeah," Kael said. "Definitely, yes. Get the surprise." She sat up and gave Anna an eager grin.

Matt jogged over to the bedroom door and poked his head into the hallway. "Hey, Isabella. Come on in."

When a pretty teenage girl with short blonde hair walked into the room with a squirming golden puppy in her arms, Anna beamed.

"Oh my...Is that a puppy? A golden retriever?" Elin stepped forward as the girl placed the puppy down on the bed.

Anna grinned so hard her cheeks hurt. *A golden retriever, huh? Elin and her books.* She turned to Kael to find glittering indigo eyes staring back at her. "You didn't show her yet?"

Kael shook her head. "I wanted to wait for you."

Anna bit her lip in an effort not to start crying then and there. "I love you, Kael."

Kael leaned close and gave her a sweet, lingering kiss. "I love you, too."

"He's so tiny." Elin patted his bottom with her hand, smiling after him as he bounded across the comforter to cover Anna's face with wet kisses.

"What are you talking about, tiny?" Anna asked through Zep's frantic tongue bath. "He's huge! I swear he's gained at least two pounds since I last saw him."

Elin laughed in delight as the puppy stopped licking Anna's face to roll over onto his back so she could scratch his belly. "He likes you, Anna."

"He should. She found the little mutt." Kael's voice was full of gruff affection. "She insisted we keep him so we could give him to you."

Elin's mouth dropped open, making her look very much like an excited child. "He's ours?" Elin squeaked.

Anna's heart swelled at the sight of Elin's joy. "Kael named him already. We tried to think of something you'd like. Zep. Short for Led Zeppelin."

Elin looked from Anna to Kael with tear-filled hazel eyes. "He's perfect."

She settled down on the bed next to Anna, who welcomed her lover's gentle weight pressed against her other side. Between Kael and Elin, she felt happy and protected. Her whole body felt warm at the love that surrounded her. "Yes, ma'am, he is."

Matt cleared his throat and, with an awkward glance at

Isabella, said, "Um, I wanted to talk to you guys about something."

"What's up, Matt?" Elin asked.

"I, uh..." Matt looked again at Isabella, who gave him a subtle nod. "I was wondering if...well, Jen told me that she and Caroline are going to travel with you guys when you leave. And Heidi also said something about maybe traveling with you now that her husband is gone. Do you think—"

Anna felt her eyes growing wider during Matt's rambling speech. *Kael knows that all these people want to travel with us?* She tried to reconcile the idea of the stoic loner traveling with a makeshift community.

Kael's lip twitched with amusement. "Safety in numbers." Giving Matt a friendly nod, she added, "We'd be happy to have you for as long as we're going the same way, my friend."

Matt relaxed into a crooked smile. "And Isabella?"

"Is more than welcome, too." Elin gave both young people a warm smile. "I've never belonged to a tribe before."

"I thought you belonged to *our* tribe," Anna said, gesturing between Kael and herself. "What, we weren't good enough to be a tribe?"

"A *civilized* tribe, I meant." Elin stuck her tongue out at them, eyes sparkling.

"I'm civilized." Kael pinched Elin's tongue between her fingertips. "Anyway, I thought you girls liked me wild. All the time."

The quiet click of the bedroom door alerted Anna to Matt and Isabella's departure. *Probably best. When we're on a roll, it's hard to stop us.* Turning to Elin, she affected a thoughtful look. "He's got you there, sweet girl."

And they were on a roll.

Epilogue

ANNA WRAPPED HER arms around her knees and stared out at blue-gray water sparkling in the late afternoon sunlight. Two days on the coast, and she still couldn't get over it. Who knew the ocean would be so big?

Twenty yards down the beach, Jen and Caroline knelt in the sand collecting seashells. She and Jen had scoured the beach nonstop over the past couple of days, taking breaks only to steal away and make love.

While the new couple hadn't yet made an official announcement about their status, Anna was well aware that their intimate friendship, formed in a small red tent in the Procreationist camp, had grown into something more. Anna was happy for them, especially because she knew that Caroline had been taken from a loveless relationship with a man who offered her modest protection and nothing more. Jen treated her like a queen, and it warmed Anna's heart to see them so happy.

They weren't the only ones. Anna glanced over her shoulder at the sound of playful laughter and found Matt tossing a Frisbee to Isabella, the blonde girl they'd rescued from the second contingent. As she watched, the couple exchanged a look of pure devotion. *The two of them are becoming fast friends, aren't they?*

Heidi played with them. She laughed as she caught a wild toss from Matt, then executed a perfect throw to Isabella. She, too, had become a friend, and though Anna sometimes felt bad that Heidi had no one to love in a romantic way—her husband having been killed only weeks before she was captured by the Procreationists—she knew that their makeshift family was a genuine source of joy for her.

As it is for me. She took a deep breath and dropped her hands to rest on the warm sand. *I'm beginning to think that having people to love, as scary as it is, makes all the difference in the world.* Distractedly, she dug into the sand with her fingers then lifted up, allowing the soft grains to sift through them. After the ocean, sand was the most amazing.

"Hey, Anna!" Matt jogged over to plop down on the sand beside her. "So where are Kael and Elin?"

"Walking Zep," Anna said. "Or rather, I think he's walking them." The puppy was growing by leaps and bounds and was a ball of unbridled energy, always eager to run and play. The beaches of South Carolina had sent him straight over the edge.

Matt laughed. "That sounds about right."

"Well, I hope you don't mind us crashing your party." Heidi joined them and wrapped a slim arm around Anna's shoulders.

"Not at all." Anna looked back at the ocean. "I was just admiring the view."

"Funny," a deep voice said from behind them. "So was I."

Breaking into a grin, Anna tilted her head to gaze up at Kael. Elin stood beside her, wearing a green bikini and a green and blue sarong, which Anna found breathtaking. Kael's indigo eyes were shaded by dark sunglasses, and she wore a gray T-shirt and faded cut-off shorts.

"Sweet talker."

"No, he's right. It's a very nice view." Elin didn't bother to hide her obvious appraisal of Anna's body. Anna wore a modest yellow bathing suit and a loose white T-shirt. The scar on her shoulder was still raw, and she didn't want to expose it to the sun.

"You guys had a nice walk?" Anna asked.

"It would've been nicer if you'd been with us," Kael said. "How's the ocean?"

"Amazing." Anna stared at the blue-gray expanse. Her dark, curly hair blew around her face in the gentle breeze that carried the vague smell of salt to shore. She smiled. She could feel the silent approval of the friends around her, their respect for the love she shared with Kael and Elin. It warmed her whole body.

Kael offered a hand. "We need you, sweetheart."

Elin nodded in agreement. "We definitely need you."

Anna's whole face went hot with embarrassed pleasure. Her desire flared at the look in Elin's eyes. *Play it cool, Anna. You've got an audience here.*

Kael stepped closer. "Please, Anna-baby?"

Anna stared at her own reflection in Kael's sunglasses, in awe of the naked emotion in her lover's voice. Since rescuing Elin and nursing Anna back to health, Kael had been openly demonstrative to the extent that Anna never had to doubt exactly how she felt. It was clear in every action and every word.

Anna took Kael's hand and allowed her lover to pull her to her feet. She brushed sand from her bottom, casting Matt an apologetic look as a few grains fell onto his lap. He gave her a carefree smile in return.

"You guys don't mind if we steal Anna for a while, do you?" Elin asked.

"Not at all," Matt said. "You want us to keep watch so you can have some time?" He stroked Zep's head. "We'll even keep the little beast entertained."

Kael grinned. "That'd be great, man."

Anna's heart raced at the thought of private time with her lovers. *I've had enough healing over the past month and a half. It's time for some loving.* In perfect synch with her thoughts, Anna felt an insistent throbbing begin between her legs. She locked eyes with Elin.

"I like you in that." Anna nodded to the bikini and sarong and fingered the silky material wrapped around Elin's waist.

"You'll like me even better out of it," Elin replied softly.

"I'm sure you're right." Anna licked her lips as she stared at Elin's creamy throat.

"All right, girls." Kael took Anna's hand in one of hers, Elin's in the other. "We need to go. Now."

"You okay, Anna?" Elin peered across Kael's chest and waggled her eyebrows. "You look a little unsteady."

"I'll be fine," Anna muttered. "I'm just so ready to love you two that it hurts."

"How's your shoulder doing?" Kael asked.

"Not bad, actually. Better every day." She peered at Kael's eyes past the side of her sunglasses. "How about you? Headaches?"

"I haven't had one in two days." Kael smiled. "I'm feeling really...good, actually."

"Good." Anna released Kael's hand and snaked her arm around her lean back, reaching out to touch Elin's side. "How about you, baby?"

At her question, Kael led them over a sandy incline, then down to a secluded beach house Anna had only observed from a distance. "It's getting easier. I'm sleeping better."

Since her kidnapping, Elin had been plagued by intense nightmares. They'd increased in frequency when they'd left Lana and her mother in a small town thirty miles east of the Procreationist camp, after having located Lana's father. He was banged up, but thrilled to see the family he thought he'd lost. While Anna knew that Elin was happy about the reunion, she also knew her lover missed the devoted little girl.

Elin hadn't spoken much about the nightmares, but Anna knew that Trey played a prominent role in them. Judging from some of the tortured whimpering she'd heard late at night, so did Brian. Having suffered through bad dreams of her own, Anna's heart ached for her lover.

"It does get easier, baby, I promise." Kael held the door open to let Anna and Elin inside and pulled off her sunglasses as she followed. "Doesn't it, Anna?"

"It does. Please remember that you can talk to us, always."

"I remember. It's just..." Elin dropped her gaze to the ground. "I think I'm always going to be a little different after what happened. I know it could've been so much worse, but...it scared me. A lot."

"I'll always be a little different, too," Kael said. "I think we all will. That doesn't change anything about the way any of us feel about one another. Except I think that I love both of you even more now, if that's possible."

Anna kissed Elin's cheek, nuzzling into her fragrant red hair. "I wish you hadn't ever had to feel that kind of fear. But like Kael said, the fact that it affected you isn't going to change anything. We'll grow with you."

Elin nodded. "I think...I have a whole new appreciation for how strong and brave both of you are. In so many ways."

"You're strong, too," Anna murmured into Elin's ear. "And so, so brave."

"I, uh...have something I wanted to give to both of you," Kael said. Color rose on her cheeks. "I think maybe this is a good time."

Elin pulled away from the circle of Anna's arms, breaking into a genuine smile. "Don't you think we should go into the bedroom for that, stud?" She winked at Anna, clearly enjoying yet another opportunity to tease.

"Behave," Kael admonished quietly. She extracted three velvet-covered boxes from her pockets. One was slightly bigger than the rest, and Kael kept that one as she handed the other two to Anna and Elin. "Just, uh...open them."

"Where did this come from?" Anna asked. She met Kael's eyes, then dropped her gaze to the small box she held. She glanced at Elin, who examined her own box with a similar expression of dazed awe.

Kael shrugged. "It doesn't matter. Just open them, please? This is killing me."

At Anna's nod, they both cracked open their boxes, releasing simultaneous noises of hushed pleasure. In each box sat a gold ring shaped like a continuous, three-sided knot. Anna looked up at Kael, startled by the delicate beauty of the gift.

"Oh, Kael," Elin breathed. She held her ring up to her face for a closer look.

Kael's eyes lit up at Elin's reaction, and she looked to Anna, who said, "They're gorgeous."

"They're trinity rings," Kael said. "I thought it might be nice...well, I mean, if you guys want to wear them...I thought it could be a nice symbol—"

"I love it," Anna said. Her eyes filled with happy tears.

"So do I," Elin murmured. "Kael, will you put mine on?"

Anna watched Elin give her ring to Kael, who took Elin's hand and, with great care, slipped the golden band on her left ring finger. Elin kissed Kael's cheek before turning to Anna.

"May I?" Elin stared at Anna with love-filled hazel eyes.

"Please," Anna said.

Elin took Anna's ring and held Anna's left hand in her own. Slipping the delicate band on Anna's finger, she smiled when Anna planted a sweet kiss on her pale cheek. "It looks wonderful on you, sweetheart," Elin whispered.

"It does. On both of you." Kael hesitated, then reached out to offer Anna her own ring. "Would you?"

"I'm honored." Anna took Kael's large left hand in both of her own and slipped the ring on her finger, then grinned over at Elin. "We're lucky to have such a romantic tough guy, aren't we?"

Elin regarded them with a watery grin. "Oh, yes."

They stood quietly for long moments until Kael released them from the embrace. Kael cleared her throat, swiped at her eyes with the back of her hand, and asked, "Why don't you come see the bed they have in here, Anna?"

Elin lit up at the suggestion. "Yeah, come see. It's amazing."

Kael led Anna and Elin into the master bedroom. She hung back as Anna stepped forward to survey her surroundings with awe. The walls were sage, lined with paintings of sunsets, boats, and dolphins. Two large, curtained windows offered a partially obscured view of the ocean.

It looked like an incredible place to sleep. *And do other things.* The king-sized bed was covered with a fluffy down comforter that was already turned down at the top. Anna smiled and turned to gaze at Elin. *It's time to start fixing what those men caused.*

"Will you let us help you forget, Elin?" Anna asked.

Elin grinned and raised up on her toes to kiss the tip of Anna's nose. "I'm counting on it. However, I think Kael and I were hoping to concentrate on your pleasure first today."

"Me?"

"You, sweetheart. On our walk, we talked about how much we both miss touching you. We're, uh..." Elin managed a sheepish shrug. "Desperate, quite honestly."

"I can't think of any good reason to complain about that," Anna said, wondering how much longer her legs would support her.

"Lucky us." Kael cupped Anna's bottom through her one-piece bathing suit and gave her a gentle squeeze.

Elin lifted an eyebrow at Anna. "Are you up to it, sweetheart? Will your shoulder be okay?"

Anna let one hand drop to Elin's waist, where she deftly untied the green and blue sarong and let it fall to the ground. She looped her arms around Elin's middle, slipping her hands into her bikini bottoms so she could cup one smooth cheek in each palm.

"It'll be just fine," she said.

The wet, lingering kiss that Elin laid on her at that, the reverent stroking of her stomach and upper thighs by Kael's sure fingers, the overwhelming heat that infused her body at the reestablishment of contact with both of them, showed her just how accurate that statement was. Anna knew, without a doubt, that everything would be just fine.

For all three of them.

The End

OTHER MEGHAN O'BRIEN TITLES

Infinite Loop

How does a casual encounter become true love?

When shy software developer, Regan O'Riley is dragged into a straight bar by her workmates, the last person she expects to meet is the woman of her dreams. Off-duty cop, Mel Raines is tall, dark and gorgeous but has no plans to enter a committed relationship any time soon. Despite their differing agendas, Mel and Regan can't deny an instant, overwhelming attraction.

Both their lives are about to change drastically, when a tragedy forces Mel to rethink her emotional isolation and face inner demons rooted in her past. She cannot make this journey alone, and Regan's decision to share it with her has consequences neither woman expects.

More than an erotic road novel, *Infinite Loop* explores the choices we make, the families we build, and the power of love to transform lives.

ISBN 1-932300-42-2
(987-1-932300-42-0)

FORTHCOMING TITLES

published by
Quest Books

Mind Games
by Nancy Griffis

Betrayed and almost killed by her police partner, PsiAgent Rebecca Curtains is understandably reluctant to take on a new one, despite the danger in working alone. When she finds out that the Violent Crimes loner, Detective Genie marshall, is scheduled to be the replacement, reluctance turns to outright apprehension.

In becoming partners with the resident telepath, Detective Genie Marshall has been given a second chance to become a 'real' cop again, and she knows it. After the death of her last partner, Genie has worked alone, not wanting to risk herself like that again. It won't make her any more popular with the other detectives, but then, being popular has never been on Genie's list. Get the job done right, and with as little bloodshed as possible, has always been her motto.

After a rocky start, the two women forge a strong partnership that allows them to solve crimes faster and more accurately than ever. The partnership grows into something deeper than friendship as they begin a journey that brings the hidden aspects of their lives to the surface. When Rebecca is attacked, telepathically and physically, it's a race to discover who's behind it; the leader of UnderTEM, a group bent on wiping out all telepaths, or a random psycho with telepathic powers of his or her own.

It is only by trusting in each other, and their new bond, that they'll find the killer. If they don't, Rebecca's very sanity will be the cost of failure.

Never Wake
by Gabrielle Goldsby

Emma Webster hasn't left her house in over two years. After a brutal attack, she holed up inside, living a safe and quiet life, until the world goes quiet on June 5, 2008. At least, that's when Emma first notices the stillness. She can't be sure of the exact date because she's been cloistered for so long, but even a recluse such as Emma can sense when things aren't exactly right. It starts when her grocery delivery doesn't arrive. Then with some annoyance she notices that there have been no new posts to her formerly popular web blog. She searches other blogs in her web ring and notes that they, too, have been abandoned. Emma's unease grows as her food supply diminishes, expensive vehicles appear to be abandoned in front of her home, and the stray cat she usually feeds stops coming around. In desperation she posts a frightened, "Where is everyone?" to her blog.

Troy Nanson is a recovering alcoholic who awakens in a hospital with a headache and no memory of how she got there. When her calls to the nursing station go unanswered, Troy leaves her bed to search for hospital staff only to find them passed out in the hospital lounge. She tries to telephone her only living relative, but no one answers. Troy is forced to make her way home through the hushed streets of Portland, Oregon, where she passes a patrolman slumped forward in his car, several eerily still young men sleeping on a sidewalk, and a well-dressed man curled up on a bench at a train stop. At her brother's house, she finds him, as well as her dog, in a coma-like state. 911 won't answer, and a trip to a neighbor's confirm what Troy has begun to suspect - everyone else is inexplicably in a coma. Desperate and suddenly faced with her worst fear, Troy uses her brother's computer to search the Internet for an explanation of the phenomenon and instead comes upon Emma's post: "Where is everyone?"

What has happened and how long can their tranced-out neighbors last? Believing they are the only two people left awake, Troy and Emma meet. How can they solve this puzzle and make a difference when Troy has an overwhelming urge to drink, and Emma is terrified of physical and emotional contact with others? Two frightened women with the weight of the world on their shoulders must face their worst fears with only one another to help.

Will they manage to confront their fears? Or will their fright result in the destruction of all they know and love?

Other QUEST Publications

Gabrielle Goldsby	Wall of Silence	1-932300-01-5	$ 20.95
Trish Kocialski	Blue Holes To Terror	1-930928-61-0	$ 16.99
Trish Kocialski	Deadly Challenge	1-930928-76-9	$ 14.95
Trish Kocialski	Forces of Evil	1-932300-10-4	$ 14.95
Trish Kocialski	The Visitors	1-932300-27-9	$ 14.95
Lori L. Lake	Gun Shy	1-930928-43-2	$ 18.95
Lori L. Lake	Have Gun We'll Travel	1-932300-33-3	$ 18.95
Lori L. Lake	Under the Gun	1-930928-44-0	$ 22.95
Helen M. Macpherson	Colder Than Ice	1-932300-29-5	$ 18.95
C. Paradee	Deep Cover	1-932300-23-6	$ 17.95
John F. Parker	Come Clean	978-1-932300-43-7	$ 19.95
Talaran	Vendetta	1-930928-56-4	$ 15.99
C N Winters	Irrefutable Evidence	1-930928-88-2	$ 15.95

Meghan O'Brien recently relocated to Northern California from her native Michigan. Though she graduated from the University of Michigan Business School with a degree in CIS and currently works as a software developer, her real passion is writing fiction. And video games – we can't forget video games.

When she's not writing or playing Halo 2 online, Meghan enjoys spending time with her friends, wrangling her cats, and exploring her new home. She is 27 years old, and hopes to keep writing lesbian fiction into the indefinite future. Her first novel, *Infinite Loop*, is also available from Regal Crest Enterprises (Yellow Rose Books). You can find her online at http://www.meghanobrien.com.

Printed in the United States
51320LVS00003B/77

9 781932 300512